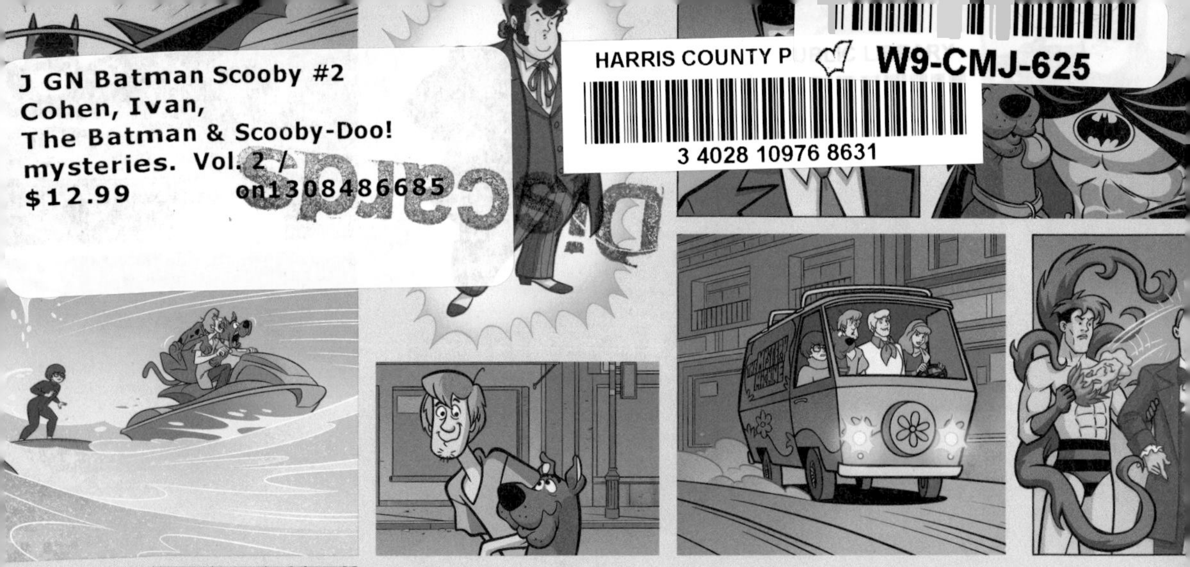

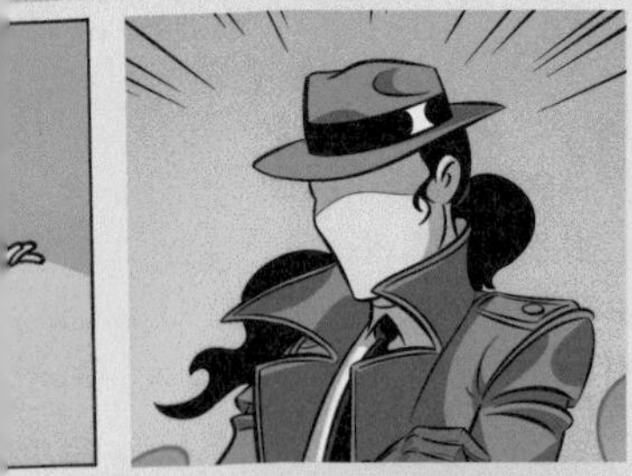

IVAN COHEN, SHOLLY FISCH WRITERS

DARIO BRIZUELA, RANDY ELLIOTT, SCOTT JERALDS ARTISTS

FRANCO RIESCO, CARRIE STRACHAN COLORISTS

SAIDA TEMOFONTE, WES ABBOTT LETTERERS

DARIO BRIZUELA AND FRANCO RIESCO COLLECTION COVER ARTISTS

BATMAN CREATED BY BOB KANE WITH BILL FINGER

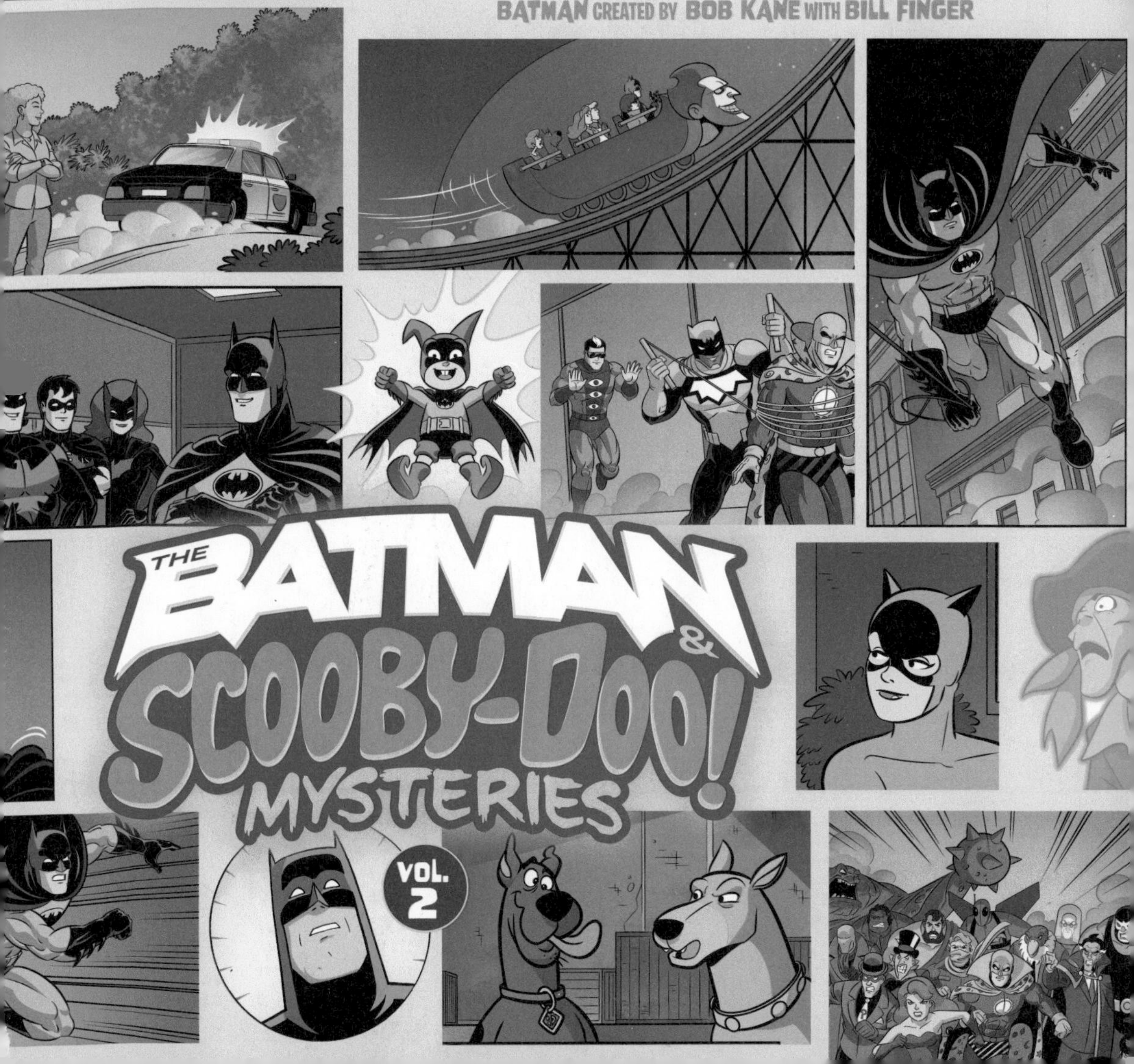
THE BATMAN & SCOOBY-DOO! MYSTERIES
VOL. 2

KRISTY QUINN Editor - Original Series & Collected Edition
STEVE COOK Design Director - Books
AMIE BROCKWAY-METCALF Publication Design
SUZANNAH ROWNTREE Publication Production

MARIE JAVINS Editor-in-Chief, DC Comics

ANNE DePIES Senior VP - General Manager
JIM LEE Publisher & Chief Creative Officer
DON FALLETTI VP - Manufacturing Operations
& Workflow Management
LAWRENCE GANEM VP - Talent Services
ALISON GILL Senior VP - Manufacturing & Operations
JEFFREY KAUFMAN VP - Editorial Strategy & Programming
NICK J. NAPOLITANO VP - Manufacturing Administration & Design
NANCY SPEARS VP - Revenue

THE BATMAN & SCOOBY-DOO MYSTERIES VOL. 2

Published by DC Comics. Compilation and all new material Copyright © 2022 DC Comics and Warner Bros. Entertainment Inc. All Rights Reserved.
Originally published in single magazine form in *The Batman & Scooby-Doo Mysteries 7-12*. Copyright © 2021, 2022 DC Comics and Warner Bros. Entertainment Inc. DC logo, BATMAN, and all related characters and elements are trademarks of DC Comics. The stories, characters, and incidents featured in this publication are entirely fictional. DC Comics does not read or accept unsolicited submissions of ideas, stories, or artwork.

All Hanna-Barbera characters and elements Copyright © and ™ Warner Bros. Entertainment Inc.

WB SHIELD: ™ & © WBEI (s22)

DC Comics, 2900 West Alameda Ave., Burbank, CA 91505

Printed by LSC Communications, Owensville, MO, USA. 6/10/22. First Printing.

ISBN: 978-1-77951-428-8

Library of Congress Cataloging-in-Publication Data is available.

PEFC Certified
This product is from sustainably managed forests and controlled sources
PEFC/29-31-337   www.pefc.org

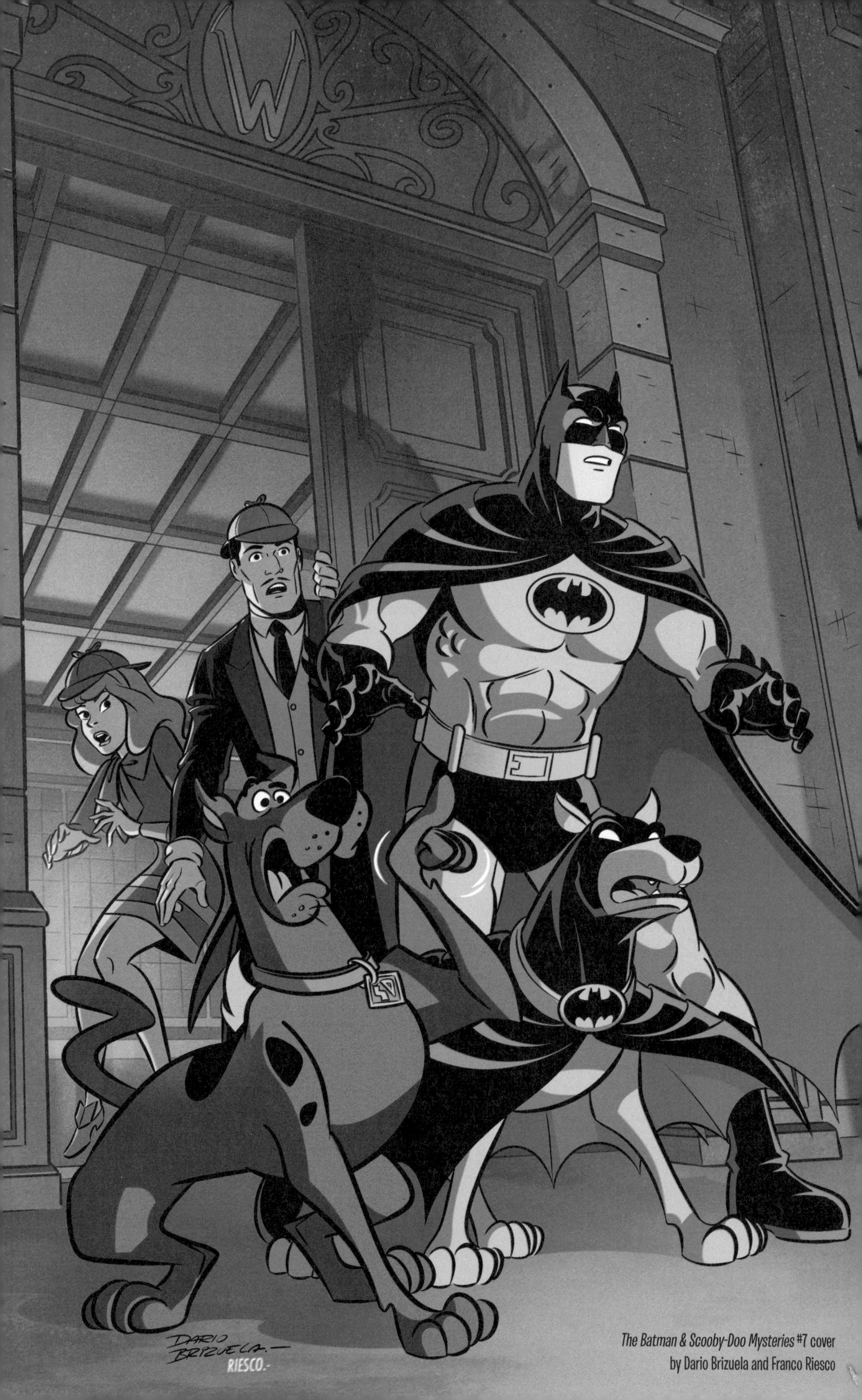
DARIO BRIZUELA.—
RIESCO.-

The Batman & Scooby-Doo Mysteries #7 cover
by Dario Brizuela and Franco Riesco

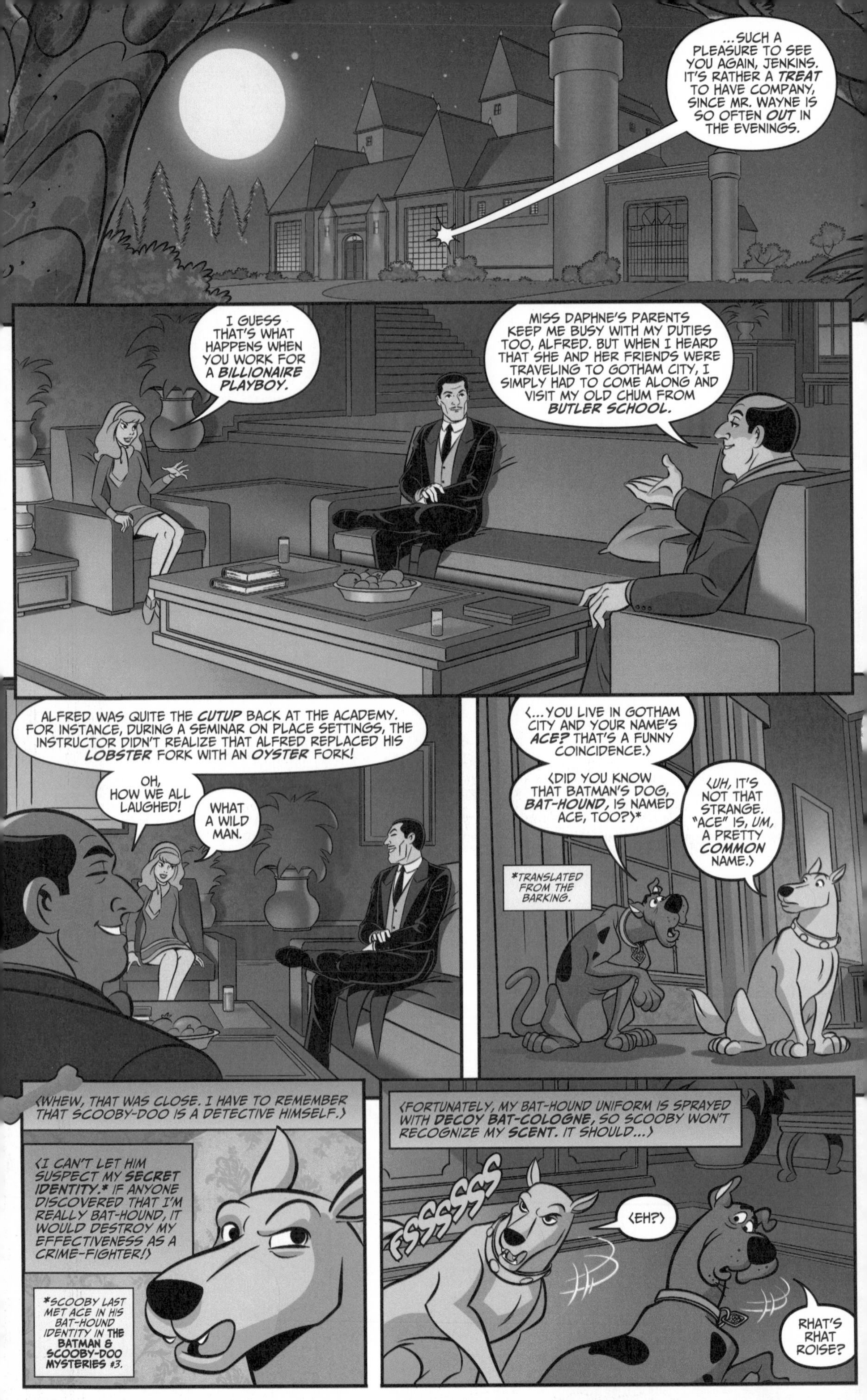
...SUCH A PLEASURE TO SEE YOU AGAIN, JENKINS. IT'S RATHER A TREAT TO HAVE COMPANY, SINCE MR. WAYNE IS SO OFTEN OUT IN THE EVENINGS.
I GUESS THAT'S WHAT HAPPENS WHEN YOU WORK FOR A BILLIONAIRE PLAYBOY.
MISS DAPHNE'S PARENTS KEEP ME BUSY WITH MY DUTIES TOO, ALFRED. BUT WHEN I HEARD THAT SHE AND HER FRIENDS WERE TRAVELING TO GOTHAM CITY, I SIMPLY HAD TO COME ALONG AND VISIT MY OLD CHUM FROM BUTLER SCHOOL.
ALFRED WAS QUITE THE CUTUP BACK AT THE ACADEMY. FOR INSTANCE, DURING A SEMINAR ON PLACE SETTINGS, THE INSTRUCTOR DIDN'T REALIZE THAT ALFRED REPLACED HIS LOBSTER FORK WITH AN OYSTER FORK!
OH, HOW WE ALL LAUGHED!
WHAT A WILD MAN.
‹...YOU LIVE IN GOTHAM CITY AND YOUR NAME'S ACE? THAT'S A FUNNY COINCIDENCE.›
‹DID YOU KNOW THAT BATMAN'S DOG, BAT-HOUND, IS NAMED ACE, TOO?›*
‹UH, IT'S NOT THAT STRANGE. "ACE" IS, UM, A PRETTY COMMON NAME.›
*TRANSLATED FROM THE BARKING.
‹WHEW, THAT WAS CLOSE. I HAVE TO REMEMBER THAT SCOOBY-DOO IS A DETECTIVE HIMSELF.›
‹I CAN'T LET HIM SUSPECT MY SECRET IDENTITY.* IF ANYONE DISCOVERED THAT I'M REALLY BAT-HOUND, IT WOULD DESTROY MY EFFECTIVENESS AS A CRIME-FIGHTER!›
*SCOOBY LAST MET ACE IN HIS BAT-HOUND IDENTITY IN THE BATMAN & SCOOBY-DOO MYSTERIES #3.
‹FORTUNATELY, MY BAT-HOUND UNIFORM IS SPRAYED WITH DECOY BAT-COLOGNE, SO SCOOBY WON'T RECOGNIZE MY SCENT. IT SHOULD...›
FSSSSSS
‹EH?›
RHAT'S RHAT ROISE?

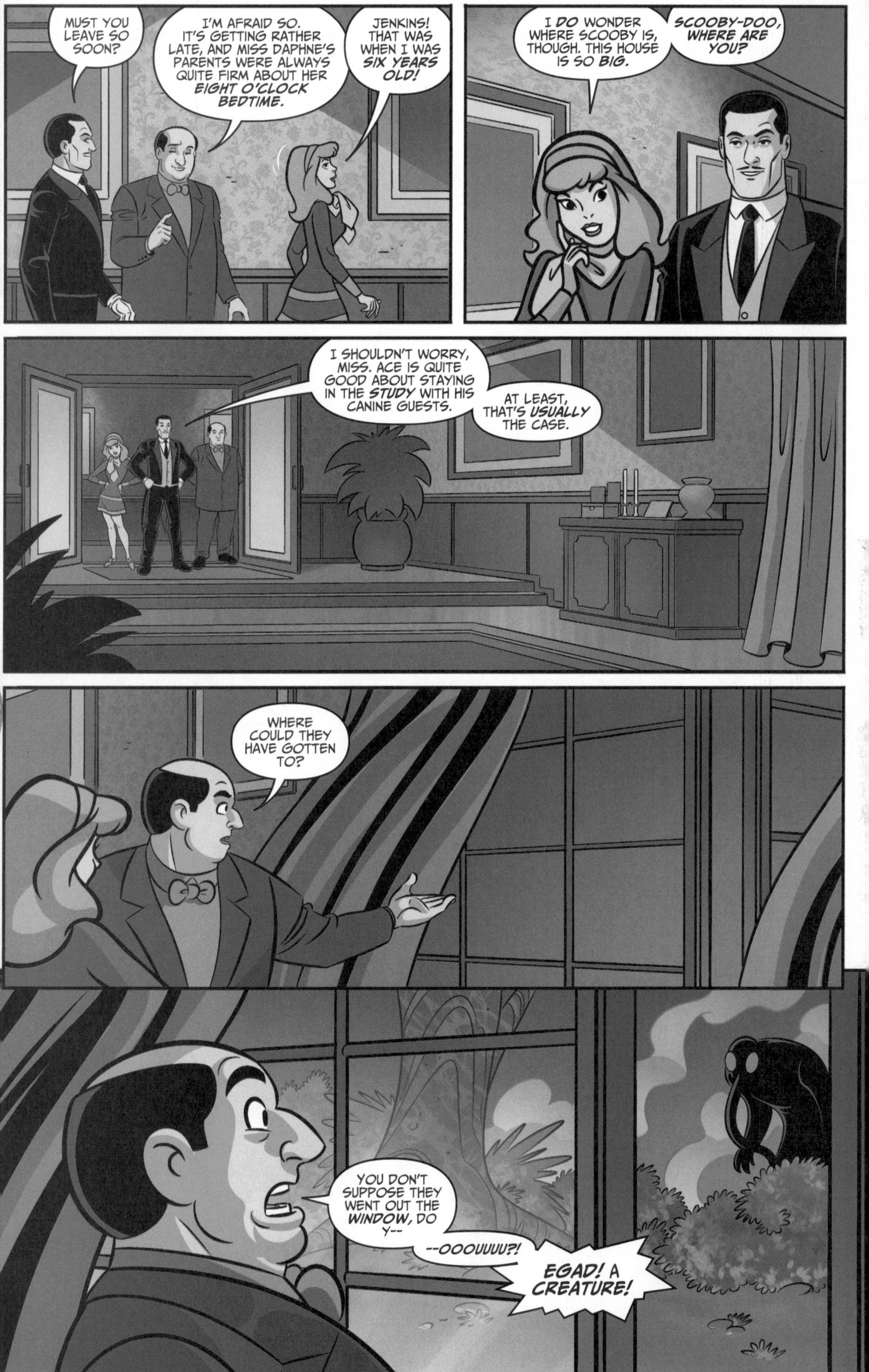
MUST YOU LEAVE SO SOON?
I'M AFRAID SO. IT'S GETTING RATHER LATE, AND MISS DAPHNE'S PARENTS WERE ALWAYS QUITE FIRM ABOUT HER EIGHT O'CLOCK BEDTIME.
JENKINS! THAT WAS WHEN I WAS SIX YEARS OLD!
I DO WONDER WHERE SCOOBY IS, THOUGH. THIS HOUSE IS SO BIG.
SCOOBY-DOO, WHERE ARE YOU?
I SHOULDN'T WORRY, MISS. ACE IS QUITE GOOD ABOUT STAYING IN THE STUDY WITH HIS CANINE GUESTS.
AT LEAST, THAT'S USUALLY THE CASE.
WHERE COULD THEY HAVE GOTTEN TO?
YOU DON'T SUPPOSE THEY WENT OUT THE WINDOW, DO Y--
--OOOUUUU?!
EGAD! A CREATURE!

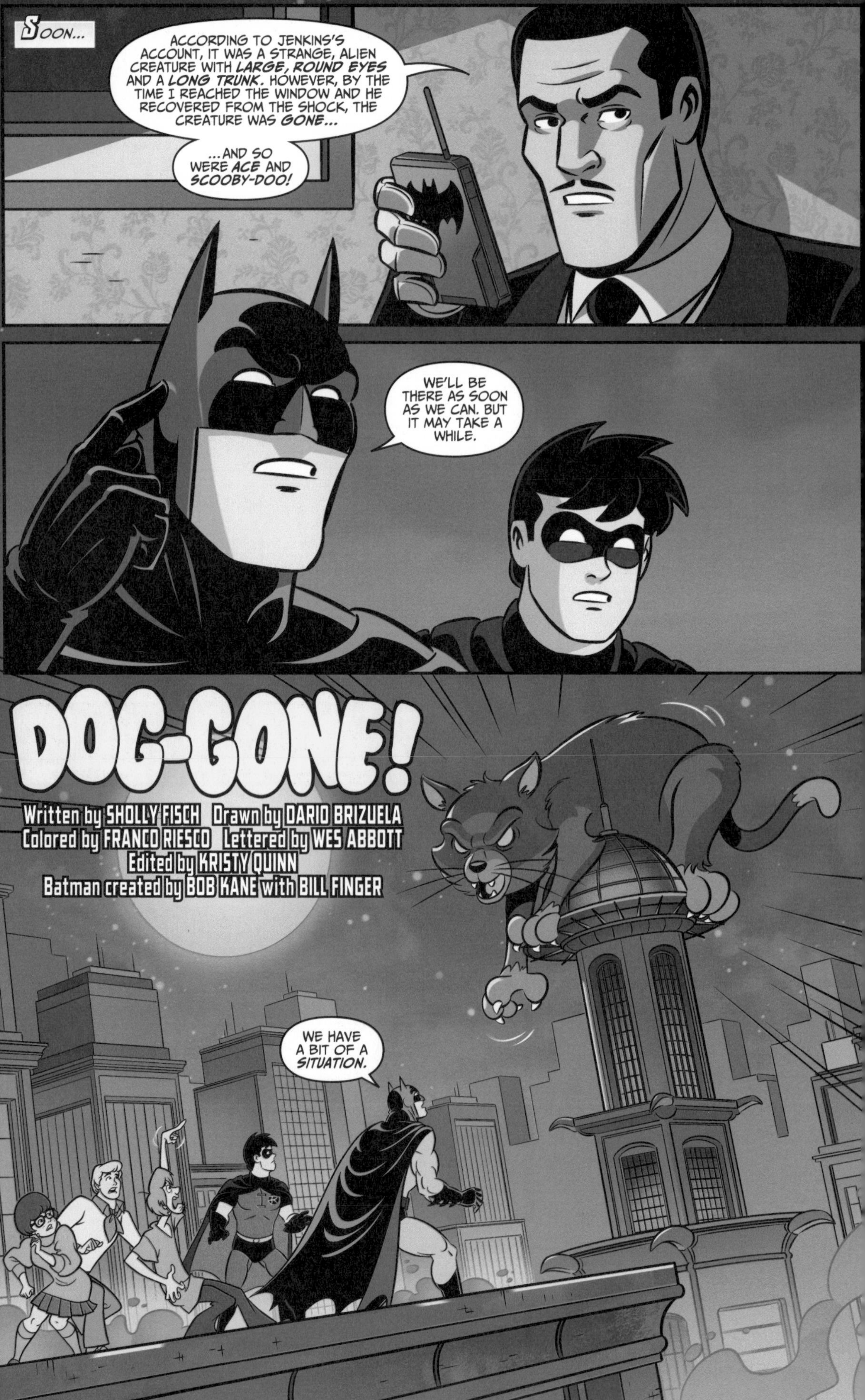
SOON...
ACCORDING TO JENKINS'S ACCOUNT, IT WAS A STRANGE, ALIEN CREATURE WITH LARGE, ROUND EYES AND A LONG TRUNK. HOWEVER, BY THE TIME I REACHED THE WINDOW AND HE RECOVERED FROM THE SHOCK, THE CREATURE WAS GONE...
...AND SO WERE ACE AND SCOOBY-DOO!
WE'LL BE THERE AS SOON AS WE CAN. BUT IT MAY TAKE A WHILE.
DOG-GONE!
Written by SHOLLY FISCH Drawn by DARIO BRIZUELA
Colored by FRANCO RIESCO Lettered by WES ABBOTT
Edited by KRISTY QUINN
Batman created by BOB KANE with BILL FINGER
WE HAVE A BIT OF A SITUATION.

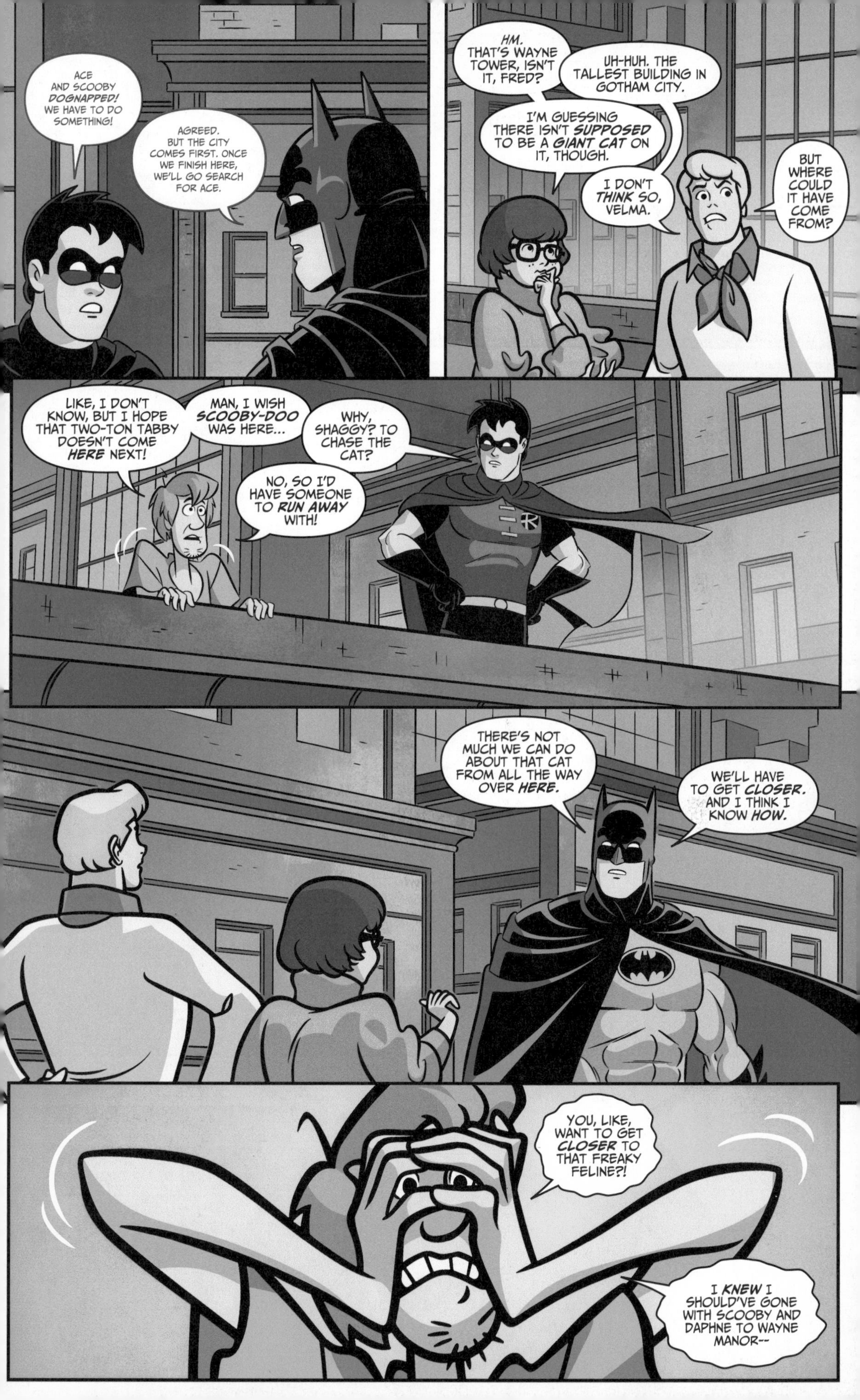
ACE AND SCOOBY DOGNAPPED! WE HAVE TO DO SOMETHING!
AGREED. BUT THE CITY COMES FIRST. ONCE WE FINISH HERE, WE'LL GO SEARCH FOR ACE.
HM. THAT'S WAYNE TOWER, ISN'T IT, FRED?
UH-HUH. THE TALLEST BUILDING IN GOTHAM CITY.
I'M GUESSING THERE ISN'T SUPPOSED TO BE A GIANT CAT ON IT, THOUGH.
I DON'T THINK SO, VELMA.
BUT WHERE COULD IT HAVE COME FROM?
LIKE, I DON'T KNOW, BUT I HOPE THAT TWO-TON TABBY DOESN'T COME HERE NEXT!
MAN, I WISH SCOOBY-DOO WAS HERE...
WHY, SHAGGY? TO CHASE THE CAT?
NO, SO I'D HAVE SOMEONE TO RUN AWAY WITH!
THERE'S NOT MUCH WE CAN DO ABOUT THAT CAT FROM ALL THE WAY OVER HERE.
WE'LL HAVE TO GET CLOSER. AND I THINK I KNOW HOW.
YOU, LIKE, WANT TO GET CLOSER TO THAT FREAKY FELINE?!
I KNEW I SHOULD'VE GONE WITH SCOOBY AND DAPHNE TO WAYNE MANOR--

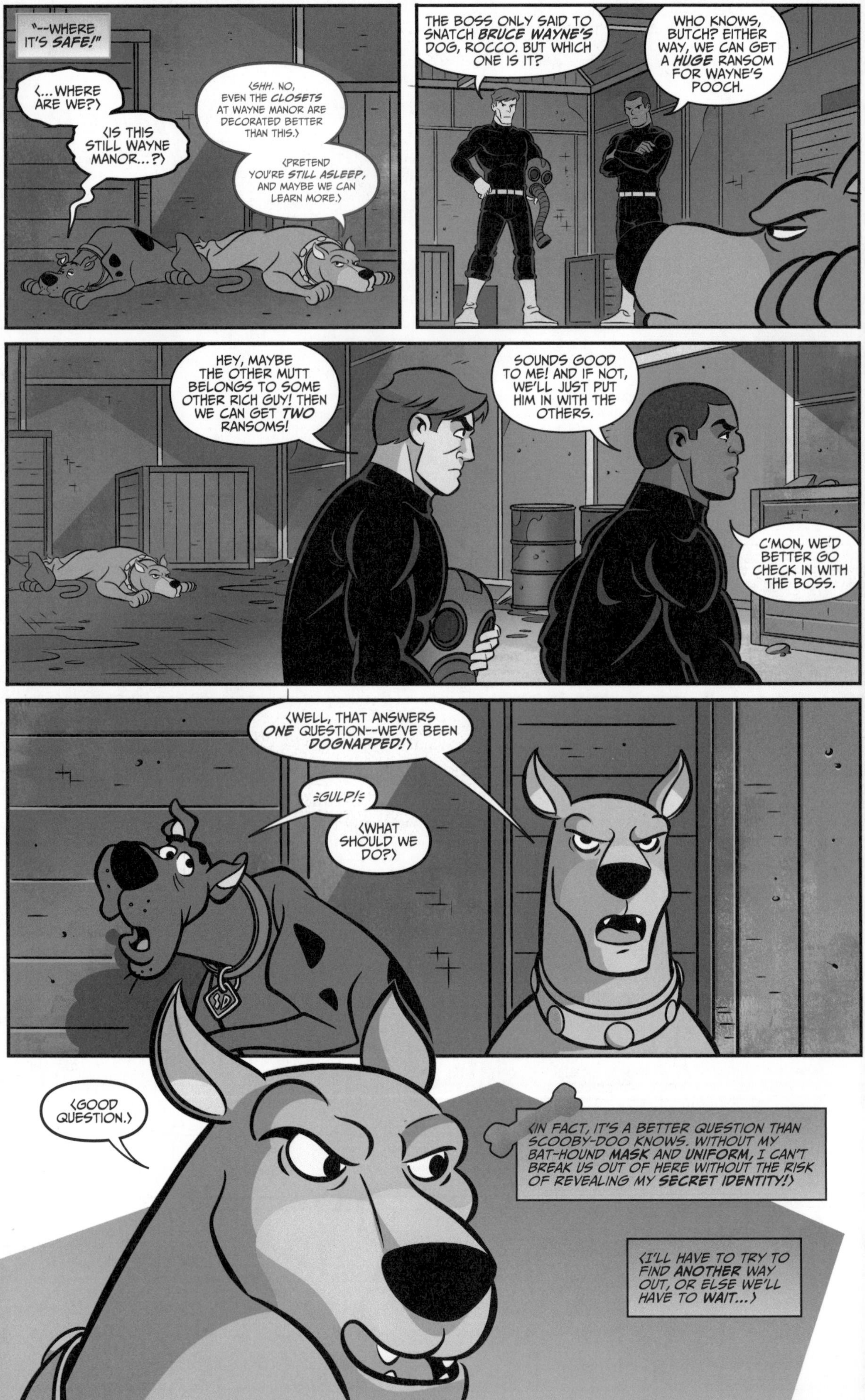
"--WHERE IT'S SAFE!"
‹...WHERE ARE WE?›
‹IS THIS STILL WAYNE MANOR...?›
‹SHH. NO, EVEN THE CLOSETS AT WAYNE MANOR ARE DECORATED BETTER THAN THIS.›
‹PRETEND YOU'RE STILL ASLEEP, AND MAYBE WE CAN LEARN MORE.›
THE BOSS ONLY SAID TO SNATCH BRUCE WAYNE'S DOG, ROCCO. BUT WHICH ONE IS IT?
WHO KNOWS, BUTCH? EITHER WAY, WE CAN GET A HUGE RANSOM FOR WAYNE'S POOCH.
HEY, MAYBE THE OTHER MUTT BELONGS TO SOME OTHER RICH GUY! THEN WE CAN GET TWO RANSOMS!
SOUNDS GOOD TO ME! AND IF NOT, WE'LL JUST PUT HIM IN WITH THE OTHERS.
C'MON, WE'D BETTER GO CHECK IN WITH THE BOSS.
‹WELL, THAT ANSWERS ONE QUESTION--WE'VE BEEN DOGNAPPED!›
GULP!
‹WHAT SHOULD WE DO?›
‹GOOD QUESTION.›
‹IN FACT, IT'S A BETTER QUESTION THAN SCOOBY-DOO KNOWS. WITHOUT MY BAT-HOUND MASK AND UNIFORM, I CAN'T BREAK US OUT OF HERE WITHOUT THE RISK OF REVEALING MY SECRET IDENTITY!›
‹I'LL HAVE TO TRY TO FIND ANOTHER WAY OUT, OR ELSE WE'LL HAVE TO WAIT...›

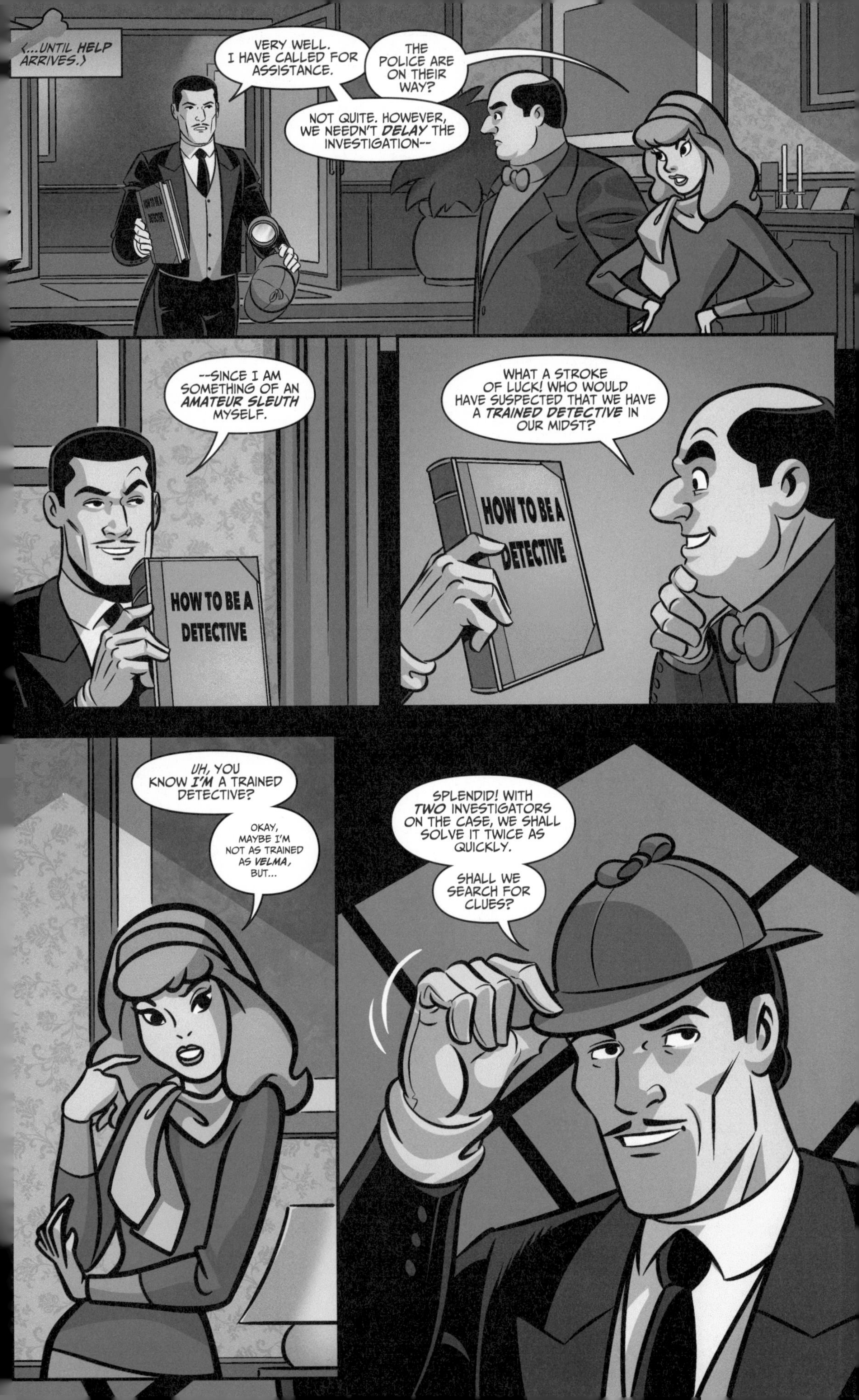

‹...UNTIL HELP ARRIVES.›
VERY WELL. I HAVE CALLED FOR ASSISTANCE.
THE POLICE ARE ON THEIR WAY?
NOT QUITE. HOWEVER, WE NEEDN'T DELAY THE INVESTIGATION--
HOW TO BE A DETECTIVE
--SINCE I AM SOMETHING OF AN AMATEUR SLEUTH MYSELF.
HOW TO BE A DETECTIVE
WHAT A STROKE OF LUCK! WHO WOULD HAVE SUSPECTED THAT WE HAVE A TRAINED DETECTIVE IN OUR MIDST?
HOW TO BE A DETECTIVE
UH, YOU KNOW I'M A TRAINED DETECTIVE?
OKAY, MAYBE I'M NOT AS TRAINED AS VELMA, BUT...
SPLENDID! WITH TWO INVESTIGATORS ON THE CASE, WE SHALL SOLVE IT TWICE AS QUICKLY.
SHALL WE SEARCH FOR CLUES?

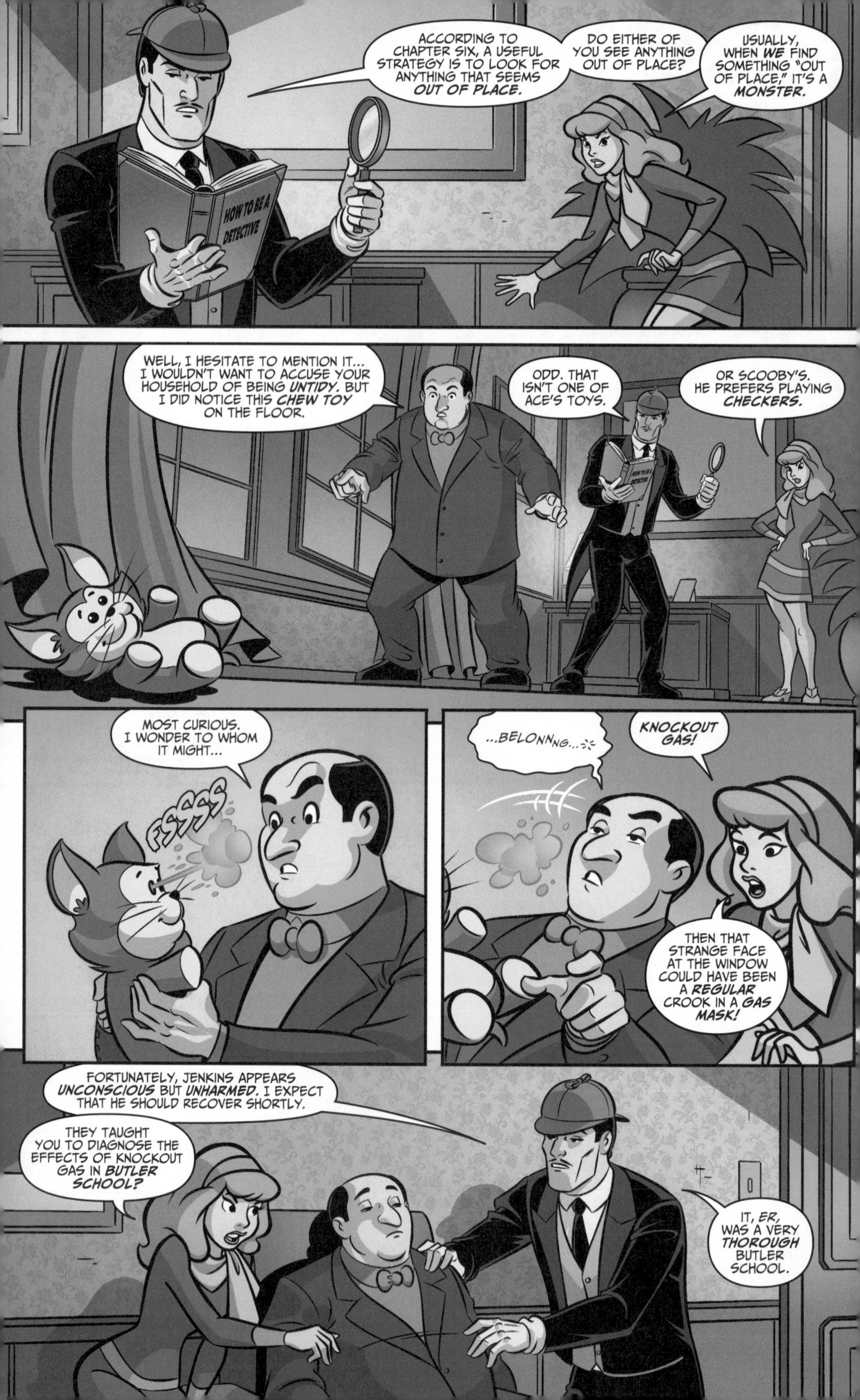
ACCORDING TO CHAPTER SIX, A USEFUL STRATEGY IS TO LOOK FOR ANYTHING THAT SEEMS OUT OF PLACE.
DO EITHER OF YOU SEE ANYTHING OUT OF PLACE?
USUALLY, WHEN WE FIND SOMETHING "OUT OF PLACE," IT'S A MONSTER.
HOW TO BE A DETECTIVE
WELL, I HESITATE TO MENTION IT... I WOULDN'T WANT TO ACCUSE YOUR HOUSEHOLD OF BEING UNTIDY. BUT I DID NOTICE THIS CHEW TOY ON THE FLOOR.
ODD. THAT ISN'T ONE OF ACE'S TOYS.
OR SCOOBY'S. HE PREFERS PLAYING CHECKERS.
MOST CURIOUS. I WONDER TO WHOM IT MIGHT...
FSSSS
...BELONNNG...
KNOCKOUT GAS!
THEN THAT STRANGE FACE AT THE WINDOW COULD HAVE BEEN A REGULAR CROOK IN A GAS MASK!
FORTUNATELY, JENKINS APPEARS UNCONSCIOUS BUT UNHARMED. I EXPECT THAT HE SHOULD RECOVER SHORTLY.
THEY TAUGHT YOU TO DIAGNOSE THE EFFECTS OF KNOCKOUT GAS IN BUTLER SCHOOL?
IT, ER, WAS A VERY THOROUGH BUTLER SCHOOL.

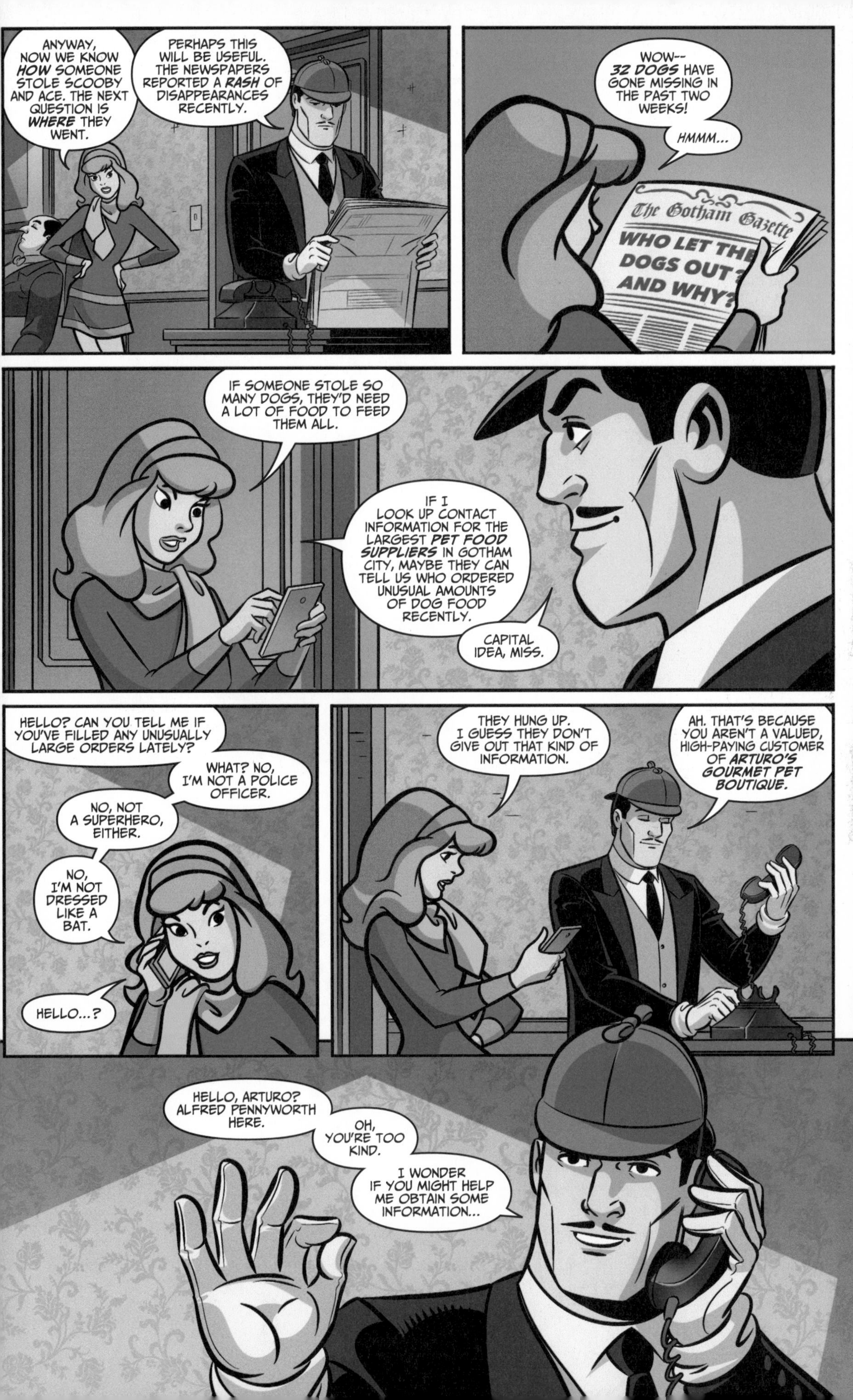
ANYWAY, NOW WE KNOW HOW SOMEONE STOLE SCOOBY AND ACE. THE NEXT QUESTION IS WHERE THEY WENT.
PERHAPS THIS WILL BE USEFUL. THE NEWSPAPERS REPORTED A RASH OF DISAPPEARANCES RECENTLY.
WOW-- 32 DOGS HAVE GONE MISSING IN THE PAST TWO WEEKS!
HMMM...
The Gotham Gazette
WHO LET THE DOGS OUT? AND WHY?
IF SOMEONE STOLE SO MANY DOGS, THEY'D NEED A LOT OF FOOD TO FEED THEM ALL.
IF I LOOK UP CONTACT INFORMATION FOR THE LARGEST PET FOOD SUPPLIERS IN GOTHAM CITY, MAYBE THEY CAN TELL US WHO ORDERED UNUSUAL AMOUNTS OF DOG FOOD RECENTLY.
CAPITAL IDEA, MISS.
HELLO? CAN YOU TELL ME IF YOU'VE FILLED ANY UNUSUALLY LARGE ORDERS LATELY?
WHAT? NO, I'M NOT A POLICE OFFICER.
NO, NOT A SUPERHERO, EITHER.
NO, I'M NOT DRESSED LIKE A BAT.
HELLO...?
THEY HUNG UP. I GUESS THEY DON'T GIVE OUT THAT KIND OF INFORMATION.
AH. THAT'S BECAUSE YOU AREN'T A VALUED, HIGH-PAYING CUSTOMER OF ARTURO'S GOURMET PET BOUTIQUE.
HELLO, ARTURO? ALFRED PENNYWORTH HERE.
OH, YOU'RE TOO KIND.
I WONDER IF YOU MIGHT HELP ME OBTAIN SOME INFORMATION...

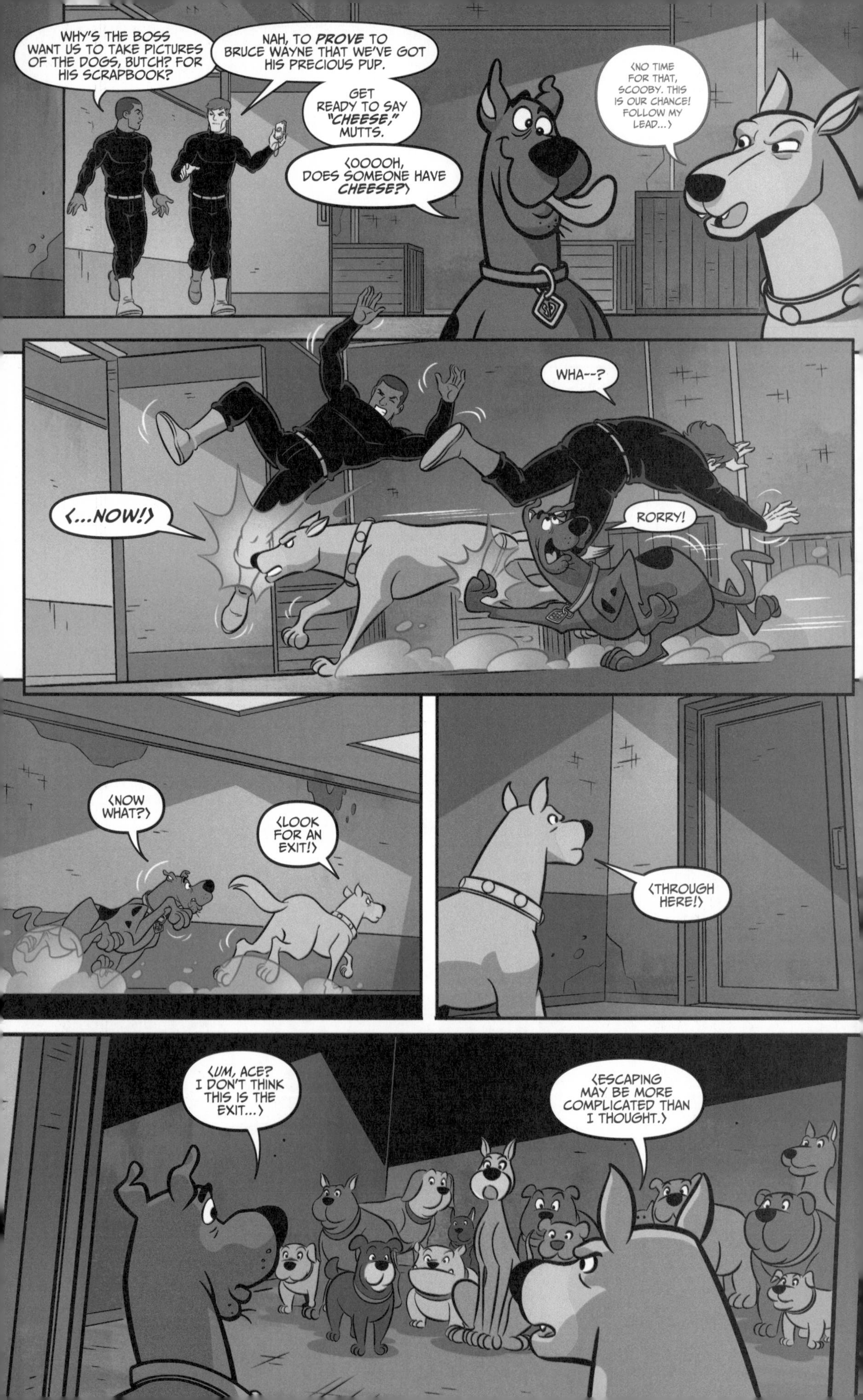
WHY'S THE BOSS WANT US TO TAKE PICTURES OF THE DOGS, BUTCH? FOR HIS SCRAPBOOK?
NAH, TO *PROVE* TO BRUCE WAYNE THAT WE'VE GOT HIS PRECIOUS PUP.
GET READY TO SAY *"CHEESE,"* MUTTS.
‹OOOOH, DOES SOMEONE HAVE *CHEESE?*›
‹NO TIME FOR THAT, SCOOBY. THIS IS OUR CHANCE! FOLLOW MY LEAD...›
WHA--?
‹...NOW!›
RORRY!
‹NOW WHAT?›
‹LOOK FOR AN EXIT!›
‹THROUGH HERE!›
‹*UM*, ACE? I DON'T THINK THIS IS THE EXIT...›
‹ESCAPING MAY BE MORE COMPLICATED THAN I THOUGHT.›

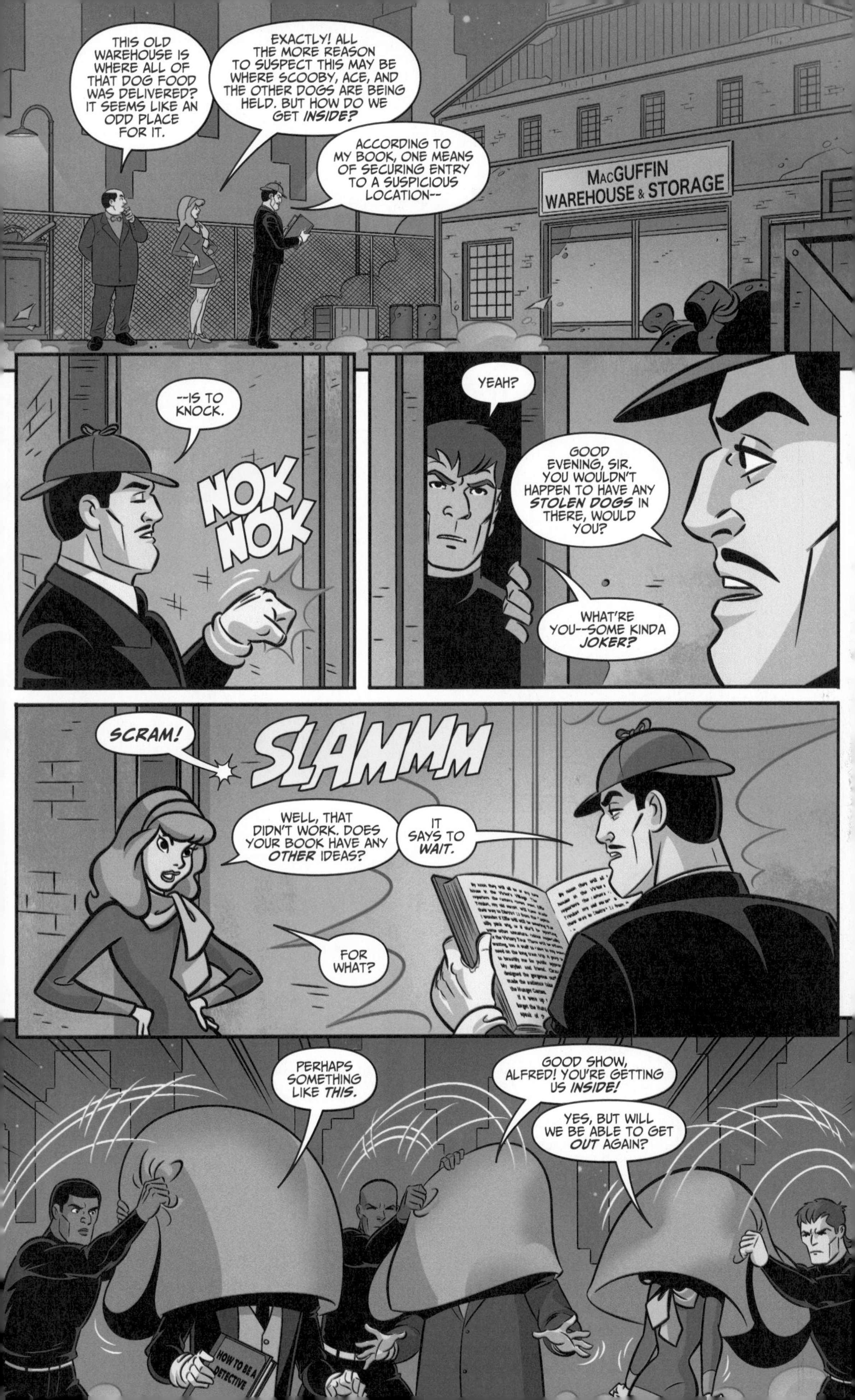
THIS OLD WAREHOUSE IS WHERE ALL OF THAT DOG FOOD WAS DELIVERED? IT SEEMS LIKE AN ODD PLACE FOR IT.
EXACTLY! ALL THE MORE REASON TO SUSPECT THIS MAY BE WHERE SCOOBY, ACE, AND THE OTHER DOGS ARE BEING HELD. BUT HOW DO WE GET INSIDE?
MacGUFFIN WAREHOUSE & STORAGE
ACCORDING TO MY BOOK, ONE MEANS OF SECURING ENTRY TO A SUSPICIOUS LOCATION--
--IS TO KNOCK.
NOK NOK
YEAH?
GOOD EVENING, SIR. YOU WOULDN'T HAPPEN TO HAVE ANY STOLEN DOGS IN THERE, WOULD YOU?
WHAT'RE YOU--SOME KINDA JOKER?
SCRAM!
SLAMMM
WELL, THAT DIDN'T WORK. DOES YOUR BOOK HAVE ANY OTHER IDEAS?
IT SAYS TO WAIT.
FOR WHAT?
PERHAPS SOMETHING LIKE THIS.
GOOD SHOW, ALFRED! YOU'RE GETTING US INSIDE!
YES, BUT WILL WE BE ABLE TO GET OUT AGAIN?
HOW TO BE A DETECTIVE

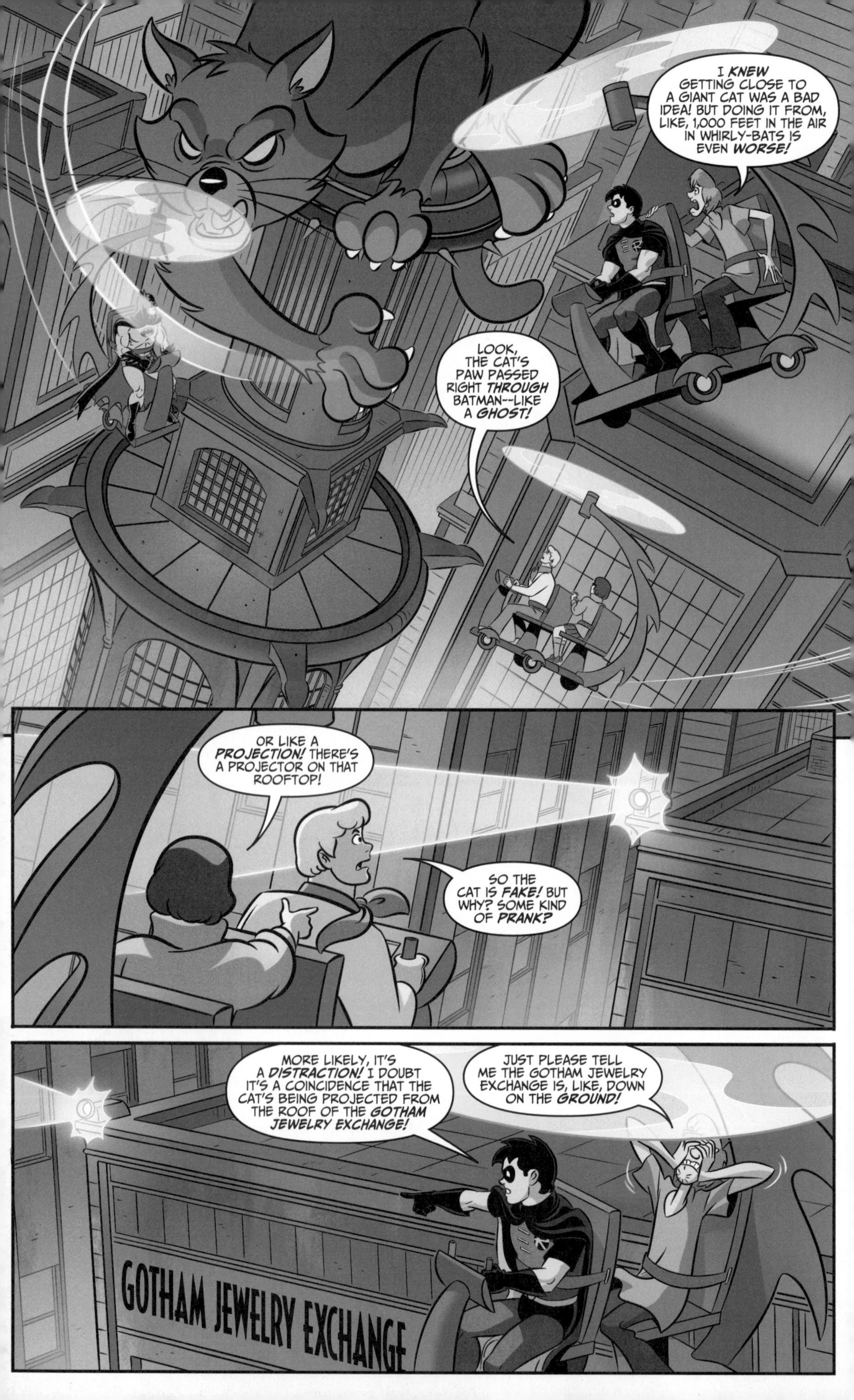
I KNEW GETTING CLOSE TO A GIANT CAT WAS A BAD IDEA! BUT DOING IT FROM, LIKE, 1,000 FEET IN THE AIR IN WHIRLY-BATS IS EVEN WORSE!
LOOK, THE CAT'S PAW PASSED RIGHT THROUGH BATMAN--LIKE A GHOST!
OR LIKE A PROJECTION! THERE'S A PROJECTOR ON THAT ROOFTOP!
SO THE CAT IS FAKE! BUT WHY? SOME KIND OF PRANK?
MORE LIKELY, IT'S A DISTRACTION! I DOUBT IT'S A COINCIDENCE THAT THE CAT'S BEING PROJECTED FROM THE ROOF OF THE GOTHAM JEWELRY EXCHANGE!
JUST PLEASE TELL ME THE GOTHAM JEWELRY EXCHANGE IS, LIKE, DOWN ON THE GROUND!
GOTHAM JEWELRY EXCHANGE

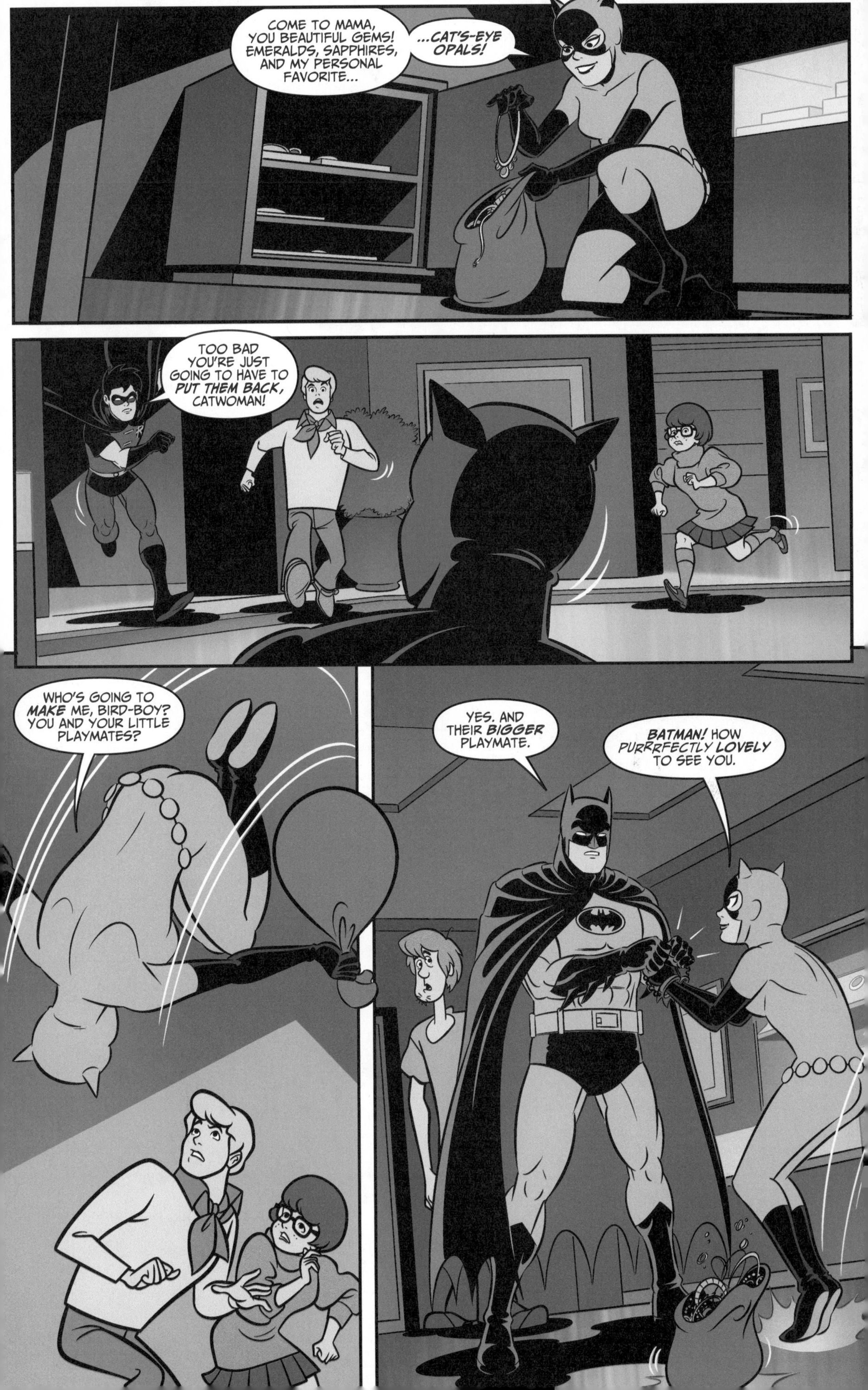
COME TO MAMA, YOU BEAUTIFUL GEMS! EMERALDS, SAPPHIRES, AND MY PERSONAL FAVORITE...
...CAT'S-EYE OPALS!
TOO BAD YOU'RE JUST GOING TO HAVE TO PUT THEM BACK, CATWOMAN!
WHO'S GOING TO MAKE ME, BIRD-BOY? YOU AND YOUR LITTLE PLAYMATES?
YES. AND THEIR BIGGER PLAYMATE.
BATMAN! HOW PURRRFECTLY LOVELY TO SEE YOU.

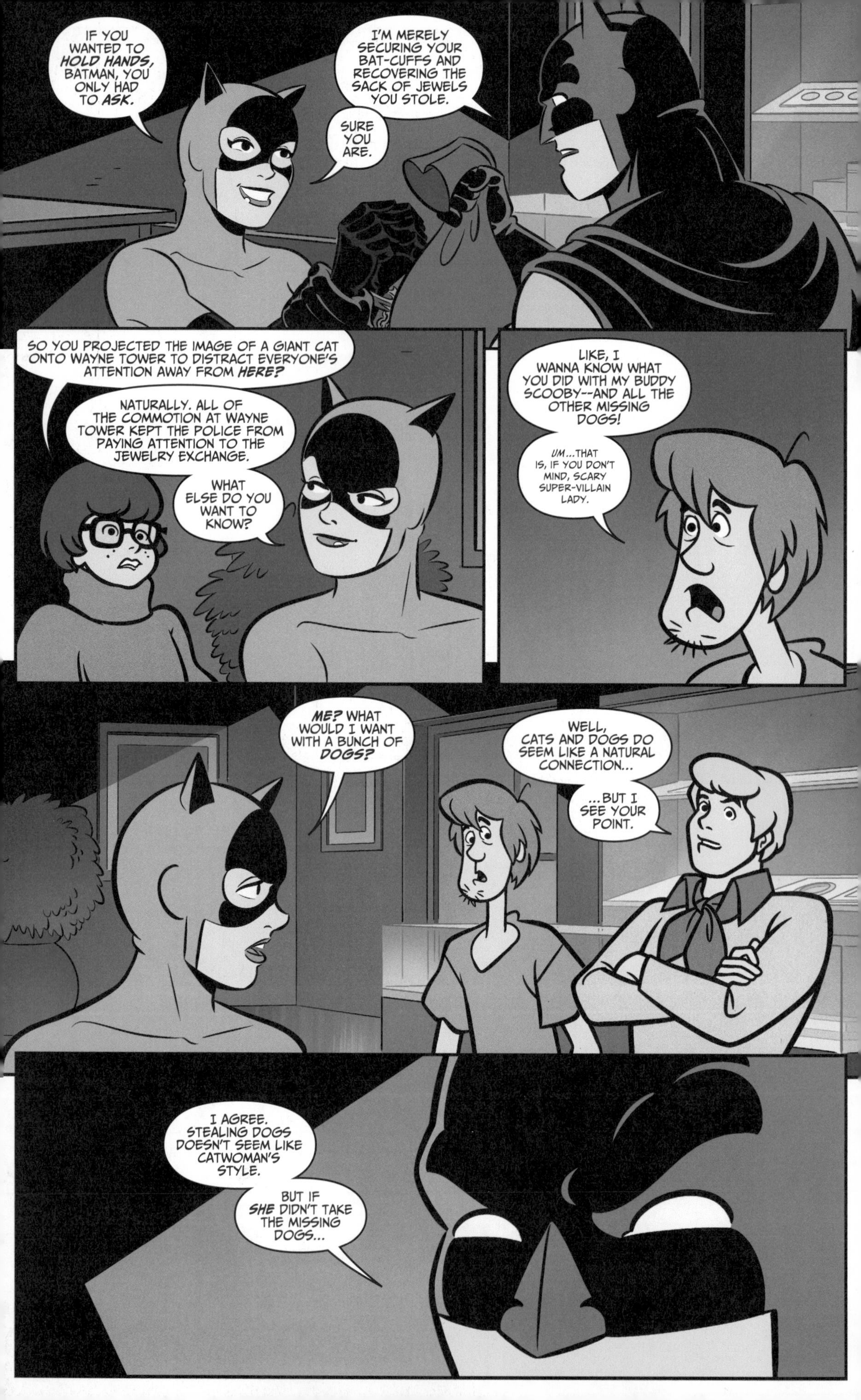
IF YOU WANTED TO HOLD HANDS, BATMAN, YOU ONLY HAD TO ASK.
I'M MERELY SECURING YOUR BAT-CUFFS AND RECOVERING THE SACK OF JEWELS YOU STOLE.
SURE YOU ARE.
SO YOU PROJECTED THE IMAGE OF A GIANT CAT ONTO WAYNE TOWER TO DISTRACT EVERYONE'S ATTENTION AWAY FROM HERE?
NATURALLY. ALL OF THE COMMOTION AT WAYNE TOWER KEPT THE POLICE FROM PAYING ATTENTION TO THE JEWELRY EXCHANGE.
WHAT ELSE DO YOU WANT TO KNOW?
LIKE, I WANNA KNOW WHAT YOU DID WITH MY BUDDY SCOOBY--AND ALL THE OTHER MISSING DOGS!
UM...THAT IS, IF YOU DON'T MIND, SCARY SUPER-VILLAIN LADY.
ME? WHAT WOULD I WANT WITH A BUNCH OF DOGS?
WELL, CATS AND DOGS DO SEEM LIKE A NATURAL CONNECTION...
...BUT I SEE YOUR POINT.
I AGREE. STEALING DOGS DOESN'T SEEM LIKE CATWOMAN'S STYLE.
BUT IF SHE DIDN'T TAKE THE MISSING DOGS...

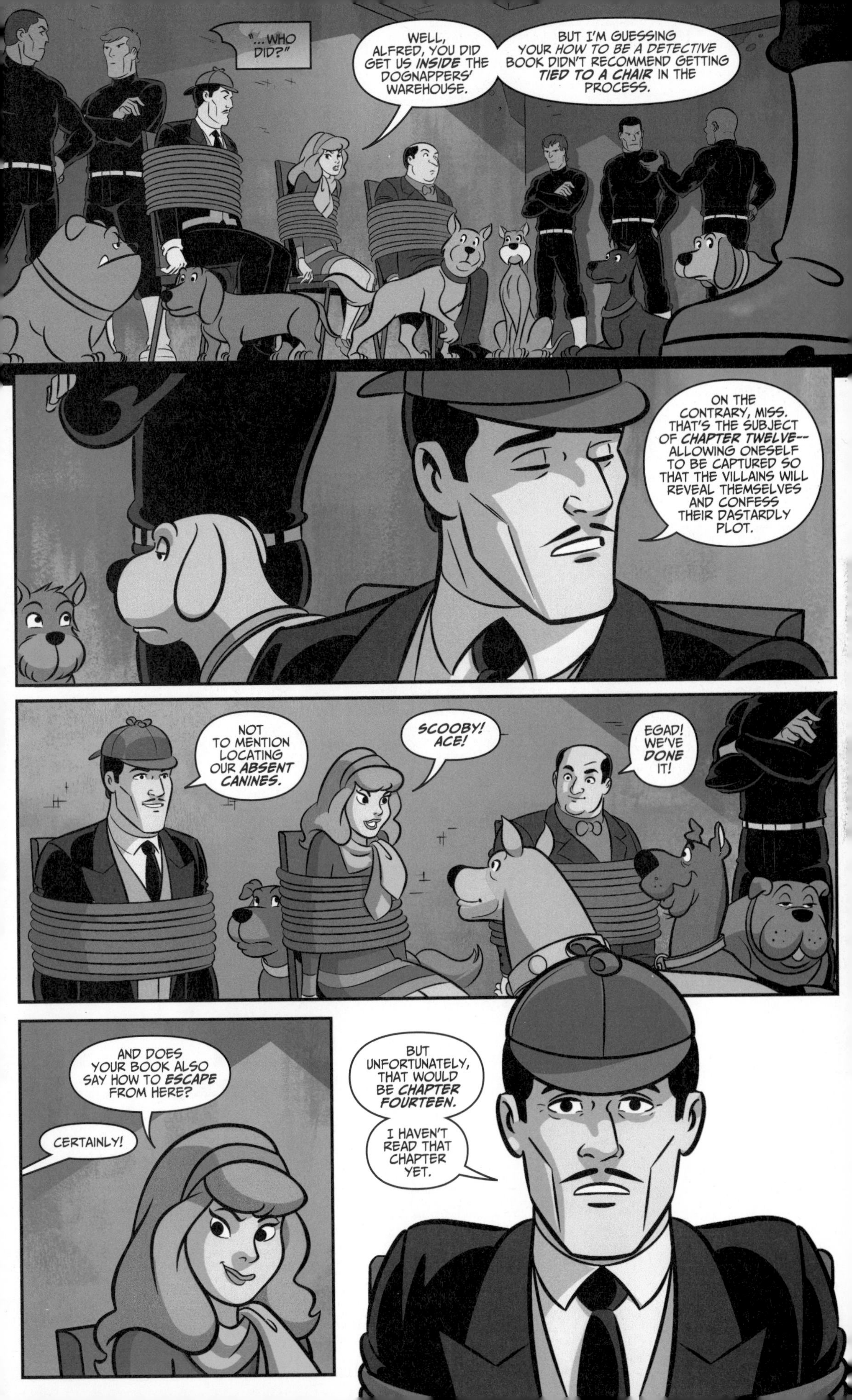
"...WHO DID?"
WELL, ALFRED, YOU DID GET US INSIDE THE DOGNAPPERS' WAREHOUSE.
BUT I'M GUESSING YOUR HOW TO BE A DETECTIVE BOOK DIDN'T RECOMMEND GETTING TIED TO A CHAIR IN THE PROCESS.
ON THE CONTRARY, MISS. THAT'S THE SUBJECT OF CHAPTER TWELVE-- ALLOWING ONESELF TO BE CAPTURED SO THAT THE VILLAINS WILL REVEAL THEMSELVES AND CONFESS THEIR DASTARDLY PLOT.
NOT TO MENTION LOCATING OUR ABSENT CANINES.
SCOOBY! ACE!
EGAD! WE'VE DONE IT!
AND DOES YOUR BOOK ALSO SAY HOW TO ESCAPE FROM HERE?
CERTAINLY!
BUT UNFORTUNATELY, THAT WOULD BE CHAPTER FOURTEEN.
I HAVEN'T READ THAT CHAPTER YET.

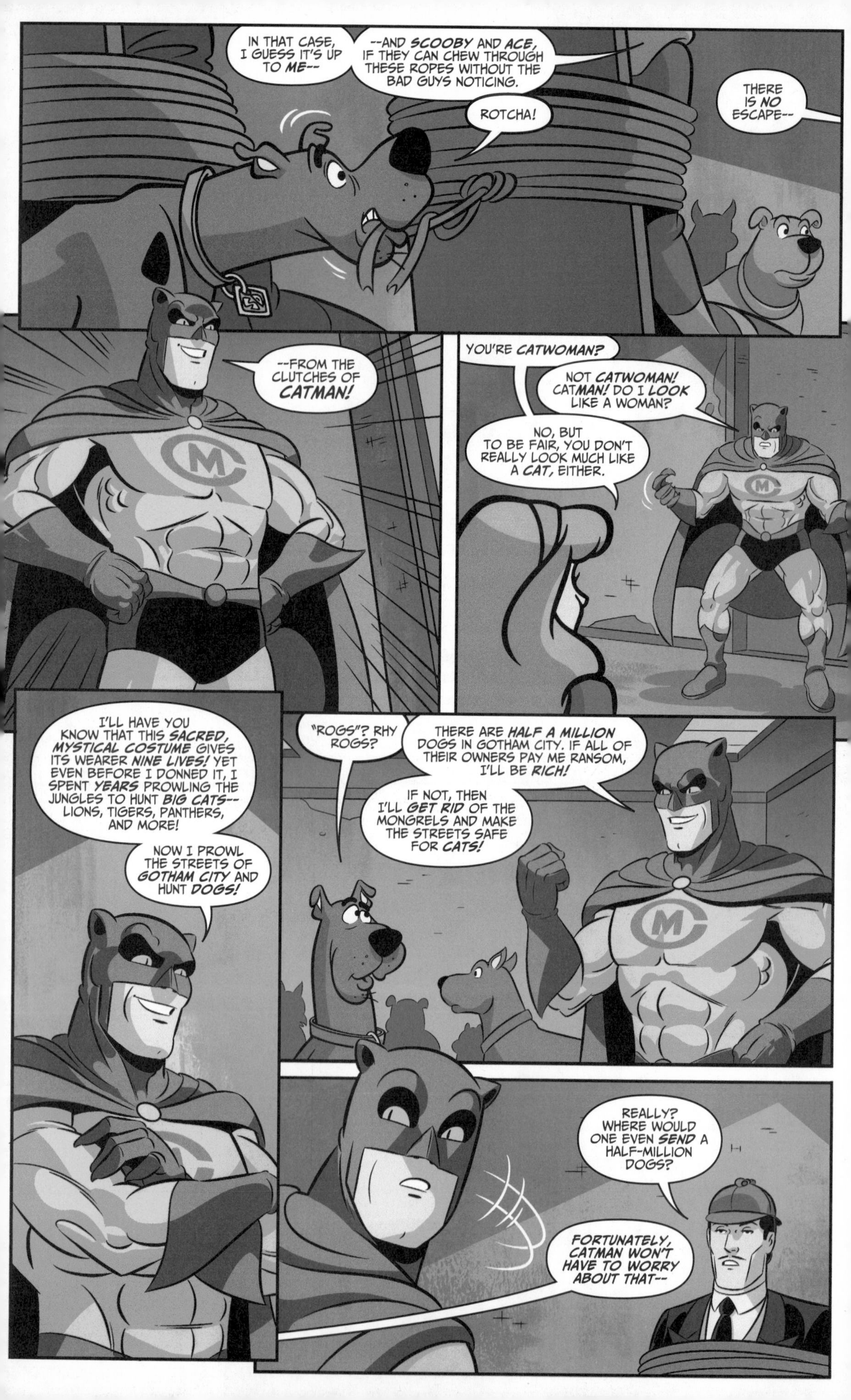
IN THAT CASE, I GUESS IT'S UP TO ME--
--AND SCOOBY AND ACE, IF THEY CAN CHEW THROUGH THESE ROPES WITHOUT THE BAD GUYS NOTICING.
ROTCHA!
THERE IS NO ESCAPE--
--FROM THE CLUTCHES OF CATMAN!
YOU'RE CATWOMAN?
NOT CATWOMAN! CATMAN! DO I LOOK LIKE A WOMAN?
NO, BUT TO BE FAIR, YOU DON'T REALLY LOOK MUCH LIKE A CAT, EITHER.
I'LL HAVE YOU KNOW THAT THIS SACRED, MYSTICAL COSTUME GIVES ITS WEARER NINE LIVES! YET EVEN BEFORE I DONNED IT, I SPENT YEARS PROWLING THE JUNGLES TO HUNT BIG CATS-- LIONS, TIGERS, PANTHERS, AND MORE!
NOW I PROWL THE STREETS OF GOTHAM CITY AND HUNT DOGS!
"ROGS"? RHY ROGS?
THERE ARE HALF A MILLION DOGS IN GOTHAM CITY. IF ALL OF THEIR OWNERS PAY ME RANSOM, I'LL BE RICH!
IF NOT, THEN I'LL GET RID OF THE MONGRELS AND MAKE THE STREETS SAFE FOR CATS!
REALLY? WHERE WOULD ONE EVEN SEND A HALF-MILLION DOGS?
FORTUNATELY, CATMAN WON'T HAVE TO WORRY ABOUT THAT--

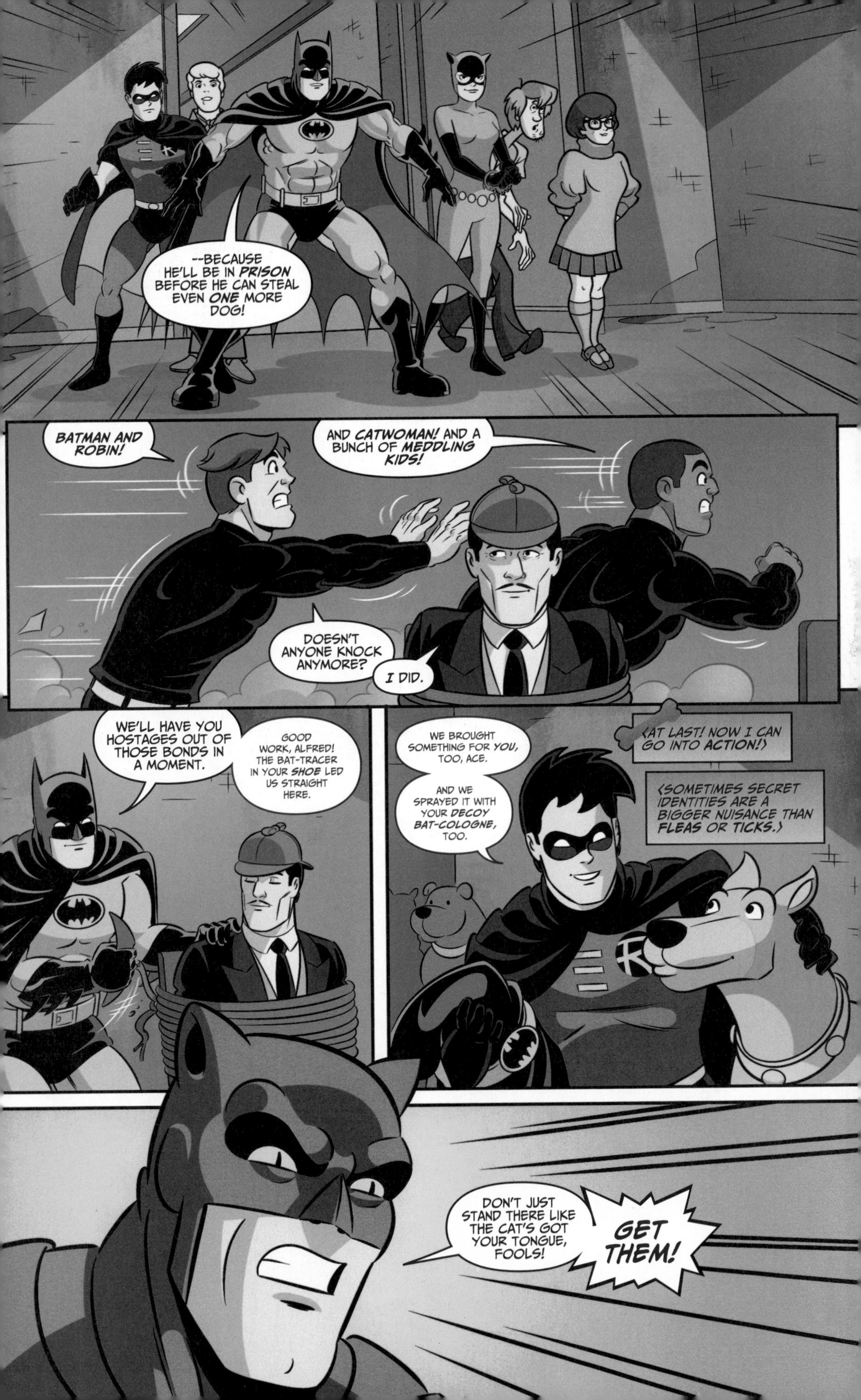
--BECAUSE HE'LL BE IN PRISON BEFORE HE CAN STEAL EVEN ONE MORE DOG!
BATMAN AND ROBIN!
AND CATWOMAN! AND A BUNCH OF MEDDLING KIDS!
DOESN'T ANYONE KNOCK ANYMORE?
I DID.
WE'LL HAVE YOU HOSTAGES OUT OF THOSE BONDS IN A MOMENT.
GOOD WORK, ALFRED! THE BAT-TRACER IN YOUR SHOE LED US STRAIGHT HERE.
WE BROUGHT SOMETHING FOR YOU, TOO, ACE.
AND WE SPRAYED IT WITH YOUR DECOY BAT-COLOGNE, TOO.
<AT LAST! NOW I CAN GO INTO ACTION!>
<SOMETIMES SECRET IDENTITIES ARE A BIGGER NUISANCE THAN FLEAS OR TICKS.>
DON'T JUST STAND THERE LIKE THE CAT'S GOT YOUR TONGUE, FOOLS!
GET THEM!

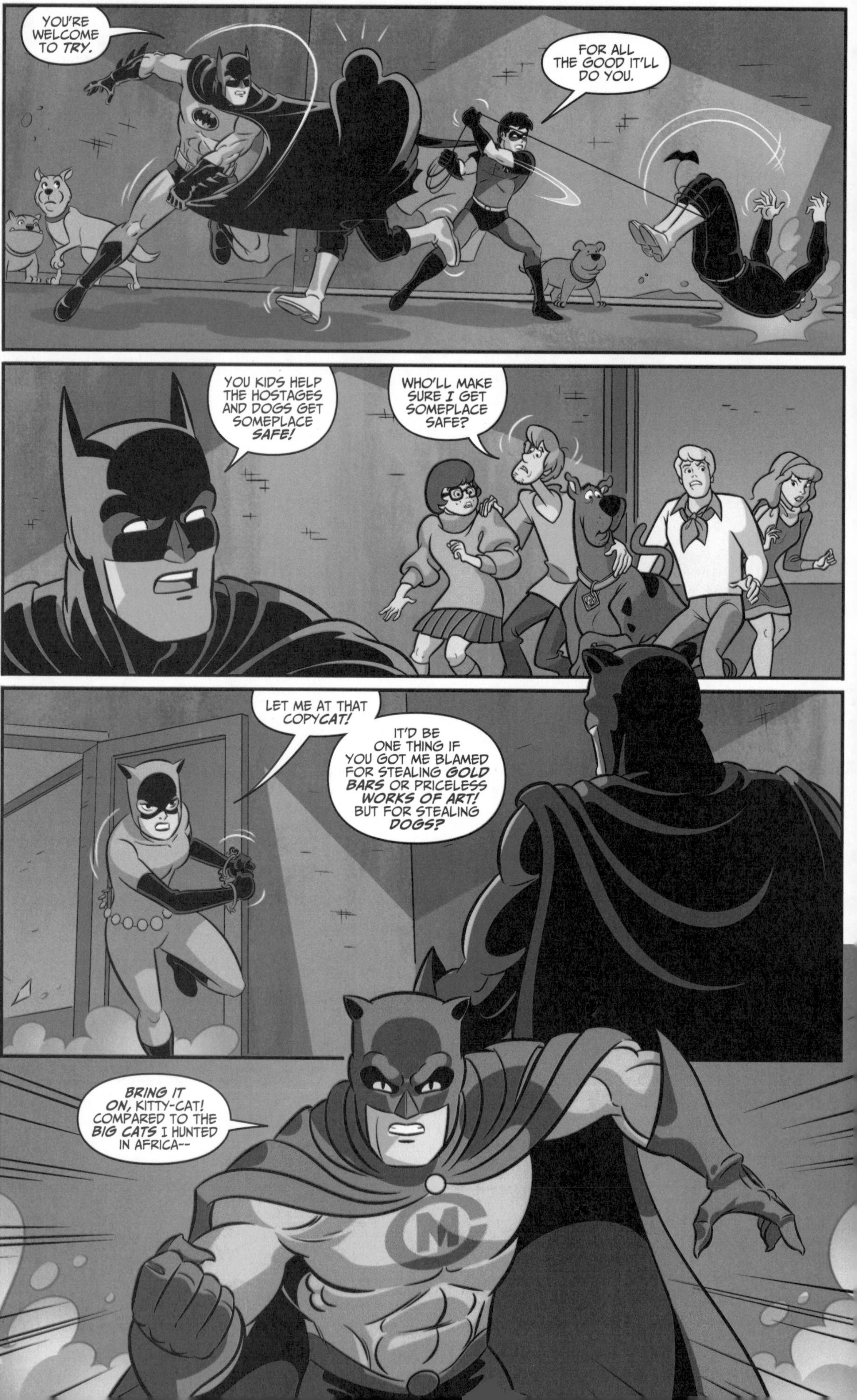

YOU'RE WELCOME TO TRY.
FOR ALL THE GOOD IT'LL DO YOU.
YOU KIDS HELP THE HOSTAGES AND DOGS GET SOMEPLACE SAFE!
WHO'LL MAKE SURE I GET SOMEPLACE SAFE?
LET ME AT THAT COPYCAT!
IT'D BE ONE THING IF YOU GOT ME BLAMED FOR STEALING GOLD BARS OR PRICELESS WORKS OF ART! BUT FOR STEALING DOGS?
BRING IT ON, KITTY-CAT! COMPARED TO THE BIG CATS I HUNTED IN AFRICA--

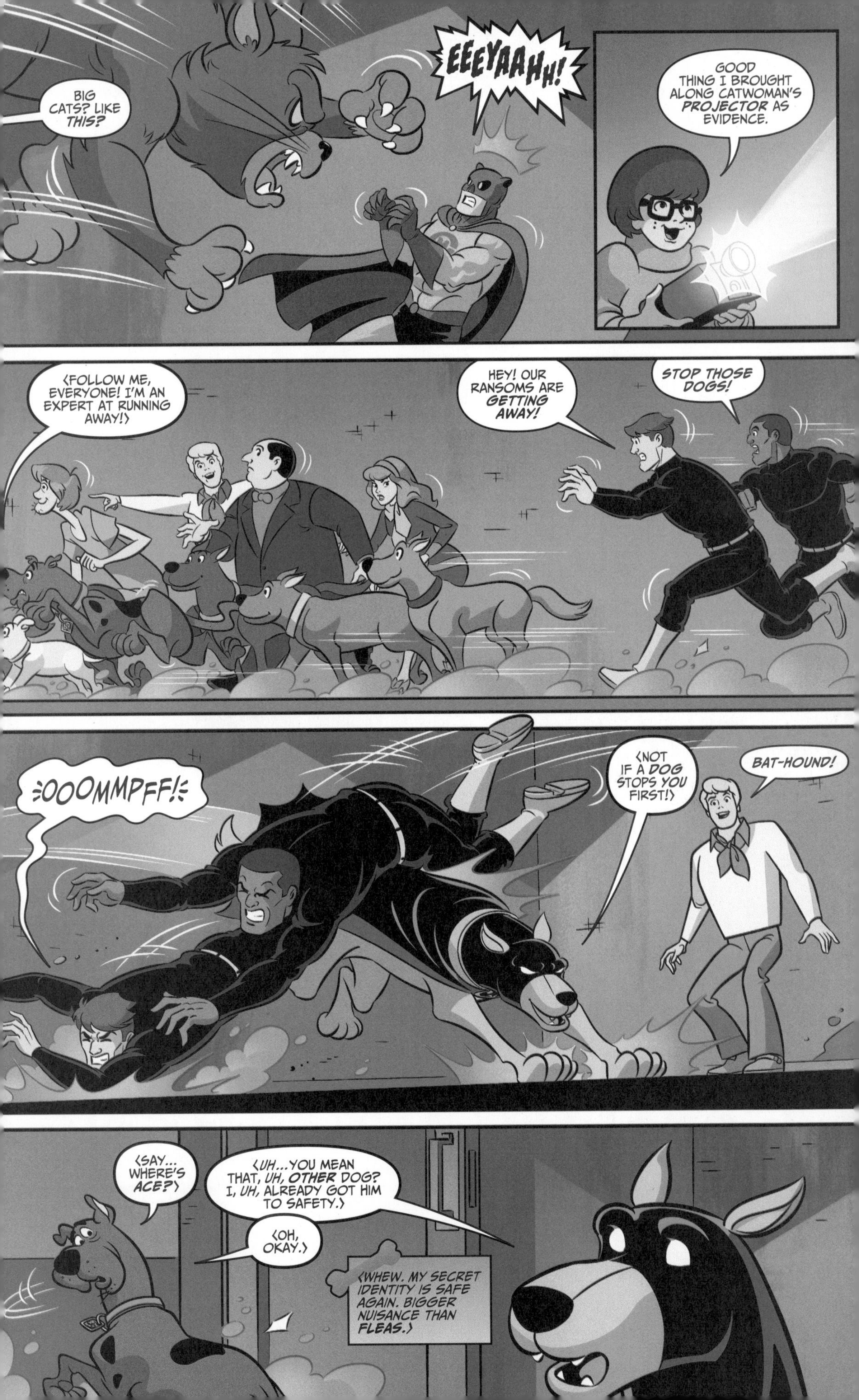
BIG CATS? LIKE THIS?
EEEYAAHH!
GOOD THING I BROUGHT ALONG CATWOMAN'S PROJECTOR AS EVIDENCE.
⟨FOLLOW ME, EVERYONE! I'M AN EXPERT AT RUNNING AWAY!⟩
HEY! OUR RANSOMS ARE GETTING AWAY!
STOP THOSE DOGS!
OOOMMPFF!
⟨NOT IF A DOG STOPS YOU FIRST!⟩
BAT-HOUND!
⟨SAY... WHERE'S ACE?⟩
⟨UH...YOU MEAN THAT, UH, OTHER DOG? I, UH, ALREADY GOT HIM TO SAFETY.⟩
⟨OH, OKAY.⟩
⟨WHEW. MY SECRET IDENTITY IS SAFE AGAIN. BIGGER NUISANCE THAN FLEAS.⟩

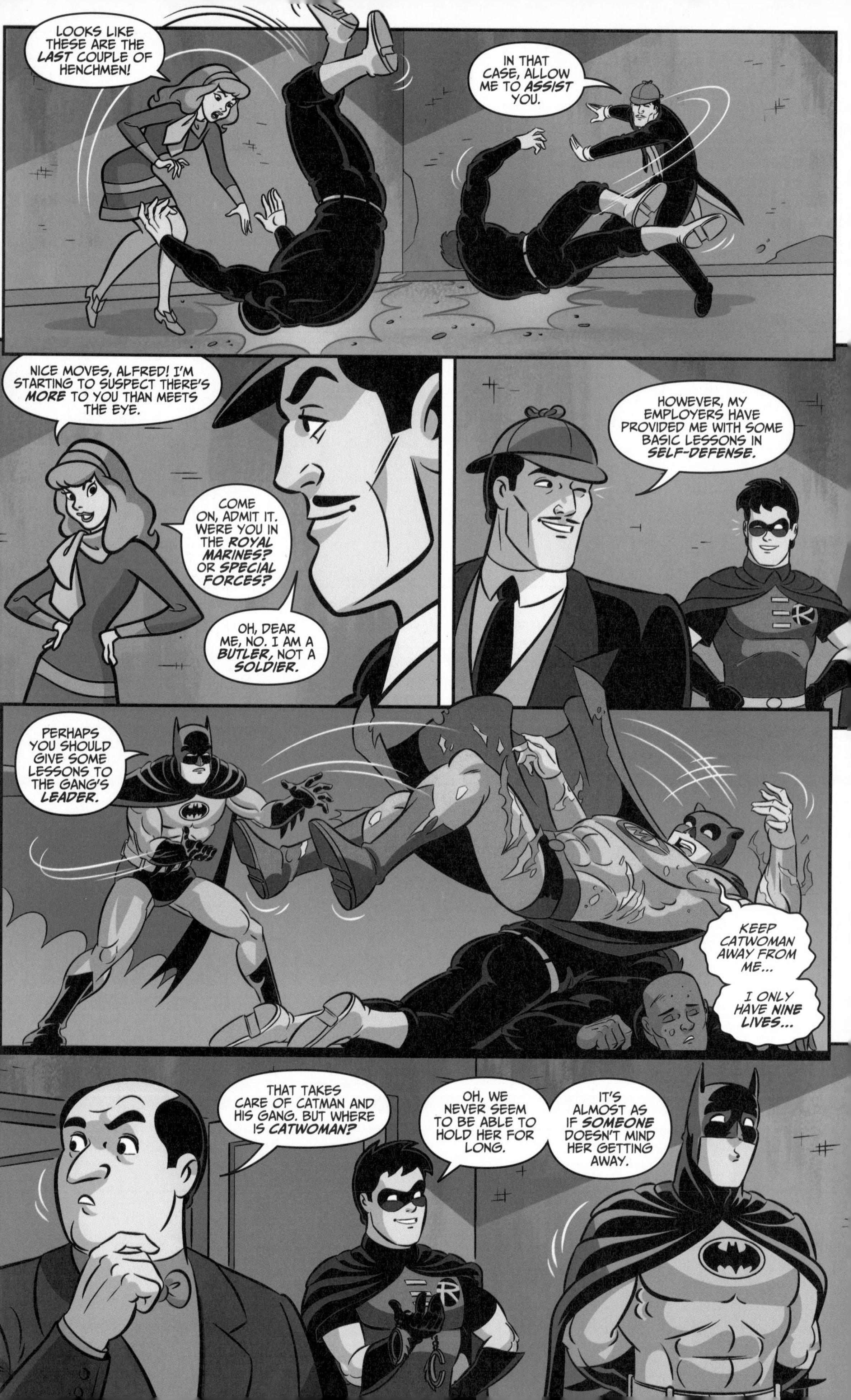
LOOKS LIKE THESE ARE THE LAST COUPLE OF HENCHMEN!
IN THAT CASE, ALLOW ME TO ASSIST YOU.
NICE MOVES, ALFRED! I'M STARTING TO SUSPECT THERE'S MORE TO YOU THAN MEETS THE EYE.
COME ON, ADMIT IT. WERE YOU IN THE ROYAL MARINES? OR SPECIAL FORCES?
OH, DEAR ME, NO. I AM A BUTLER, NOT A SOLDIER.
HOWEVER, MY EMPLOYERS HAVE PROVIDED ME WITH SOME BASIC LESSONS IN SELF-DEFENSE.
PERHAPS YOU SHOULD GIVE SOME LESSONS TO THE GANG'S LEADER.
KEEP CATWOMAN AWAY FROM ME...
I ONLY HAVE NINE LIVES...
THAT TAKES CARE OF CATMAN AND HIS GANG. BUT WHERE IS CATWOMAN?
OH, WE NEVER SEEM TO BE ABLE TO HOLD HER FOR LONG.
IT'S ALMOST AS IF SOMEONE DOESN'T MIND HER GETTING AWAY.

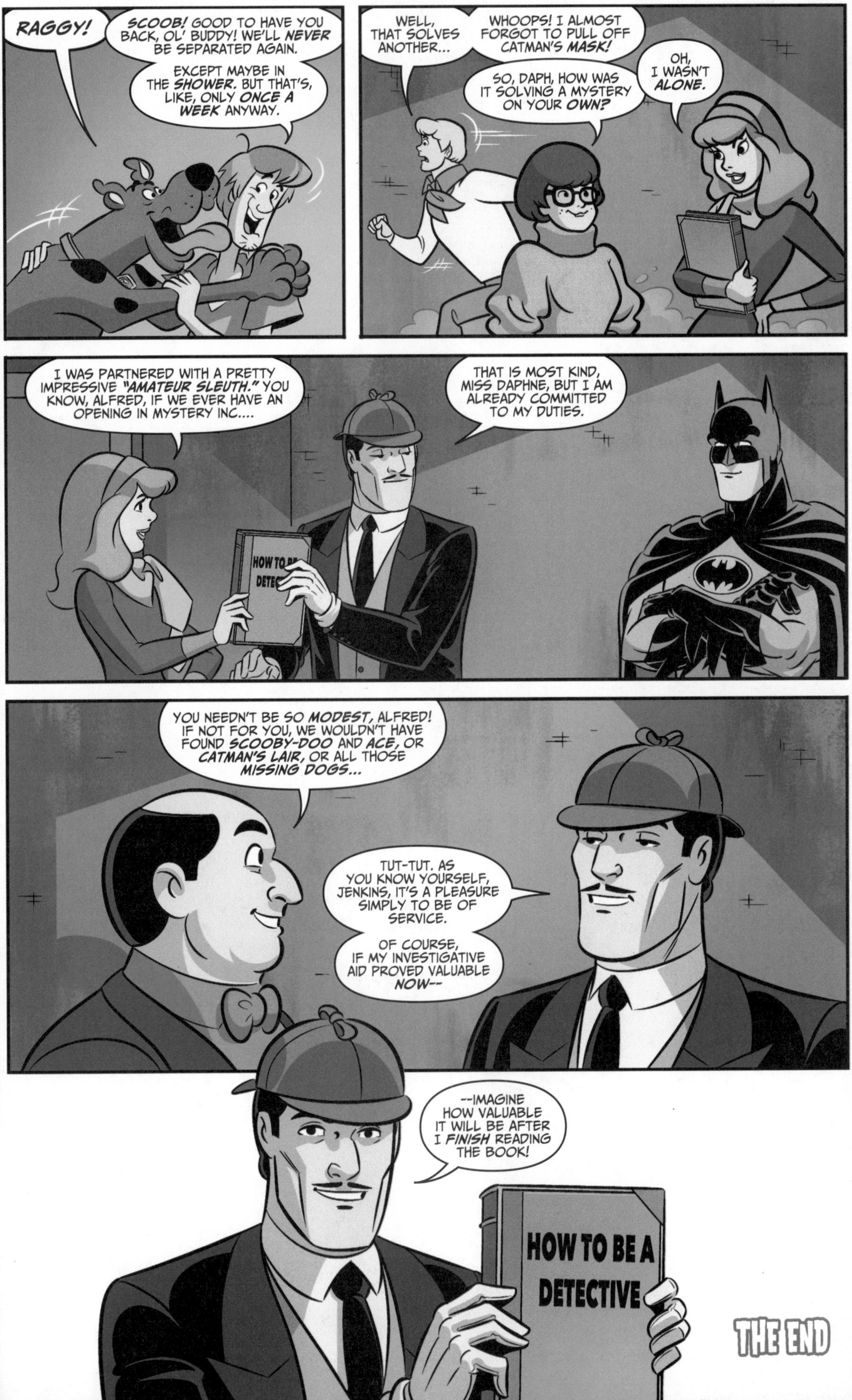
RAGGY!
SCOOB! GOOD TO HAVE YOU BACK, OL' BUDDY! WE'LL NEVER BE SEPARATED AGAIN.
EXCEPT MAYBE IN THE SHOWER. BUT THAT'S, LIKE, ONLY ONCE A WEEK ANYWAY.
WELL, THAT SOLVES ANOTHER...
WHOOPS! I ALMOST FORGOT TO PULL OFF CATMAN'S MASK!
SO, DAPH, HOW WAS IT SOLVING A MYSTERY ON YOUR OWN?
OH, I WASN'T ALONE.
I WAS PARTNERED WITH A PRETTY IMPRESSIVE "AMATEUR SLEUTH." YOU KNOW, ALFRED, IF WE EVER HAVE AN OPENING IN MYSTERY INC....
THAT IS MOST KIND, MISS DAPHNE, BUT I AM ALREADY COMMITTED TO MY DUTIES.
YOU NEEDN'T BE SO MODEST, ALFRED! IF NOT FOR YOU, WE WOULDN'T HAVE FOUND SCOOBY-DOO AND ACE, OR CATMAN'S LAIR, OR ALL THOSE MISSING DOGS...
TUT-TUT. AS YOU KNOW YOURSELF, JENKINS, IT'S A PLEASURE SIMPLY TO BE OF SERVICE.
OF COURSE, IF MY INVESTIGATIVE AID PROVED VALUABLE NOW--
--IMAGINE HOW VALUABLE IT WILL BE AFTER I FINISH READING THE BOOK!
HOW TO BE A DETECTIVE
THE END

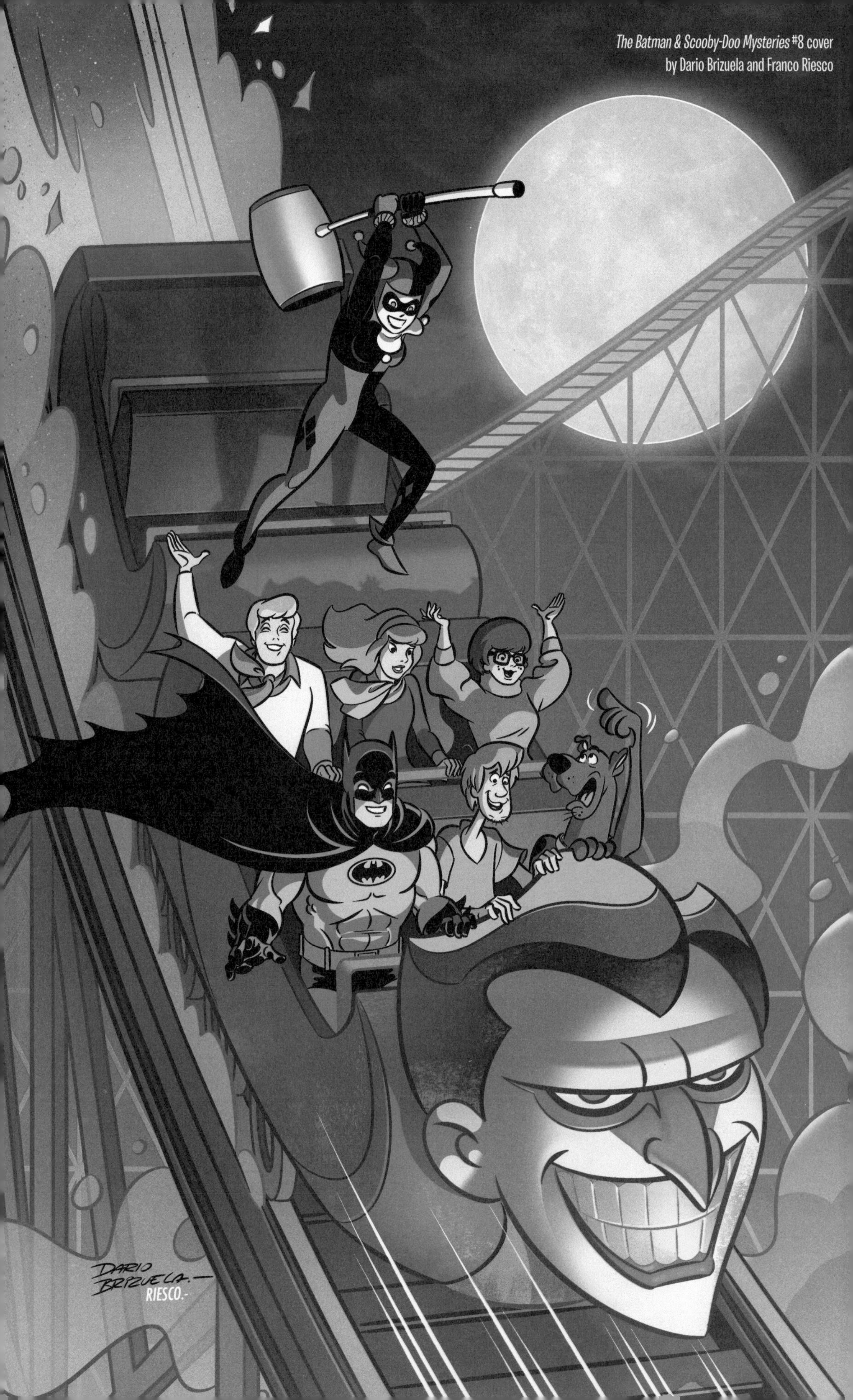
DARIO BRIZUELA.—
RIESCO.-

The Batman & Scooby-Doo Mysteries #8 cover
by Dario Brizuela and Franco Riesco

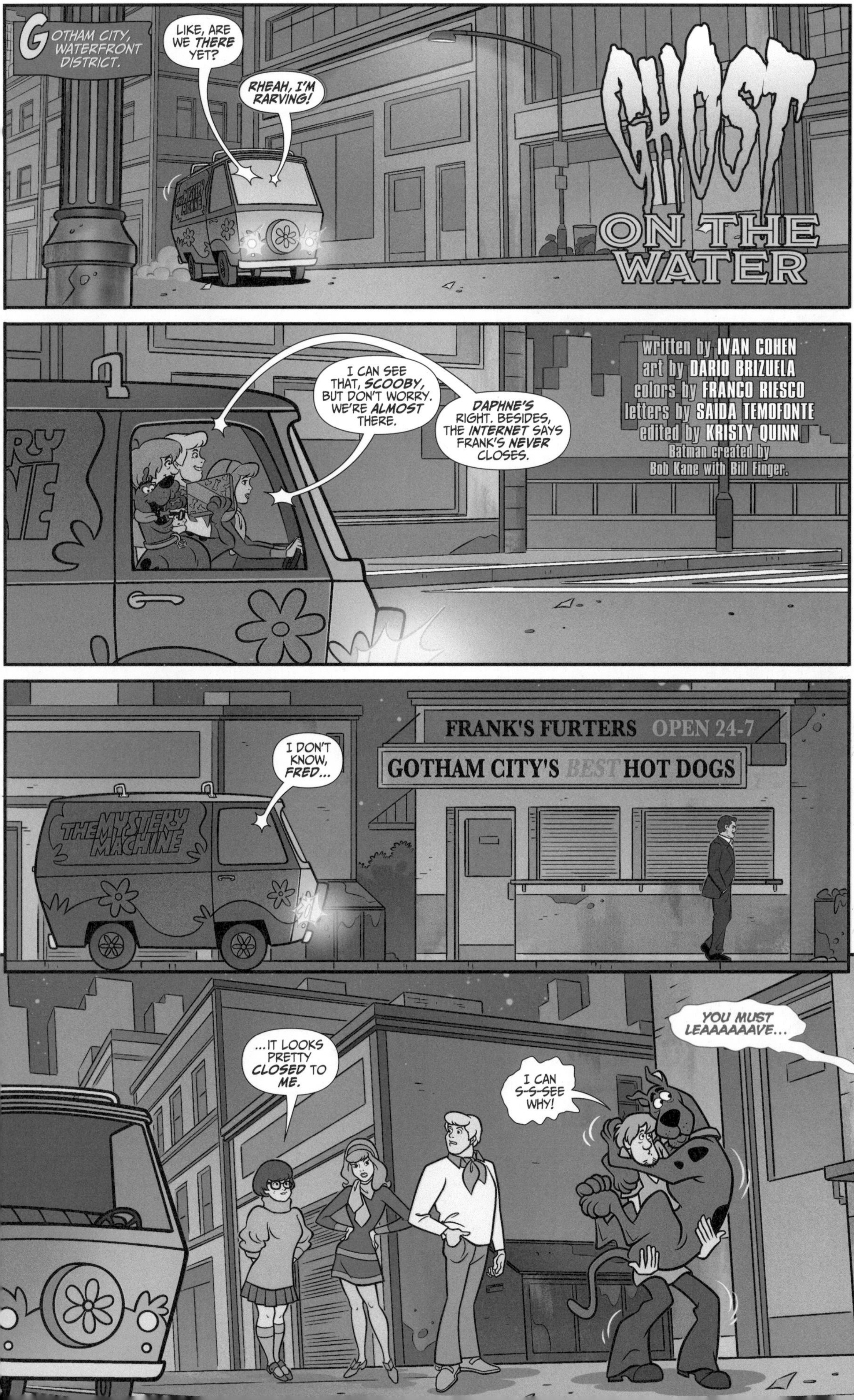
GOTHAM CITY, WATERFRONT DISTRICT.
LIKE, ARE WE THERE YET?
RHEAH, I'M RARVING!
GHOST ON THE WATER
THE MYSTERY MACHINE
I CAN SEE THAT, SCOOBY, BUT DON'T WORRY. WE'RE ALMOST THERE.
DAPHNE'S RIGHT. BESIDES, THE INTERNET SAYS FRANK'S NEVER CLOSES.
written by IVAN COHEN
art by DARIO BRIZUELA
colors by FRANCO RIESCO
letters by SAIDA TEMOFONTE
edited by KRISTY QUINN
Batman created by Bob Kane with Bill Finger.
FRANK'S FURTERS OPEN 24-7
GOTHAM CITY'S BEST HOT DOGS
THE MYSTERY MACHINE
I DON'T KNOW, FRED...
...IT LOOKS PRETTY CLOSED TO ME.
YOU MUST LEAAAAAAVE...
I CAN S-S-SEE WHY!

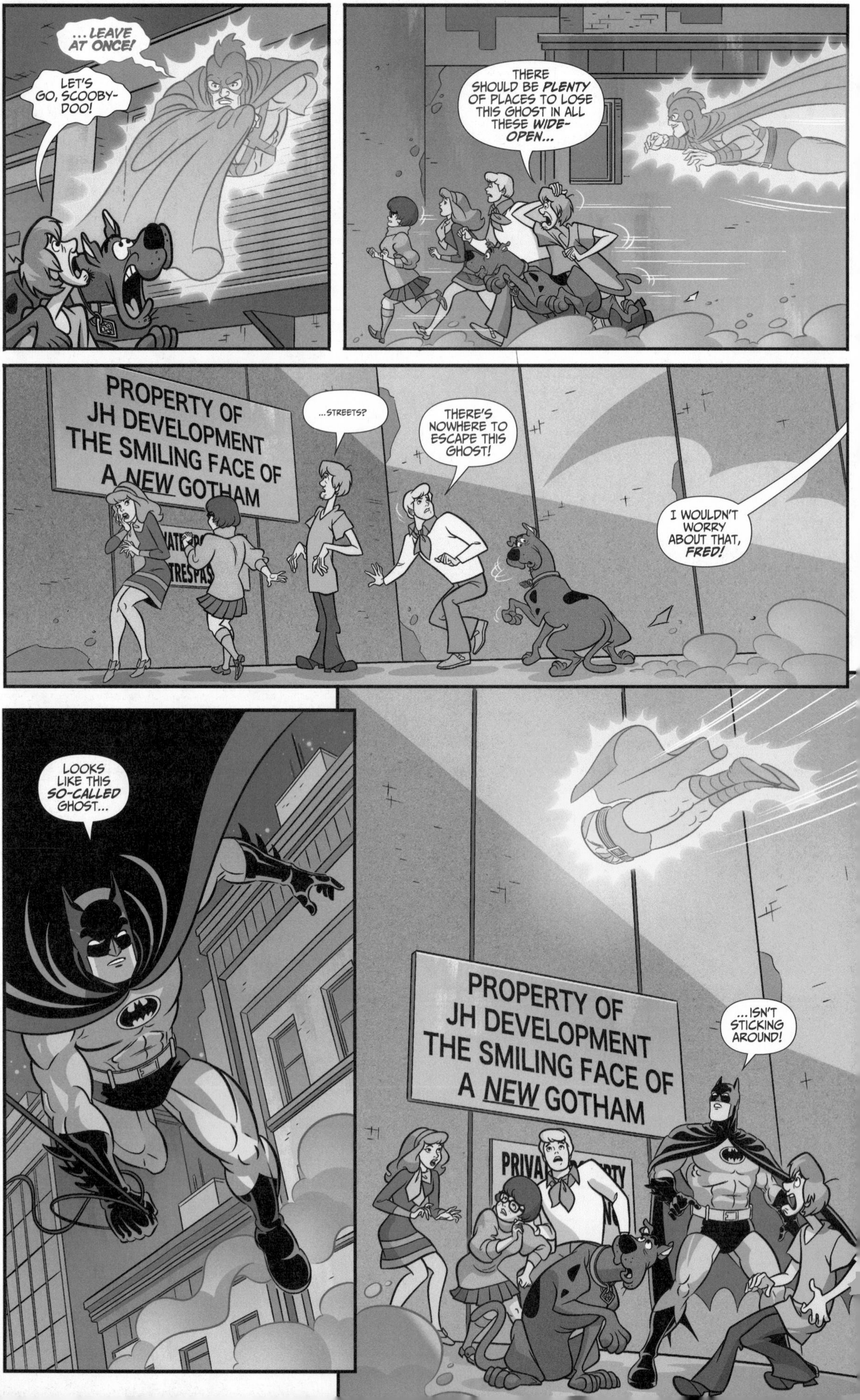

...LEAVE AT ONCE!
LET'S GO, SCOOBY-DOO!
THERE SHOULD BE PLENTY OF PLACES TO LOSE THIS GHOST IN ALL THESE WIDE-OPEN...
PROPERTY OF JH DEVELOPMENT THE SMILING FACE OF A NEW GOTHAM
...STREETS?
THERE'S NOWHERE TO ESCAPE THIS GHOST!
I WOULDN'T WORRY ABOUT THAT, FRED!
LOOKS LIKE THIS SO-CALLED GHOST...
PROPERTY OF JH DEVELOPMENT THE SMILING FACE OF A NEW GOTHAM
...ISN'T STICKING AROUND!

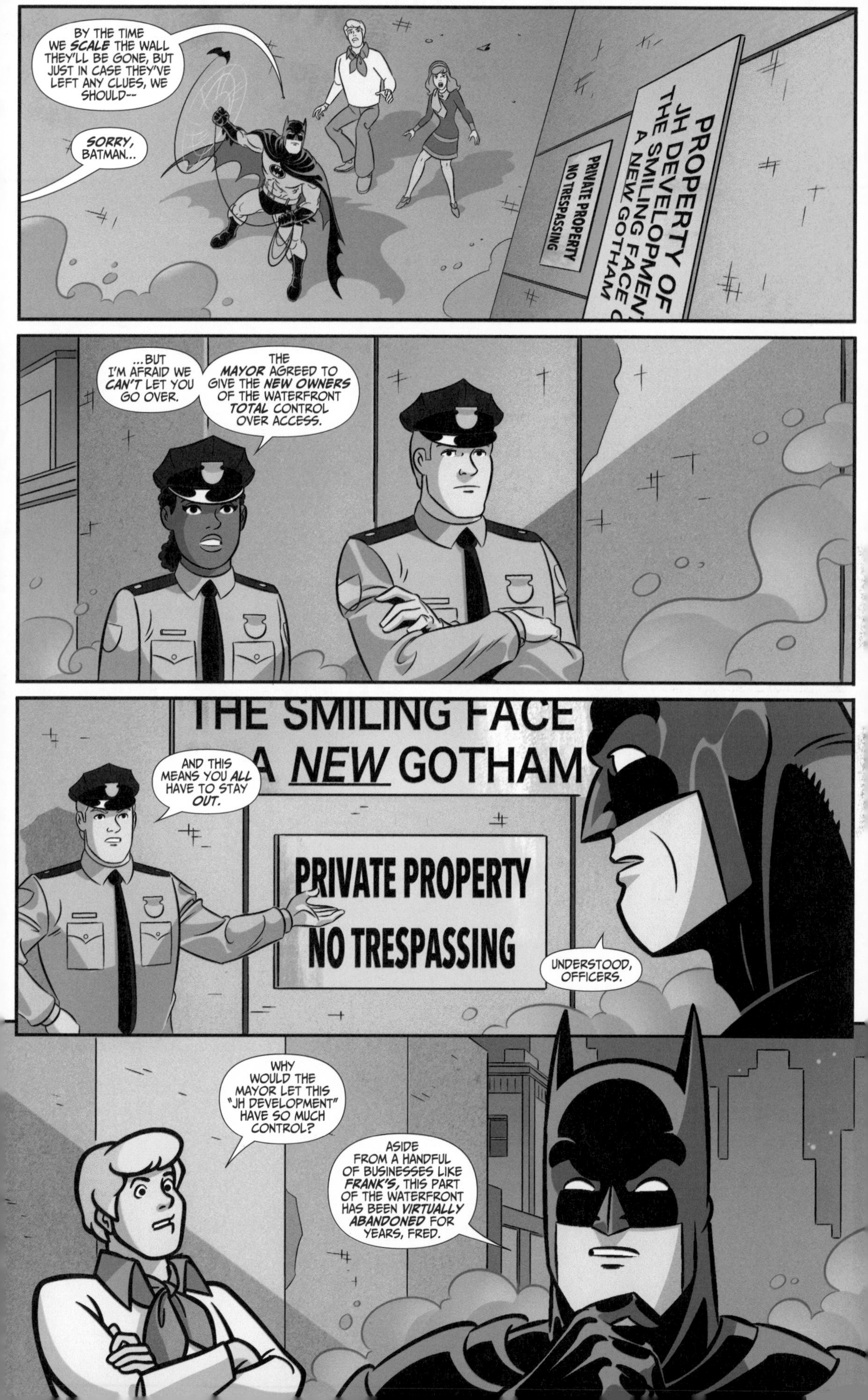
BY THE TIME WE SCALE THE WALL THEY'LL BE GONE, BUT JUST IN CASE THEY'VE LEFT ANY CLUES, WE SHOULD--
SORRY, BATMAN...
PROPERTY OF JH DEVELOPMEN THE SMILING FACE A NEW GOTHAM
PRIVATE PROPERTY NO TRESPASSING
...BUT I'M AFRAID WE CAN'T LET YOU GO OVER.
THE MAYOR AGREED TO GIVE THE NEW OWNERS OF THE WATERFRONT TOTAL CONTROL OVER ACCESS.
THE SMILING FACE
A NEW GOTHAM
AND THIS MEANS YOU ALL HAVE TO STAY OUT.
PRIVATE PROPERTY
NO TRESPASSING
UNDERSTOOD, OFFICERS.
WHY WOULD THE MAYOR LET THIS "JH DEVELOPMENT" HAVE SO MUCH CONTROL?
ASIDE FROM A HANDFUL OF BUSINESSES LIKE FRANK'S, THIS PART OF THE WATERFRONT HAS BEEN VIRTUALLY ABANDONED FOR YEARS, FRED.

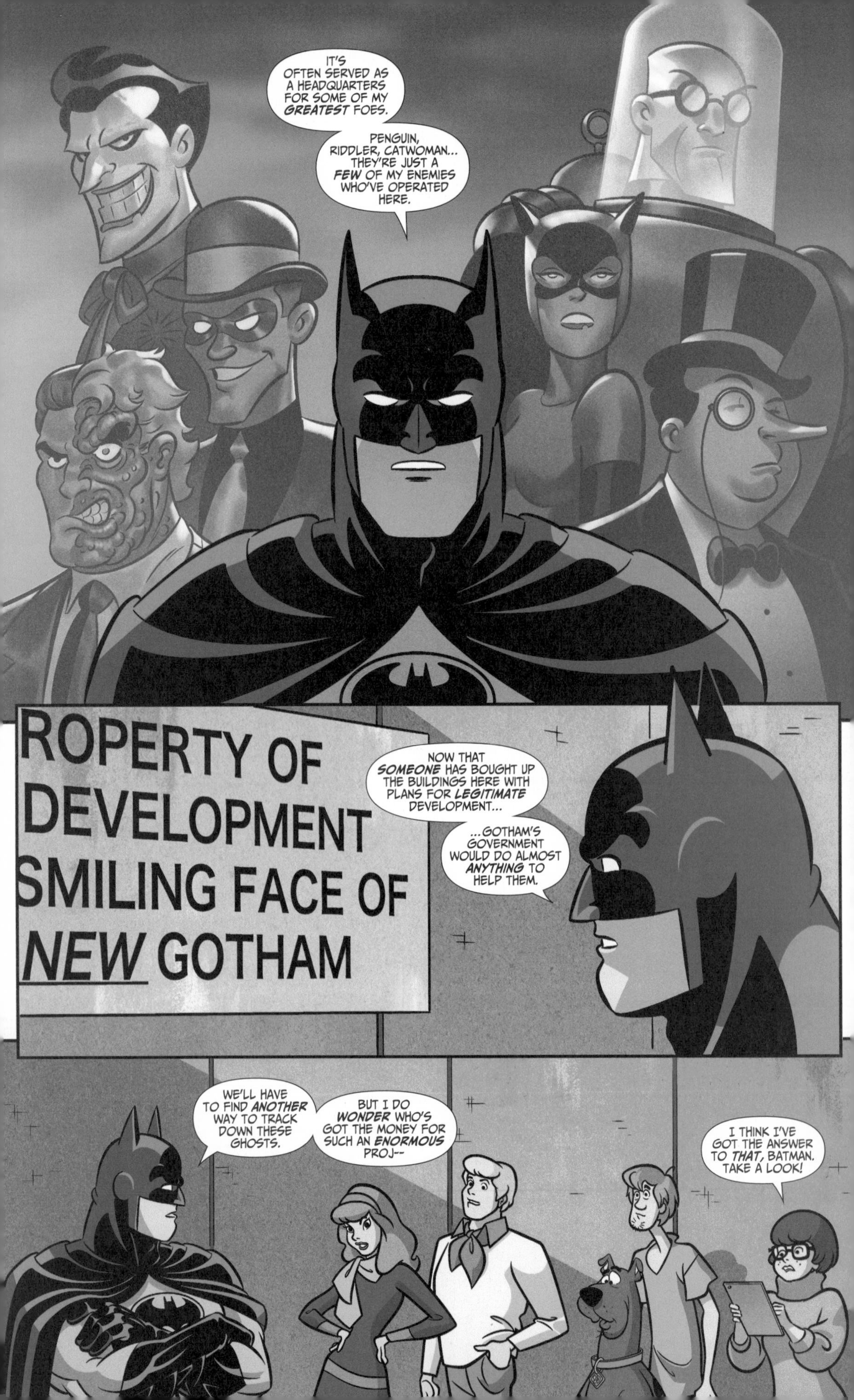
IT'S OFTEN SERVED AS A HEADQUARTERS FOR SOME OF MY GREATEST FOES.
PENGUIN, RIDDLER, CATWOMAN... THEY'RE JUST A FEW OF MY ENEMIES WHO'VE OPERATED HERE.
ROPERTY OF DEVELOPMENT SMILING FACE OF NEW GOTHAM
NOW THAT SOMEONE HAS BOUGHT UP THE BUILDINGS HERE WITH PLANS FOR LEGITIMATE DEVELOPMENT...
...GOTHAM'S GOVERNMENT WOULD DO ALMOST ANYTHING TO HELP THEM.
WE'LL HAVE TO FIND ANOTHER WAY TO TRACK DOWN THESE GHOSTS.
BUT I DO WONDER WHO'S GOT THE MONEY FOR SUCH AN ENORMOUS PROJ--
I THINK I'VE GOT THE ANSWER TO THAT, BATMAN. TAKE A LOOK!

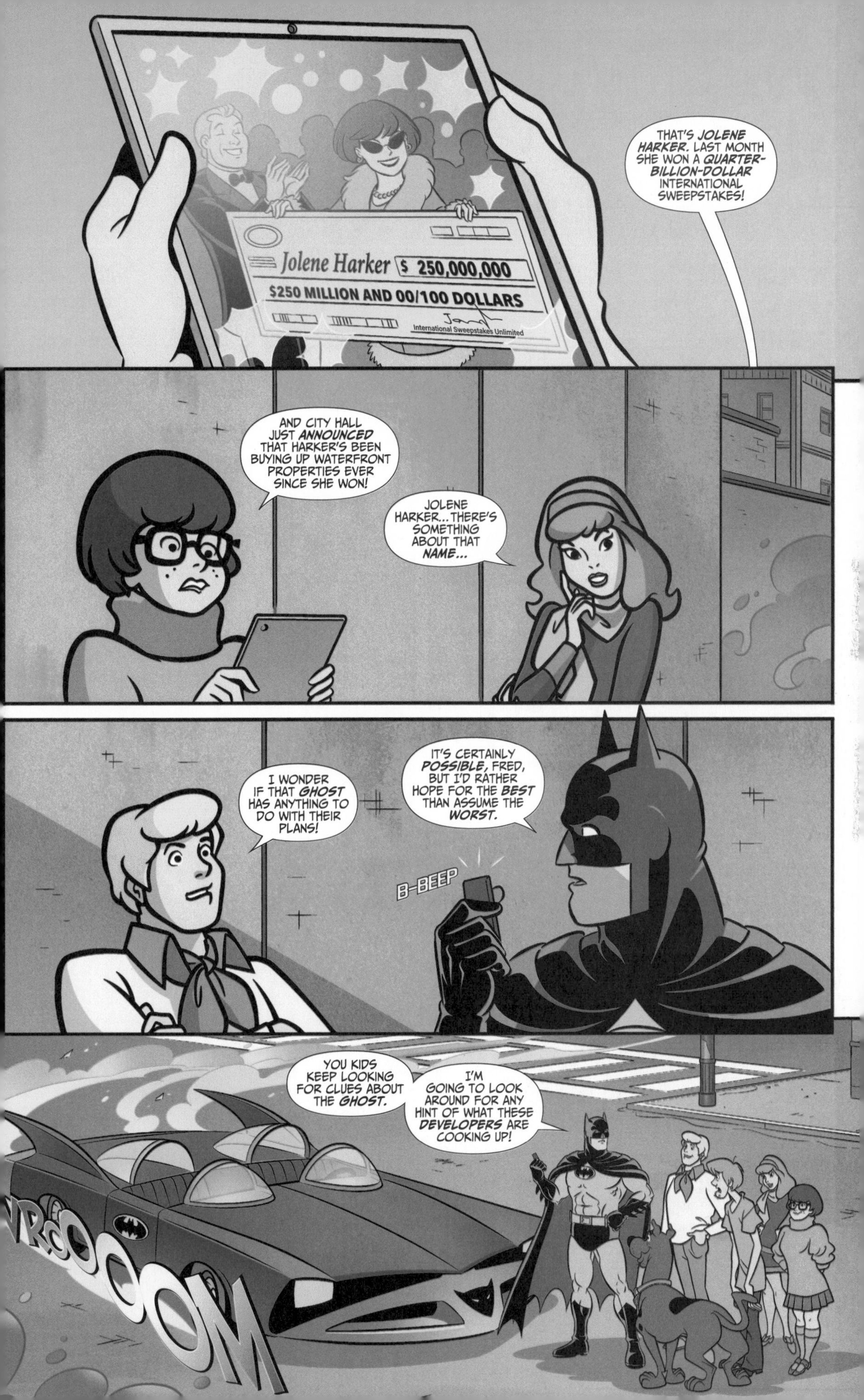
Jolene Harker $ 250,000,000
$250 MILLION AND 00/100 DOLLARS
International Sweepstakes Unlimited
THAT'S JOLENE HARKER. LAST MONTH SHE WON A QUARTER-BILLION-DOLLAR INTERNATIONAL SWEEPSTAKES!
AND CITY HALL JUST ANNOUNCED THAT HARKER'S BEEN BUYING UP WATERFRONT PROPERTIES EVER SINCE SHE WON!
JOLENE HARKER... THERE'S SOMETHING ABOUT THAT NAME...
I WONDER IF THAT GHOST HAS ANYTHING TO DO WITH THEIR PLANS!
IT'S CERTAINLY POSSIBLE, FRED, BUT I'D RATHER HOPE FOR THE BEST THAN ASSUME THE WORST.
B-BEEP
YOU KIDS KEEP LOOKING FOR CLUES ABOUT THE GHOST.
I'M GOING TO LOOK AROUND FOR ANY HINT OF WHAT THESE DEVELOPERS ARE COOKING UP!
VRoOOOM

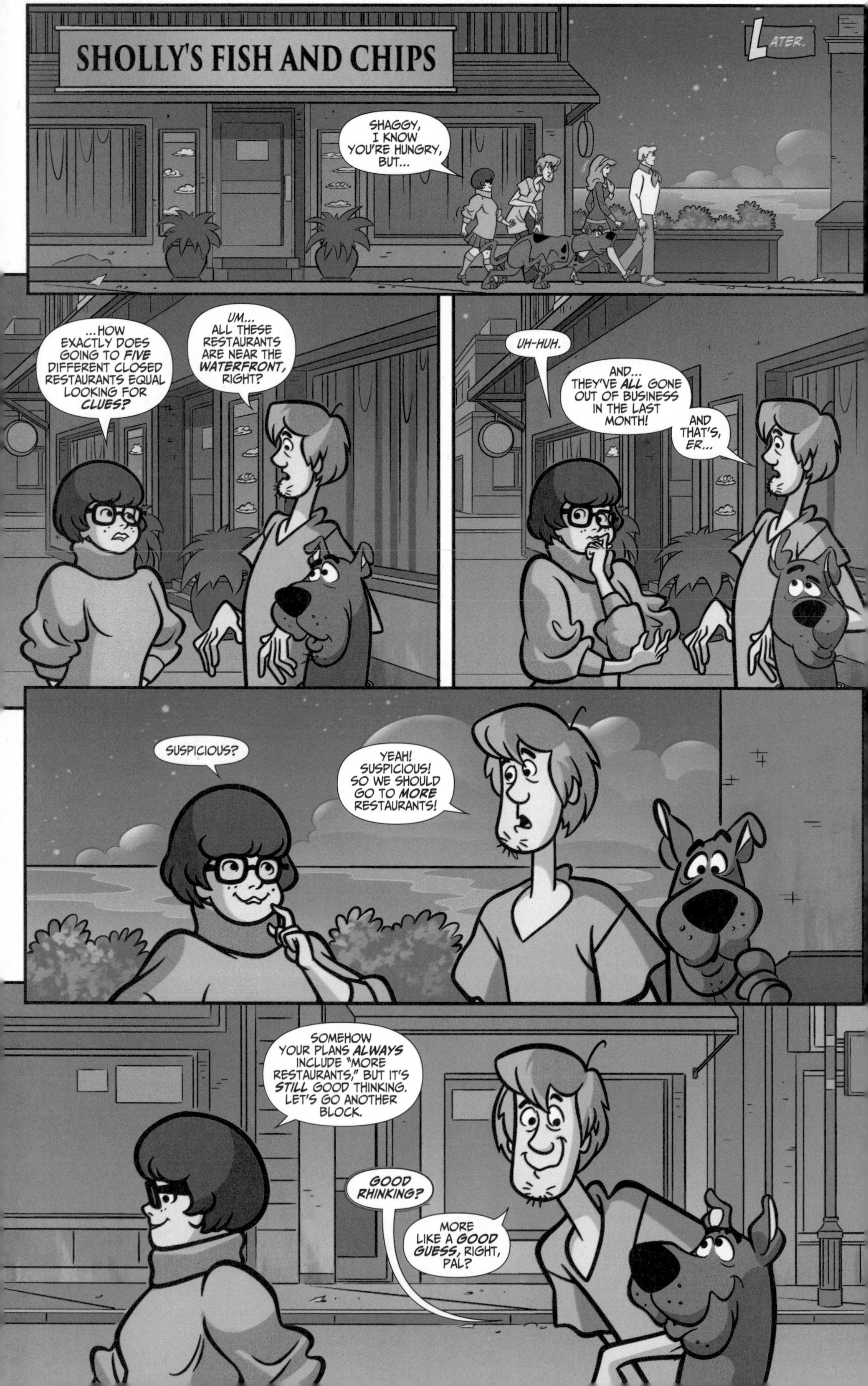
SHOLLY'S FISH AND CHIPS
LATER.
SHAGGY, I KNOW YOU'RE HUNGRY, BUT...
...HOW EXACTLY DOES GOING TO *FIVE* DIFFERENT CLOSED RESTAURANTS EQUAL LOOKING FOR *CLUES?*
UM... ALL THESE RESTAURANTS ARE NEAR THE *WATERFRONT,* RIGHT?
UH-HUH.
AND... THEY'VE *ALL* GONE OUT OF BUSINESS IN THE LAST MONTH!
AND THAT'S, ER...
SUSPICIOUS?
YEAH! SUSPICIOUS! SO WE SHOULD GO TO *MORE* RESTAURANTS!
SOMEHOW YOUR PLANS *ALWAYS* INCLUDE "MORE RESTAURANTS," BUT IT'S *STILL* GOOD THINKING. LET'S GO ANOTHER BLOCK.
GOOD RHINKING?
MORE LIKE A *GOOD GUESS,* RIGHT, PAL?

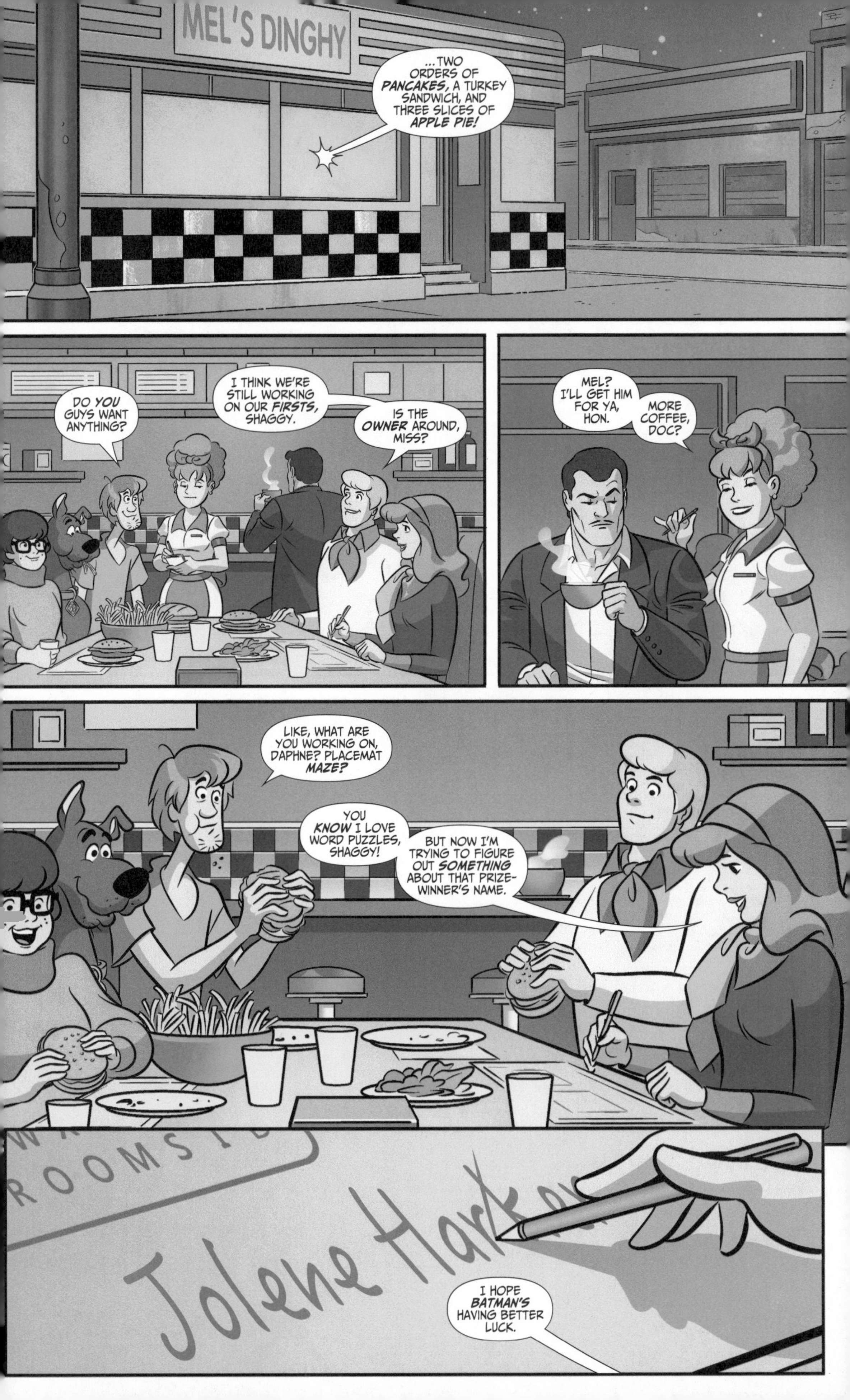
MEL'S DINGHY
...TWO ORDERS OF PANCAKES, A TURKEY SANDWICH, AND THREE SLICES OF APPLE PIE!
DO YOU GUYS WANT ANYTHING?
I THINK WE'RE STILL WORKING ON OUR FIRSTS, SHAGGY.
IS THE OWNER AROUND, MISS?
MEL? I'LL GET HIM FOR YA, HON.
MORE COFFEE, DOC?
LIKE, WHAT ARE YOU WORKING ON, DAPHNE? PLACEMAT MAZE?
YOU KNOW I LOVE WORD PUZZLES, SHAGGY!
BUT NOW I'M TRYING TO FIGURE OUT SOMETHING ABOUT THAT PRIZE-WINNER'S NAME.
I HOPE BATMAN'S HAVING BETTER LUCK.

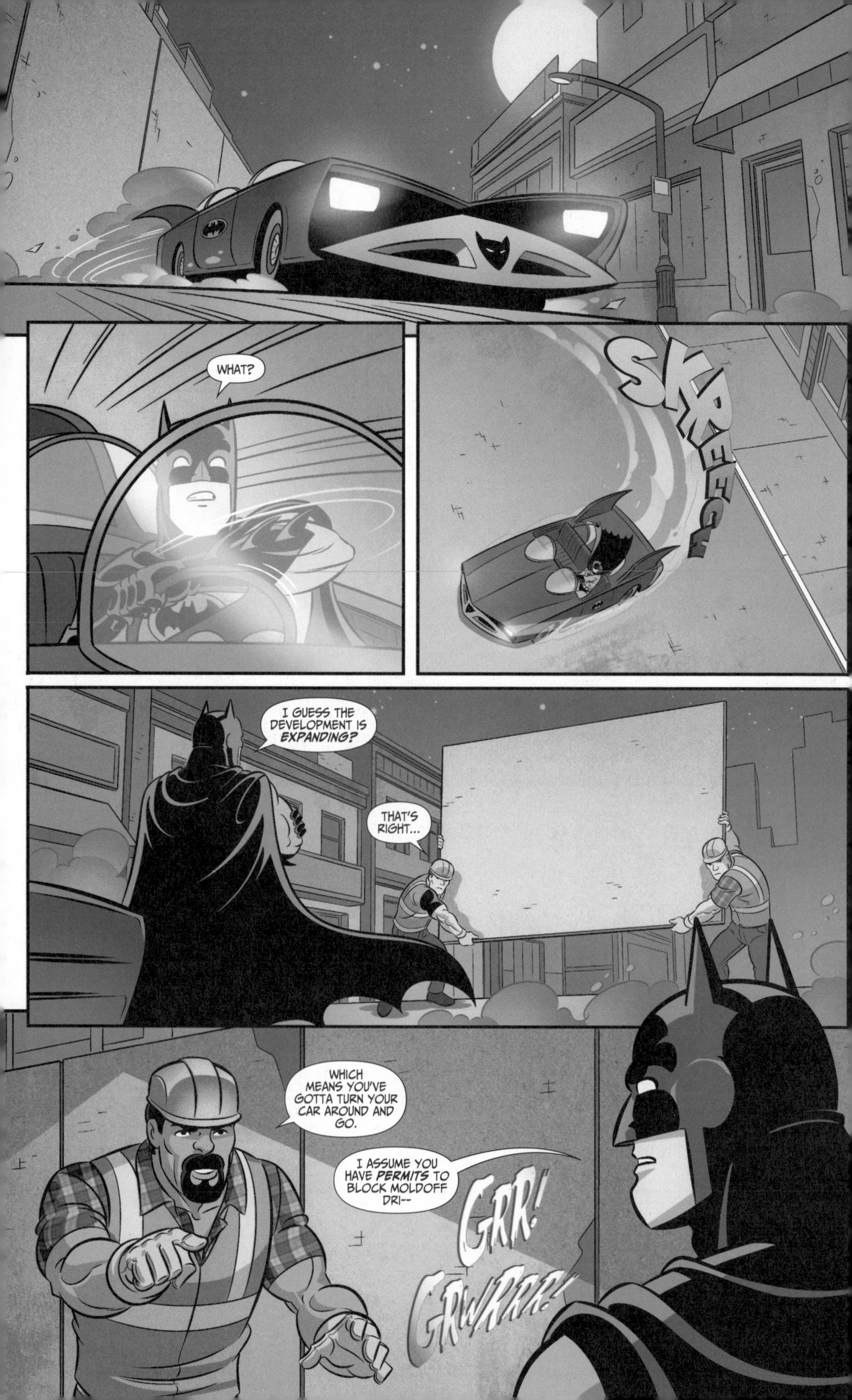
WHAT?
SKREEEECH
I GUESS THE DEVELOPMENT IS *EXPANDING?*
THAT'S RIGHT...
WHICH MEANS YOU'VE GOTTA TURN YOUR CAR AROUND AND GO.
I ASSUME YOU HAVE *PERMITS* TO BLOCK MOLDOFF DRI--
GRR!
GRWRRR!

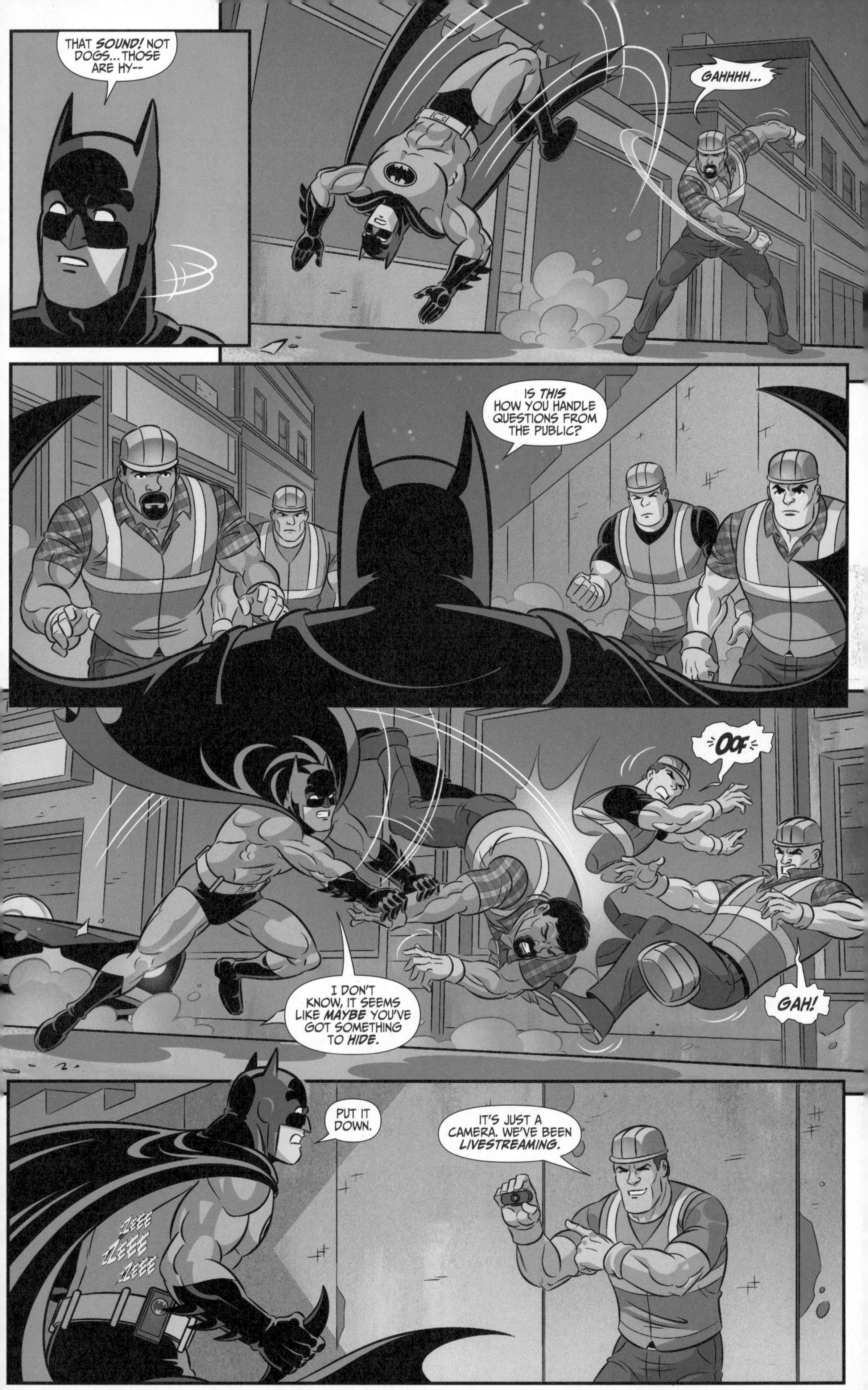
THAT SOUND! NOT DOGS... THOSE ARE HY--
GAHHHH...
IS THIS HOW YOU HANDLE QUESTIONS FROM THE PUBLIC?
OOF
I DON'T KNOW, IT SEEMS LIKE MAYBE YOU'VE GOT SOMETHING TO HIDE.
GAH!
PUT IT DOWN.
IT'S JUST A CAMERA. WE'VE BEEN LIVESTREAMING.
ZEEE
ZEEE
ZEEE

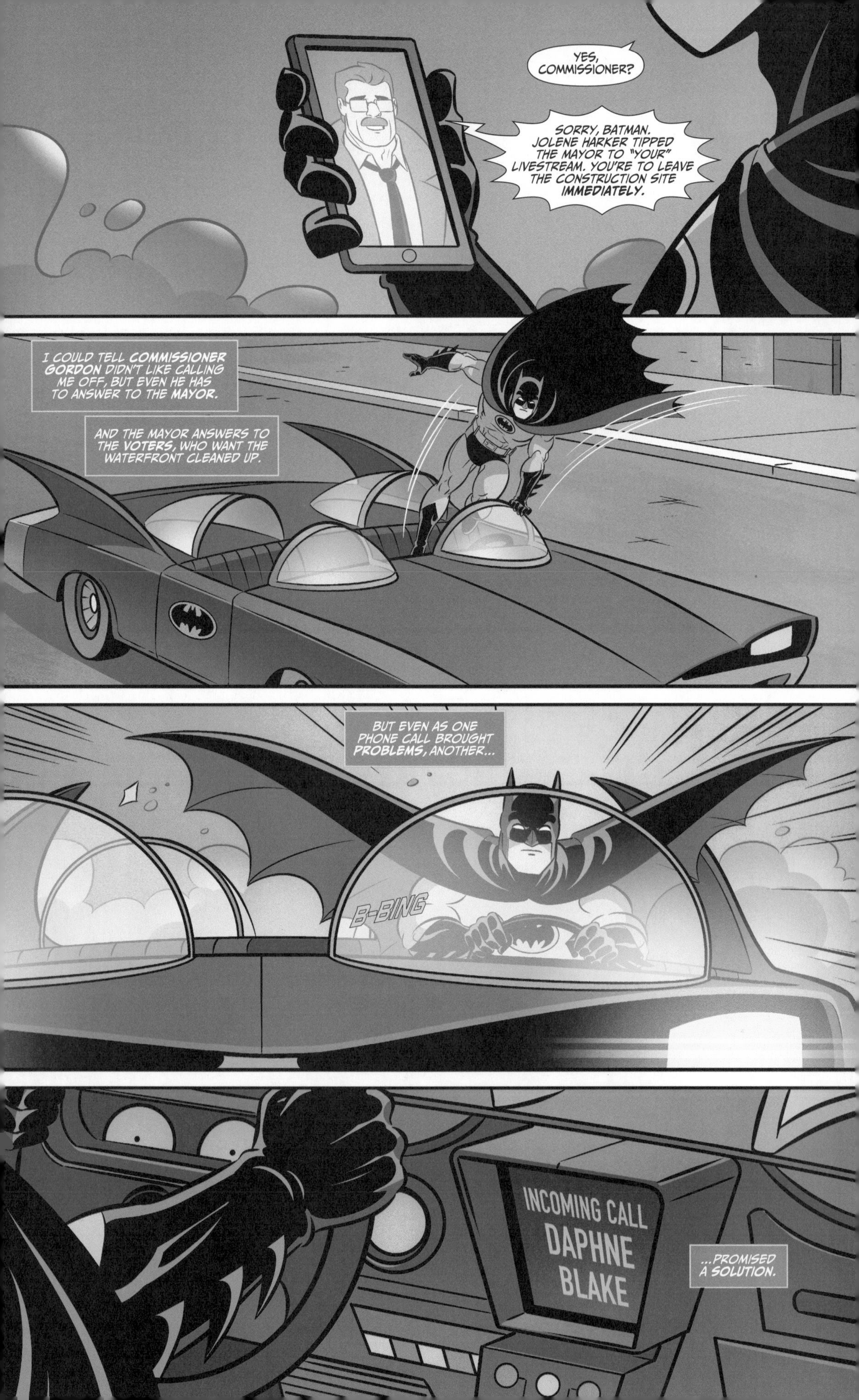
YES, COMMISSIONER?
SORRY, BATMAN. JOLENE HARKER TIPPED THE MAYOR TO "YOUR" LIVESTREAM. YOU'RE TO LEAVE THE CONSTRUCTION SITE IMMEDIATELY.
I COULD TELL COMMISSIONER GORDON DIDN'T LIKE CALLING ME OFF, BUT EVEN HE HAS TO ANSWER TO THE MAYOR.
AND THE MAYOR ANSWERS TO THE VOTERS, WHO WANT THE WATERFRONT CLEANED UP.
BUT EVEN AS ONE PHONE CALL BROUGHT PROBLEMS, ANOTHER...
B-BING
INCOMING CALL DAPHNE BLAKE
...PROMISED A SOLUTION.

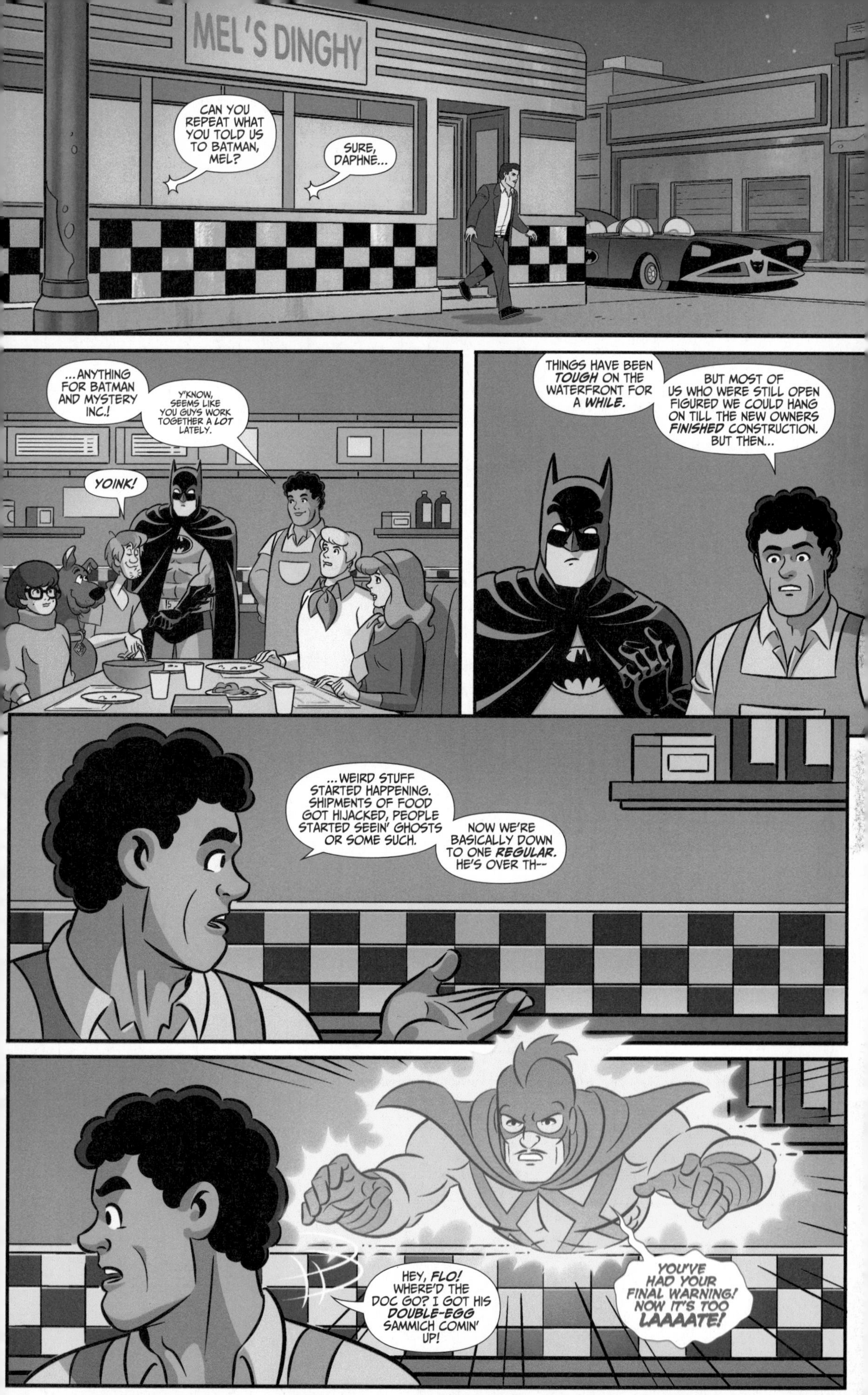
MEL'S DINGHY
CAN YOU REPEAT WHAT YOU TOLD US TO BATMAN, MEL?
SURE, DAPHNE...
...ANYTHING FOR BATMAN AND MYSTERY INC.!
Y'KNOW, SEEMS LIKE YOU GUYS WORK TOGETHER A LOT LATELY.
YOINK!
THINGS HAVE BEEN TOUGH ON THE WATERFRONT FOR A WHILE.
BUT MOST OF US WHO WERE STILL OPEN FIGURED WE COULD HANG ON TILL THE NEW OWNERS FINISHED CONSTRUCTION. BUT THEN...
...WEIRD STUFF STARTED HAPPENING. SHIPMENTS OF FOOD GOT HIJACKED, PEOPLE STARTED SEEIN' GHOSTS OR SOME SUCH.
NOW WE'RE BASICALLY DOWN TO ONE REGULAR. HE'S OVER TH--
HEY, FLO! WHERE'D THE DOC GO? I GOT HIS DOUBLE-EGG SAMMICH COMIN' UP!
YOU'VE HAD YOUR FINAL WARNING! NOW IT'S TOO LAAAATE!

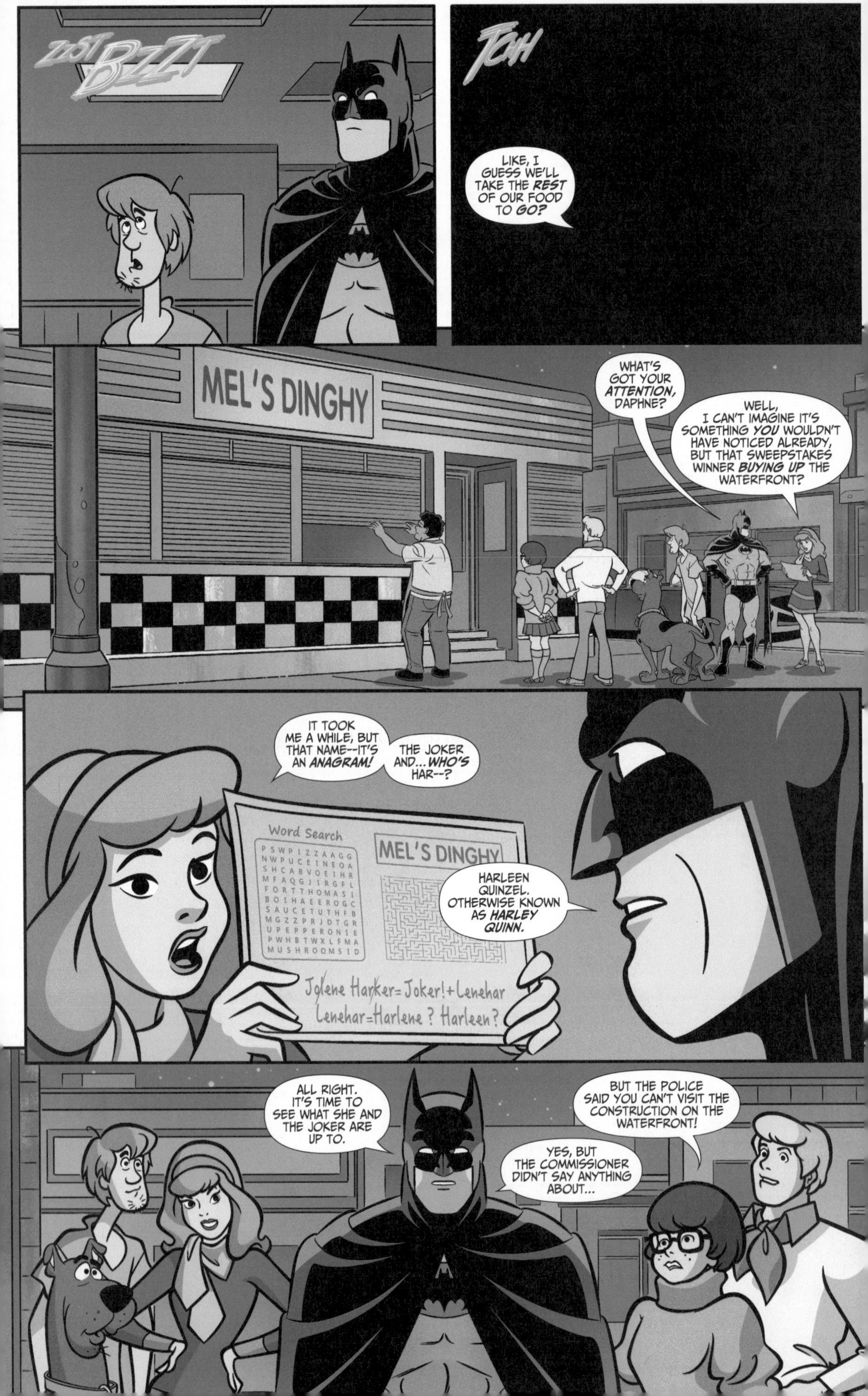
ZZST BZZZT
TCHH
LIKE, I GUESS WE'LL TAKE THE *REST* OF OUR FOOD TO *GO?*
MEL'S DINGHY
WHAT'S GOT YOUR *ATTENTION,* DAPHNE?
WELL, I CAN'T IMAGINE IT'S SOMETHING *YOU* WOULDN'T HAVE NOTICED ALREADY, BUT THAT SWEEPSTAKES WINNER *BUYING UP* THE WATERFRONT?
IT TOOK ME A WHILE, BUT THAT NAME--IT'S AN *ANAGRAM!*
THE JOKER AND... *WHO'S* HAR--?
Word Search
MEL'S DINGHY
Jolene Harker= Joker!+ Lenehar
Lenehar=Harlene ? Harleen?
HARLEEN QUINZEL. OTHERWISE KNOWN AS *HARLEY QUINN.*
ALL RIGHT. IT'S TIME TO SEE WHAT SHE AND THE JOKER ARE UP TO.
BUT THE POLICE SAID YOU CAN'T VISIT THE CONSTRUCTION ON THE WATERFRONT!
YES, BUT THE COMMISSIONER DIDN'T SAY ANYTHING ABOUT...

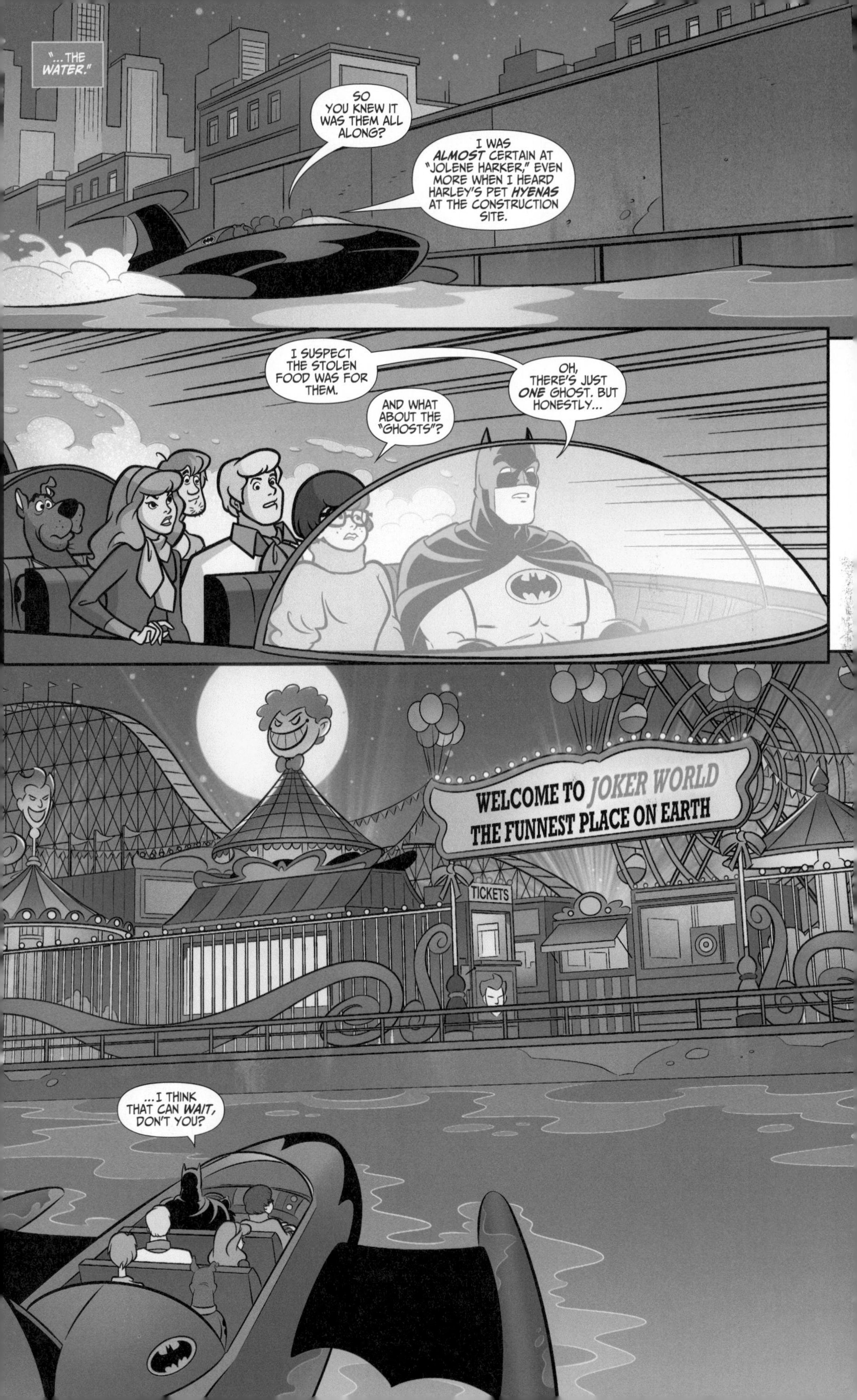
"...THE WATER."
SO YOU KNEW IT WAS THEM ALL ALONG?
I WAS ALMOST CERTAIN AT "JOLENE HARKER," EVEN MORE WHEN I HEARD HARLEY'S PET HYENAS AT THE CONSTRUCTION SITE.
I SUSPECT THE STOLEN FOOD WAS FOR THEM.
AND WHAT ABOUT THE "GHOSTS"?
OH, THERE'S JUST ONE GHOST. BUT HONESTLY...
WELCOME TO JOKER WORLD
THE FUNNEST PLACE ON EARTH
TICKETS
...I THINK THAT CAN WAIT, DON'T YOU?

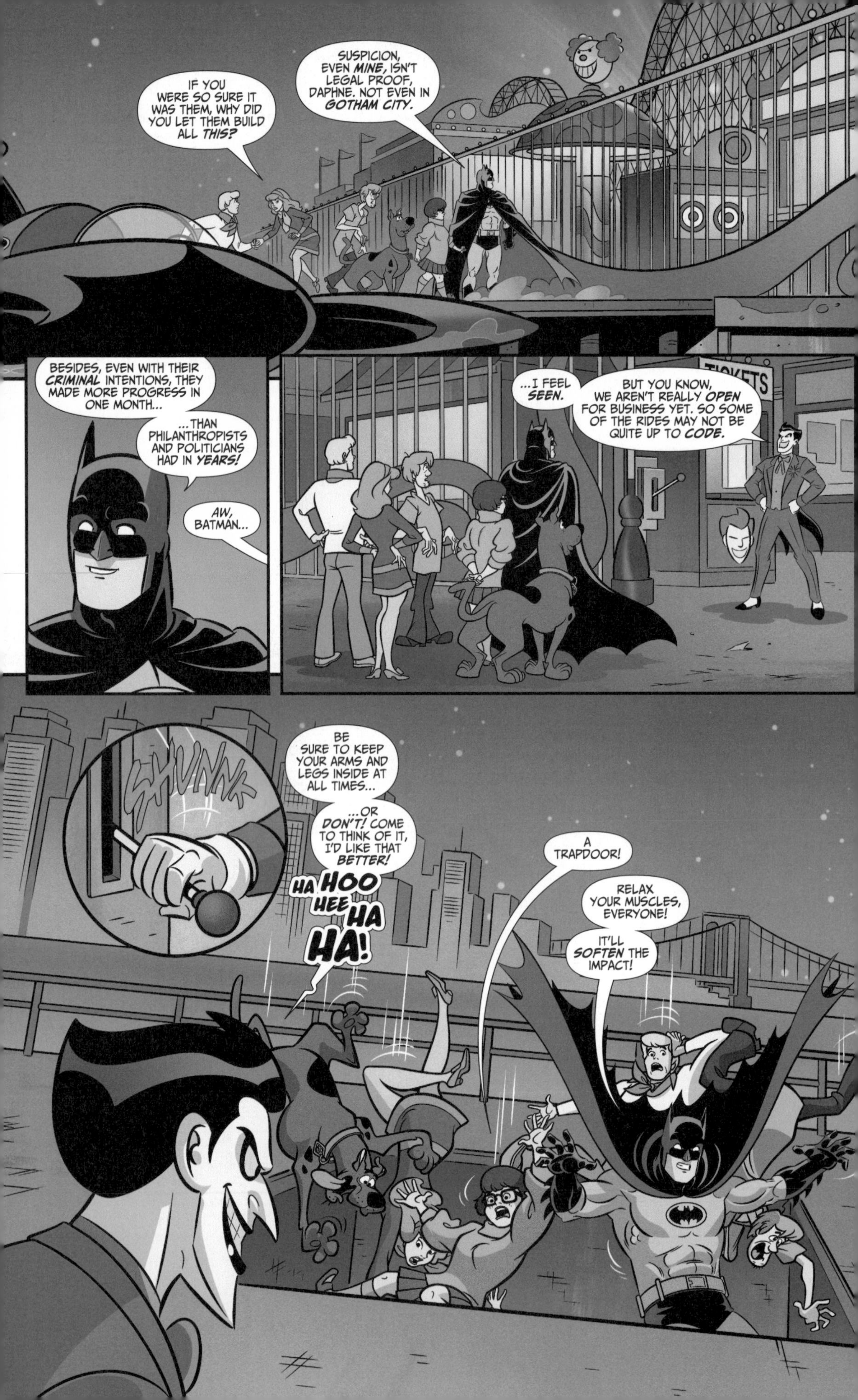
IF YOU WERE SO SURE IT WAS THEM, WHY DID YOU LET THEM BUILD ALL THIS?
SUSPICION, EVEN MINE, ISN'T LEGAL PROOF, DAPHNE. NOT EVEN IN GOTHAM CITY.
BESIDES, EVEN WITH THEIR CRIMINAL INTENTIONS, THEY MADE MORE PROGRESS IN ONE MONTH...
...THAN PHILANTHROPISTS AND POLITICIANS HAD IN YEARS!
AW, BATMAN...
...I FEEL SEEN.
TICKETS
BUT YOU KNOW, WE AREN'T REALLY OPEN FOR BUSINESS YET. SO SOME OF THE RIDES MAY NOT BE QUITE UP TO CODE.
SHUNNK
BE SURE TO KEEP YOUR ARMS AND LEGS INSIDE AT ALL TIMES...
...OR DON'T! COME TO THINK OF IT, I'D LIKE THAT BETTER!
HA HOO HEE HA HA!
A TRAPDOOR!
RELAX YOUR MUSCLES, EVERYONE!
IT'LL SOFTEN THE IMPACT!

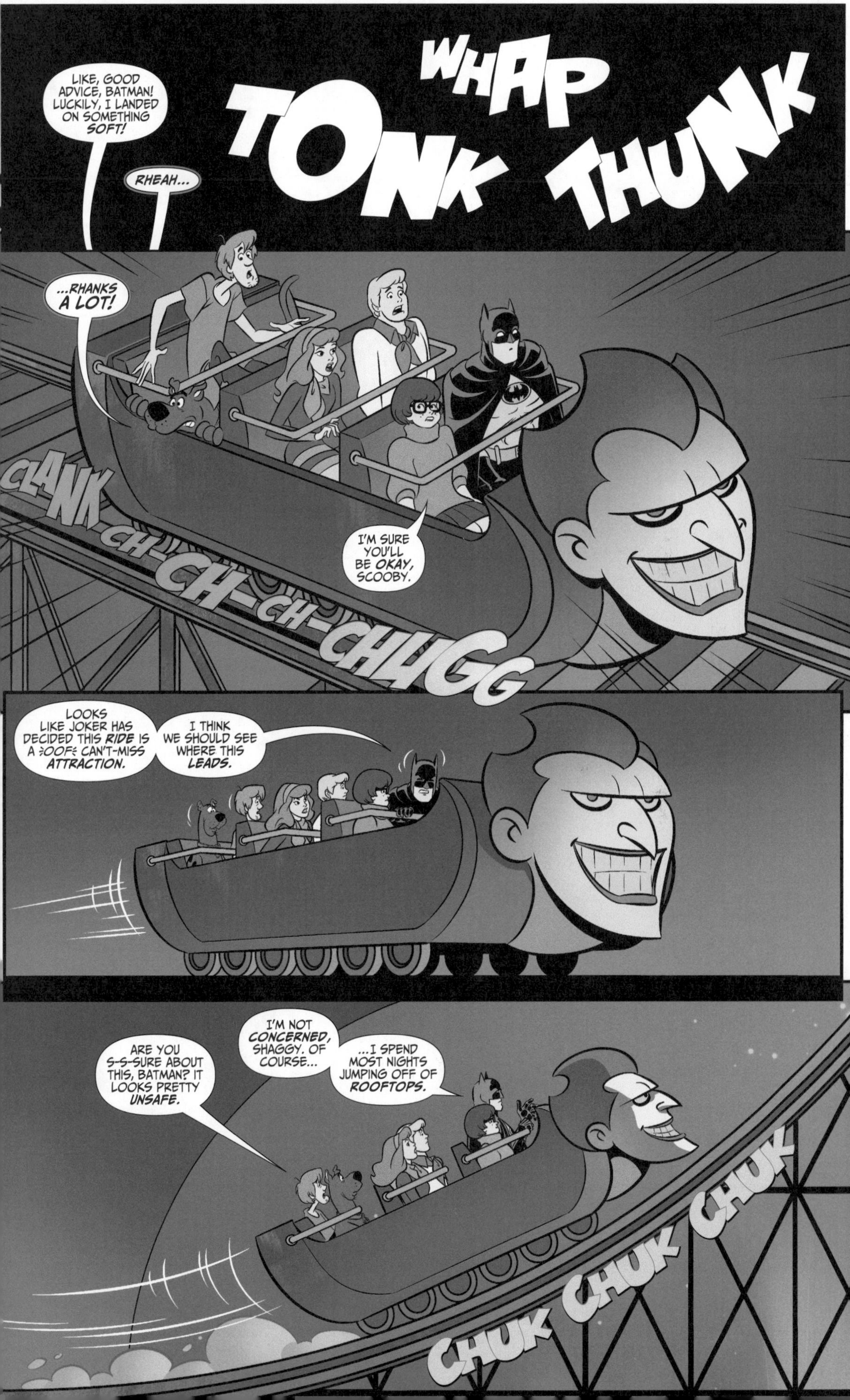
LIKE, GOOD ADVICE, BATMAN! LUCKILY, I LANDED ON SOMETHING SOFT!
RHEAH...
WHAP
TONK
THUNK
...RHANKS A LOT!
I'M SURE YOU'LL BE OKAY, SCOOBY.
CLANK
CH-CH-CH-CHUGG
LOOKS LIKE JOKER HAS DECIDED THIS RIDE IS A *OOF* CAN'T-MISS ATTRACTION.
I THINK WE SHOULD SEE WHERE THIS LEADS.
ARE YOU S-S-SURE ABOUT THIS, BATMAN? IT LOOKS PRETTY UNSAFE.
I'M NOT CONCERNED, SHAGGY. OF COURSE...
...I SPEND MOST NIGHTS JUMPING OFF OF ROOFTOPS.
CHUK CHUK CHUK CHUK

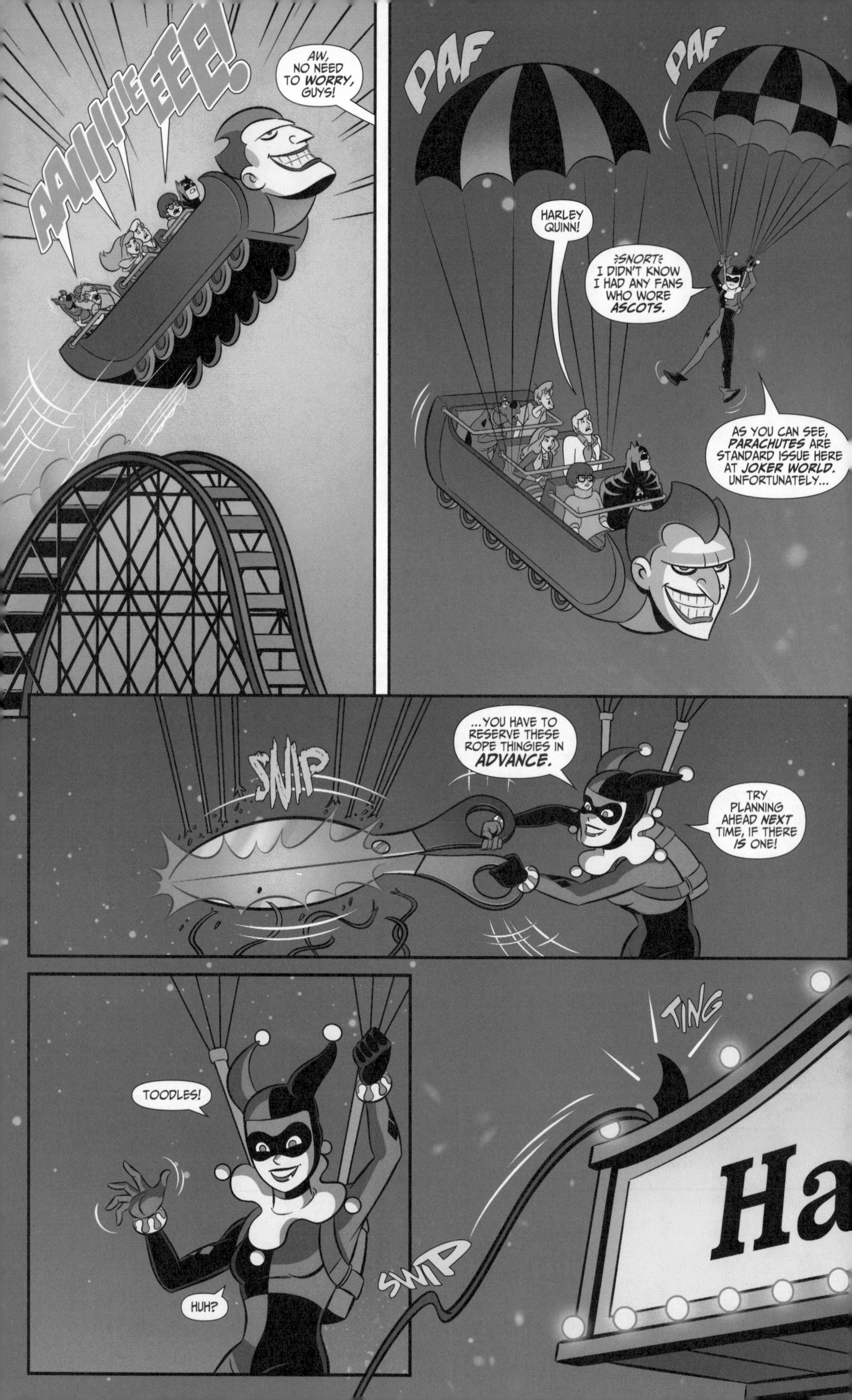
AAIIIIIEEEE!
AW, NO NEED TO WORRY, GUYS!
PAF
PAF
HARLEY QUINN!
SNORT
I DIDN'T KNOW I HAD ANY FANS WHO WORE ASCOTS.
AS YOU CAN SEE, PARACHUTES ARE STANDARD ISSUE HERE AT JOKER WORLD. UNFORTUNATELY...
...YOU HAVE TO RESERVE THESE ROPE THINGIES IN ADVANCE.
SNIP
TRY PLANNING AHEAD NEXT TIME, IF THERE IS ONE!
TOODLES!
HUH?
TING
SWIP
Ha

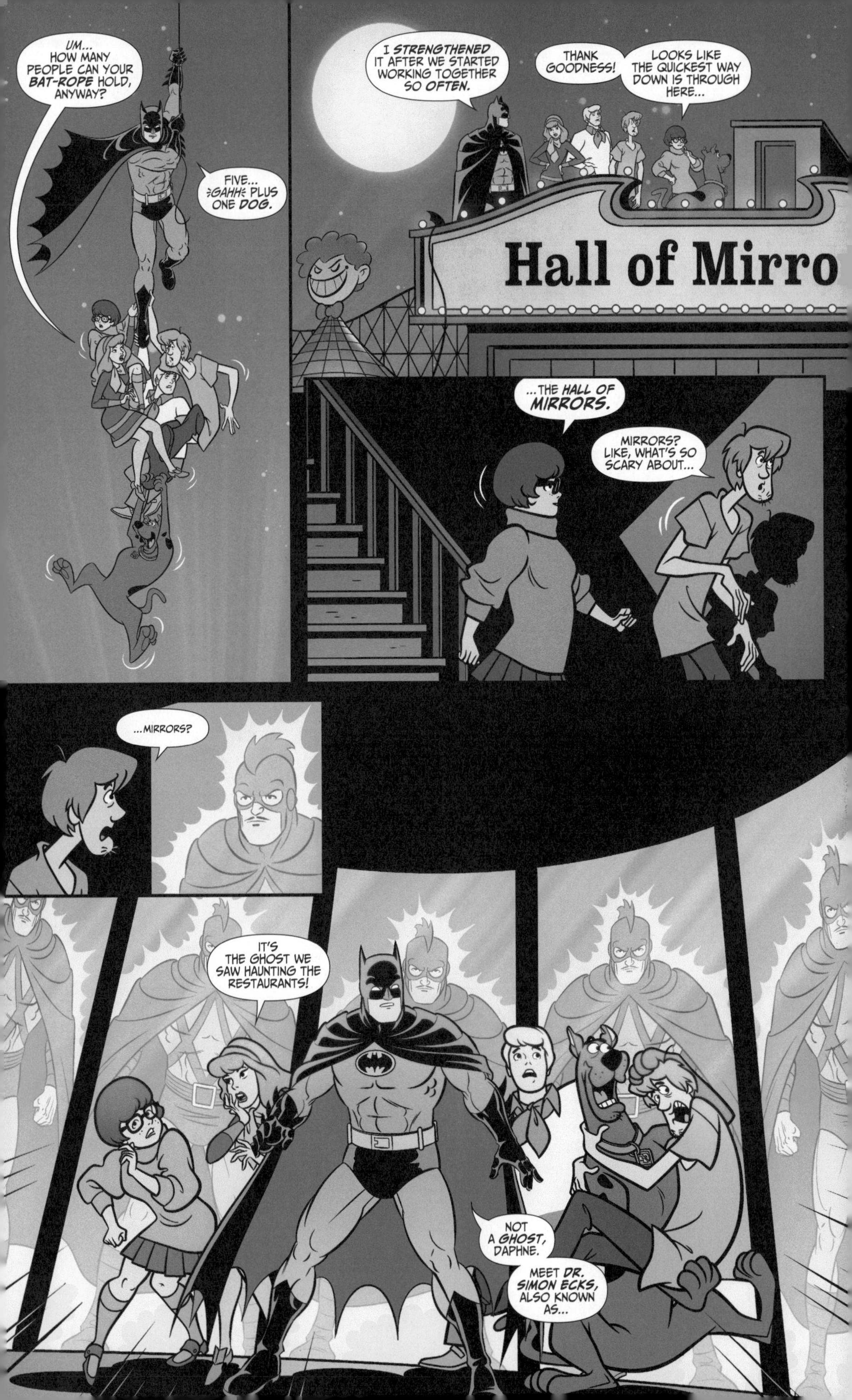
UM... HOW MANY PEOPLE CAN YOUR BAT-ROPE HOLD, ANYWAY?
FIVE... GAHH PLUS ONE DOG.
I STRENGTHENED IT AFTER WE STARTED WORKING TOGETHER SO OFTEN.
THANK GOODNESS!
LOOKS LIKE THE QUICKEST WAY DOWN IS THROUGH HERE...
Hall of Mirro
...THE HALL OF MIRRORS.
MIRRORS? LIKE, WHAT'S SO SCARY ABOUT...
...MIRRORS?
IT'S THE GHOST WE SAW HAUNTING THE RESTAURANTS!
NOT A GHOST, DAPHNE.
MEET DR. SIMON ECKS, ALSO KNOWN AS...

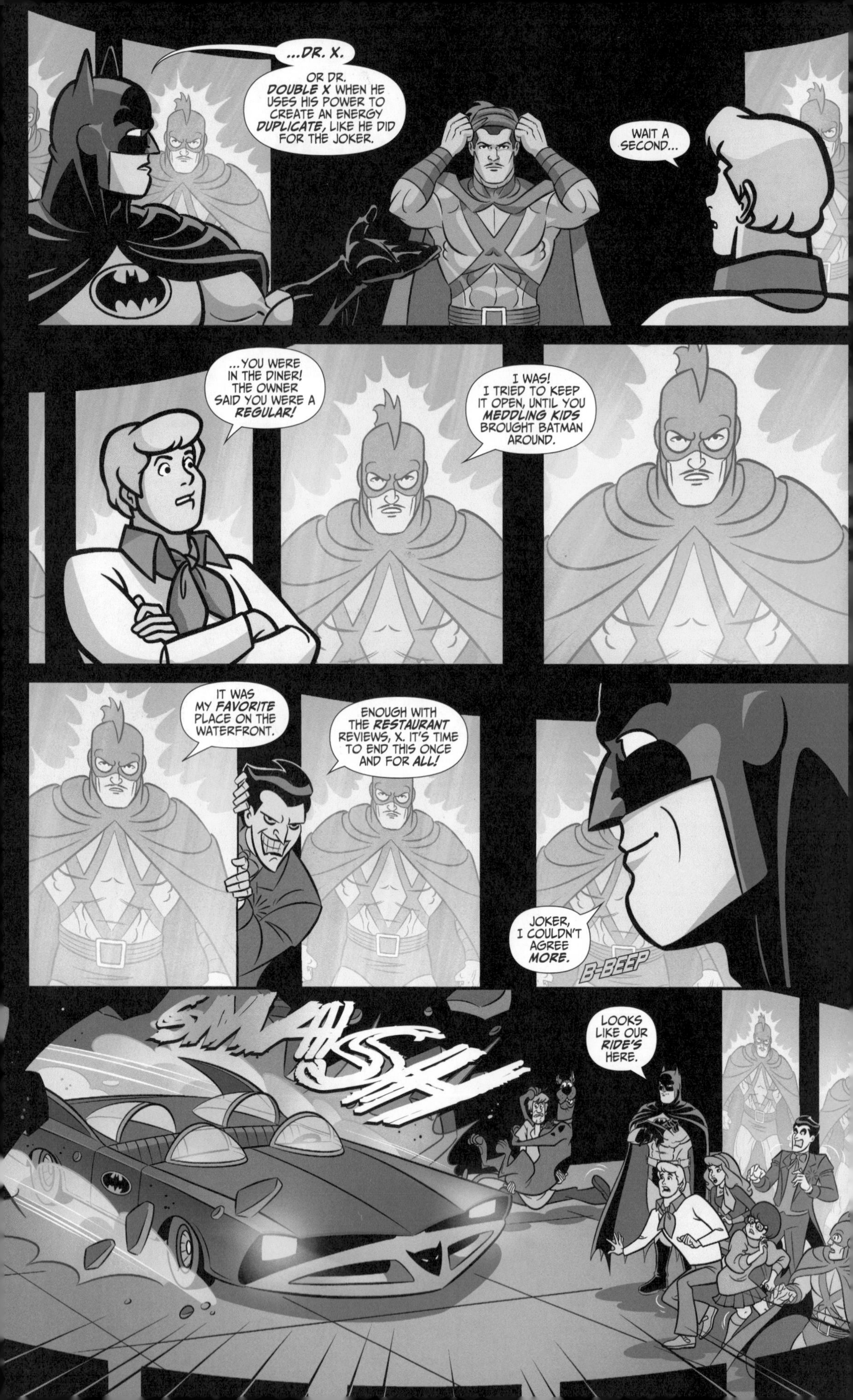
...DR. X.
OR DR. DOUBLE X WHEN HE USES HIS POWER TO CREATE AN ENERGY DUPLICATE, LIKE HE DID FOR THE JOKER.
WAIT A SECOND...
...YOU WERE IN THE DINER! THE OWNER SAID YOU WERE A REGULAR!
I WAS! I TRIED TO KEEP IT OPEN, UNTIL YOU MEDDLING KIDS BROUGHT BATMAN AROUND.
IT WAS MY FAVORITE PLACE ON THE WATERFRONT.
ENOUGH WITH THE RESTAURANT REVIEWS, X. IT'S TIME TO END THIS ONCE AND FOR ALL!
JOKER, I COULDN'T AGREE MORE.
B-BEEP
SMASH
LOOKS LIKE OUR RIDE'S HERE.

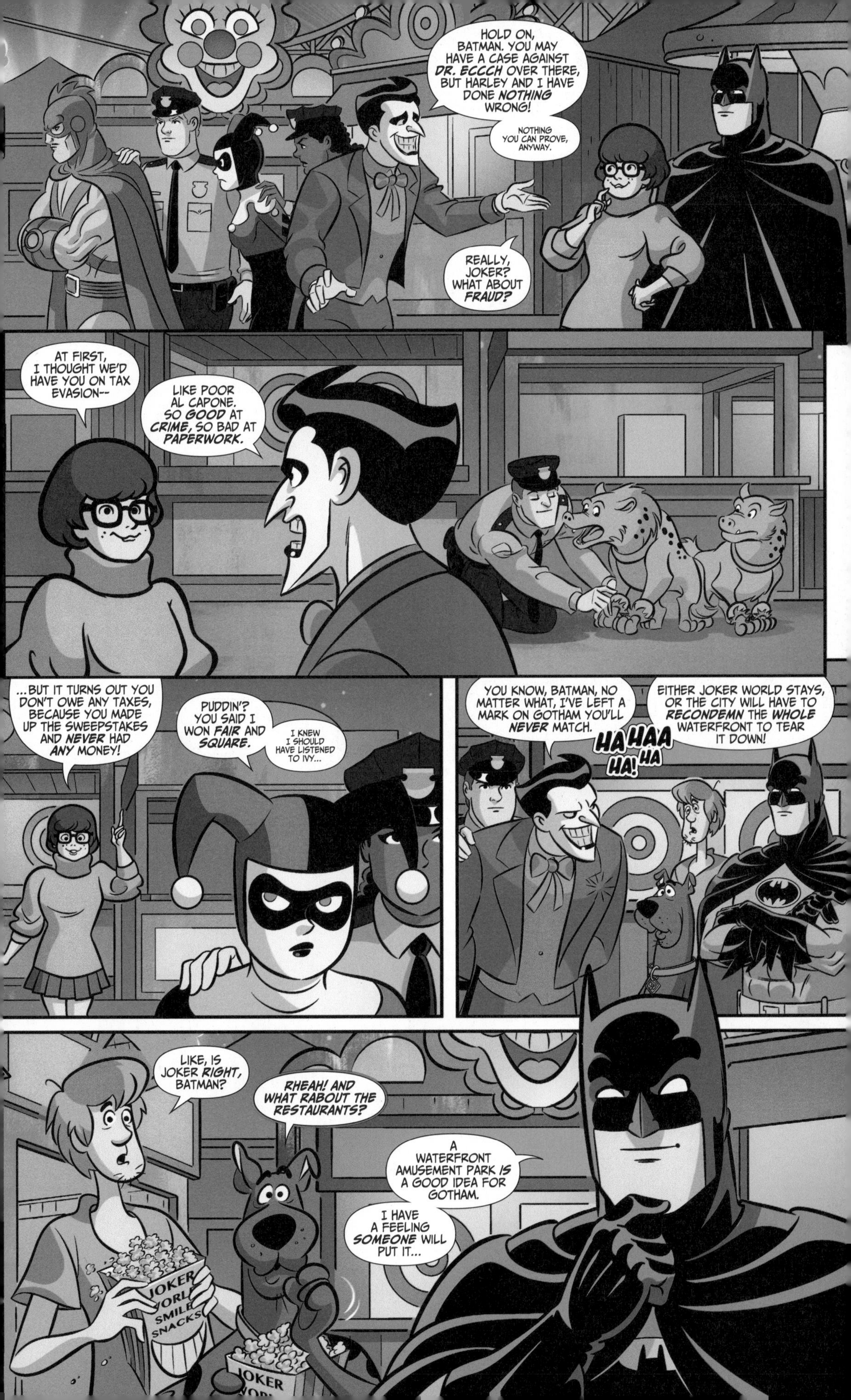
HOLD ON, BATMAN. YOU MAY HAVE A CASE AGAINST DR. ECCCH OVER THERE, BUT HARLEY AND I HAVE DONE NOTHING WRONG!
NOTHING YOU CAN PROVE, ANYWAY.
REALLY, JOKER? WHAT ABOUT FRAUD?
AT FIRST, I THOUGHT WE'D HAVE YOU ON TAX EVASION--
LIKE POOR AL CAPONE. SO GOOD AT CRIME, SO BAD AT PAPERWORK.
...BUT IT TURNS OUT YOU DON'T OWE ANY TAXES, BECAUSE YOU MADE UP THE SWEEPSTAKES AND NEVER HAD ANY MONEY!
PUDDIN'? YOU SAID I WON FAIR AND SQUARE.
I KNEW I SHOULD HAVE LISTENED TO IVY...
YOU KNOW, BATMAN, NO MATTER WHAT, I'VE LEFT A MARK ON GOTHAM YOU'LL NEVER MATCH.
HA HAA HA HA!
EITHER JOKER WORLD STAYS, OR THE CITY WILL HAVE TO RECONDEMN THE WHOLE WATERFRONT TO TEAR IT DOWN!
LIKE, IS JOKER RIGHT, BATMAN?
RHEAH! AND WHAT RABOUT THE RESTAURANTS?
A WATERFRONT AMUSEMENT PARK IS A GOOD IDEA FOR GOTHAM.
I HAVE A FEELING SOMEONE WILL PUT IT...
JOKER WORLD SMILE SNACKS
JOKER

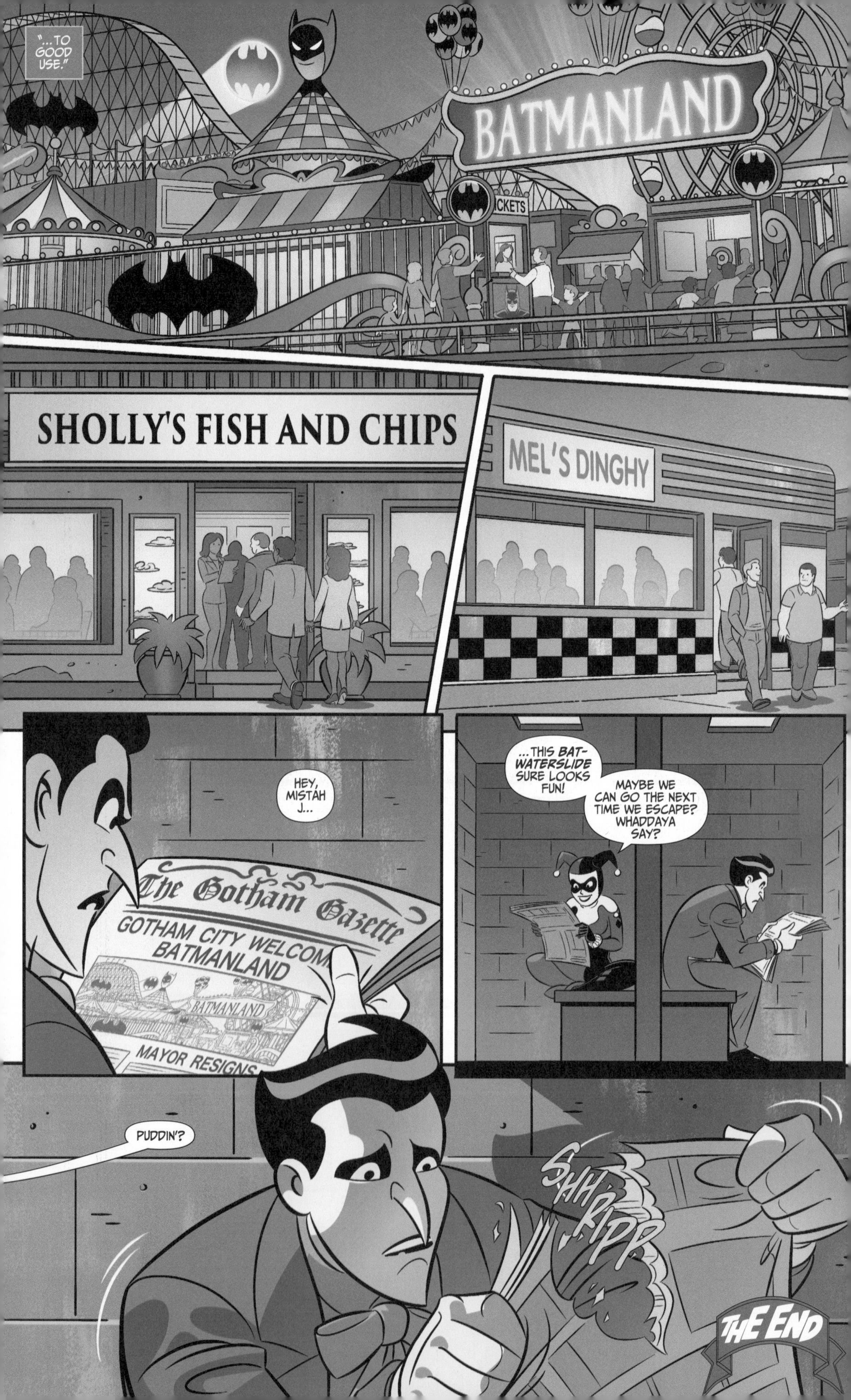
"...TO GOOD USE."
BATMANLAND
TICKETS
SHOLLY'S FISH AND CHIPS
MEL'S DINGHY
HEY, MISTAH J...
The Gotham Gazette
GOTHAM CITY WELCOM
BATMANLAND
BATMANLAND
MAYOR RESIGNS
...THIS BAT-WATERSLIDE SURE LOOKS FUN!
MAYBE WE CAN GO THE NEXT TIME WE ESCAPE? WHADDAYA SAY?
PUDDIN'?
SHHRIPP
THE END

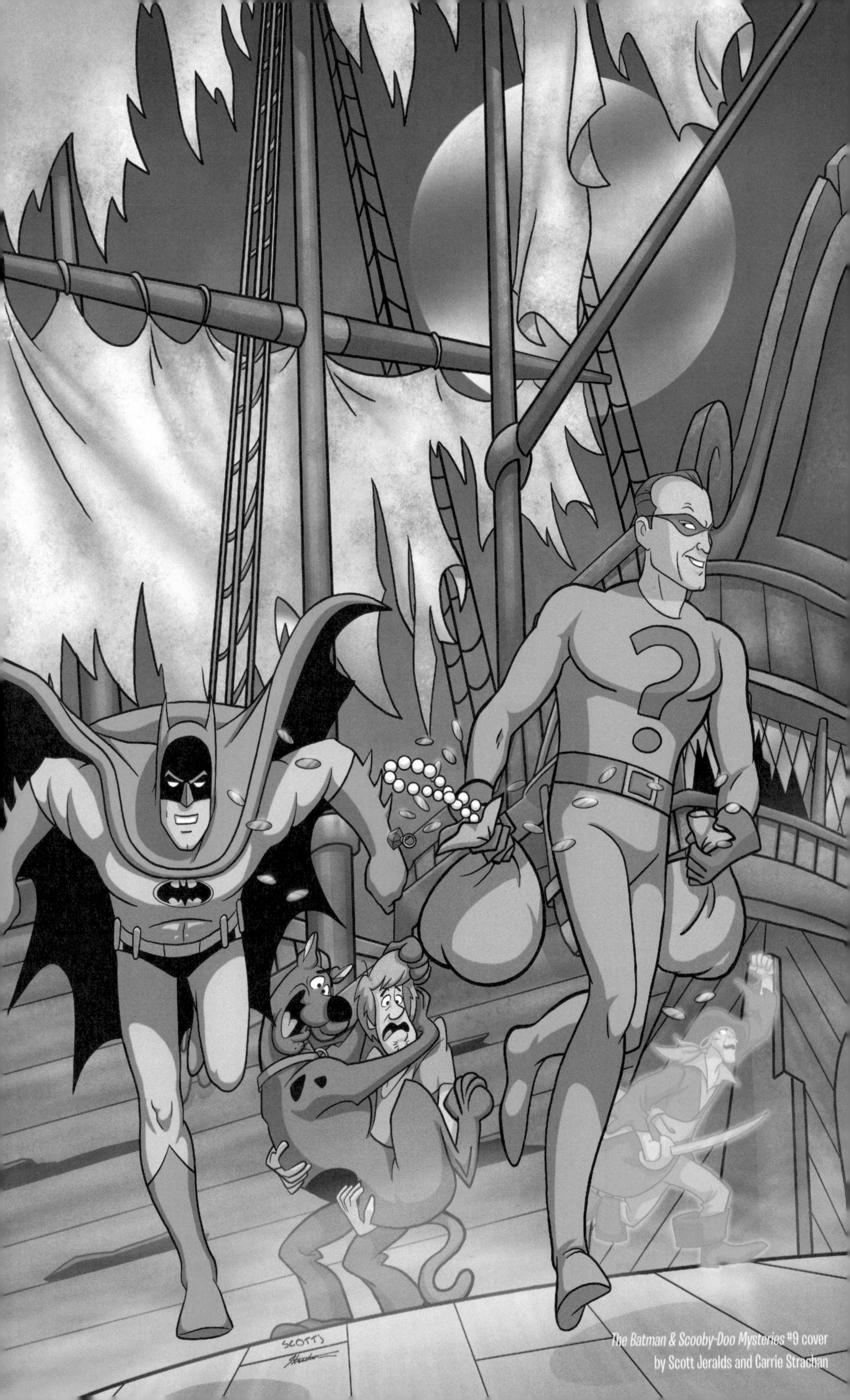

The Batman & Scooby-Doo Mysteries #9 cover
by Scott Jeralds and Carrie Strachan

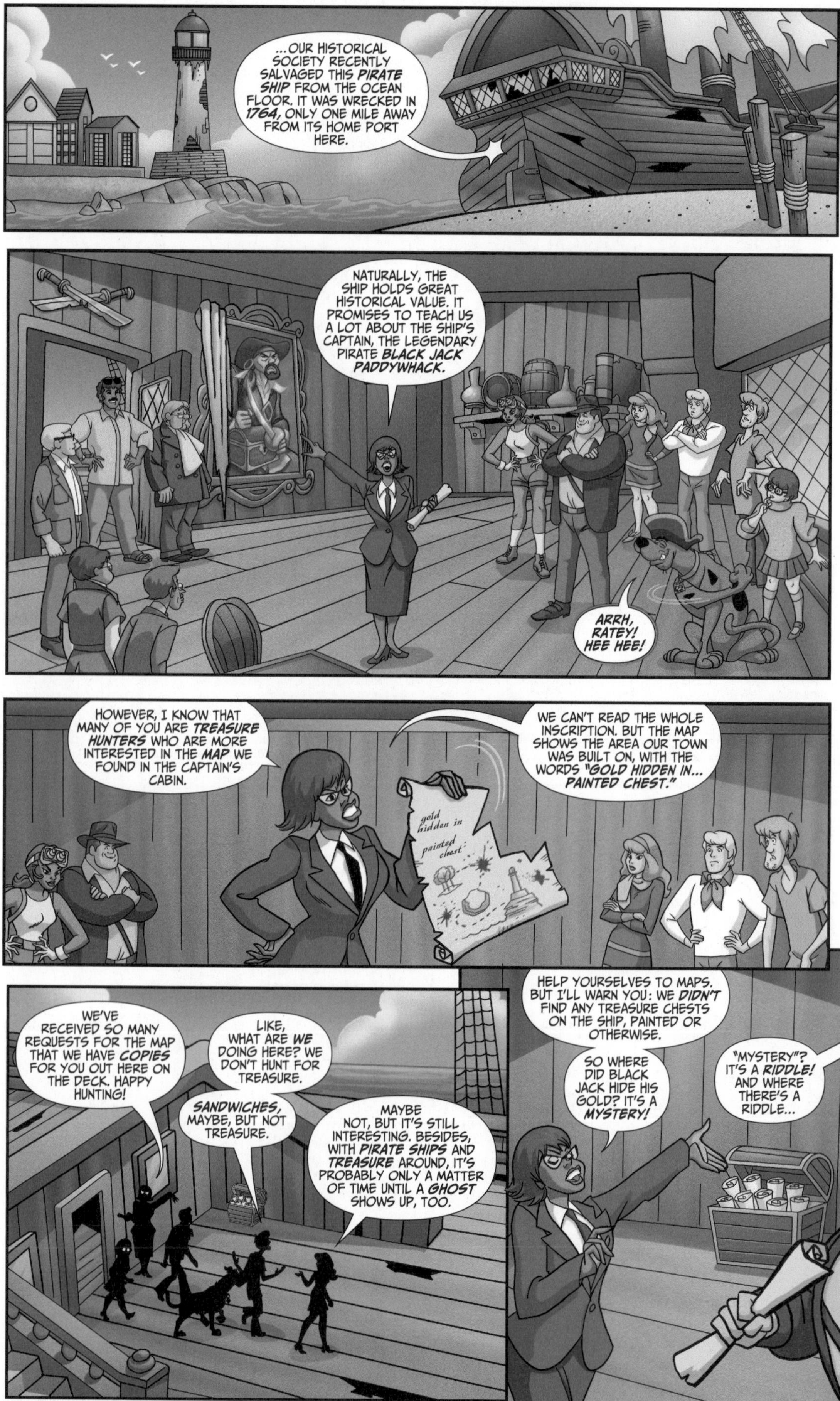
...OUR HISTORICAL SOCIETY RECENTLY SALVAGED THIS PIRATE SHIP FROM THE OCEAN FLOOR. IT WAS WRECKED IN 1764, ONLY ONE MILE AWAY FROM ITS HOME PORT HERE.
NATURALLY, THE SHIP HOLDS GREAT HISTORICAL VALUE. IT PROMISES TO TEACH US A LOT ABOUT THE SHIP'S CAPTAIN, THE LEGENDARY PIRATE BLACK JACK PADDYWHACK.
ARRH, RATEY! HEE HEE!
HOWEVER, I KNOW THAT MANY OF YOU ARE TREASURE HUNTERS WHO ARE MORE INTERESTED IN THE MAP WE FOUND IN THE CAPTAIN'S CABIN.
WE CAN'T READ THE WHOLE INSCRIPTION. BUT THE MAP SHOWS THE AREA OUR TOWN WAS BUILT ON, WITH THE WORDS "GOLD HIDDEN IN... PAINTED CHEST."
gold hidden in
painted chest
WE'VE RECEIVED SO MANY REQUESTS FOR THE MAP THAT WE HAVE COPIES FOR YOU OUT HERE ON THE DECK. HAPPY HUNTING!
LIKE, WHAT ARE WE DOING HERE? WE DON'T HUNT FOR TREASURE.
SANDWICHES, MAYBE, BUT NOT TREASURE.
MAYBE NOT, BUT IT'S STILL INTERESTING. BESIDES, WITH PIRATE SHIPS AND TREASURE AROUND, IT'S PROBABLY ONLY A MATTER OF TIME UNTIL A GHOST SHOWS UP, TOO.
HELP YOURSELVES TO MAPS. BUT I'LL WARN YOU: WE DIDN'T FIND ANY TREASURE CHESTS ON THE SHIP, PAINTED OR OTHERWISE.
SO WHERE DID BLACK JACK HIDE HIS GOLD? IT'S A MYSTERY!
"MYSTERY"? IT'S A RIDDLE! AND WHERE THERE'S A RIDDLE...

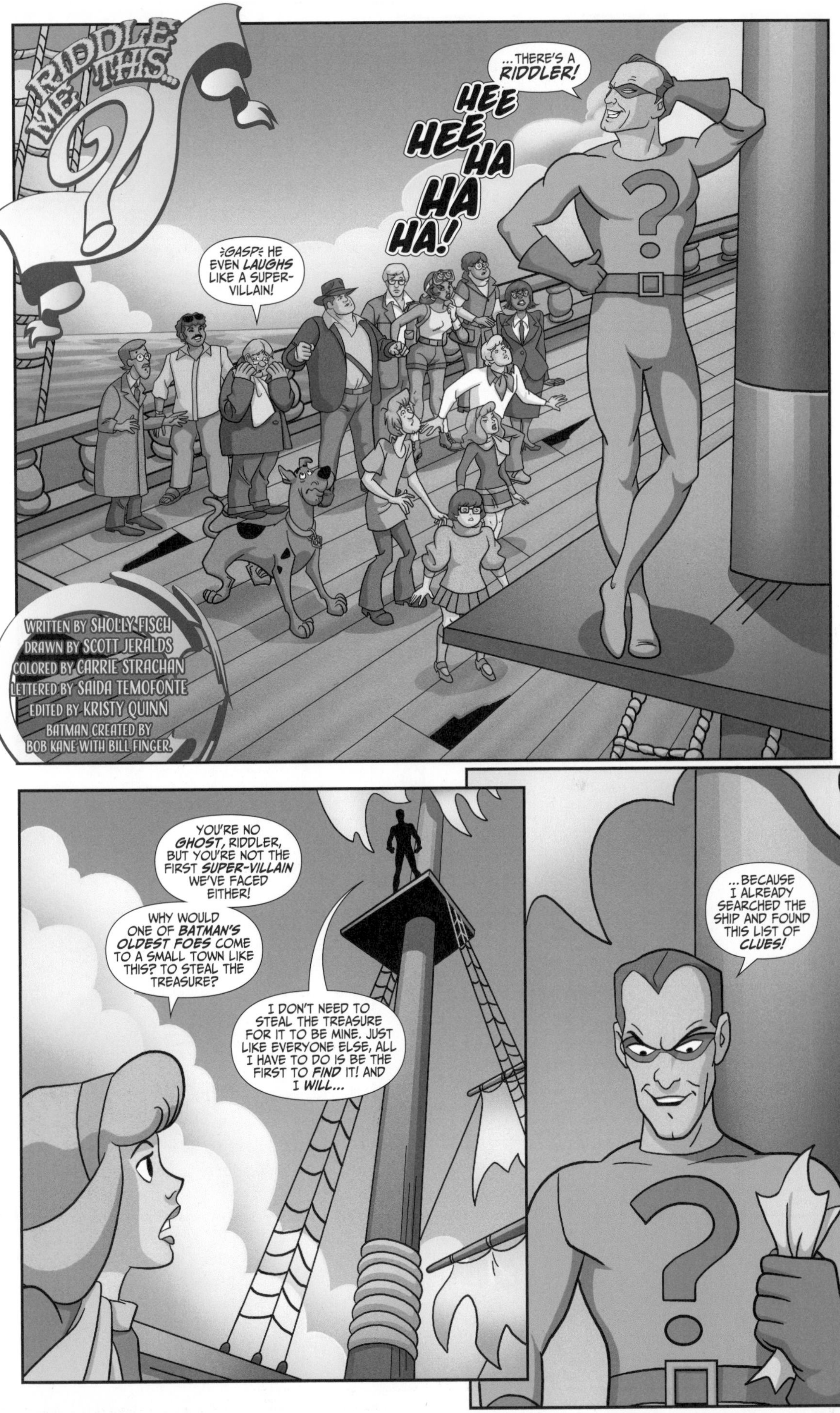
RIDDLE ME THIS...
...THERE'S A RIDDLER!
HEE HEE HA HA HA!
⁼GASP⁼ HE EVEN LAUGHS LIKE A SUPER-VILLAIN!
WRITTEN BY SHOLLY FISCH
DRAWN BY SCOTT JERALDS
COLORED BY CARRIE STRACHAN
LETTERED BY SAIDA TEMOFONTE
EDITED BY KRISTY QUINN
BATMAN CREATED BY BOB KANE WITH BILL FINGER.
YOU'RE NO GHOST, RIDDLER, BUT YOU'RE NOT THE FIRST SUPER-VILLAIN WE'VE FACED EITHER!
WHY WOULD ONE OF BATMAN'S OLDEST FOES COME TO A SMALL TOWN LIKE THIS? TO STEAL THE TREASURE?
I DON'T NEED TO STEAL THE TREASURE FOR IT TO BE MINE. JUST LIKE EVERYONE ELSE, ALL I HAVE TO DO IS BE THE FIRST TO FIND IT! AND I WILL...
...BECAUSE I ALREADY SEARCHED THE SHIP AND FOUND THIS LIST OF CLUES!

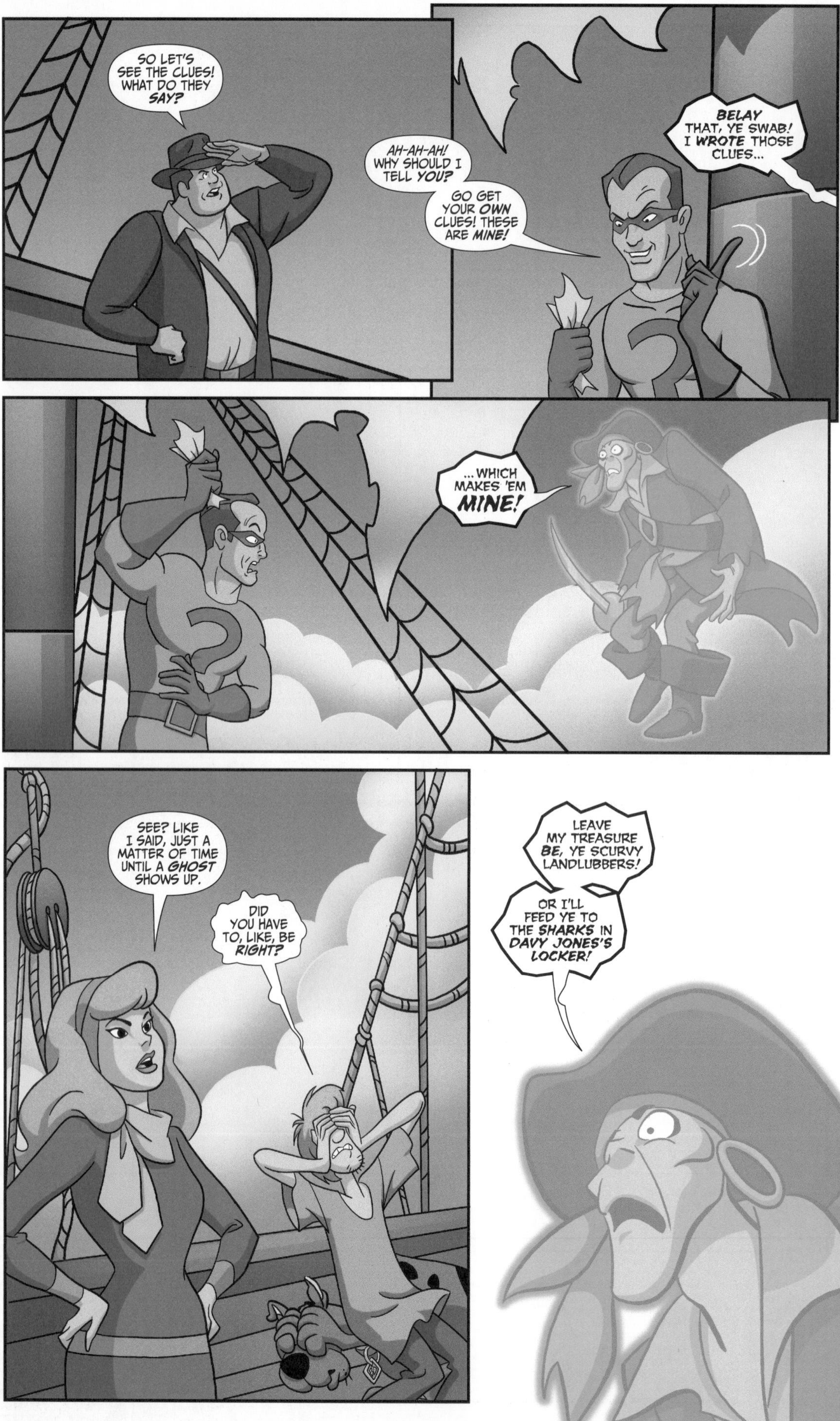
SO LET'S SEE THE CLUES! WHAT DO THEY SAY?
AH-AH-AH! WHY SHOULD I TELL YOU?
GO GET YOUR OWN CLUES! THESE ARE MINE!
BELAY THAT, YE SWAB! I WROTE THOSE CLUES...
...WHICH MAKES 'EM MINE!
SEE? LIKE I SAID, JUST A MATTER OF TIME UNTIL A GHOST SHOWS UP.
DID YOU HAVE TO, LIKE, BE RIGHT?
LEAVE MY TREASURE BE, YE SCURVY LANDLUBBERS!
OR I'LL FEED YE TO THE SHARKS IN DAVY JONES'S LOCKER!

THAT'S ALL I NEED TO HEAR!

GHOSTS!

SUPER-VILLAINS!

I'M GONNA SEARCH FOR AN *EASIER* TREASURE--ONE THAT'S JUST GUARDED BY *SNAKES* AND *SCORPIONS!*

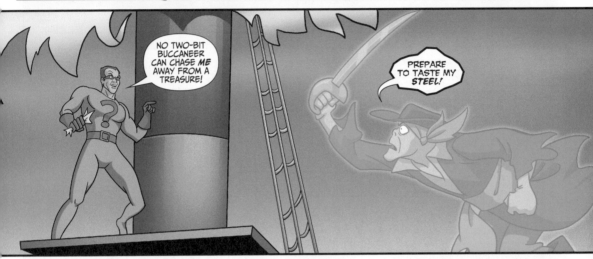

NO TWO-BIT BUCCANEER CAN CHASE *ME* AWAY FROM A TREASURE!

PREPARE TO TASTE MY *STEEL!*

ON THE OTHER HAND, WHAT TIME IS IT WHEN A *THREE-HUNDRED-YEAR-OLD GHOST* THREATENS YOU WITH A *SWORD?*

TIME FOR A *STRATEGIC WITHDRAWAL!*

LIKE, I'LL SETTLE FOR A *NOT-SO-STRATEGIC WITHDRAWAL!* C'MON, OLD BUDDY!

RUH-HUH!

THIS HIDING PLACE IS *TAKEN!*

EEP! THAT WITHDRAWAL *DEFINITELY* WASN'T STRATEGIC!

RIKES!

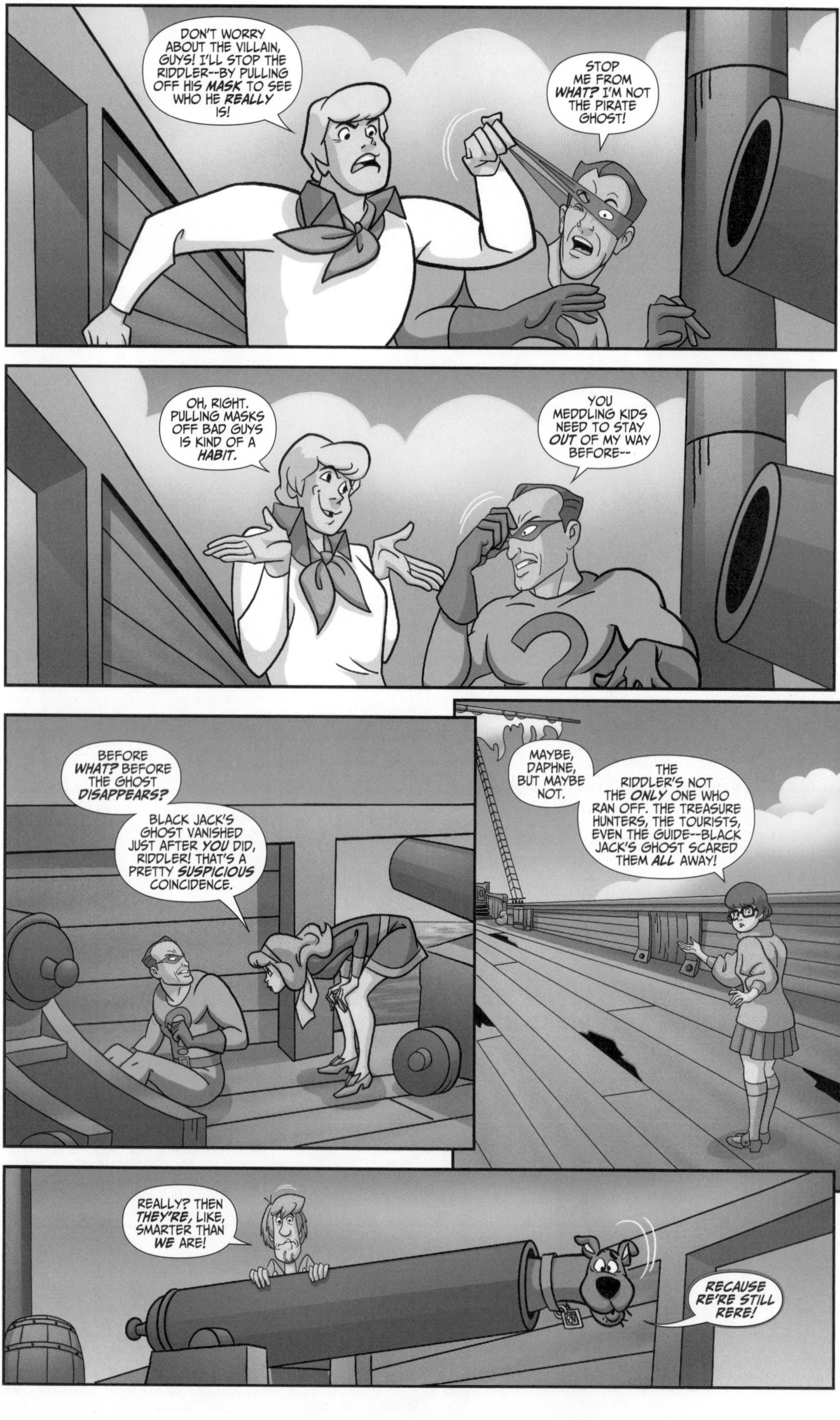
DON'T WORRY ABOUT THE VILLAIN, GUYS! I'LL STOP THE RIDDLER--BY PULLING OFF HIS MASK TO SEE WHO HE REALLY IS!
STOP ME FROM WHAT? I'M NOT THE PIRATE GHOST!
OH, RIGHT. PULLING MASKS OFF BAD GUYS IS KIND OF A HABIT.
YOU MEDDLING KIDS NEED TO STAY OUT OF MY WAY BEFORE--
BEFORE WHAT? BEFORE THE GHOST DISAPPEARS?
BLACK JACK'S GHOST VANISHED JUST AFTER YOU DID, RIDDLER! THAT'S A PRETTY SUSPICIOUS COINCIDENCE.
MAYBE, DAPHNE, BUT MAYBE NOT.
THE RIDDLER'S NOT THE ONLY ONE WHO RAN OFF. THE TREASURE HUNTERS, THE TOURISTS, EVEN THE GUIDE--BLACK JACK'S GHOST SCARED THEM ALL AWAY!
REALLY? THEN THEY'RE, LIKE, SMARTER THAN WE ARE!
RECAUSE RE'RE STILL RERE!

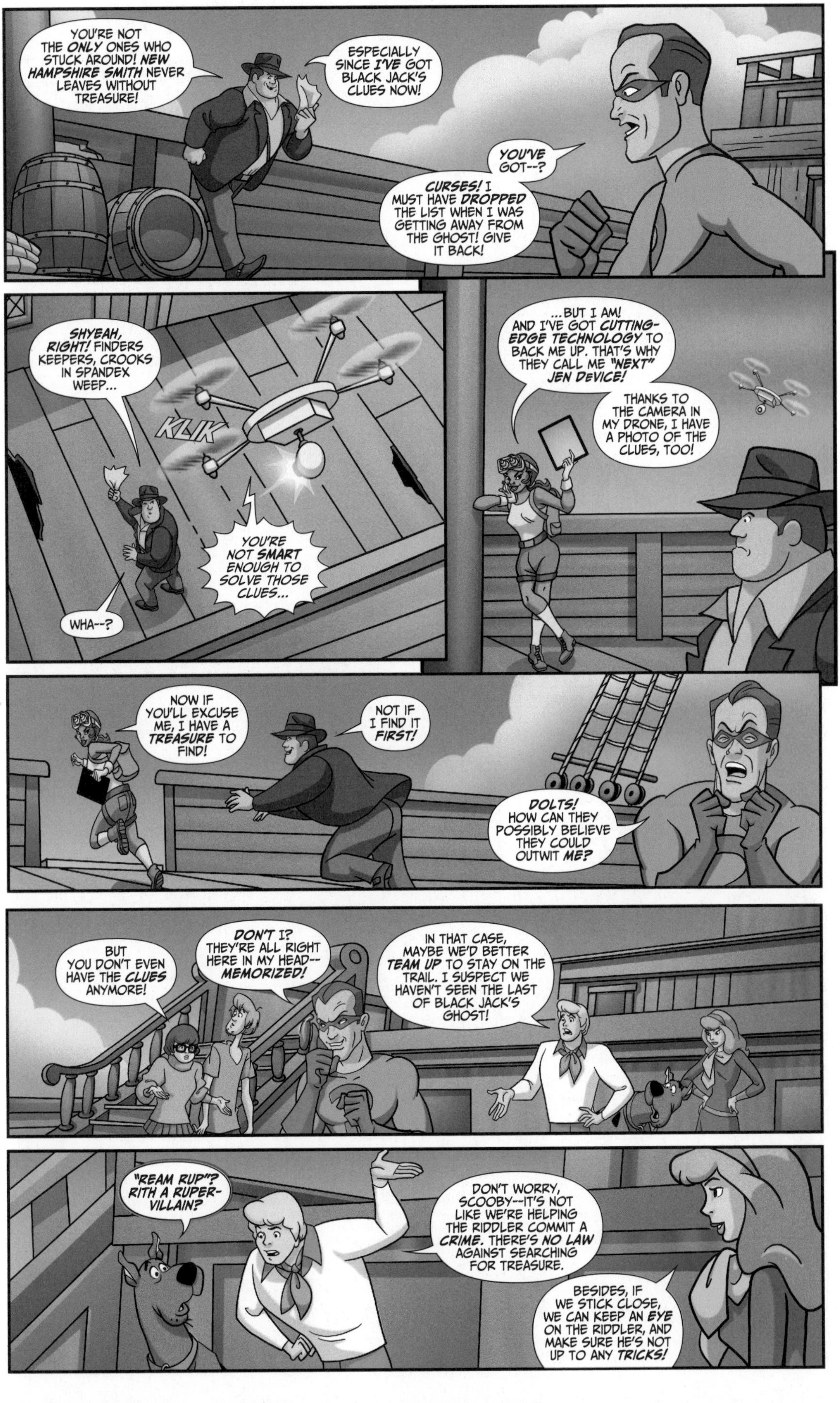
YOU'RE NOT THE ONLY ONES WHO STUCK AROUND! NEW HAMPSHIRE SMITH NEVER LEAVES WITHOUT TREASURE!
ESPECIALLY SINCE I'VE GOT BLACK JACK'S CLUES NOW!
YOU'VE GOT--?
CURSES! I MUST HAVE DROPPED THE LIST WHEN I WAS GETTING AWAY FROM THE GHOST! GIVE IT BACK!
SHYEAH, RIGHT! FINDERS KEEPERS, CROOKS IN SPANDEX WEEP...
KLIK
YOU'RE NOT SMART ENOUGH TO SOLVE THOSE CLUES...
WHA--?
...BUT I AM! AND I'VE GOT CUTTING-EDGE TECHNOLOGY TO BACK ME UP. THAT'S WHY THEY CALL ME "NEXT" JEN DEVICE!
THANKS TO THE CAMERA IN MY DRONE, I HAVE A PHOTO OF THE CLUES, TOO!
NOW IF YOU'LL EXCUSE ME, I HAVE A TREASURE TO FIND!
NOT IF I FIND IT FIRST!
DOLTS! HOW CAN THEY POSSIBLY BELIEVE THEY COULD OUTWIT ME?
BUT YOU DON'T EVEN HAVE THE CLUES ANYMORE!
DON'T I? THEY'RE ALL RIGHT HERE IN MY HEAD--MEMORIZED!
IN THAT CASE, MAYBE WE'D BETTER TEAM UP TO STAY ON THE TRAIL. I SUSPECT WE HAVEN'T SEEN THE LAST OF BLACK JACK'S GHOST!
"REAM RUP"? RITH A RUPER-VILLAIN?
DON'T WORRY, SCOOBY--IT'S NOT LIKE WE'RE HELPING THE RIDDLER COMMIT A CRIME. THERE'S NO LAW AGAINST SEARCHING FOR TREASURE.
BESIDES, IF WE STICK CLOSE, WE CAN KEEP AN EYE ON THE RIDDLER, AND MAKE SURE HE'S NOT UP TO ANY TRICKS!

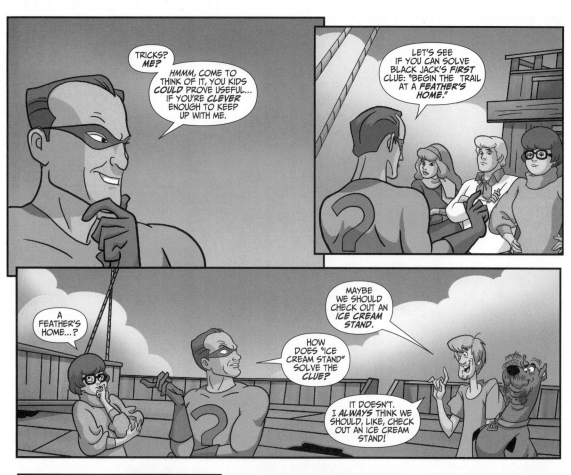

TRICKS? *ME?*

HMMM, COME TO THINK OF IT, YOU KIDS COULD PROVE USEFUL... IF YOU'RE CLEVER ENOUGH TO KEEP UP WITH ME.

LET'S SEE IF YOU CAN SOLVE BLACK JACK'S *FIRST* CLUE: "BEGIN THE TRAIL AT A *FEATHER'S HOME."*

A *FEATHER'S HOME...?*

MAYBE WE SHOULD CHECK OUT AN *ICE CREAM STAND.*

HOW DOES "ICE CREAM STAND" SOLVE THE *CLUE?*

IT DOESN'T. I *ALWAYS* THINK WE SHOULD, LIKE, CHECK OUT AN ICE CREAM STAND!

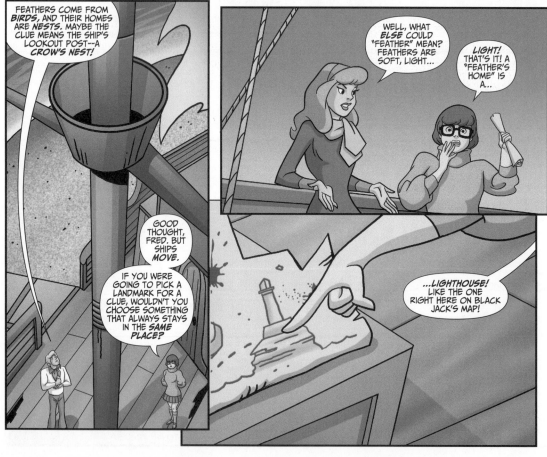

FEATHERS COME FROM *BIRDS,* AND THEIR HOMES ARE *NESTS.* MAYBE THE CLUE MEANS THE SHIP'S LOOKOUT POST--A *CROW'S NEST!*

GOOD THOUGHT, FRED. BUT SHIPS *MOVE.*

IF YOU WERE GOING TO PICK A LANDMARK FOR A CLUE, WOULDN'T YOU CHOOSE SOMETHING THAT ALWAYS STAYS IN THE *SAME PLACE?*

WELL, WHAT *ELSE* COULD "FEATHER" MEAN? FEATHERS ARE SOFT, LIGHT...

LIGHT! THAT'S IT! A "FEATHER'S HOME" IS A...

...LIGHTHOUSE! LIKE THE ONE RIGHT HERE ON BLACK JACK'S MAP!

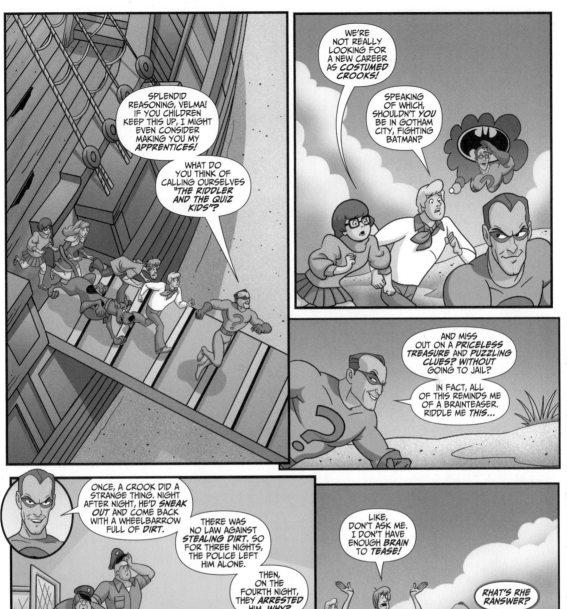

SPLENDID REASONING, VELMA! IF YOU CHILDREN KEEP THIS UP, I MIGHT EVEN CONSIDER MAKING YOU MY APPRENTICES!

WHAT DO YOU THINK OF CALLING OURSELVES "THE RIDDLER AND THE QUIZ KIDS"?

WE'RE NOT REALLY LOOKING FOR A NEW CAREER AS COSTUMED CROOKS!

SPEAKING OF WHICH, SHOULDN'T YOU BE IN GOTHAM CITY, FIGHTING BATMAN?

AND MISS OUT ON A PRICELESS TREASURE AND PUZZLING CLUES? WITHOUT GOING TO JAIL?

IN FACT, ALL OF THIS REMINDS ME OF A BRAINTEASER. RIDDLE ME THIS...

ONCE, A CROOK DID A STRANGE THING. NIGHT AFTER NIGHT, HE'D SNEAK OUT AND COME BACK WITH A WHEELBARROW FULL OF DIRT.

THERE WAS NO LAW AGAINST STEALING DIRT. SO FOR THREE NIGHTS, THE POLICE LEFT HIM ALONE.

THEN, ON THE FOURTH NIGHT, THEY ARRESTED HIM. WHY?

LIKE, DON'T ASK ME. I DON'T HAVE ENOUGH BRAIN TO TEASE!

RHAT'S RHE RANSWER?

TSK TSK. WHERE'S THE FUN IN JUST TELLING YOU THE ANSWER? I'M SURE THE SOLUTION WILL REVEAL ITSELF EVENTUALLY.

BESIDES, WE'VE REACHED THE LIGHTHOUSE!

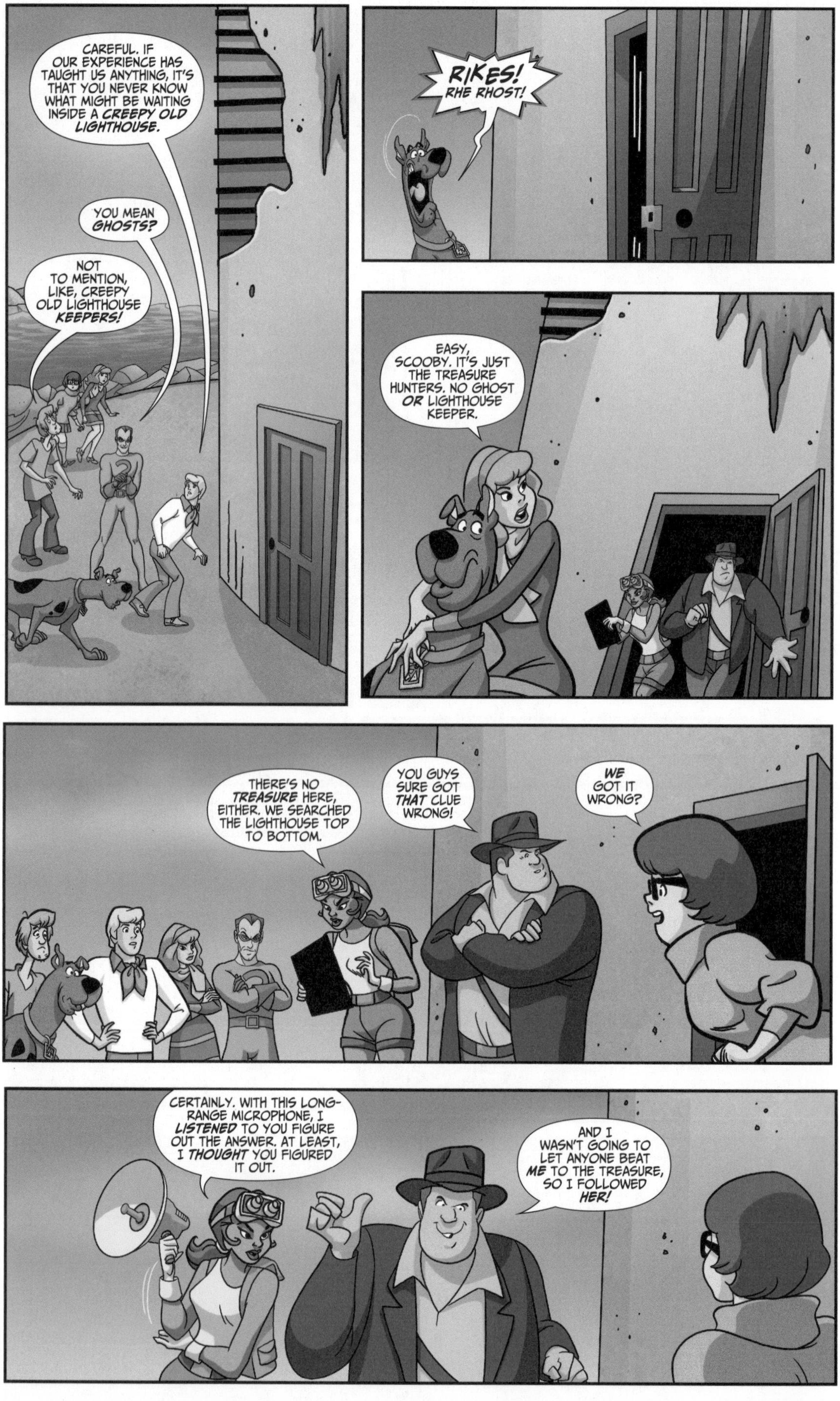

CAREFUL. IF OUR EXPERIENCE HAS TAUGHT US ANYTHING, IT'S THAT YOU NEVER KNOW WHAT MIGHT BE WAITING INSIDE A CREEPY OLD LIGHTHOUSE.
YOU MEAN GHOSTS?
NOT TO MENTION, LIKE, CREEPY OLD LIGHTHOUSE KEEPERS!
RIKES! RHE RHOST!
EASY, SCOOBY. IT'S JUST THE TREASURE HUNTERS. NO GHOST OR LIGHTHOUSE KEEPER.
THERE'S NO TREASURE HERE, EITHER. WE SEARCHED THE LIGHTHOUSE TOP TO BOTTOM.
YOU GUYS SURE GOT THAT CLUE WRONG!
WE GOT IT WRONG?
CERTAINLY. WITH THIS LONG-RANGE MICROPHONE, I LISTENED TO YOU FIGURE OUT THE ANSWER. AT LEAST, I THOUGHT YOU FIGURED IT OUT.
AND I WASN'T GOING TO LET ANYONE BEAT ME TO THE TREASURE, SO I FOLLOWED HER!

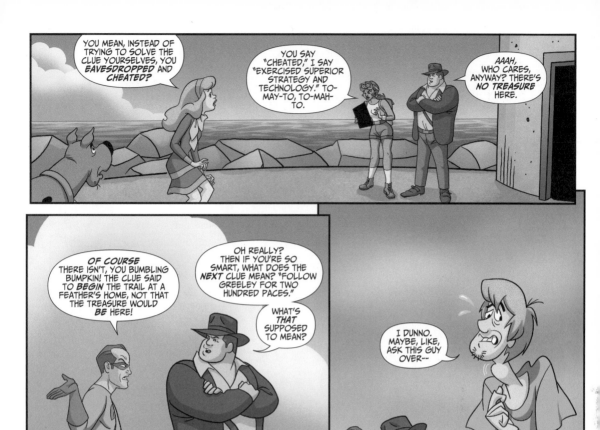

YOU MEAN, INSTEAD OF TRYING TO SOLVE THE CLUE YOURSELVES, YOU *EAVESDROPPED* AND *CHEATED?*

YOU SAY "CHEATED," I SAY "EXERCISED SUPERIOR STRATEGY AND TECHNOLOGY." TO-MAY-TO, TO-MAH-TO.

AAAH, WHO CARES, ANYWAY? THERE'S *NO TREASURE* HERE.

OF COURSE THERE ISN'T, YOU BUMBLING BUMPKIN! THE CLUE SAID TO *BEGIN* THE TRAIL AT A FEATHER'S HOME, NOT THAT THE TREASURE WOULD *BE* HERE!

OH REALLY? THEN IF YOU'RE SO SMART, WHAT DOES THE *NEXT* CLUE MEAN? "FOLLOW GREELEY FOR TWO HUNDRED PACES."

WHAT'S *THAT* SUPPOSED TO MEAN?

I DUNNO. MAYBE, LIKE, ASK THIS GUY OVER--

--HERE?!

ZOINKS! BLACK JACK'S GHOST!

YE'LL *WALK THE PLANK,* YE BARNACLE-RIDDEN BILGE RATS!

RIDDLE ME THIS: WHY DOES WATER WIN RACES?

BECAUSE IT *RUNS--* LIKE ME!

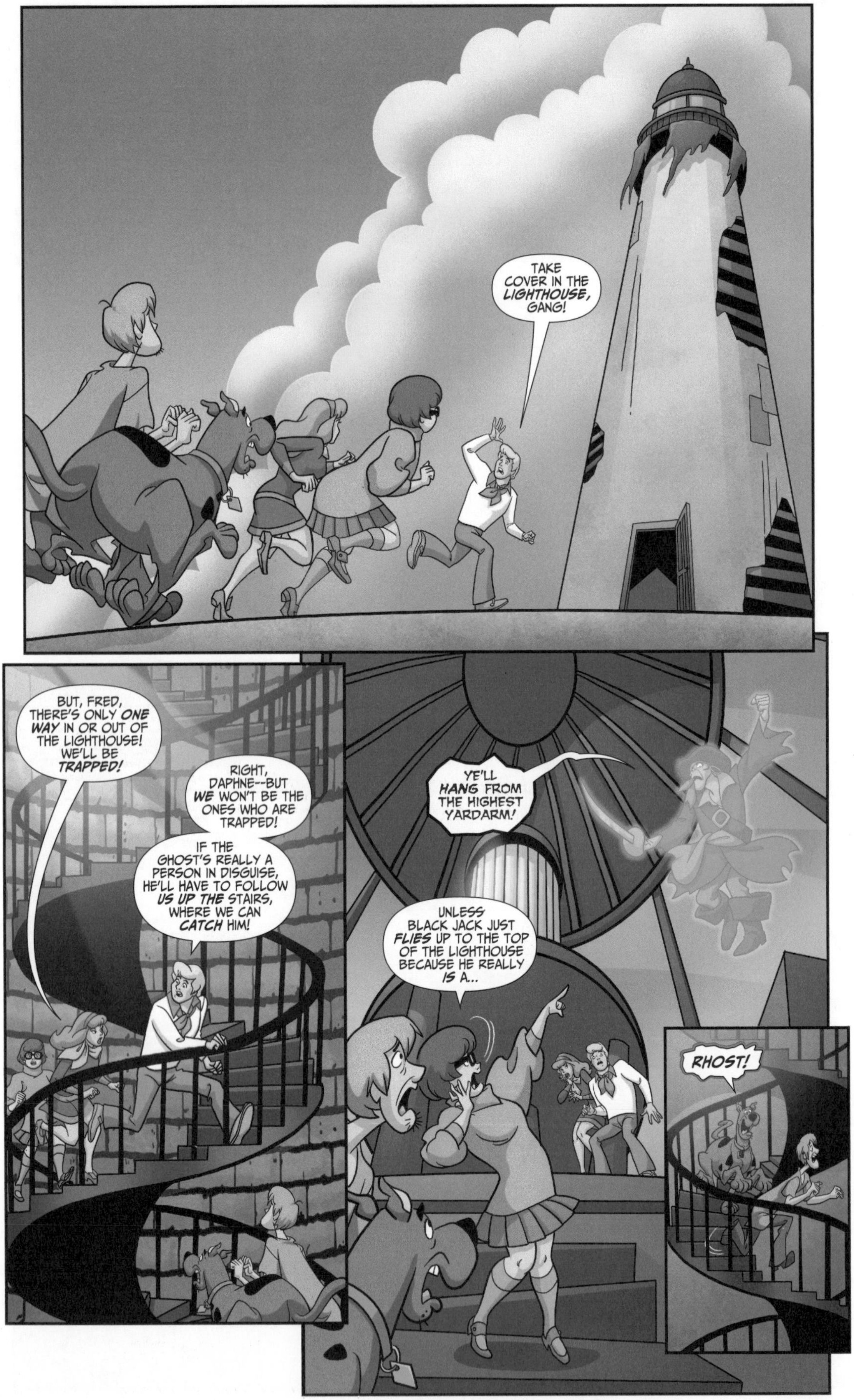

TAKE COVER IN THE LIGHTHOUSE, GANG!
BUT, FRED, THERE'S ONLY ONE WAY IN OR OUT OF THE LIGHTHOUSE! WE'LL BE TRAPPED!
RIGHT, DAPHNE--BUT WE WON'T BE THE ONES WHO ARE TRAPPED!
IF THE GHOST'S REALLY A PERSON IN DISGUISE, HE'LL HAVE TO FOLLOW US UP THE STAIRS, WHERE WE CAN CATCH HIM!
YE'LL HANG FROM THE HIGHEST YARDARM!
UNLESS BLACK JACK JUST FLIES UP TO THE TOP OF THE LIGHTHOUSE BECAUSE HE REALLY IS A...
RHOST!

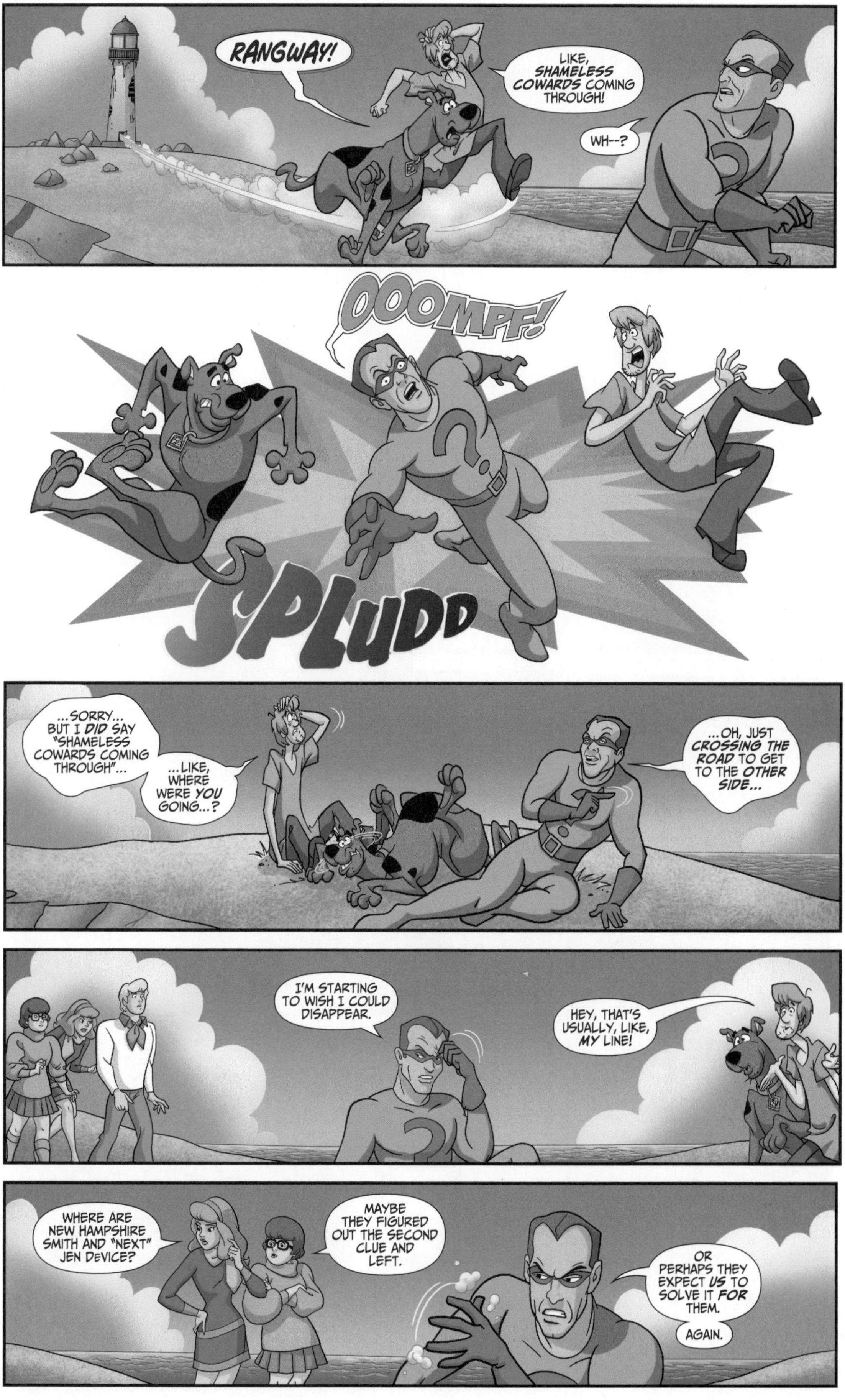
RANGWAY!
LIKE, SHAMELESS COWARDS COMING THROUGH!
WH--?
OOOMPF!
SPLUDD
...SORRY... BUT I DID SAY "SHAMELESS COWARDS COMING THROUGH"...
...LIKE, WHERE WERE YOU GOING...?
...OH, JUST CROSSING THE ROAD TO GET TO THE OTHER SIDE...
I'M STARTING TO WISH I COULD DISAPPEAR.
HEY, THAT'S USUALLY, LIKE, MY LINE!
WHERE ARE NEW HAMPSHIRE SMITH AND "NEXT" JEN DEVICE?
MAYBE THEY FIGURED OUT THE SECOND CLUE AND LEFT.
OR PERHAPS THEY EXPECT US TO SOLVE IT FOR THEM.
AGAIN.

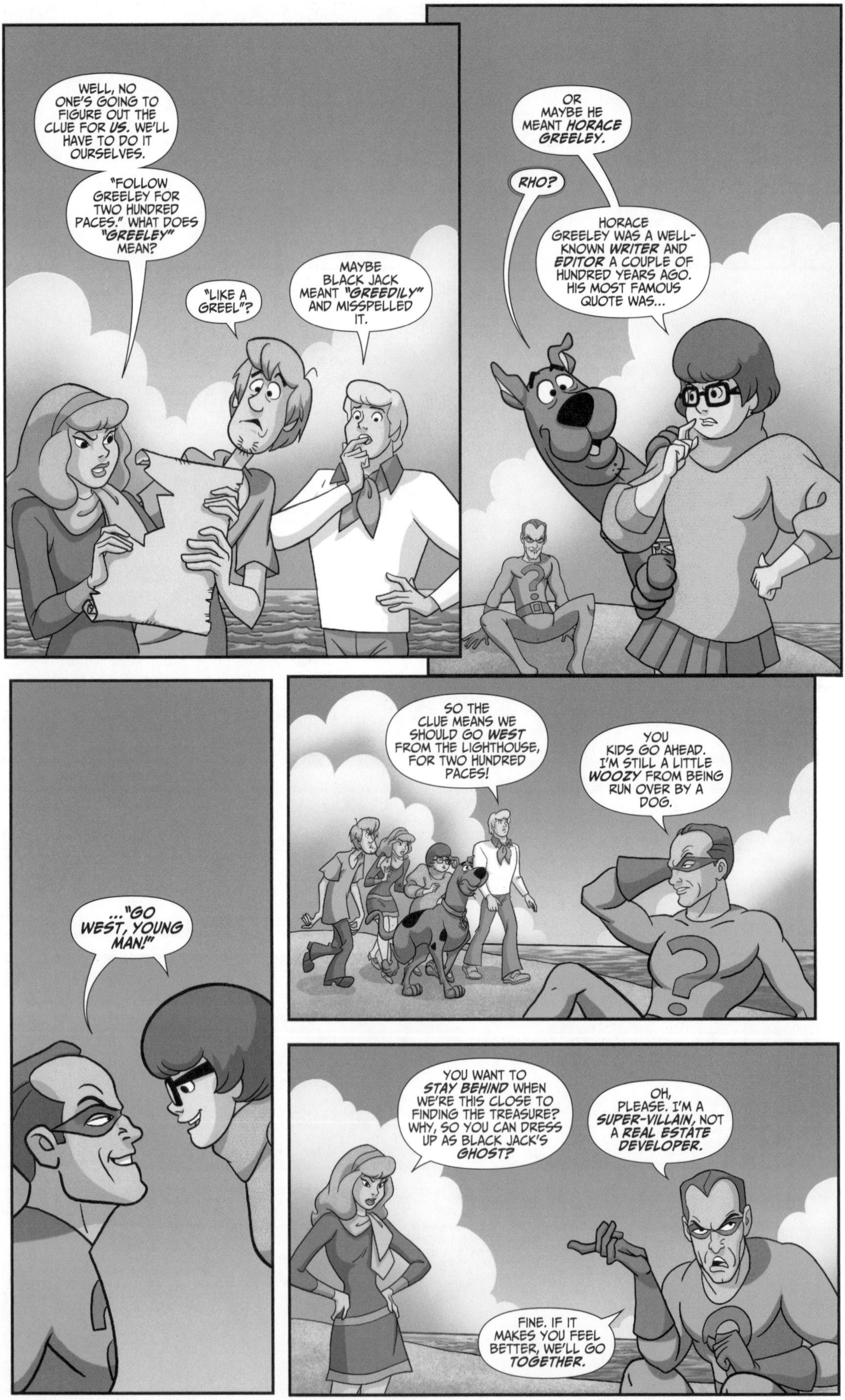
WELL, NO ONE'S GOING TO FIGURE OUT THE CLUE FOR *US.* WE'LL HAVE TO DO IT OURSELVES.
"FOLLOW GREELEY FOR TWO HUNDRED PACES." WHAT DOES *"GREELEY"* MEAN?
"LIKE A GREEL"?
MAYBE BLACK JACK MEANT *"GREEDILY"* AND MISSPELLED IT.
OR MAYBE HE MEANT *HORACE GREELEY.*
RHO?
HORACE GREELEY WAS A WELL-KNOWN *WRITER* AND *EDITOR* A COUPLE OF HUNDRED YEARS AGO. HIS MOST FAMOUS QUOTE WAS...
..."GO WEST, YOUNG MAN!"
SO THE CLUE MEANS WE SHOULD GO *WEST* FROM THE LIGHTHOUSE, FOR TWO HUNDRED PACES!
YOU KIDS GO AHEAD. I'M STILL A LITTLE *WOOZY* FROM BEING RUN OVER BY A DOG.
YOU WANT TO *STAY BEHIND* WHEN WE'RE THIS CLOSE TO FINDING THE TREASURE? WHY, SO YOU CAN DRESS UP AS BLACK JACK'S *GHOST?*
OH, PLEASE. I'M A *SUPER-VILLAIN,* NOT A *REAL ESTATE DEVELOPER.*
FINE. IF IT MAKES YOU FEEL BETTER, WE'LL GO *TOGETHER.*

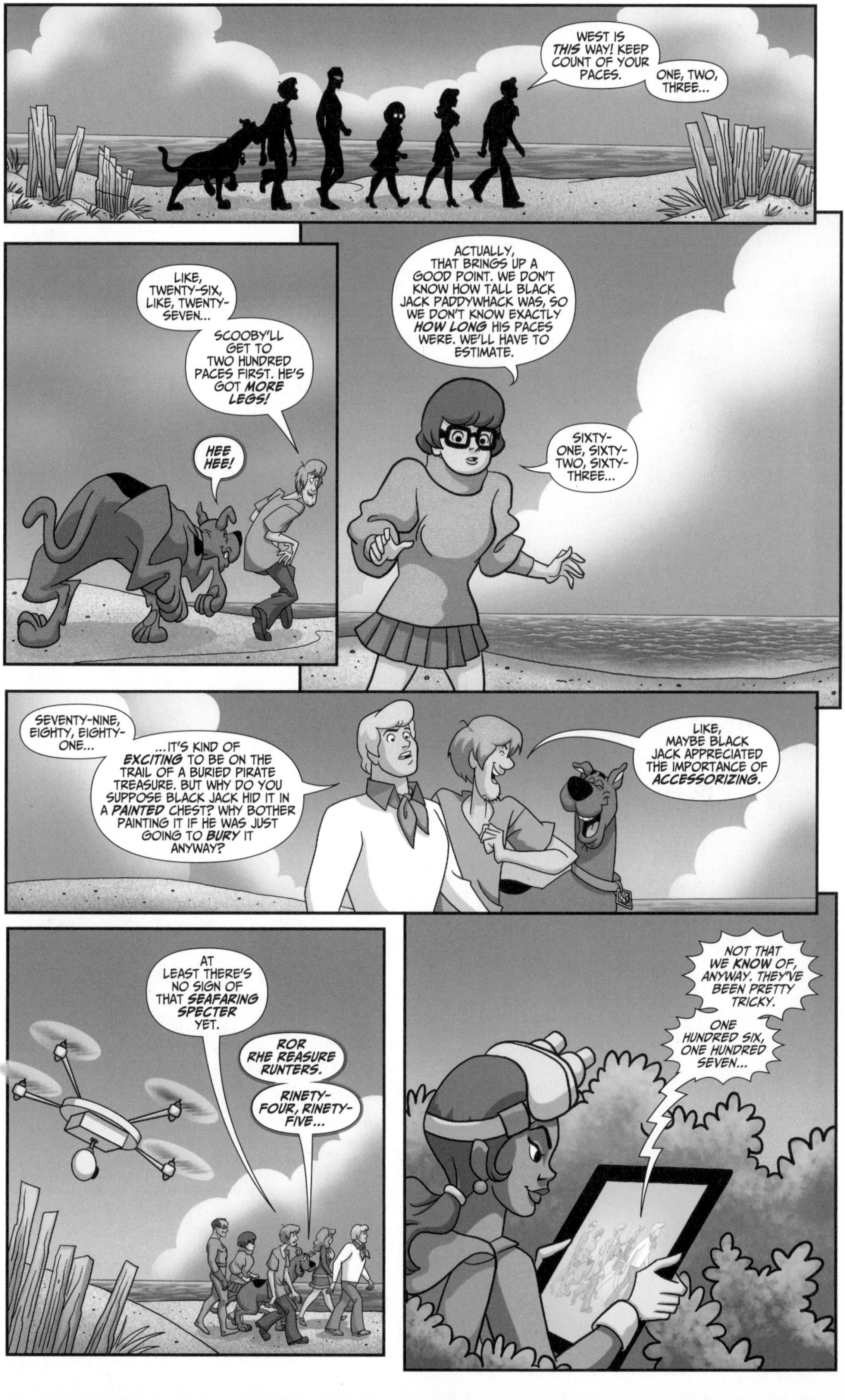
WEST IS THIS WAY! KEEP COUNT OF YOUR PACES.
ONE, TWO, THREE...
LIKE, TWENTY-SIX, LIKE, TWENTY-SEVEN...
SCOOBY'LL GET TO TWO HUNDRED PACES FIRST. HE'S GOT MORE LEGS!
HEE HEE!
ACTUALLY, THAT BRINGS UP A GOOD POINT. WE DON'T KNOW HOW TALL BLACK JACK PADDYWHACK WAS, SO WE DON'T KNOW EXACTLY HOW LONG HIS PACES WERE. WE'LL HAVE TO ESTIMATE.
SIXTY-ONE, SIXTY-TWO, SIXTY-THREE...
SEVENTY-NINE, EIGHTY, EIGHTY-ONE...
...IT'S KIND OF EXCITING TO BE ON THE TRAIL OF A BURIED PIRATE TREASURE. BUT WHY DO YOU SUPPOSE BLACK JACK HID IT IN A PAINTED CHEST? WHY BOTHER PAINTING IT IF HE WAS JUST GOING TO BURY IT ANYWAY?
LIKE, MAYBE BLACK JACK APPRECIATED THE IMPORTANCE OF ACCESSORIZING.
AT LEAST THERE'S NO SIGN OF THAT SEAFARING SPECTER YET.
ROR RHE REASURE RUNTERS.
RINETY-FOUR, RINETY-FIVE...
NOT THAT WE KNOW OF, ANYWAY. THEY'VE BEEN PRETTY TRICKY.
ONE HUNDRED SIX, ONE HUNDRED SEVEN...

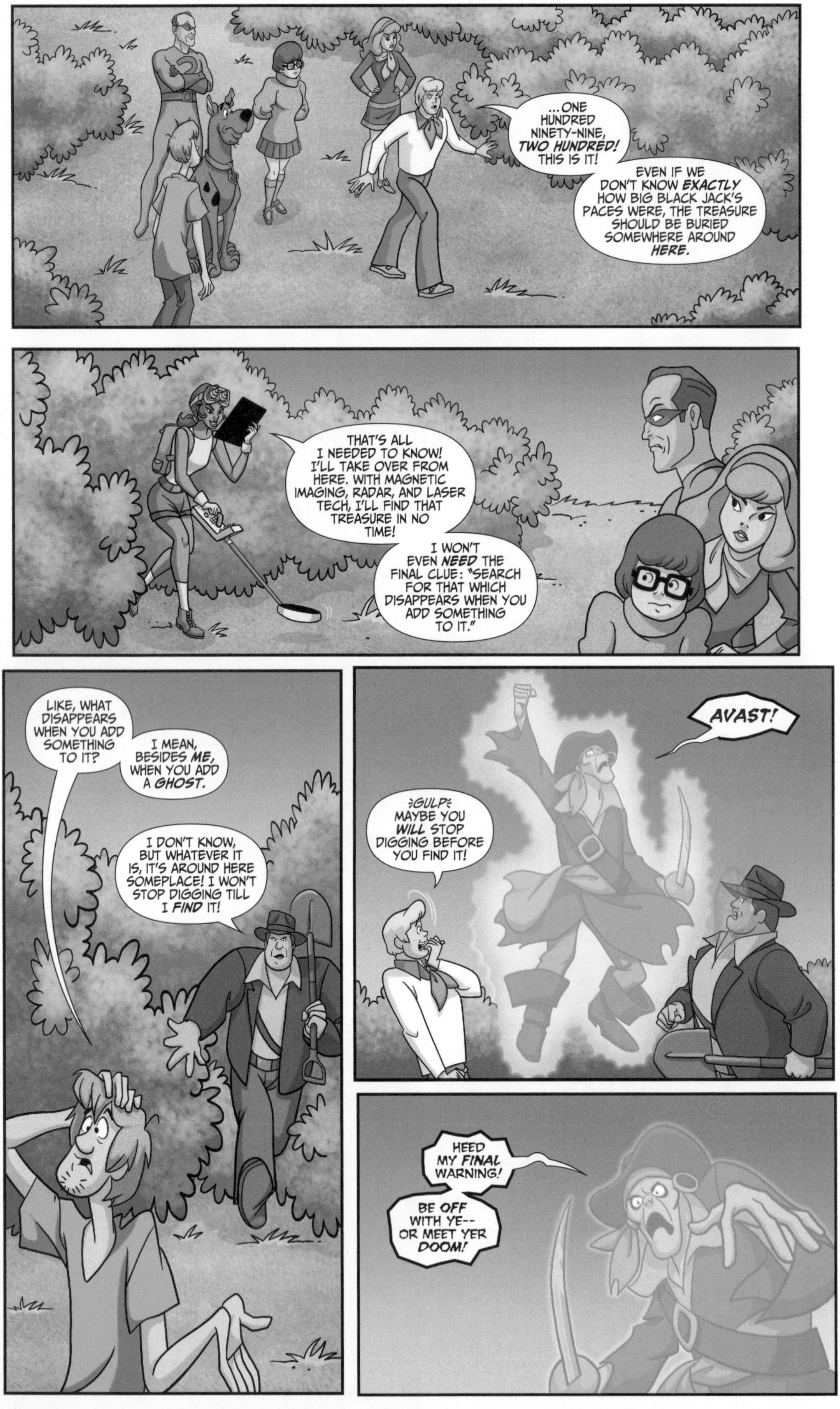
...ONE HUNDRED NINETY-NINE, TWO HUNDRED! THIS IS IT!
EVEN IF WE DON'T KNOW EXACTLY HOW BIG BLACK JACK'S PACES WERE, THE TREASURE SHOULD BE BURIED SOMEWHERE AROUND HERE.
THAT'S ALL I NEEDED TO KNOW! I'LL TAKE OVER FROM HERE. WITH MAGNETIC IMAGING, RADAR, AND LASER TECH, I'LL FIND THAT TREASURE IN NO TIME!
I WON'T EVEN NEED THE FINAL CLUE: "SEARCH FOR THAT WHICH DISAPPEARS WHEN YOU ADD SOMETHING TO IT."
LIKE, WHAT DISAPPEARS WHEN YOU ADD SOMETHING TO IT?
I MEAN, BESIDES ME, WHEN YOU ADD A GHOST.
I DON'T KNOW, BUT WHATEVER IT IS, IT'S AROUND HERE SOMEPLACE! I WON'T STOP DIGGING TILL I FIND IT!
AVAST!
GULP
MAYBE YOU WILL STOP DIGGING BEFORE YOU FIND IT!
HEED MY FINAL WARNING!
BE OFF WITH YE-- OR MEET YER DOOM!

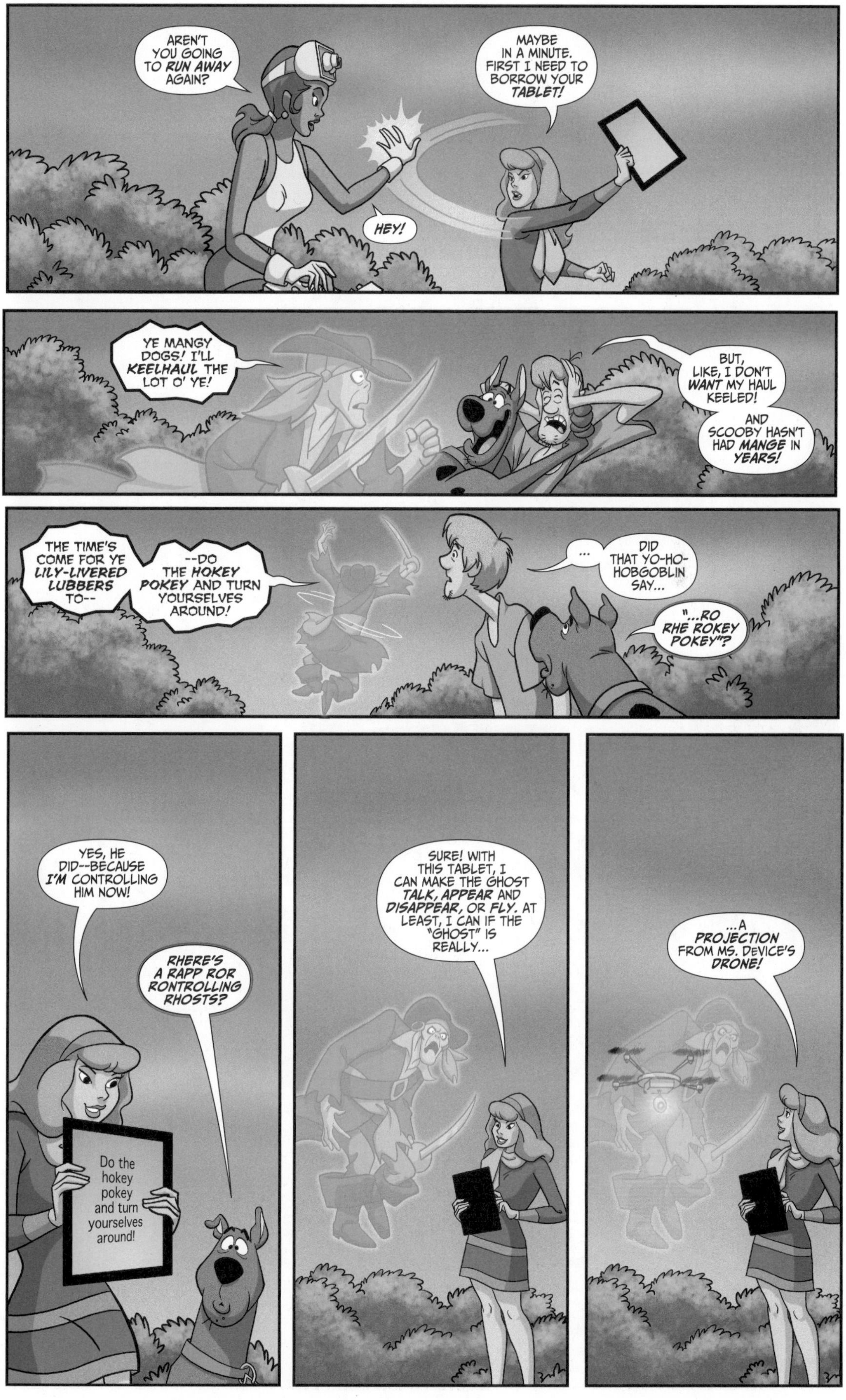
AREN'T YOU GOING TO RUN AWAY AGAIN?
MAYBE IN A MINUTE. FIRST I NEED TO BORROW YOUR TABLET!
HEY!
YE MANGY DOGS! I'LL KEELHAUL THE LOT O' YE!
BUT, LIKE, I DON'T WANT MY HAUL KEELED!
AND SCOOBY HASN'T HAD MANGE IN YEARS!
THE TIME'S COME FOR YE LILY-LIVERED LUBBERS TO--
--DO THE HOKEY POKEY AND TURN YOURSELVES AROUND!
...
DID THAT YO-HO-HOBGOBLIN SAY...
"...RO RHE ROKEY POKEY"?
YES, HE DID--BECAUSE I'M CONTROLLING HIM NOW!
RHERE'S A RAPP ROR RONTROLLING RHOSTS?
Do the hokey pokey and turn yourselves around!
SURE! WITH THIS TABLET, I CAN MAKE THE GHOST TALK, APPEAR AND DISAPPEAR, OR FLY. AT LEAST, I CAN IF THE "GHOST" IS REALLY...
...A PROJECTION FROM MS. DEVICE'S DRONE!

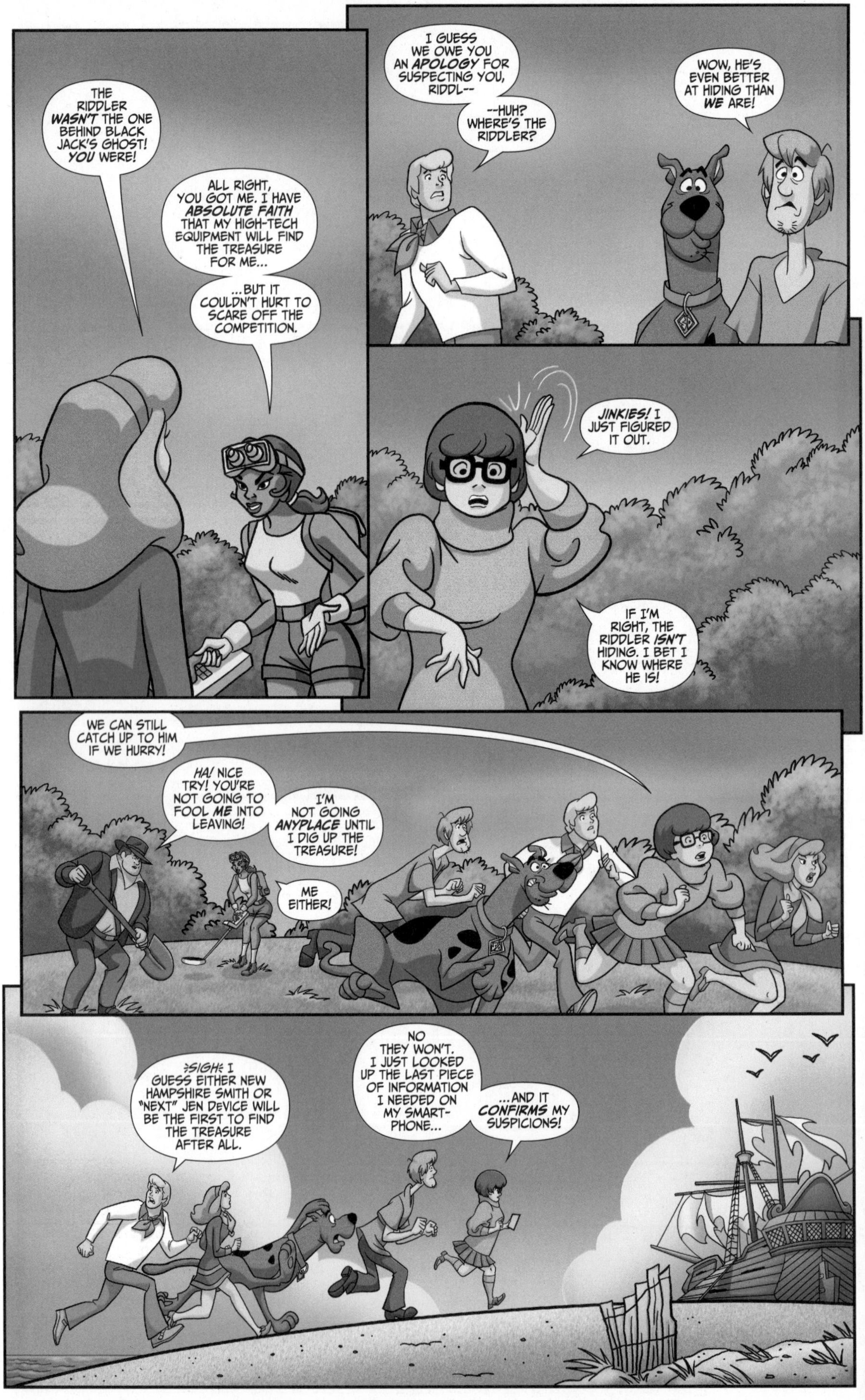
THE RIDDLER WASN'T THE ONE BEHIND BLACK JACK'S GHOST! YOU WERE!
ALL RIGHT, YOU GOT ME. I HAVE ABSOLUTE FAITH THAT MY HIGH-TECH EQUIPMENT WILL FIND THE TREASURE FOR ME...
...BUT IT COULDN'T HURT TO SCARE OFF THE COMPETITION.
I GUESS WE OWE YOU AN APOLOGY FOR SUSPECTING YOU, RIDDL--
--HUH? WHERE'S THE RIDDLER?
WOW, HE'S EVEN BETTER AT HIDING THAN WE ARE!
JINKIES! I JUST FIGURED IT OUT.
IF I'M RIGHT, THE RIDDLER ISN'T HIDING. I BET I KNOW WHERE HE IS!
WE CAN STILL CATCH UP TO HIM IF WE HURRY!
HA! NICE TRY! YOU'RE NOT GOING TO FOOL ME INTO LEAVING!
I'M NOT GOING ANYPLACE UNTIL I DIG UP THE TREASURE!
ME EITHER!
SIGH I GUESS EITHER NEW HAMPSHIRE SMITH OR "NEXT" JEN DEVICE WILL BE THE FIRST TO FIND THE TREASURE AFTER ALL.
NO THEY WON'T. I JUST LOOKED UP THE LAST PIECE OF INFORMATION I NEEDED ON MY SMART-PHONE...
...AND IT CONFIRMS MY SUSPICIONS!

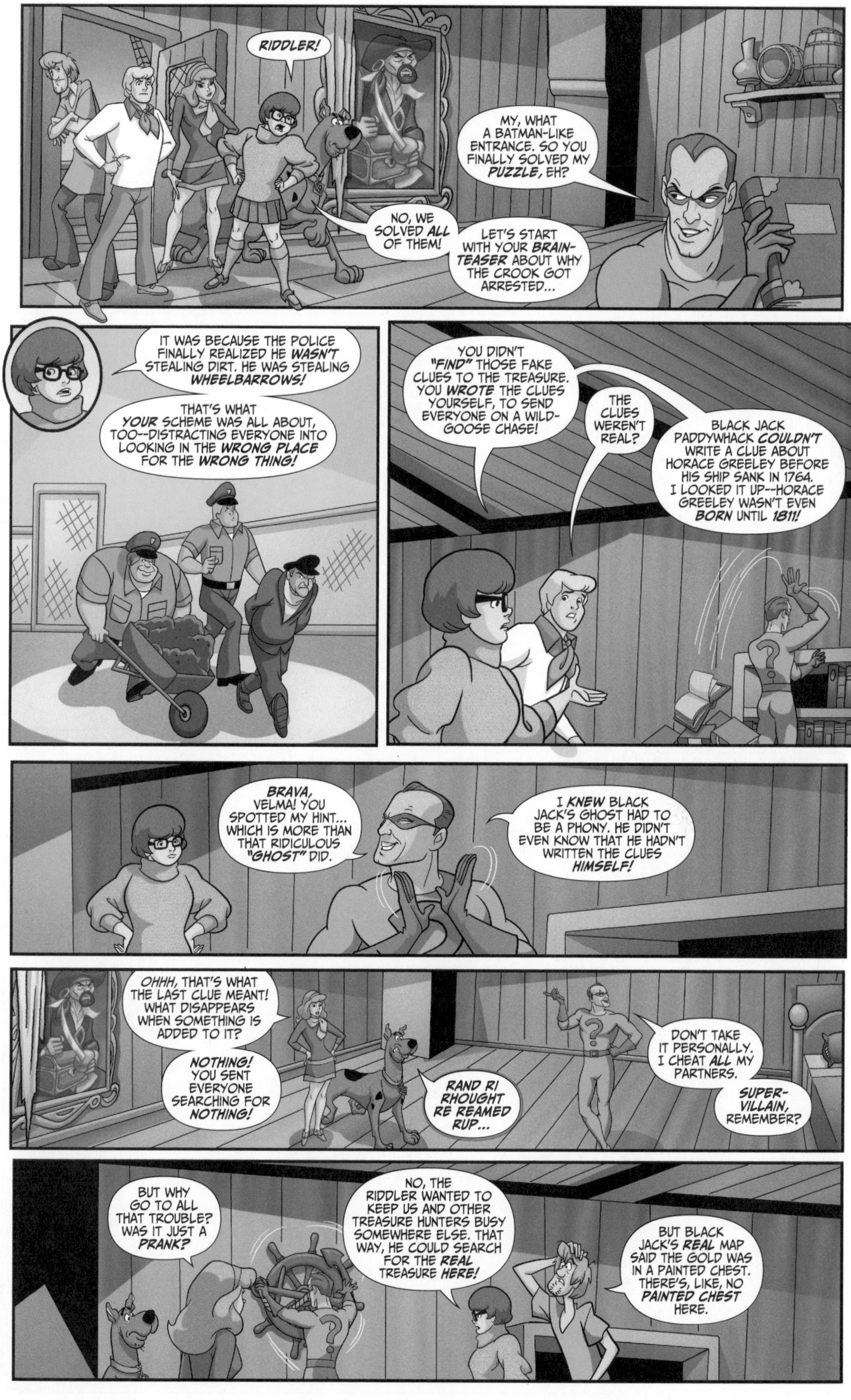
RIDDLER!
MY, WHAT A BATMAN-LIKE ENTRANCE. SO YOU FINALLY SOLVED MY PUZZLE, EH?
NO, WE SOLVED ALL OF THEM!
LET'S START WITH YOUR BRAIN-TEASER ABOUT WHY THE CROOK GOT ARRESTED...
IT WAS BECAUSE THE POLICE FINALLY REALIZED HE WASN'T STEALING DIRT. HE WAS STEALING WHEELBARROWS!
THAT'S WHAT YOUR SCHEME WAS ALL ABOUT, TOO--DISTRACTING EVERYONE INTO LOOKING IN THE WRONG PLACE FOR THE WRONG THING!
YOU DIDN'T "FIND" THOSE FAKE CLUES TO THE TREASURE. YOU WROTE THE CLUES YOURSELF, TO SEND EVERYONE ON A WILD-GOOSE CHASE!
THE CLUES WEREN'T REAL?
BLACK JACK PADDYWHACK COULDN'T WRITE A CLUE ABOUT HORACE GREELEY BEFORE HIS SHIP SANK IN 1764. I LOOKED IT UP--HORACE GREELEY WASN'T EVEN BORN UNTIL 1811!
BRAVA, VELMA! YOU SPOTTED MY HINT... WHICH IS MORE THAN THAT RIDICULOUS "GHOST" DID.
I KNEW BLACK JACK'S GHOST HAD TO BE A PHONY. HE DIDN'T EVEN KNOW THAT HE HADN'T WRITTEN THE CLUES HIMSELF!
OHHH, THAT'S WHAT THE LAST CLUE MEANT! WHAT DISAPPEARS WHEN SOMETHING IS ADDED TO IT?
NOTHING! YOU SENT EVERYONE SEARCHING FOR NOTHING!
RAND RI RHOUGHT RE REAMED RUP...
DON'T TAKE IT PERSONALLY. I CHEAT ALL MY PARTNERS.
SUPER-VILLAIN, REMEMBER?
BUT WHY GO TO ALL THAT TROUBLE? WAS IT JUST A PRANK?
NO, THE RIDDLER WANTED TO KEEP US AND OTHER TREASURE HUNTERS BUSY SOMEWHERE ELSE. THAT WAY, HE COULD SEARCH FOR THE REAL TREASURE HERE!
BUT BLACK JACK'S REAL MAP SAID THE GOLD WAS IN A PAINTED CHEST. THERE'S, LIKE, NO PAINTED CHEST HERE.

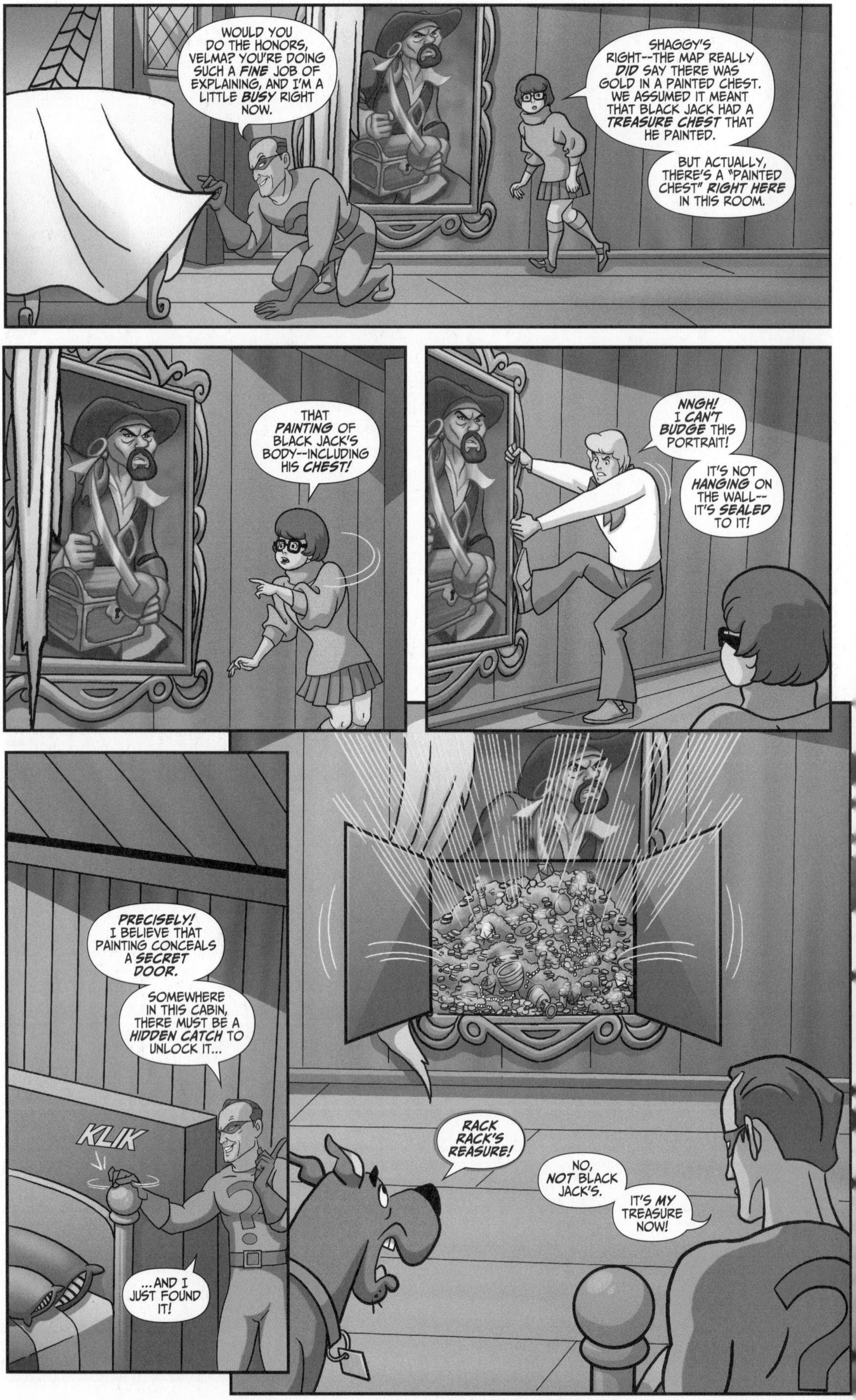
WOULD YOU DO THE HONORS, VELMA? YOU'RE DOING SUCH A FINE JOB OF EXPLAINING, AND I'M A LITTLE BUSY RIGHT NOW.
SHAGGY'S RIGHT--THE MAP REALLY DID SAY THERE WAS GOLD IN A PAINTED CHEST. WE ASSUMED IT MEANT THAT BLACK JACK HAD A TREASURE CHEST THAT HE PAINTED.
BUT ACTUALLY, THERE'S A "PAINTED CHEST" RIGHT HERE IN THIS ROOM.
THAT PAINTING OF BLACK JACK'S BODY--INCLUDING HIS CHEST!
NNGH! I CAN'T BUDGE THIS PORTRAIT!
IT'S NOT HANGING ON THE WALL--IT'S SEALED TO IT!
PRECISELY! I BELIEVE THAT PAINTING CONCEALS A SECRET DOOR.
SOMEWHERE IN THIS CABIN, THERE MUST BE A HIDDEN CATCH TO UNLOCK IT...
KLIK
...AND I JUST FOUND IT!
RACK RACK'S REASURE!
NO, NOT BLACK JACK'S.
IT'S MY TREASURE NOW!

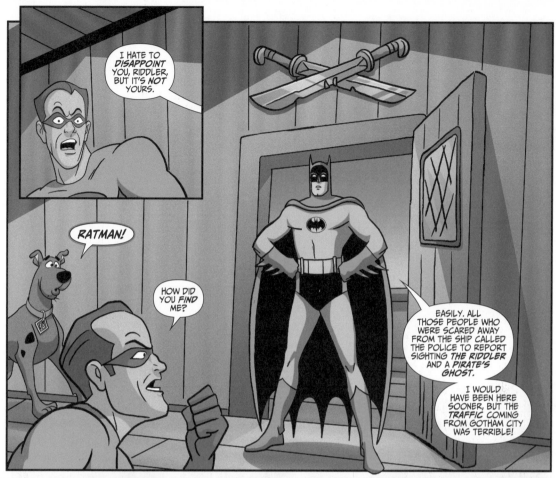

I HATE TO *DISAPPOINT* YOU, RIDDLER, BUT IT'S *NOT* YOURS.

RATMAN!

HOW DID YOU *FIND* ME?

EASILY. ALL THOSE PEOPLE WHO WERE SCARED AWAY FROM THE SHIP CALLED THE POLICE TO REPORT SIGHTING *THE RIDDLER* AND A *PIRATE'S GHOST.*

I WOULD HAVE BEEN HERE SOONER, BUT THE *TRAFFIC* COMING FROM GOTHAM CITY WAS TERRIBLE!

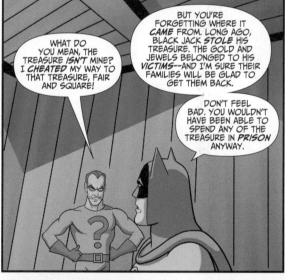

WHAT DO YOU MEAN, THE TREASURE *ISN'T* MINE? I *CHEATED* MY WAY TO THAT TREASURE, FAIR AND SQUARE!

BUT YOU'RE FORGETTING WHERE IT *CAME* FROM. LONG AGO, BLACK JACK *STOLE* HIS TREASURE. THE GOLD AND JEWELS BELONGED TO HIS *VICTIMS*--AND I'M SURE THEIR FAMILIES WILL BE GLAD TO GET THEM BACK.

DON'T FEEL BAD. YOU WOULDN'T HAVE BEEN ABLE TO SPEND ANY OF THE TREASURE IN *PRISON* ANYWAY.

PRISON?! FOR *WHAT?* THERE'S NO LAW AGAINST SEARCHING FOR *TREASURE!*

NO, BUT THERE ARE PLENTY OF LAWS AGAINST THE SEVENTEEN CRIMES YOU COMMITTED IN GOTHAM CITY *LAST* WEEK.

OH, THOSE.

I GUESS THAT'S WHAT COMES FROM A LIFE OF CRIME. BLACK JACK PADDYWHACK LOST HIS LOOT IN A SHIPWRECK, AND THE RIDDLER DIDN'T GET TO KEEP ANY OF IT EITHER.

RIDDLE ME THIS: IF A PIRATE'S MASCOT IS A *PARROT,* WHAT'S THE *RIDDLER'S* MASCOT?

YEAH, I KNOW, I KNOW. A *JAILBIRD.*

THE END

The Batman & Scooby-Doo Mysteries #10 cover
by Dario Brizuela and Franco Riesco

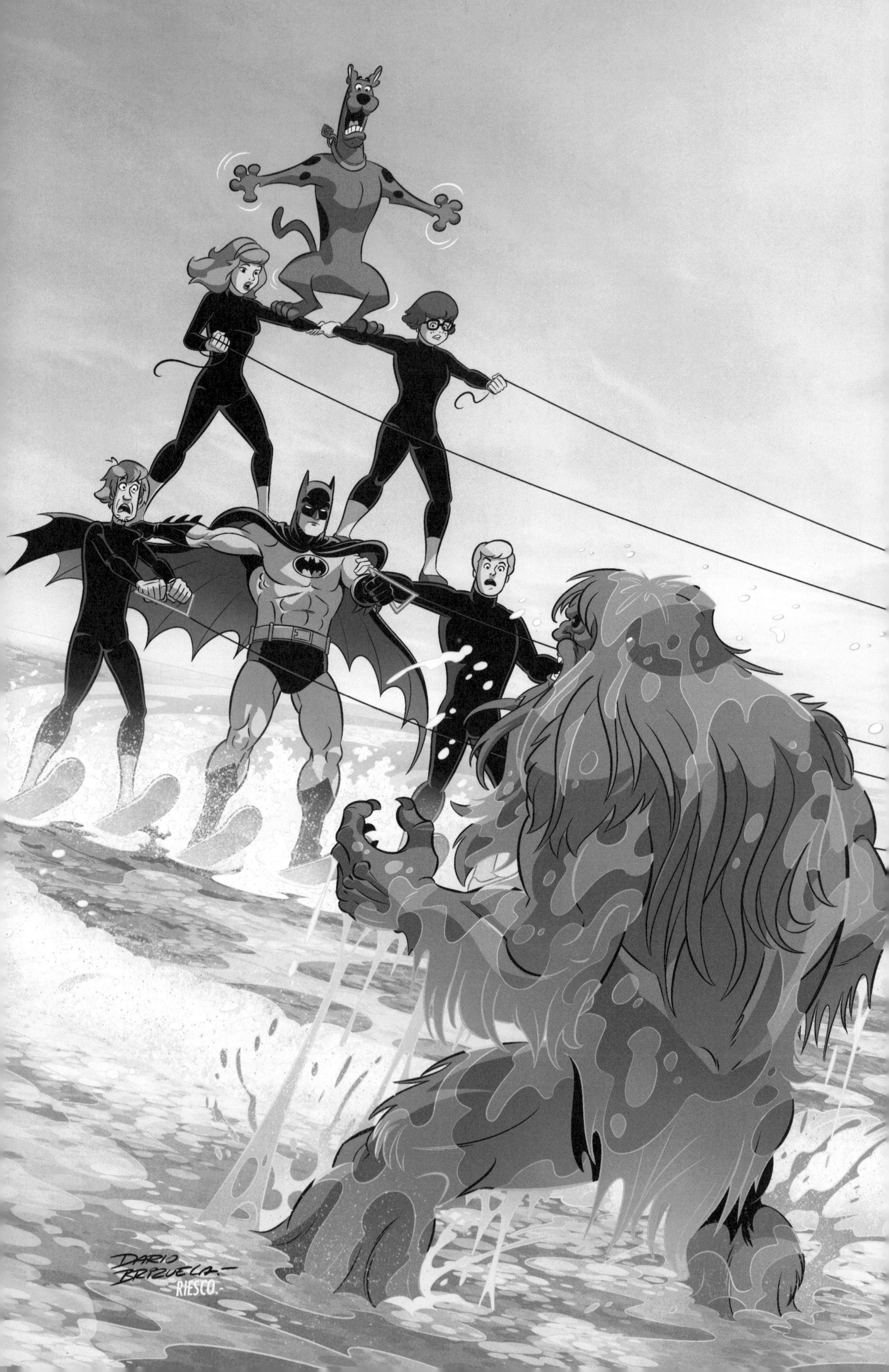
DARIO
BRIZUELA
RIESCO.

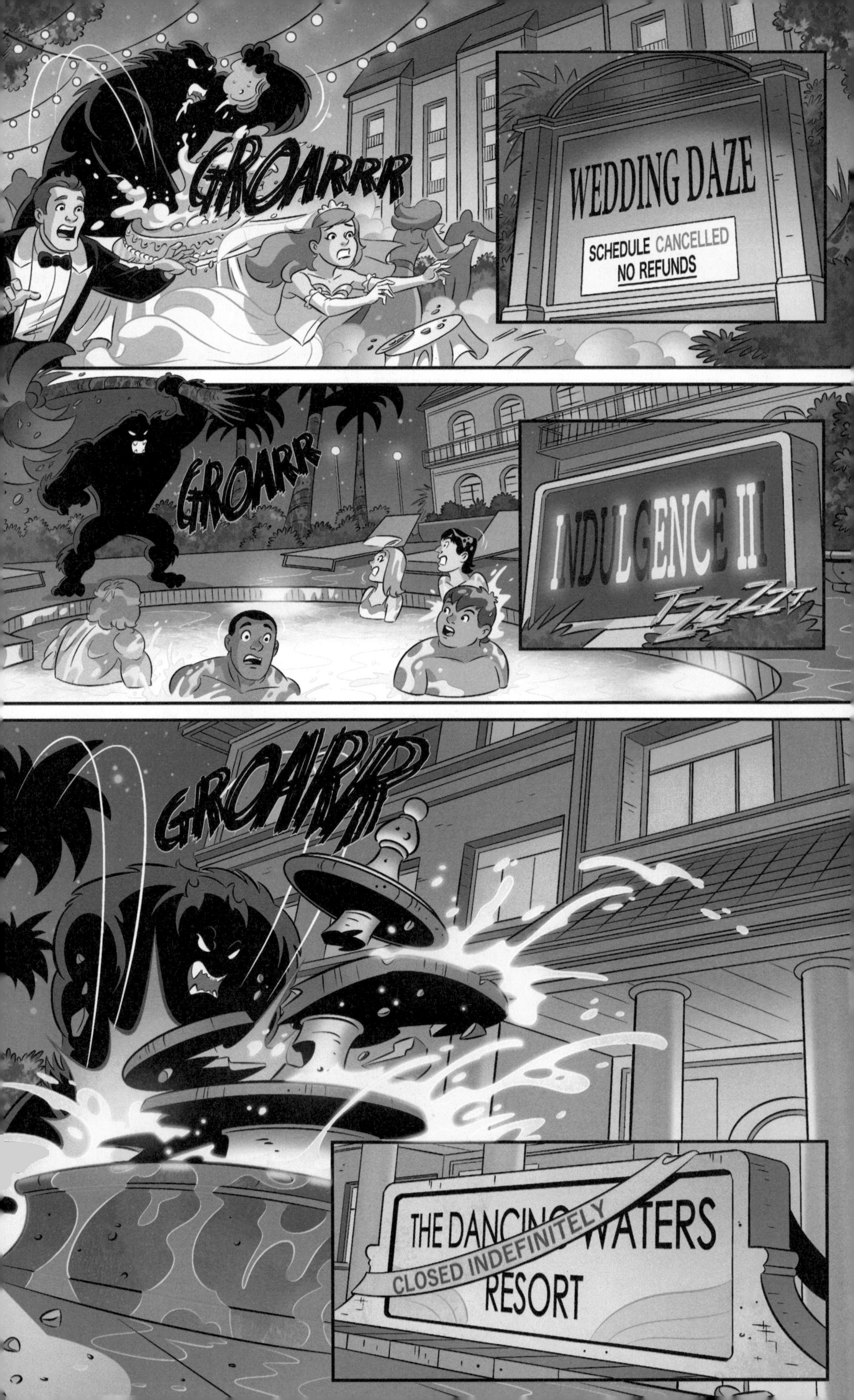
GROARRR
WEDDING DAZE
SCHEDULE CANCELLED
NO REFUNDS
GROARR
INDULGENCE II
GROARR
THE DANCING WATERS RESORT
CLOSED INDEFINITELY

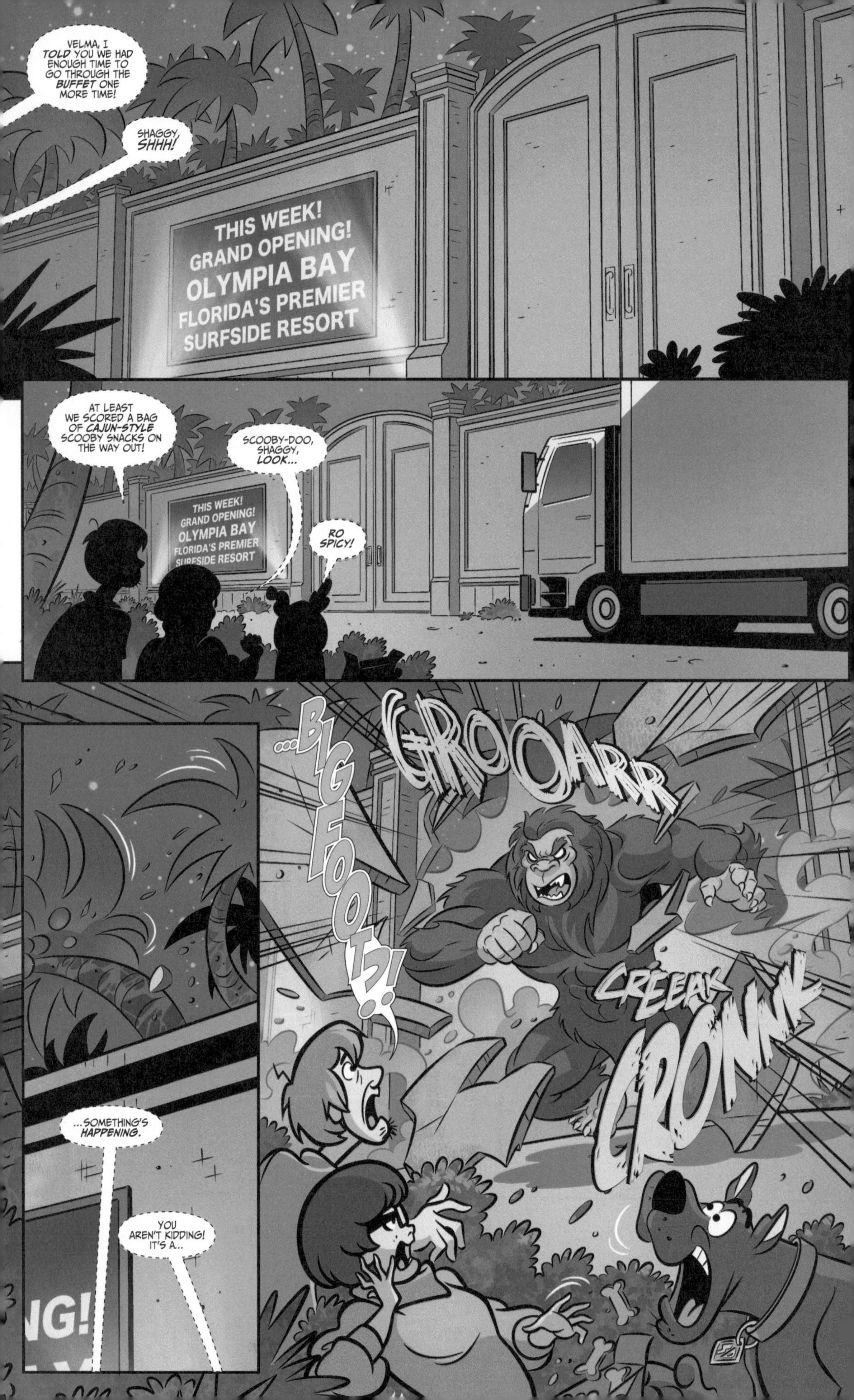

VELMA, I TOLD YOU WE HAD ENOUGH TIME TO GO THROUGH THE BUFFET ONE MORE TIME!
SHAGGY, SHHH!
THIS WEEK! GRAND OPENING! OLYMPIA BAY FLORIDA'S PREMIER SURFSIDE RESORT
AT LEAST WE SCORED A BAG OF CAJUN-STYLE SCOOBY SNACKS ON THE WAY OUT!
SCOOBY-DOO, SHAGGY, LOOK...
RO SPICY!
THIS WEEK! GRAND OPENING! OLYMPIA BAY FLORIDA'S PREMIER SURFSIDE RESORT
...SOMETHING'S HAPPENING.
YOU AREN'T KIDDING! IT'S A...
...BIGFOOT?!
GROOARR
CREEAK
CRONNK

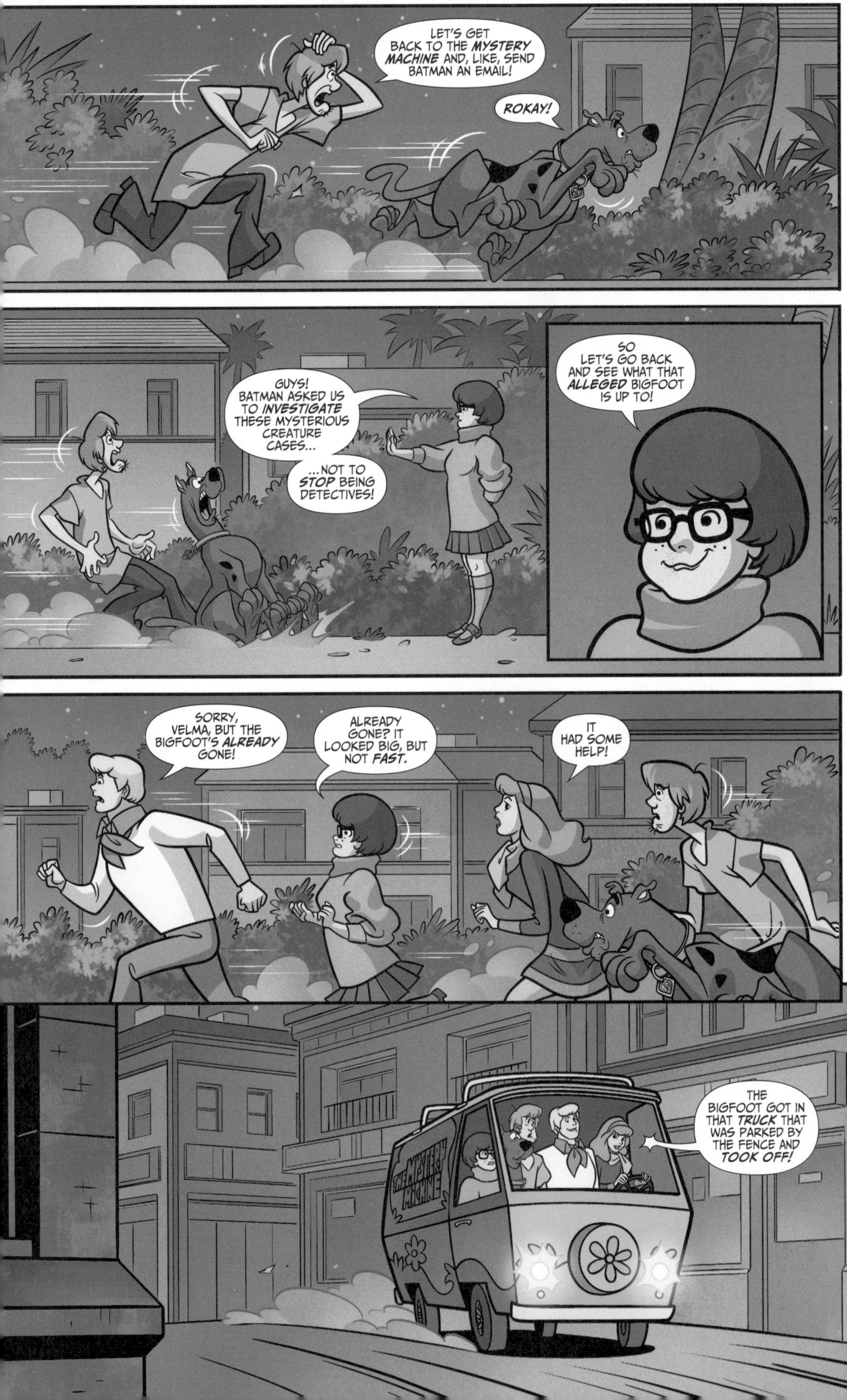
LET'S GET BACK TO THE MYSTERY MACHINE AND, LIKE, SEND BATMAN AN EMAIL!
ROKAY!
GUYS! BATMAN ASKED US TO INVESTIGATE THESE MYSTERIOUS CREATURE CASES...
...NOT TO STOP BEING DETECTIVES!
SO LET'S GO BACK AND SEE WHAT THAT ALLEGED BIGFOOT IS UP TO!
SORRY, VELMA, BUT THE BIGFOOT'S ALREADY GONE!
ALREADY GONE? IT LOOKED BIG, BUT NOT FAST.
IT HAD SOME HELP!
THE MYSTERY MACHINE
THE BIGFOOT GOT IN THAT TRUCK THAT WAS PARKED BY THE FENCE AND TOOK OFF!

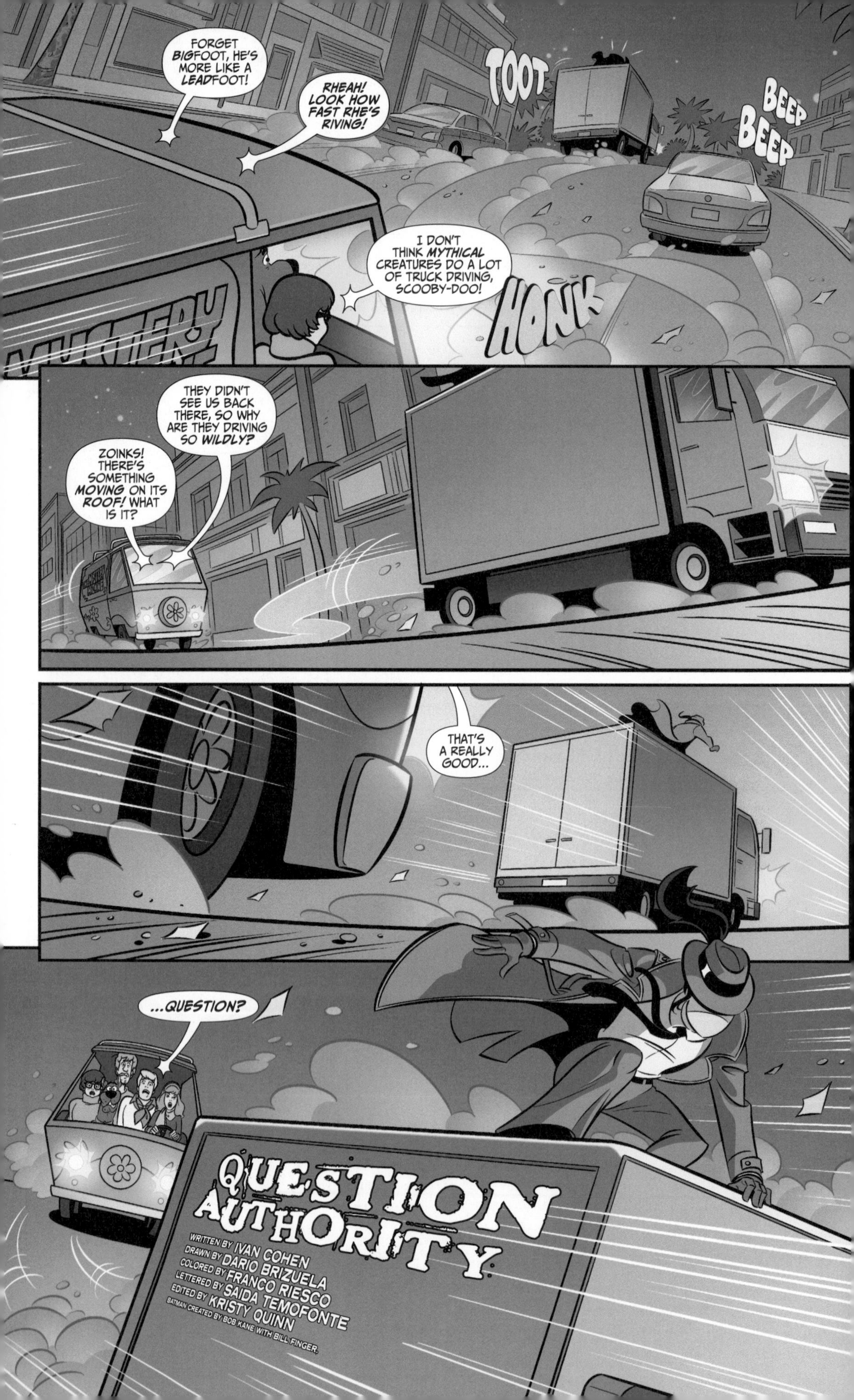

FORGET BIGFOOT, HE'S MORE LIKE A LEADFOOT!
RHEAH! LOOK HOW FAST RHE'S RIVING!
TOOT
BEEP BEEP
I DON'T THINK MYTHICAL CREATURES DO A LOT OF TRUCK DRIVING, SCOOBY-DOO!
HONK
THEY DIDN'T SEE US BACK THERE, SO WHY ARE THEY DRIVING SO WILDLY?
ZOINKS! THERE'S SOMETHING MOVING ON ITS ROOF! WHAT IS IT?
THAT'S A REALLY GOOD...
...QUESTION?
QUESTION AUTHORITY
WRITTEN BY IVAN COHEN
DRAWN BY DARIO BRIZUELA
COLORED BY FRANCO RIESCO
LETTERED BY SAIDA TEMOFONTE
EDITED BY KRISTY QUINN
BATMAN CREATED BY BOB KANE WITH BILL FINGER.

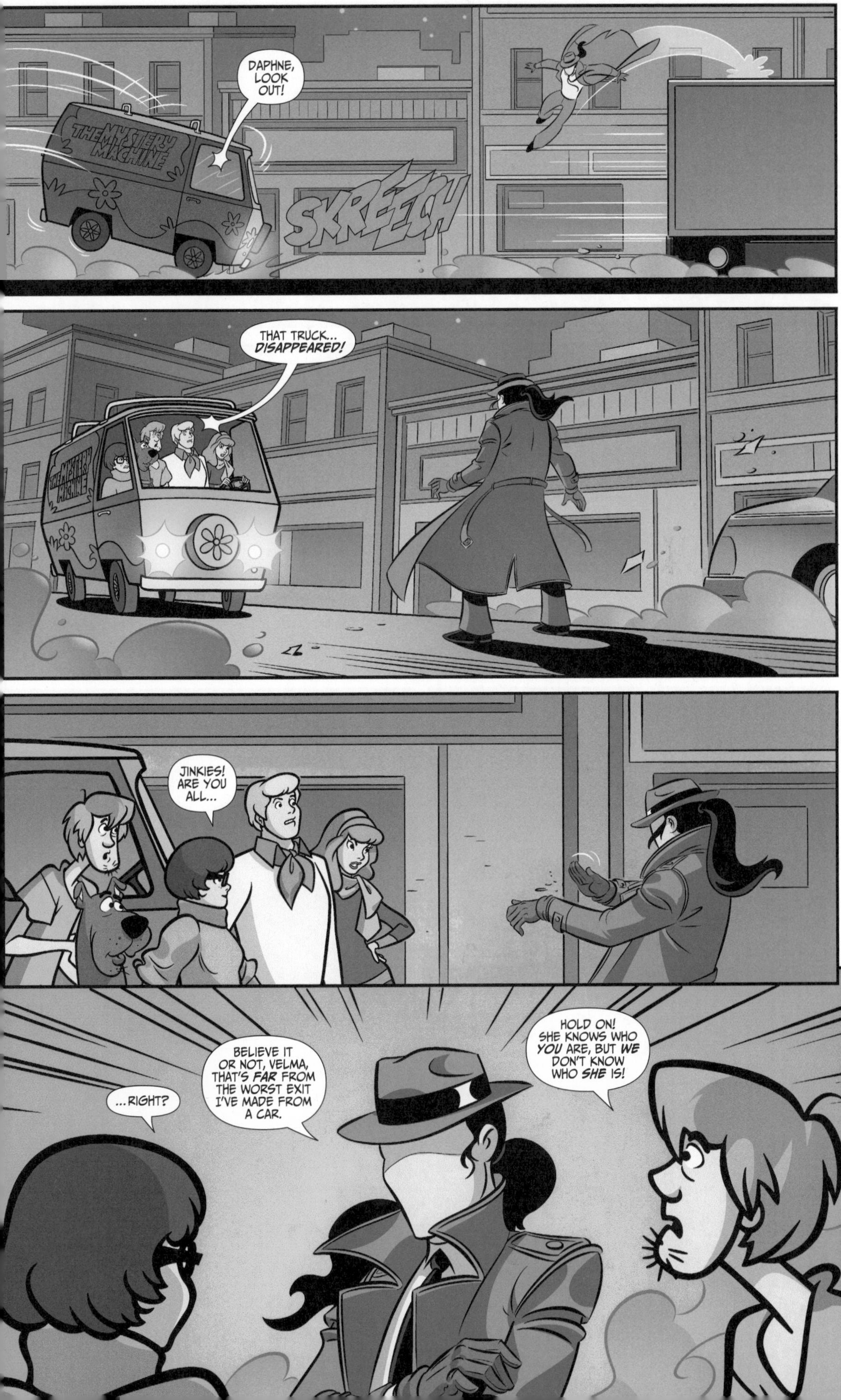
DAPHNE, LOOK OUT!
SKREECH
THE MYSTERY MACHINE
THAT TRUCK... DISAPPEARED!
JINKIES! ARE YOU ALL...
...RIGHT?
BELIEVE IT OR NOT, VELMA, THAT'S FAR FROM THE WORST EXIT I'VE MADE FROM A CAR.
HOLD ON! SHE KNOWS WHO YOU ARE, BUT WE DON'T KNOW WHO SHE IS!

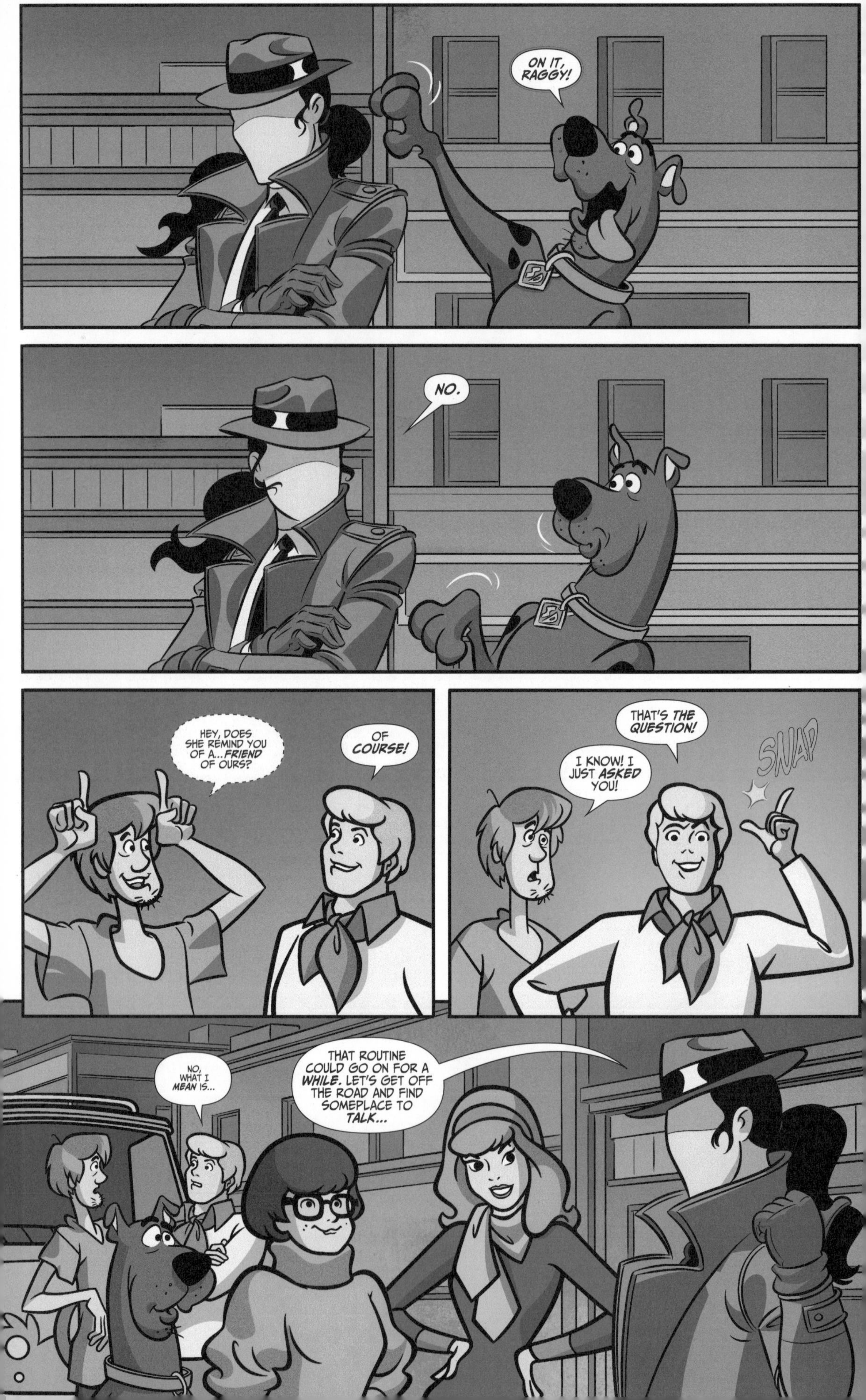
ON IT, RAGGY!
NO.
HEY, DOES SHE REMIND YOU OF A...FRIEND OF OURS?
OF COURSE!
THAT'S THE QUESTION!
I KNOW! I JUST ASKED YOU!
SNAP
NO, WHAT I MEAN IS...
THAT ROUTINE COULD GO ON FOR A WHILE. LET'S GET OFF THE ROAD AND FIND SOMEPLACE TO TALK...

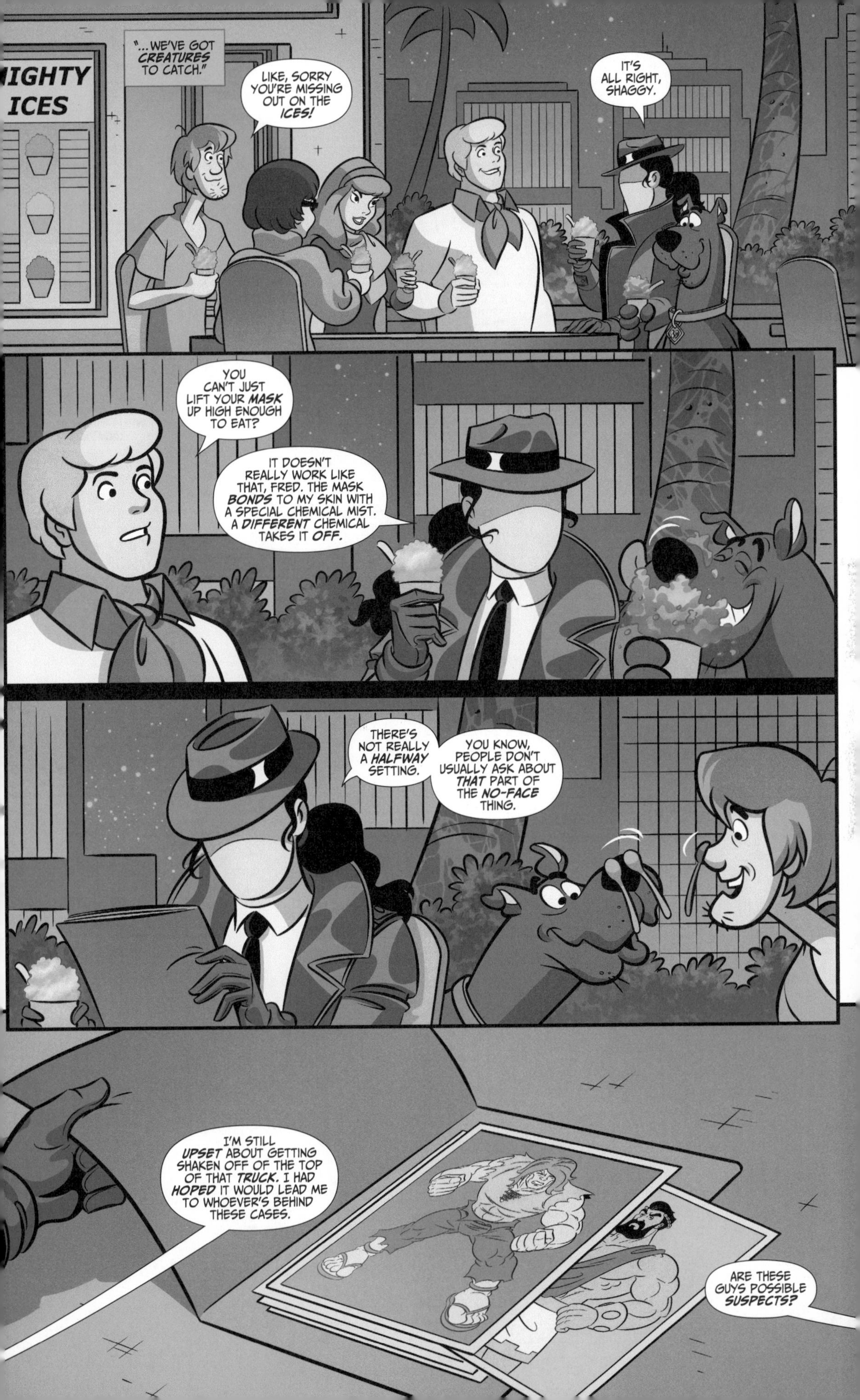

"...WE'VE GOT CREATURES TO CATCH."
IGHTY ICES
LIKE, SORRY YOU'RE MISSING OUT ON THE ICES!
IT'S ALL RIGHT, SHAGGY.
YOU CAN'T JUST LIFT YOUR MASK UP HIGH ENOUGH TO EAT?
IT DOESN'T REALLY WORK LIKE THAT, FRED. THE MASK BONDS TO MY SKIN WITH A SPECIAL CHEMICAL MIST. A DIFFERENT CHEMICAL TAKES IT OFF.
THERE'S NOT REALLY A HALFWAY SETTING.
YOU KNOW, PEOPLE DON'T USUALLY ASK ABOUT THAT PART OF THE NO-FACE THING.
I'M STILL UPSET ABOUT GETTING SHAKEN OFF OF THE TOP OF THAT TRUCK. I HAD HOPED IT WOULD LEAD ME TO WHOEVER'S BEHIND THESE CASES.
ARE THESE GUYS POSSIBLE SUSPECTS?

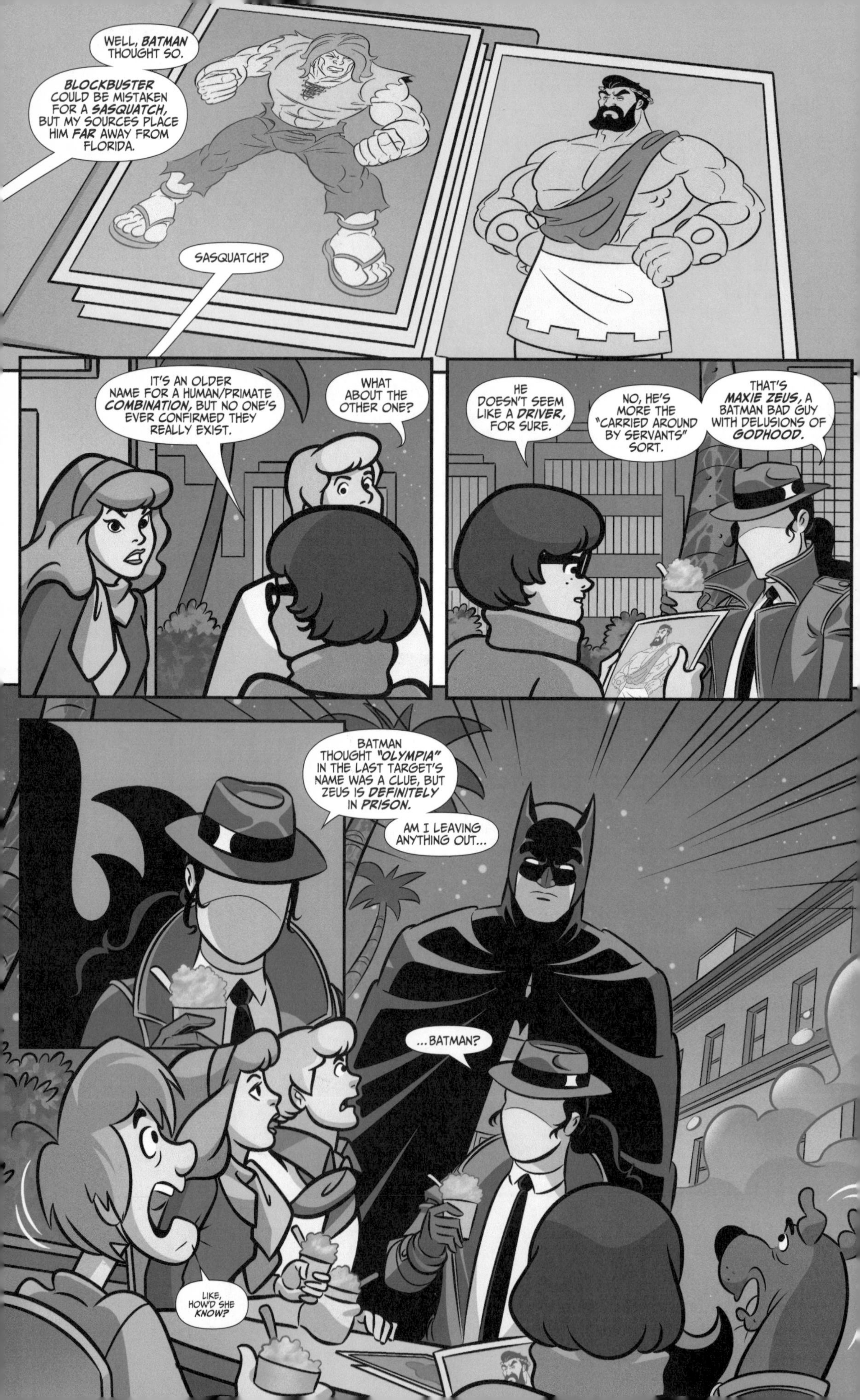

WELL, BATMAN THOUGHT SO.
BLOCKBUSTER COULD BE MISTAKEN FOR A SASQUATCH, BUT MY SOURCES PLACE HIM FAR AWAY FROM FLORIDA.
SASQUATCH?
IT'S AN OLDER NAME FOR A HUMAN/PRIMATE COMBINATION, BUT NO ONE'S EVER CONFIRMED THEY REALLY EXIST.
WHAT ABOUT THE OTHER ONE?
HE DOESN'T SEEM LIKE A DRIVER, FOR SURE.
NO, HE'S MORE THE "CARRIED AROUND BY SERVANTS" SORT.
THAT'S MAXIE ZEUS, A BATMAN BAD GUY WITH DELUSIONS OF GODHOOD.
BATMAN THOUGHT "OLYMPIA" IN THE LAST TARGET'S NAME WAS A CLUE, BUT ZEUS IS DEFINITELY IN PRISON.
AM I LEAVING ANYTHING OUT...
...BATMAN?
LIKE, HOW'D SHE KNOW?

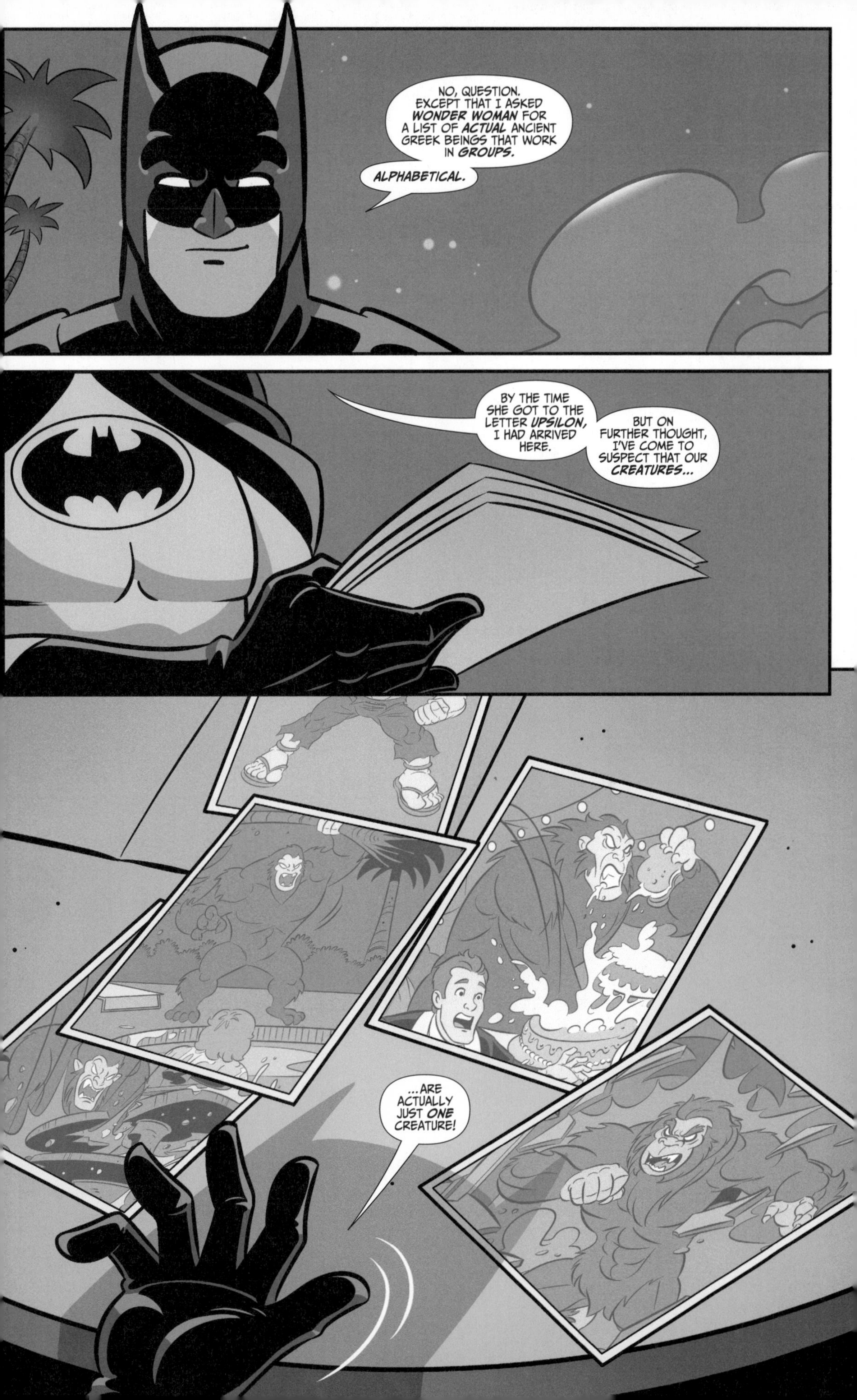
NO, QUESTION. EXCEPT THAT I ASKED WONDER WOMAN FOR A LIST OF ACTUAL ANCIENT GREEK BEINGS THAT WORK IN GROUPS.
ALPHABETICAL.
BY THE TIME SHE GOT TO THE LETTER UPSILON, I HAD ARRIVED HERE.
BUT ON FURTHER THOUGHT, I'VE COME TO SUSPECT THAT OUR CREATURES...
...ARE ACTUALLY JUST ONE CREATURE!

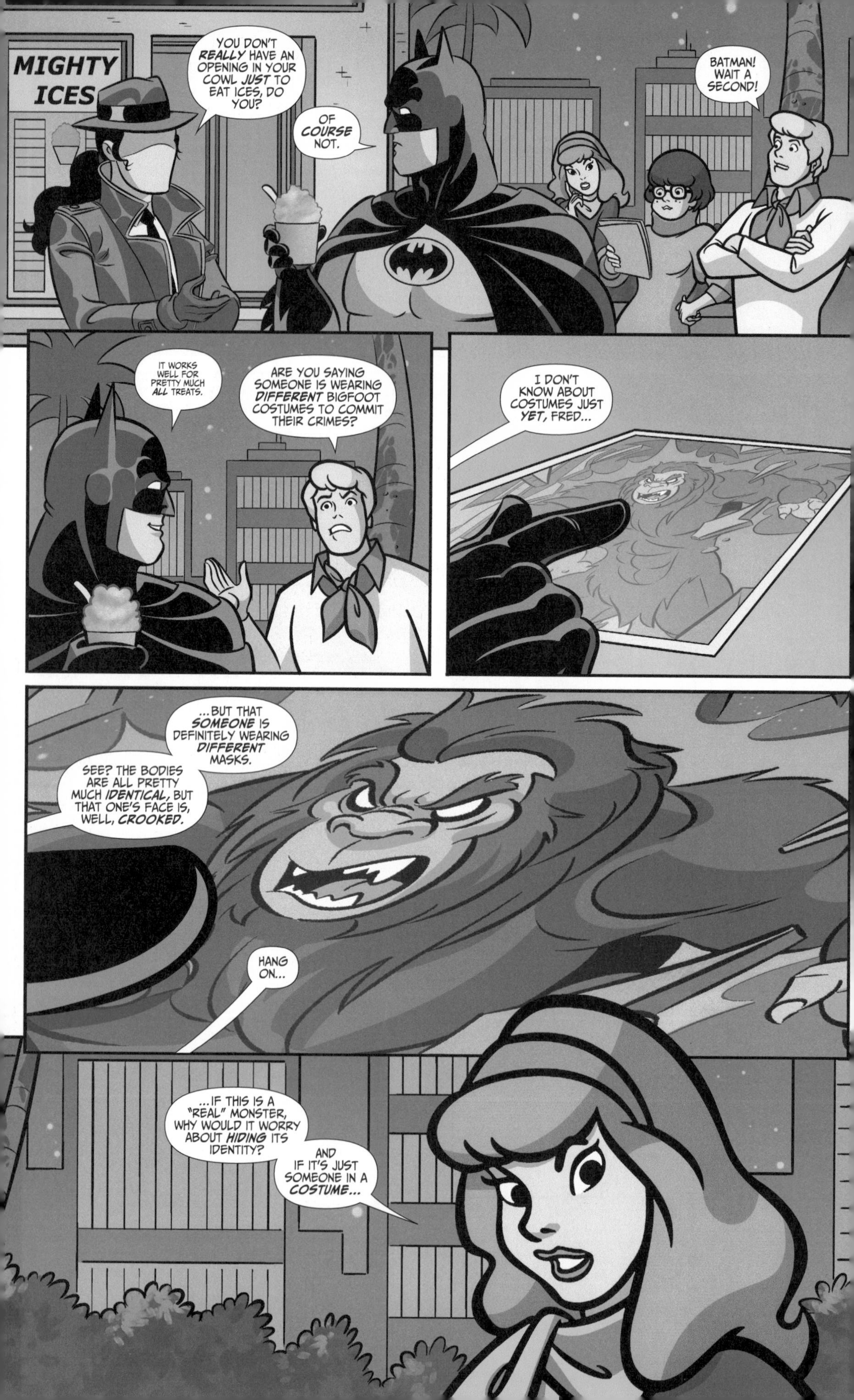
MIGHTY ICES
YOU DON'T REALLY HAVE AN OPENING IN YOUR COWL JUST TO EAT ICES, DO YOU?
OF COURSE NOT.
BATMAN! WAIT A SECOND!
IT WORKS WELL FOR PRETTY MUCH ALL TREATS.
ARE YOU SAYING SOMEONE IS WEARING DIFFERENT BIGFOOT COSTUMES TO COMMIT THEIR CRIMES?
I DON'T KNOW ABOUT COSTUMES JUST YET, FRED...
...BUT THAT SOMEONE IS DEFINITELY WEARING DIFFERENT MASKS.
SEE? THE BODIES ARE ALL PRETTY MUCH IDENTICAL, BUT THAT ONE'S FACE IS, WELL, CROOKED.
HANG ON...
...IF THIS IS A "REAL" MONSTER, WHY WOULD IT WORRY ABOUT HIDING ITS IDENTITY?
AND IF IT'S JUST SOMEONE IN A COSTUME...

...WHY WOULD THEY WANT PEOPLE TO THINK THERE WERE *MULTIPLE* MONSTERS ON THE LOOSE?

RIGHT! SOMETHING DOESN'T ADD UP.

AGREED. THAT'S WHY YOU AND QUESTION SHOULD GO VISIT *JAYE HUFF*...

"...THE OWNER OF OLYMPIA BAY."

THANKS FOR TAKING THE TIME TO MEET WITH US, MS. HUFF.

WELL, DAPHNE...

...IT'S NOT LIKE I HAVE A LOT ELSE TO DO RIGHT NOW.

APART FROM *PACKING*, I GUESS.

PACKING? ARE YOU GOING AWAY?

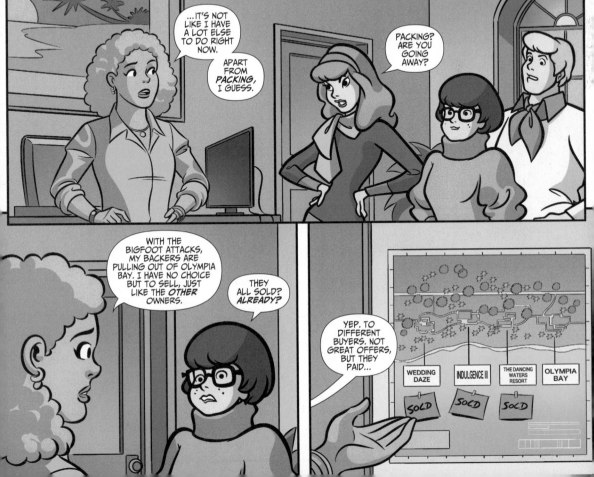

WITH THE BIGFOOT ATTACKS, MY BACKERS ARE PULLING OUT OF OLYMPIA BAY. I HAVE NO CHOICE BUT TO SELL, JUST LIKE THE *OTHER* OWNERS.

THEY ALL SOLD? *ALREADY?*

YEP. TO DIFFERENT BUYERS. NOT GREAT OFFERS, BUT THEY PAID...

WEDDING DAZE — SOLD

INDULGENCE III — SOLD

THE DANCING WATERS RESORT — SOLD

OLYMPIA BAY

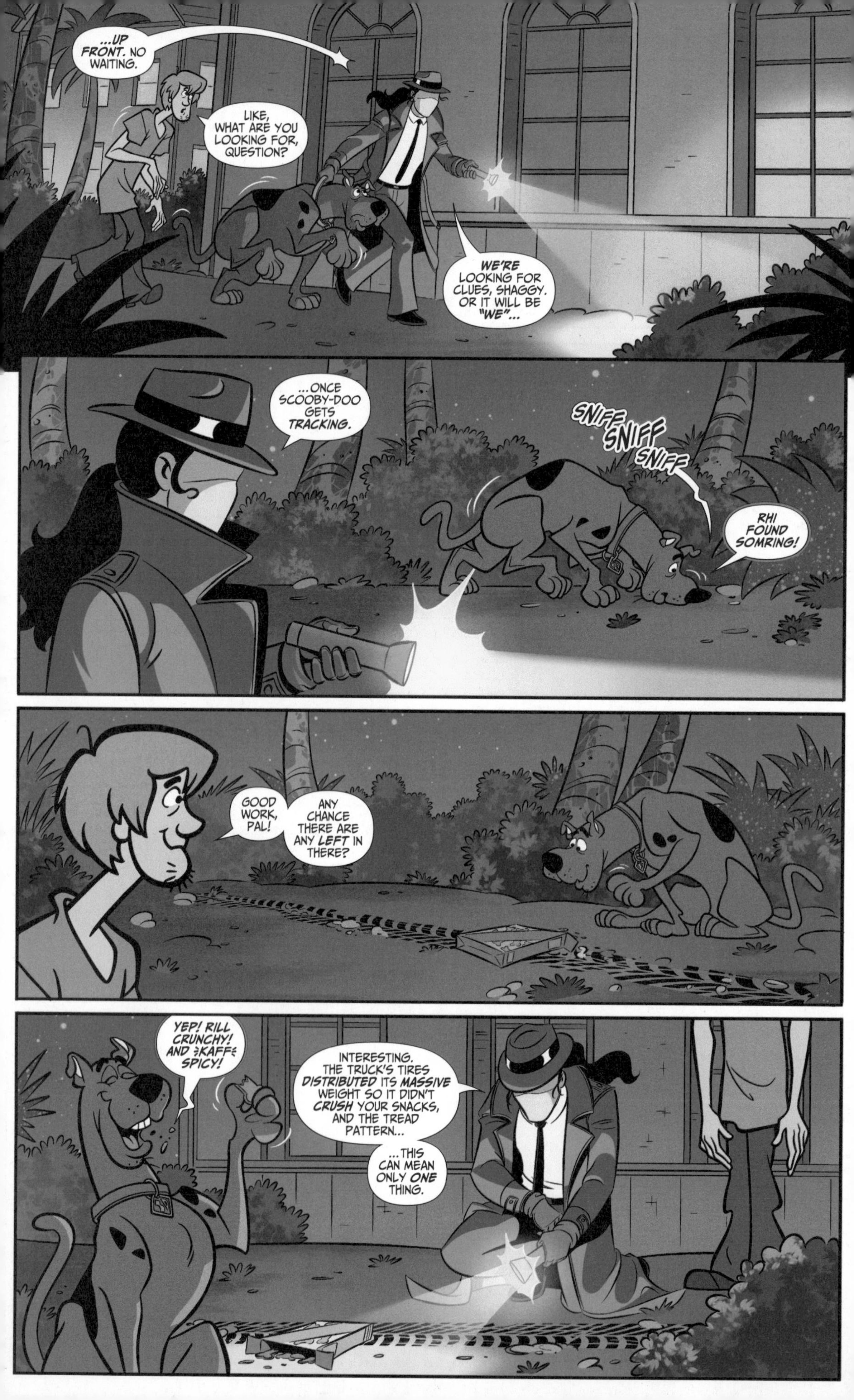
...UP FRONT. NO WAITING.
LIKE, WHAT ARE YOU LOOKING FOR, QUESTION?
WE'RE LOOKING FOR CLUES, SHAGGY. OR IT WILL BE "WE"...
...ONCE SCOOBY-DOO GETS TRACKING.
SNIFF SNIFF SNIFF
RHI FOUND SOMRING!
GOOD WORK, PAL!
ANY CHANCE THERE ARE ANY LEFT IN THERE?
YEP! RILL CRUNCHY! AND *KAFF* SPICY!
INTERESTING. THE TRUCK'S TIRES DISTRIBUTED ITS MASSIVE WEIGHT SO IT DIDN'T CRUSH YOUR SNACKS, AND THE TREAD PATTERN...
...THIS CAN MEAN ONLY ONE THING.

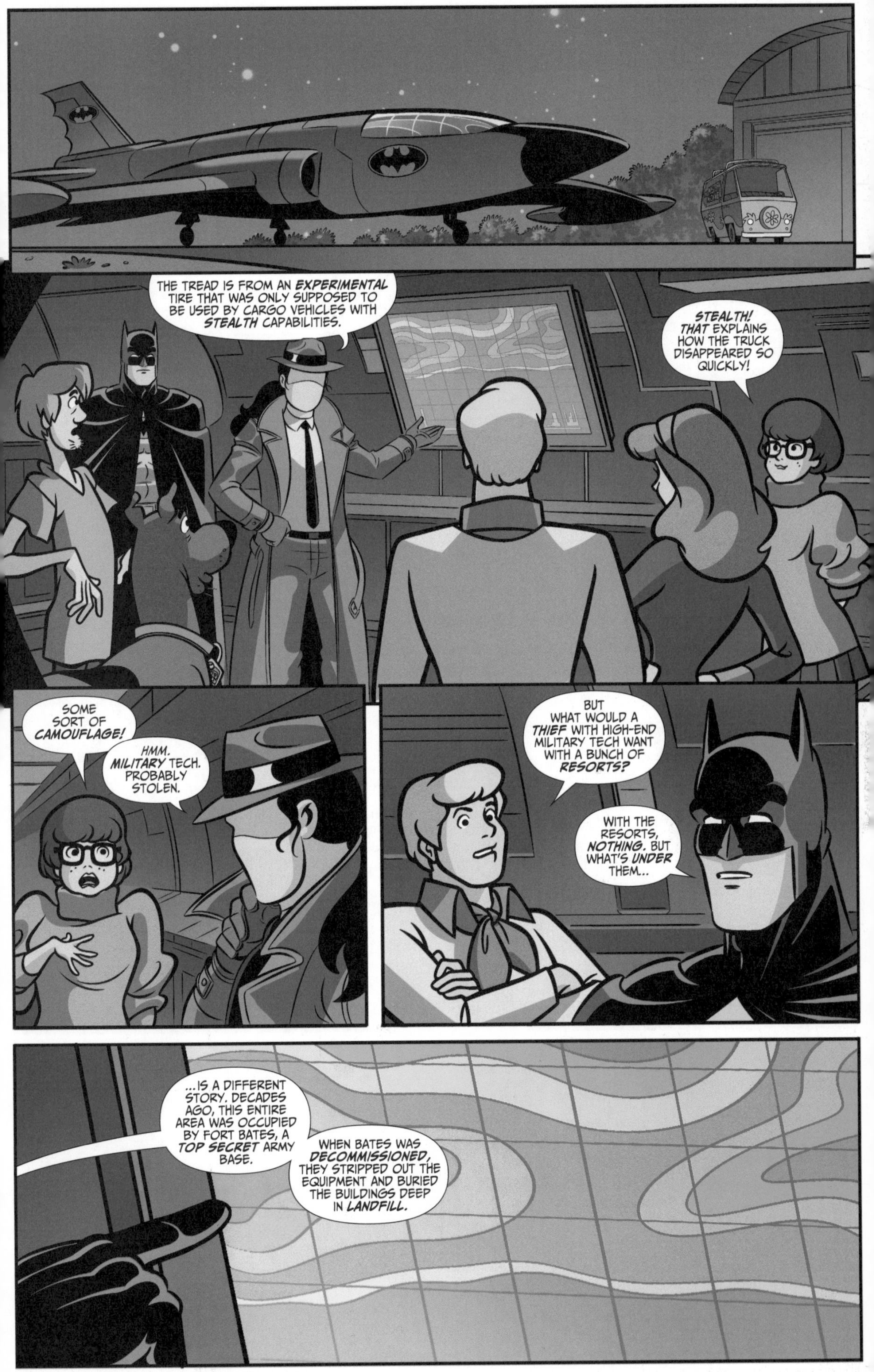
THE TREAD IS FROM AN EXPERIMENTAL TIRE THAT WAS ONLY SUPPOSED TO BE USED BY CARGO VEHICLES WITH STEALTH CAPABILITIES.
STEALTH! THAT EXPLAINS HOW THE TRUCK DISAPPEARED SO QUICKLY!
SOME SORT OF CAMOUFLAGE!
HMM. MILITARY TECH. PROBABLY STOLEN.
BUT WHAT WOULD A THIEF WITH HIGH-END MILITARY TECH WANT WITH A BUNCH OF RESORTS?
WITH THE RESORTS, NOTHING. BUT WHAT'S UNDER THEM...
...IS A DIFFERENT STORY. DECADES AGO, THIS ENTIRE AREA WAS OCCUPIED BY FORT BATES, A TOP SECRET ARMY BASE.
WHEN BATES WAS DECOMMISSIONED, THEY STRIPPED OUT THE EQUIPMENT AND BURIED THE BUILDINGS DEEP IN LANDFILL.

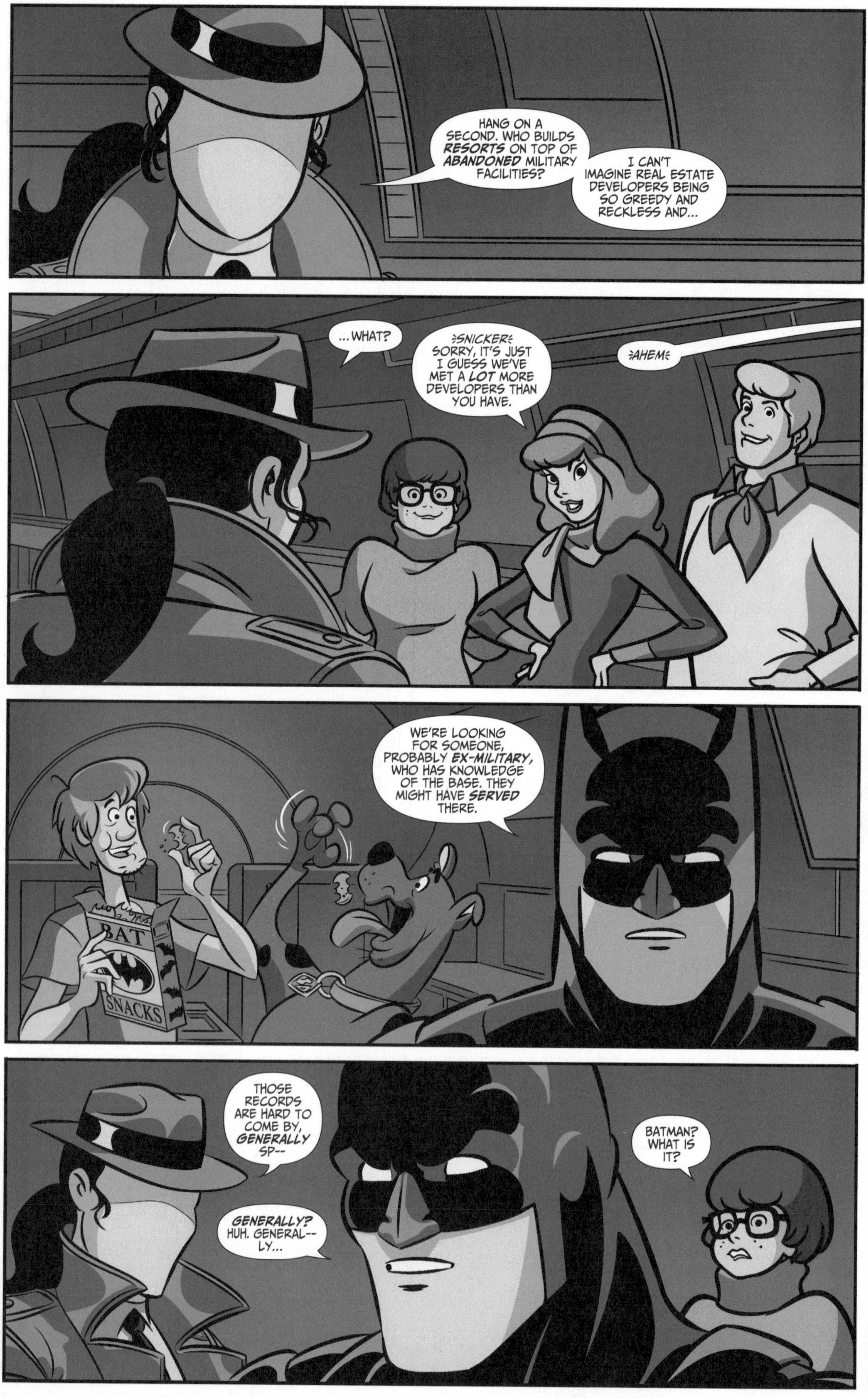
HANG ON A SECOND. WHO BUILDS RESORTS ON TOP OF ABANDONED MILITARY FACILITIES?
I CAN'T IMAGINE REAL ESTATE DEVELOPERS BEING SO GREEDY AND RECKLESS AND...
...WHAT?
SNICKER SORRY, IT'S JUST I GUESS WE'VE MET A LOT MORE DEVELOPERS THAN YOU HAVE.
AHEM
WE'RE LOOKING FOR SOMEONE, PROBABLY EX-MILITARY, WHO HAS KNOWLEDGE OF THE BASE. THEY MIGHT HAVE SERVED THERE.
BAT SNACKS
THOSE RECORDS ARE HARD TO COME BY, GENERALLY SP--
GENERALLY? HUH. GENERAL-- LY...
BATMAN? WHAT IS IT?

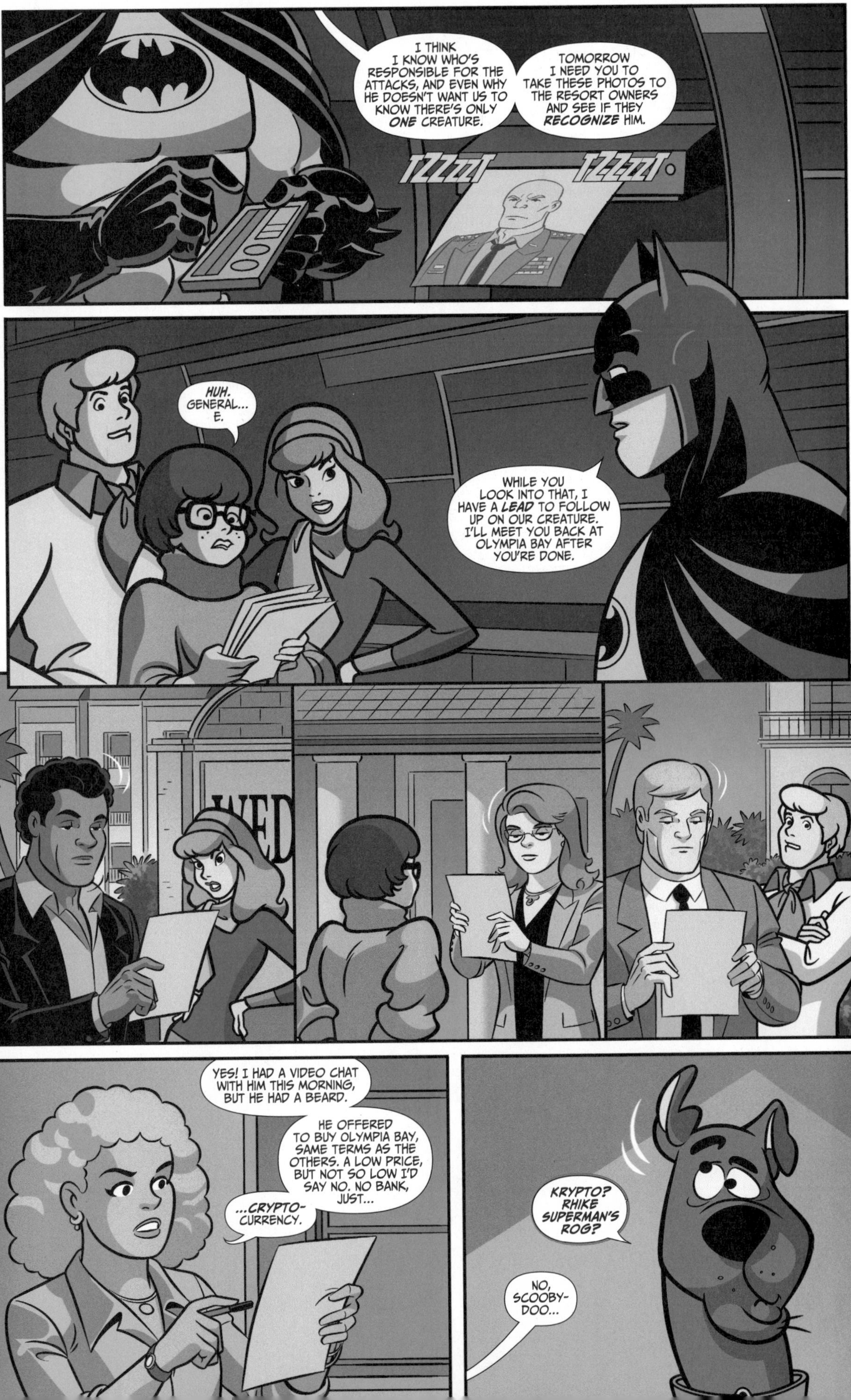
I THINK I KNOW WHO'S RESPONSIBLE FOR THE ATTACKS, AND EVEN WHY HE DOESN'T WANT US TO KNOW THERE'S ONLY ONE CREATURE.
TOMORROW I NEED YOU TO TAKE THESE PHOTOS TO THE RESORT OWNERS AND SEE IF THEY RECOGNIZE HIM.
TZZZZT
TZZZZT
HUH. GENERAL... E.
WHILE YOU LOOK INTO THAT, I HAVE A LEAD TO FOLLOW UP ON OUR CREATURE. I'LL MEET YOU BACK AT OLYMPIA BAY AFTER YOU'RE DONE.
YES! I HAD A VIDEO CHAT WITH HIM THIS MORNING, BUT HE HAD A BEARD.
HE OFFERED TO BUY OLYMPIA BAY, SAME TERMS AS THE OTHERS. A LOW PRICE, BUT NOT SO LOW I'D SAY NO. NO BANK, JUST...
...CRYPTO-CURRENCY.
KRYPTO? RHIKE SUPERMAN'S ROG?
NO, SCOOBY-DOO...

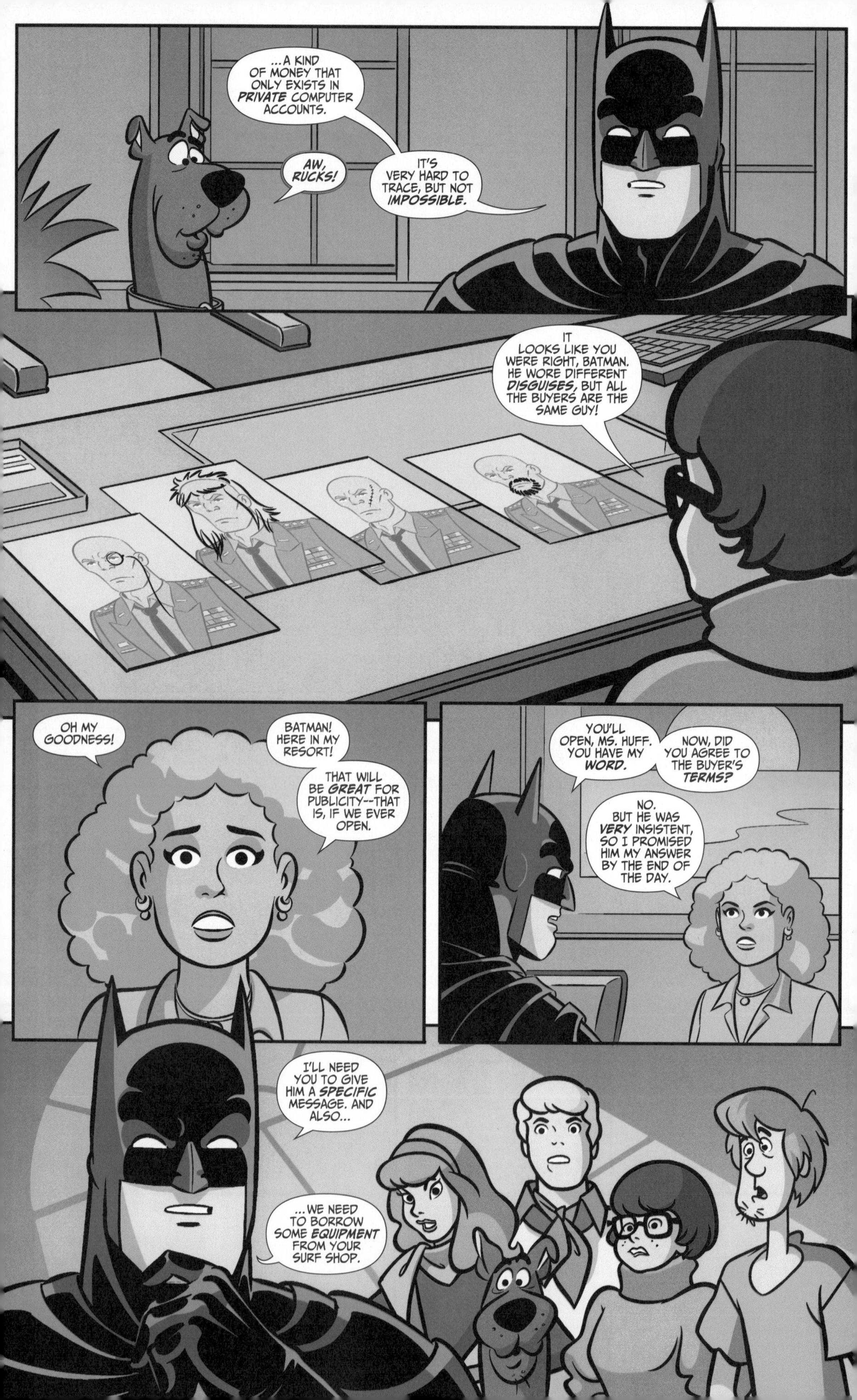
...A KIND OF MONEY THAT ONLY EXISTS IN PRIVATE COMPUTER ACCOUNTS.
AW, RUCKS!
IT'S VERY HARD TO TRACE, BUT NOT IMPOSSIBLE.
IT LOOKS LIKE YOU WERE RIGHT, BATMAN. HE WORE DIFFERENT DISGUISES, BUT ALL THE BUYERS ARE THE SAME GUY!
OH MY GOODNESS!
BATMAN! HERE IN MY RESORT!
THAT WILL BE GREAT FOR PUBLICITY--THAT IS, IF WE EVER OPEN.
YOU'LL OPEN, MS. HUFF. YOU HAVE MY WORD.
NOW, DID YOU AGREE TO THE BUYER'S TERMS?
NO. BUT HE WAS VERY INSISTENT, SO I PROMISED HIM MY ANSWER BY THE END OF THE DAY.
I'LL NEED YOU TO GIVE HIM A SPECIFIC MESSAGE. AND ALSO...
...WE NEED TO BORROW SOME EQUIPMENT FROM YOUR SURF SHOP.

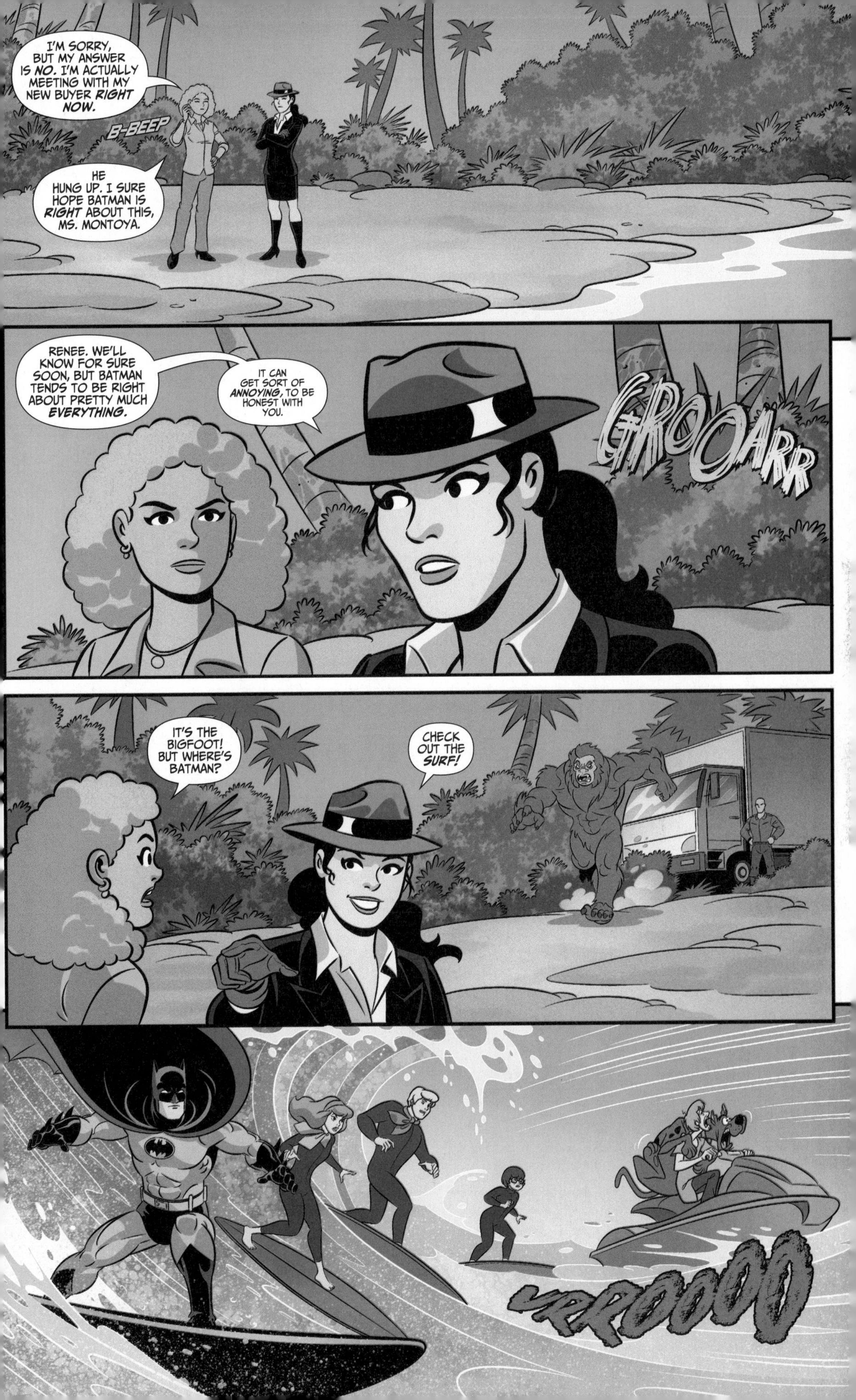
I'M SORRY, BUT MY ANSWER IS NO. I'M ACTUALLY MEETING WITH MY NEW BUYER RIGHT NOW.
B-BEEP
HE HUNG UP. I SURE HOPE BATMAN IS RIGHT ABOUT THIS, MS. MONTOYA.
RENEE. WE'LL KNOW FOR SURE SOON, BUT BATMAN TENDS TO BE RIGHT ABOUT PRETTY MUCH EVERYTHING.
IT CAN GET SORT OF ANNOYING, TO BE HONEST WITH YOU.
GROOARR
IT'S THE BIGFOOT! BUT WHERE'S BATMAN?
CHECK OUT THE SURF!
VRROOOOO

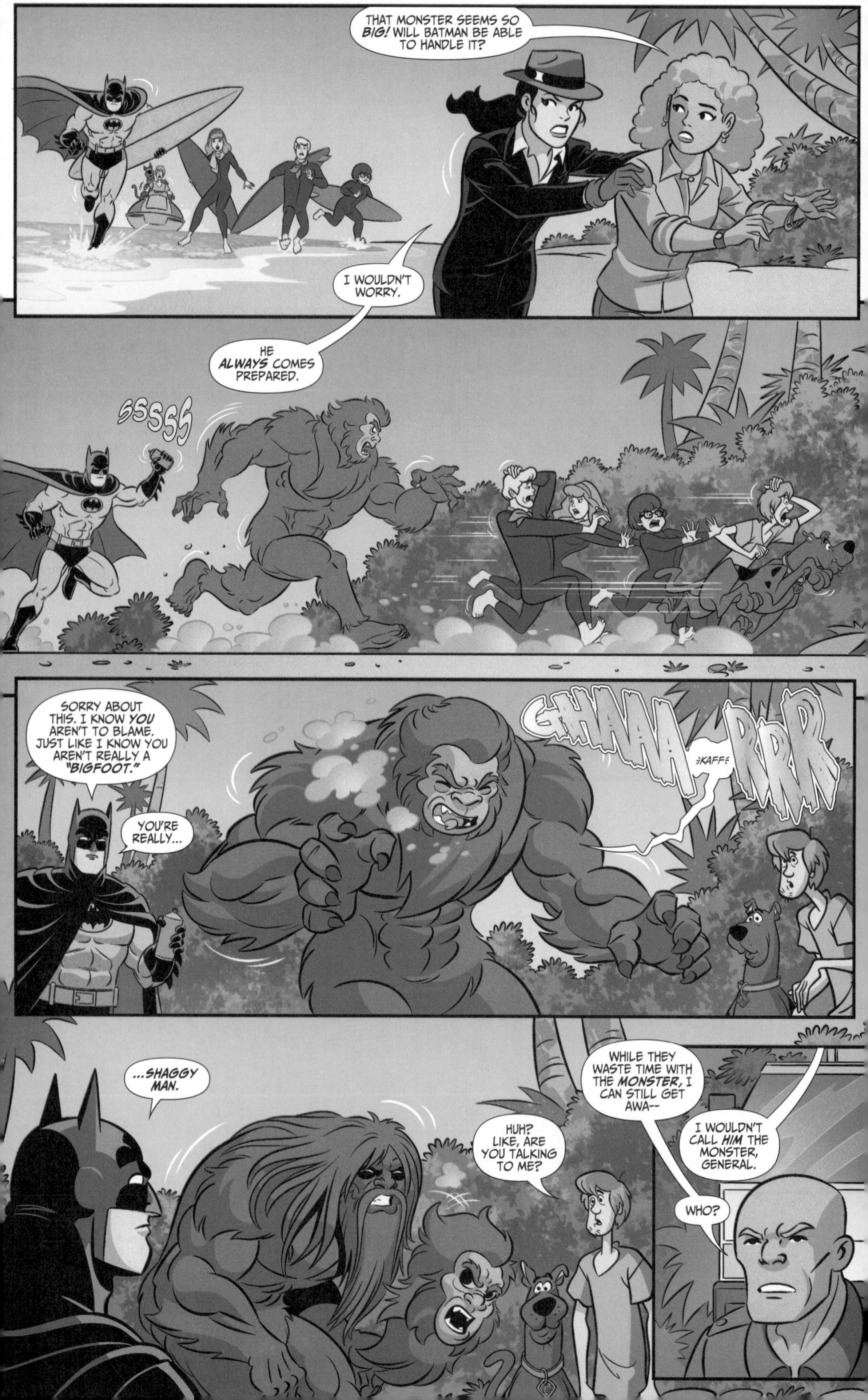
THAT MONSTER SEEMS SO BIG! WILL BATMAN BE ABLE TO HANDLE IT?
I WOULDN'T WORRY.
HE ALWAYS COMES PREPARED.
SSSSS
SORRY ABOUT THIS. I KNOW YOU AREN'T TO BLAME. JUST LIKE I KNOW YOU AREN'T REALLY A "BIGFOOT."
YOU'RE REALLY...
GHAAAA RRRR
KAFF
...SHAGGY MAN.
HUH? LIKE, ARE YOU TALKING TO ME?
WHILE THEY WASTE TIME WITH THE MONSTER, I CAN STILL GET AWA--
I WOULDN'T CALL HIM THE MONSTER, GENERAL.
WHO?

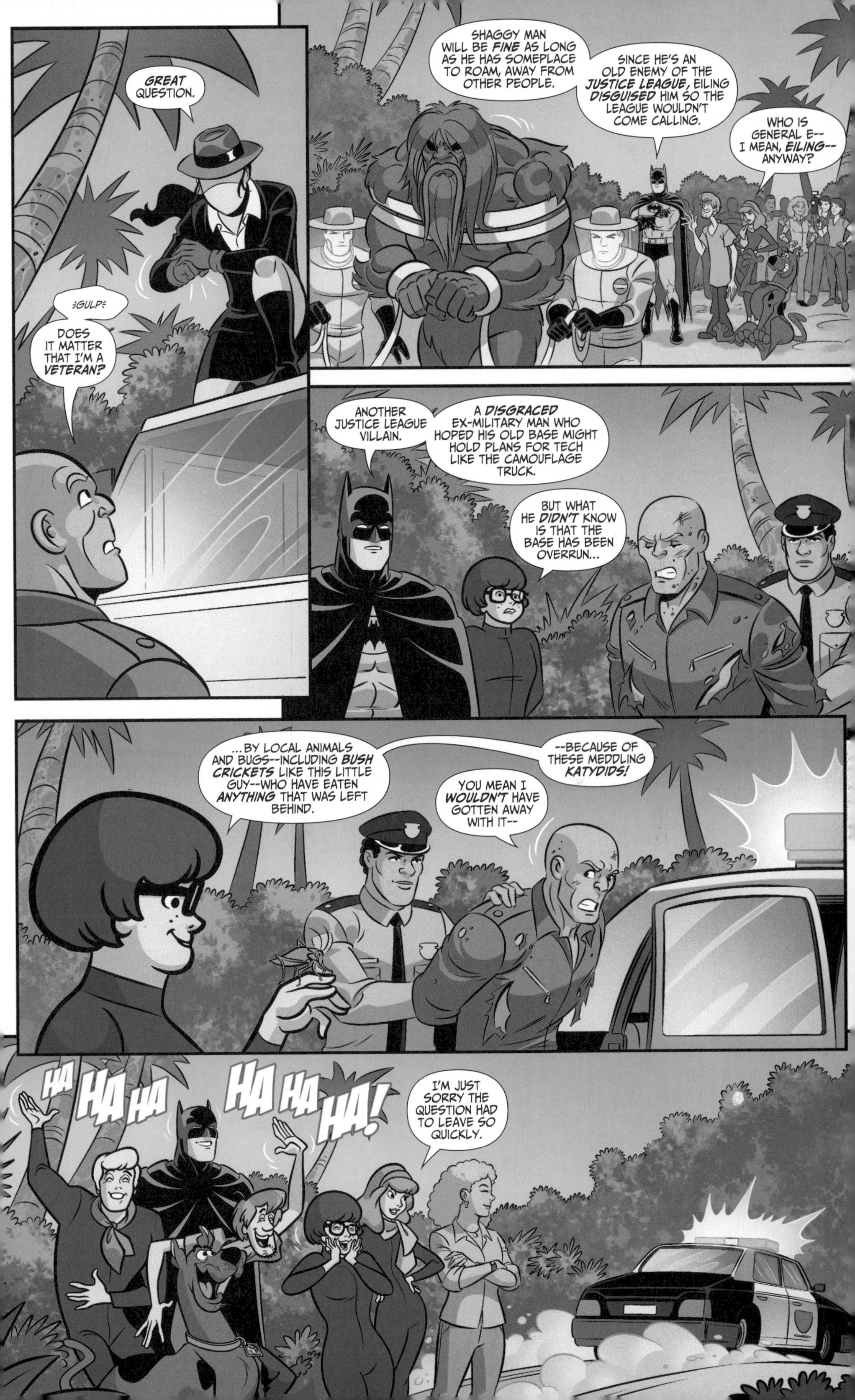
GREAT QUESTION.
SHAGGY MAN WILL BE FINE AS LONG AS HE HAS SOMEPLACE TO ROAM, AWAY FROM OTHER PEOPLE.
SINCE HE'S AN OLD ENEMY OF THE JUSTICE LEAGUE, EILING DISGUISED HIM SO THE LEAGUE WOULDN'T COME CALLING.
WHO IS GENERAL E-- I MEAN, EILING-- ANYWAY?
GULP
DOES IT MATTER THAT I'M A VETERAN?
ANOTHER JUSTICE LEAGUE VILLAIN.
A DISGRACED EX-MILITARY MAN WHO HOPED HIS OLD BASE MIGHT HOLD PLANS FOR TECH LIKE THE CAMOUFLAGE TRUCK.
BUT WHAT HE DIDN'T KNOW IS THAT THE BASE HAS BEEN OVERRUN...
...BY LOCAL ANIMALS AND BUGS--INCLUDING BUSH CRICKETS LIKE THIS LITTLE GUY--WHO HAVE EATEN ANYTHING THAT WAS LEFT BEHIND.
YOU MEAN I WOULDN'T HAVE GOTTEN AWAY WITH IT--
--BECAUSE OF THESE MEDDLING KATYDIDS!
HA HA HA
HA HA HA!
I'M JUST SORRY THE QUESTION HAD TO LEAVE SO QUICKLY.

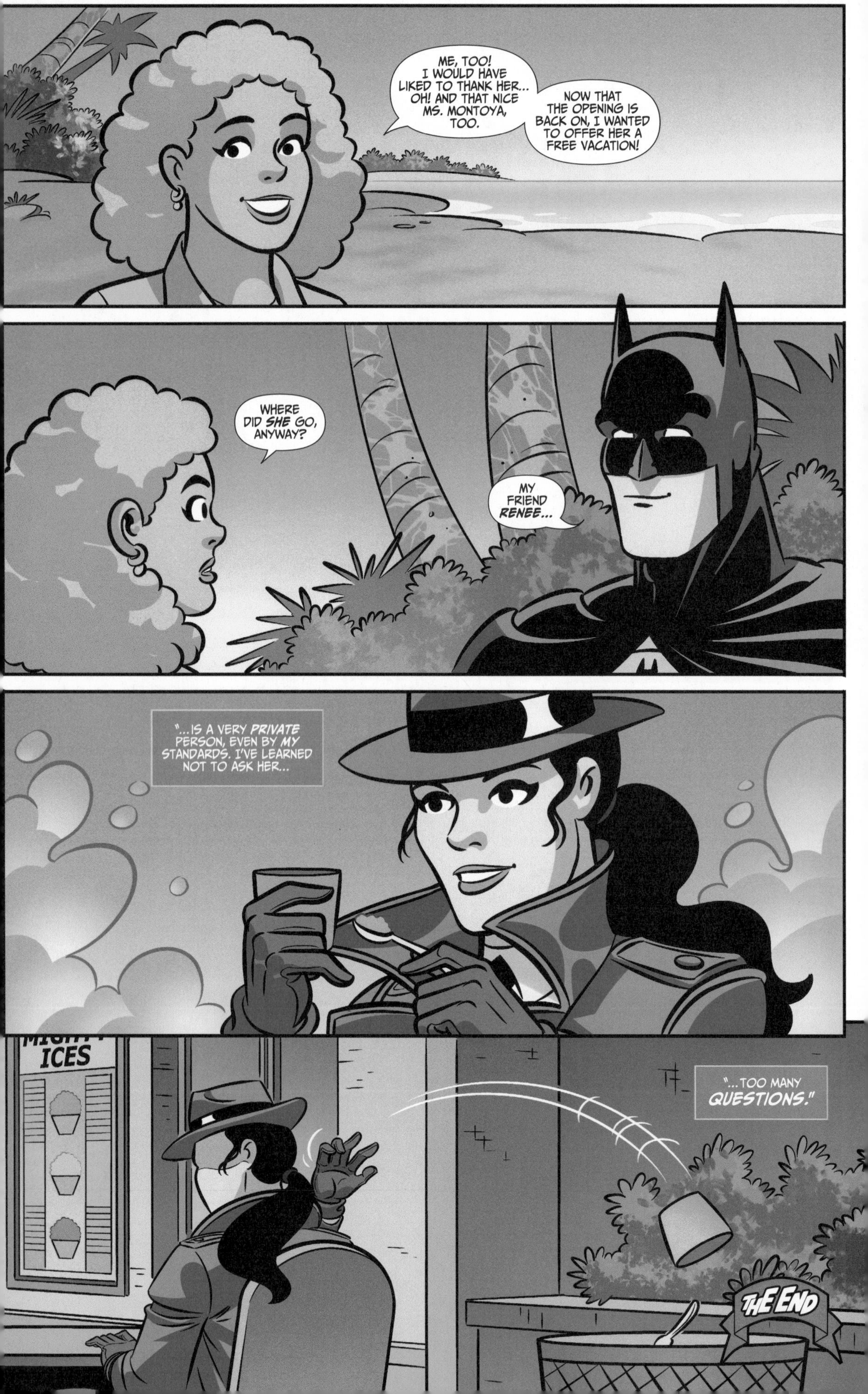
ME, TOO! I WOULD HAVE LIKED TO THANK HER... OH! AND THAT NICE MS. MONTOYA, TOO.
NOW THAT THE OPENING IS BACK ON, I WANTED TO OFFER HER A FREE VACATION!
WHERE DID SHE GO, ANYWAY?
MY FRIEND RENEE...
"...IS A VERY PRIVATE PERSON, EVEN BY MY STANDARDS. I'VE LEARNED NOT TO ASK HER...
ICES
"...TOO MANY QUESTIONS."
THE END

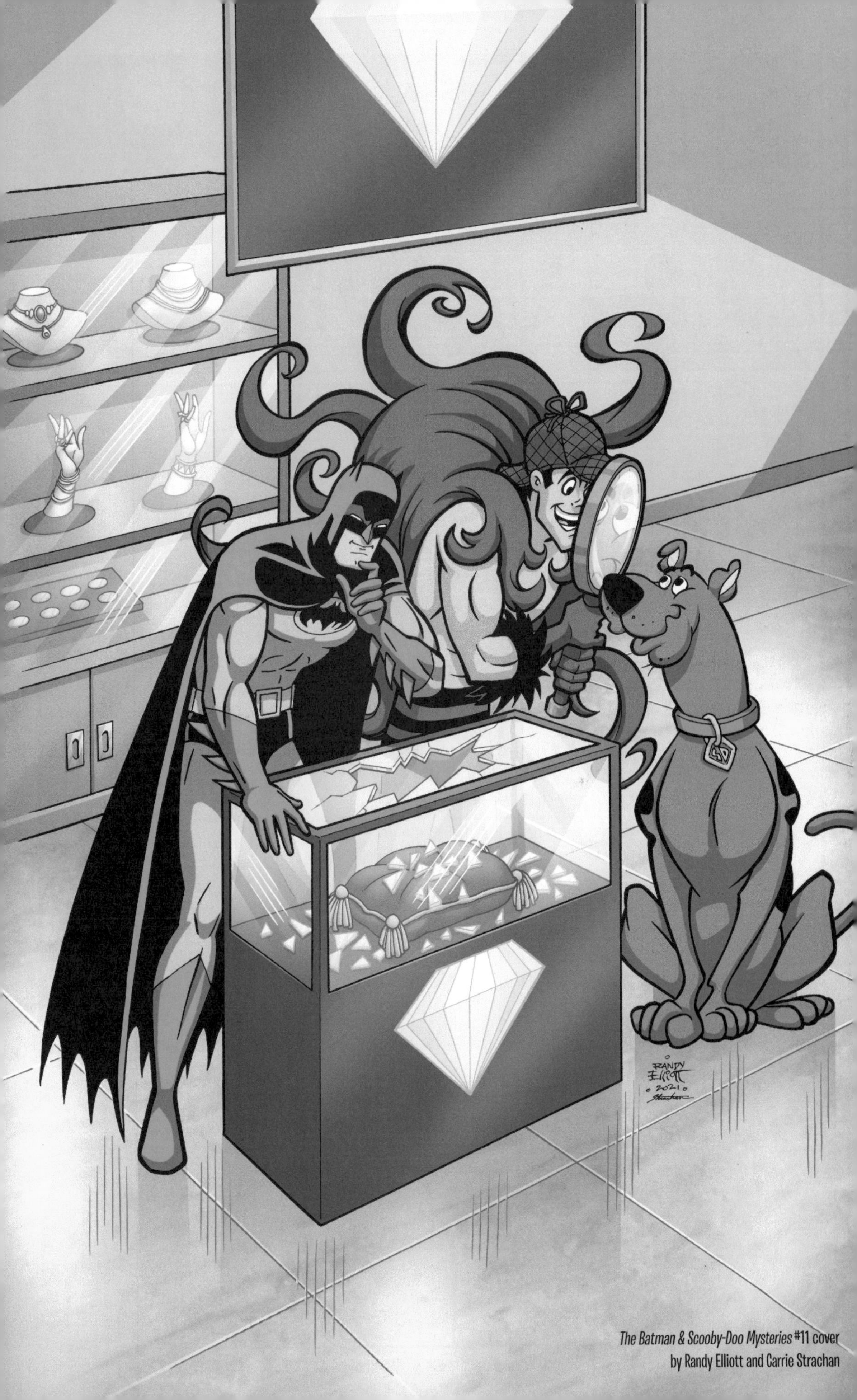
RANDY ELLIOTT
©2021
Strachan

The Batman & Scooby-Doo Mysteries #11 cover
by Randy Elliott and Carrie Strachan

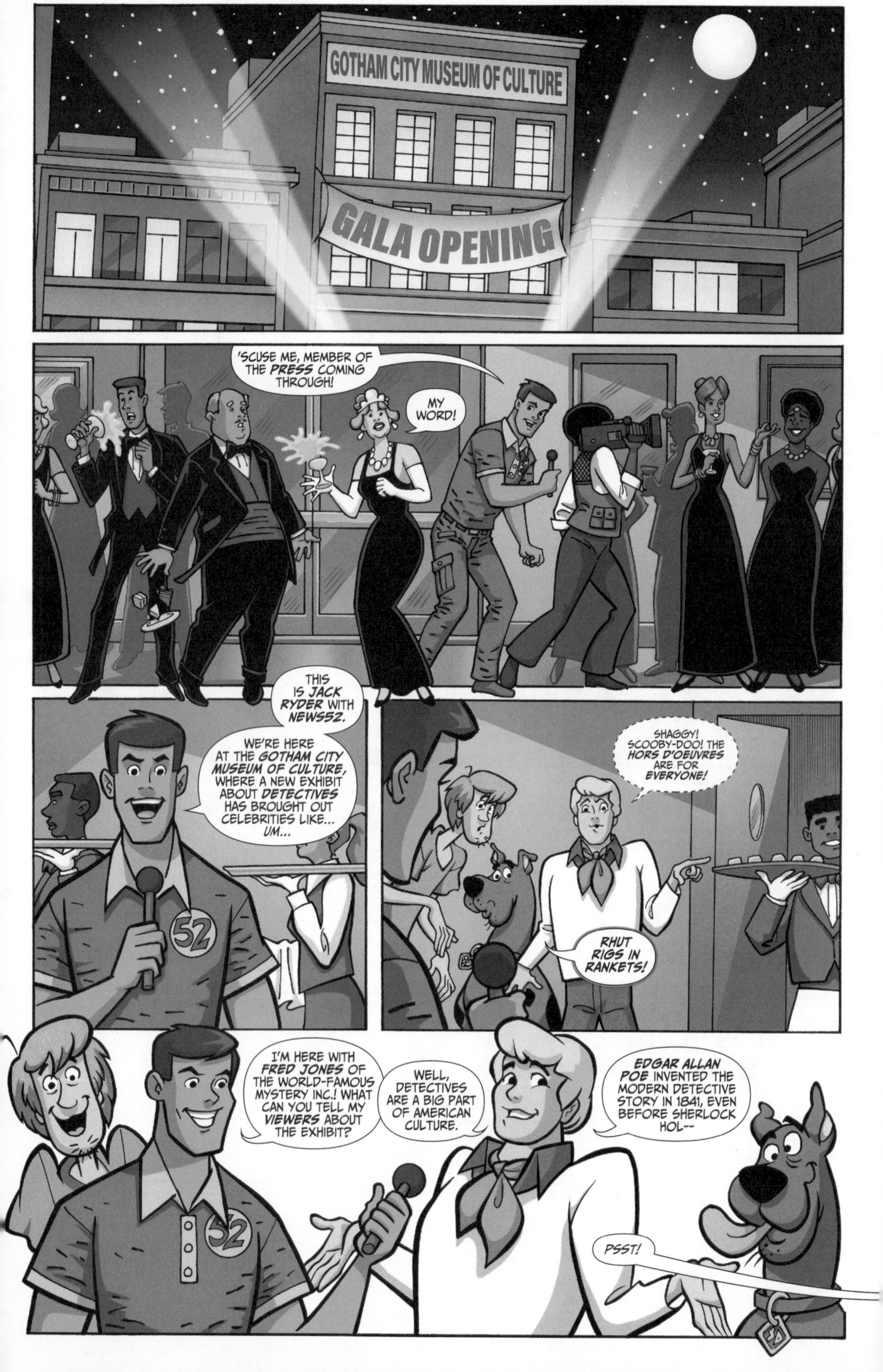
GOTHAM CITY MUSEUM OF CULTURE
GALA OPENING
'SCUSE ME, MEMBER OF THE PRESS COMING THROUGH!
MY WORD!
THIS IS JACK RYDER WITH NEWS52.
WE'RE HERE AT THE GOTHAM CITY MUSEUM OF CULTURE, WHERE A NEW EXHIBIT ABOUT DETECTIVES HAS BROUGHT OUT CELEBRITIES LIKE... UM...
SHAGGY! SCOOBY-DOO! THE HORS D'OEUVRES ARE FOR EVERYONE!
RHUT RIGS IN RANKETS!
I'M HERE WITH FRED JONES OF THE WORLD-FAMOUS MYSTERY INC.! WHAT CAN YOU TELL MY VIEWERS ABOUT THE EXHIBIT?
WELL, DETECTIVES ARE A BIG PART OF AMERICAN CULTURE.
EDGAR ALLAN POE INVENTED THE MODERN DETECTIVE STORY IN 1841, EVEN BEFORE SHERLOCK HOL--
PSST!

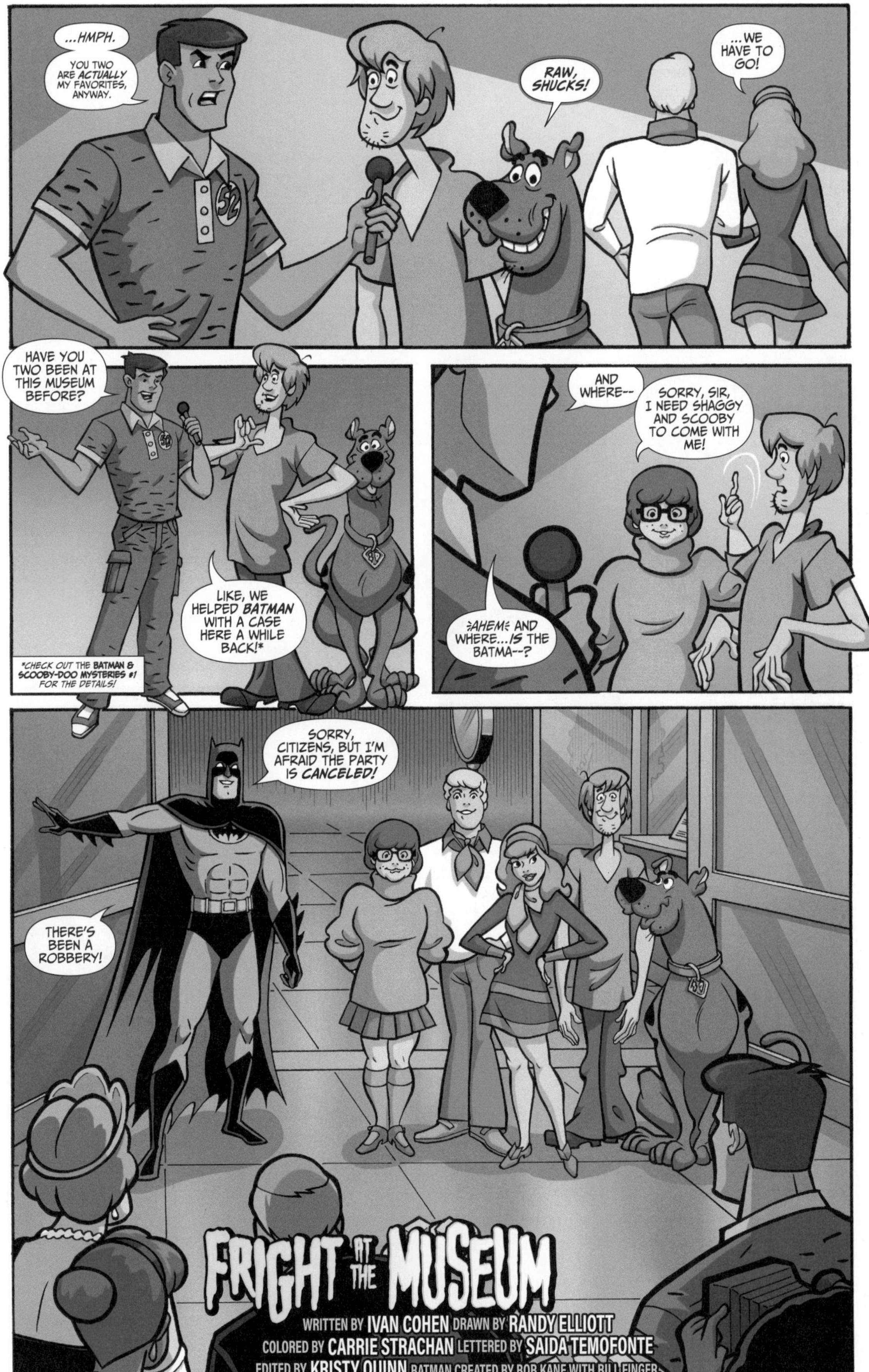
...HMPH.
YOU TWO ARE ACTUALLY MY FAVORITES, ANYWAY.
RAW, SHUCKS!
...WE HAVE TO GO!
HAVE YOU TWO BEEN AT THIS MUSEUM BEFORE?
LIKE, WE HELPED BATMAN WITH A CASE HERE A WHILE BACK!*
*CHECK OUT THE BATMAN & SCOOBY-DOO MYSTERIES #1 FOR THE DETAILS!
AND WHERE--
SORRY, SIR, I NEED SHAGGY AND SCOOBY TO COME WITH ME!
AHEM AND WHERE...IS THE BATMA--?
SORRY, CITIZENS, BUT I'M AFRAID THE PARTY IS CANCELED!
THERE'S BEEN A ROBBERY!
FRIGHT AT THE MUSEUM
WRITTEN BY IVAN COHEN DRAWN BY RANDY ELLIOTT
COLORED BY CARRIE STRACHAN LETTERED BY SAIDA TEMOFONTE
EDITED BY KRISTY QUINN BATMAN CREATED BY BOB KANE WITH BILL FINGER.

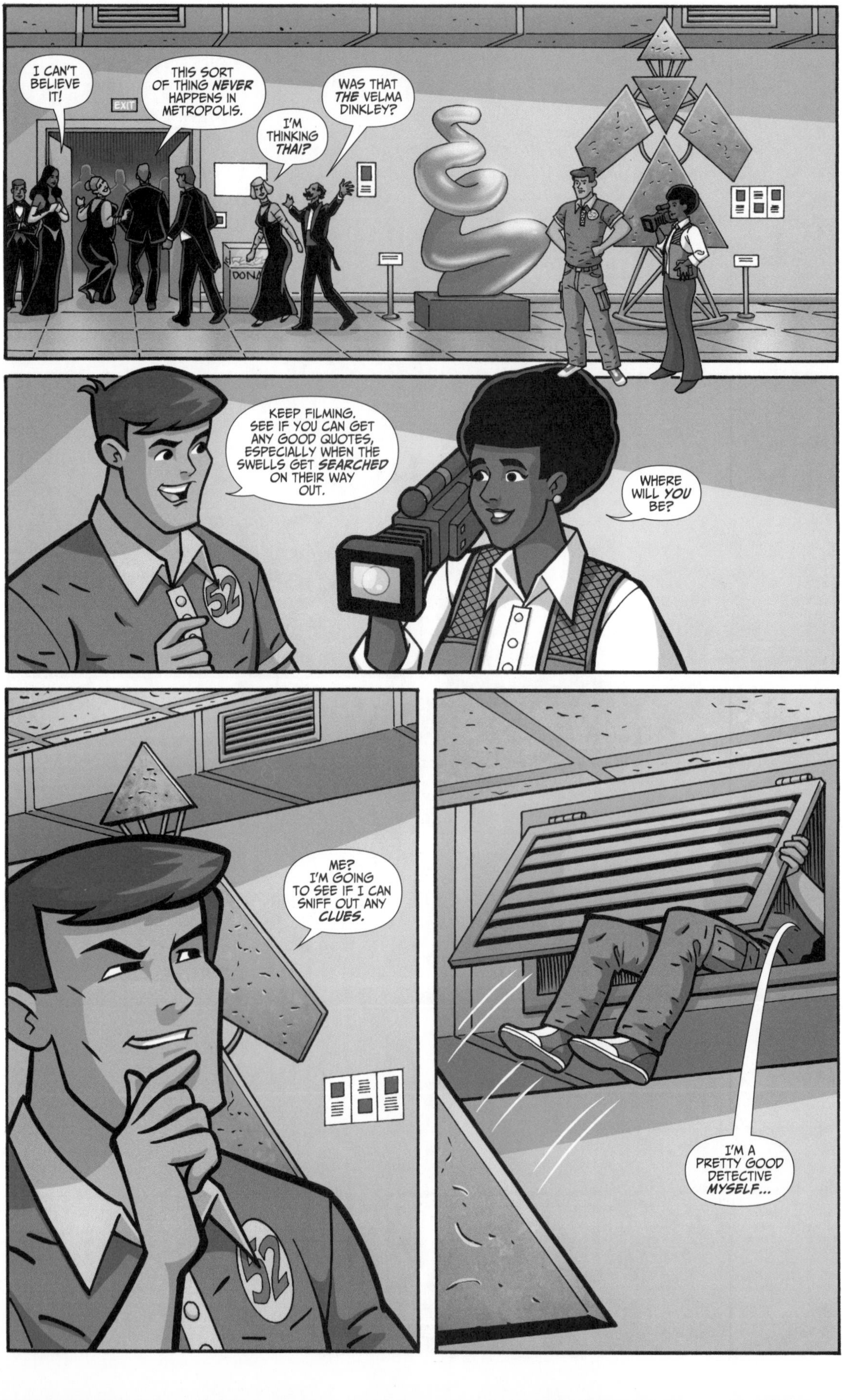
I CAN'T BELIEVE IT!
THIS SORT OF THING NEVER HAPPENS IN METROPOLIS.
I'M THINKING THAI?
WAS THAT THE VELMA DINKLEY?
EXIT
DONA
KEEP FILMING. SEE IF YOU CAN GET ANY GOOD QUOTES, ESPECIALLY WHEN THE SWELLS GET SEARCHED ON THEIR WAY OUT.
WHERE WILL YOU BE?
52
ME? I'M GOING TO SEE IF I CAN SNIFF OUT ANY CLUES.
I'M A PRETTY GOOD DETECTIVE MYSELF...

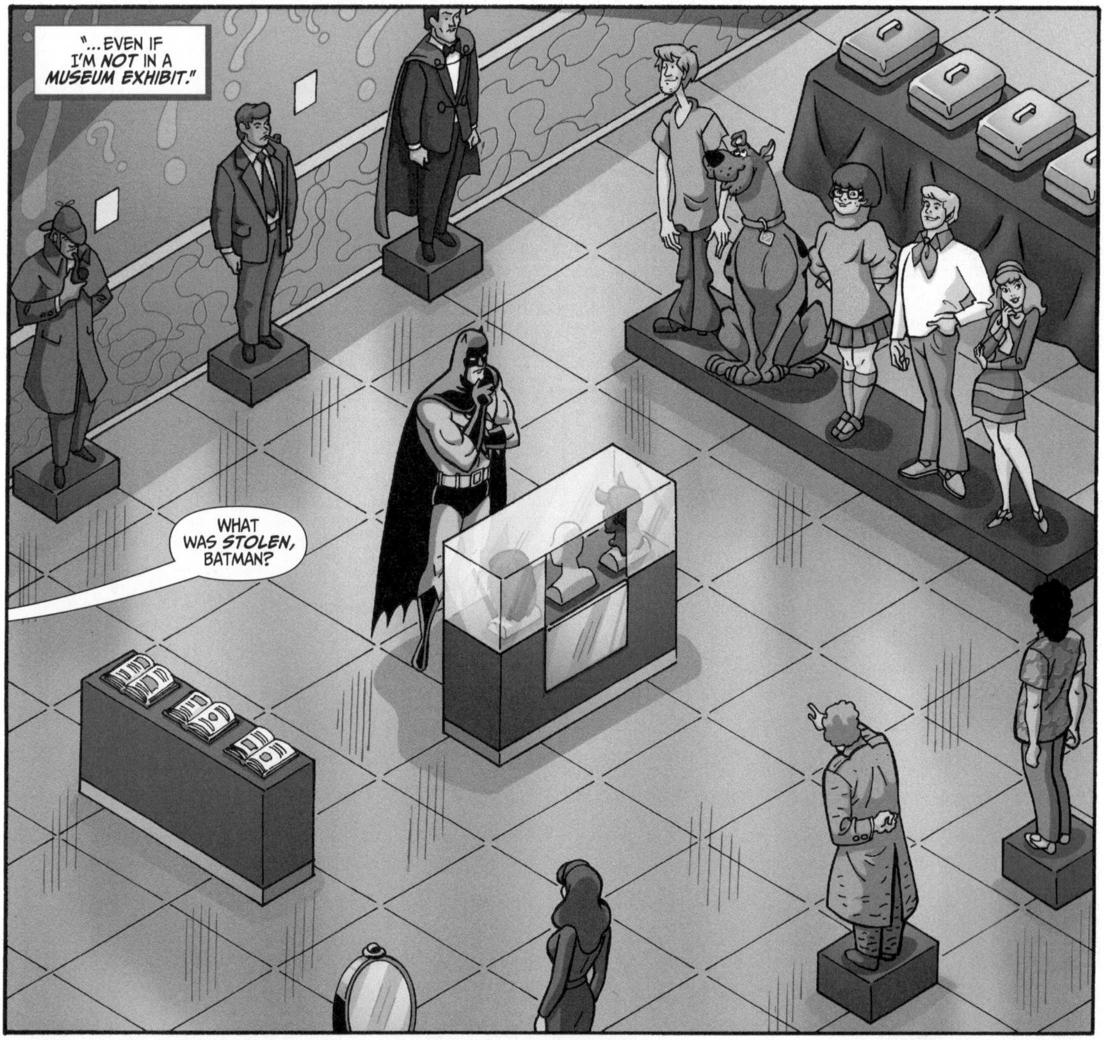
"...EVEN IF I'M NOT IN A MUSEUM EXHIBIT."
WHAT WAS STOLEN, BATMAN?

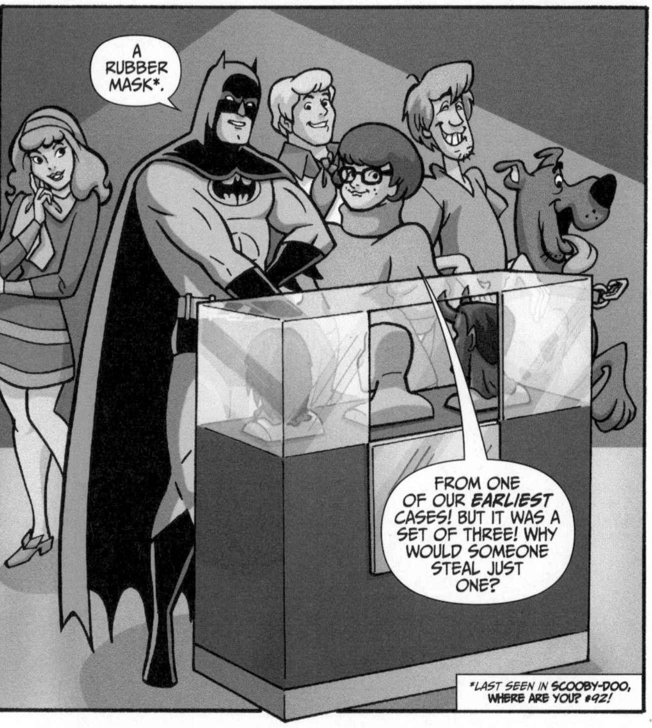
A RUBBER MASK*.
FROM ONE OF OUR EARLIEST CASES! BUT IT WAS A SET OF THREE! WHY WOULD SOMEONE STEAL JUST ONE?
*LAST SEEN IN SCOOBY-DOO, WHERE ARE YOU? #92!

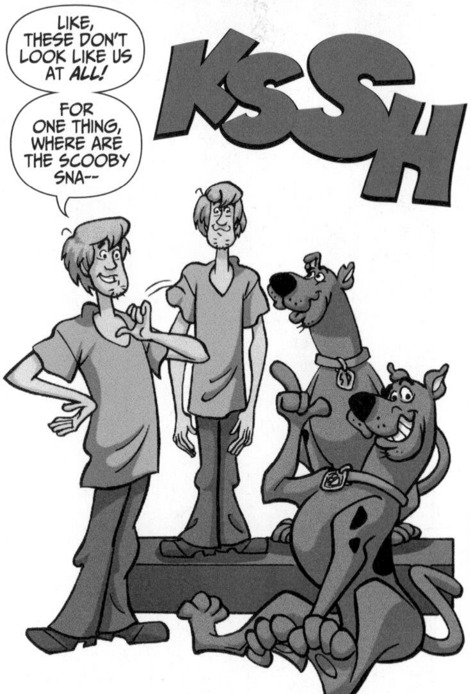
LIKE, THESE DON'T LOOK LIKE US AT ALL!
FOR ONE THING, WHERE ARE THE SCOOBY SNA--
KSSH

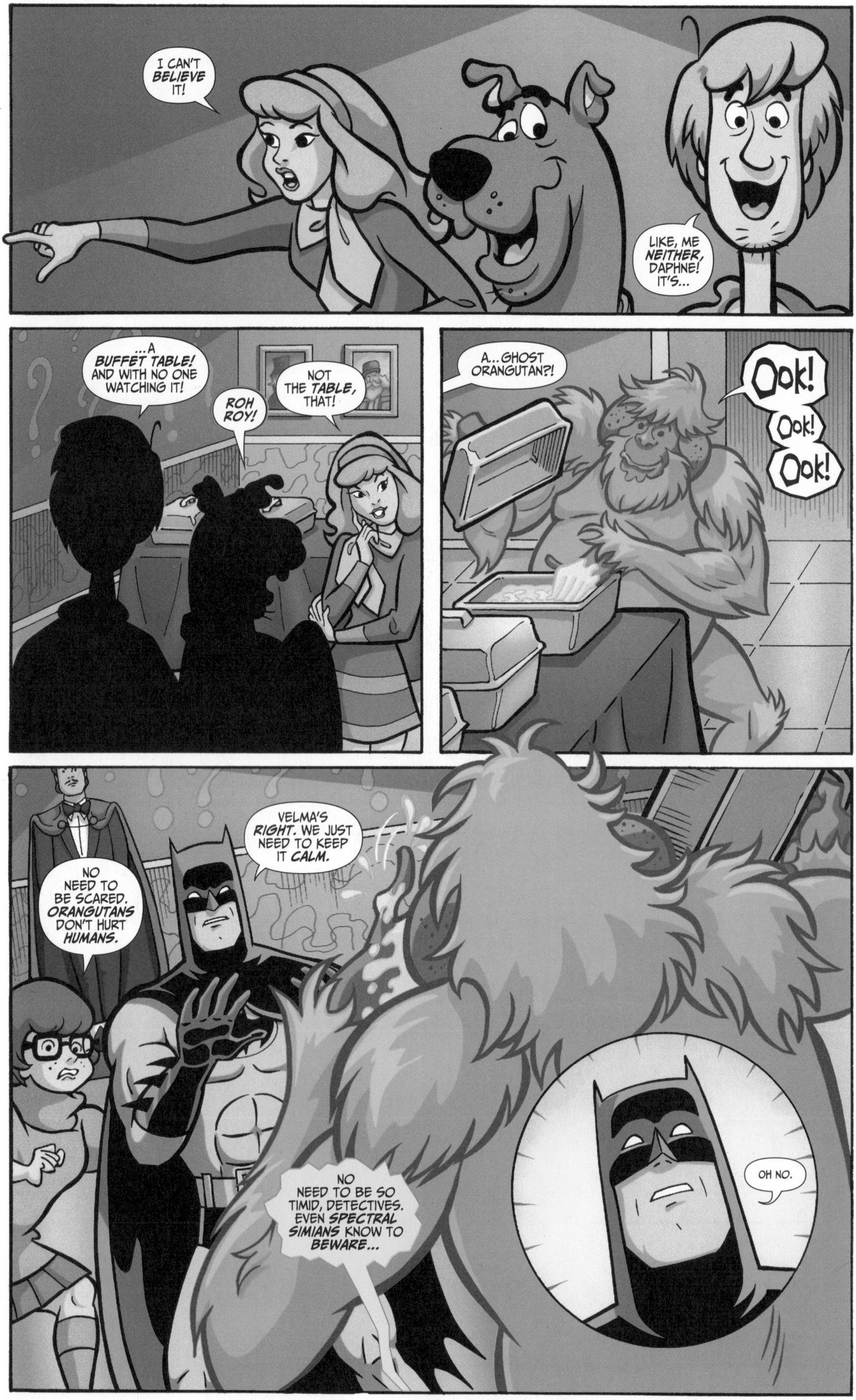
I CAN'T *BELIEVE* IT!
LIKE, ME *NEITHER*, DAPHNE! IT'S...
...A *BUFFET TABLE!* AND WITH NO ONE WATCHING IT!
ROH ROY!
NOT THE *TABLE,* THAT!
A...GHOST ORANGUTAN?!
OOK!
OOK!
OOK!
NO NEED TO BE SCARED. *ORANGUTANS* DON'T HURT *HUMANS.*
VELMA'S *RIGHT.* WE JUST NEED TO KEEP IT *CALM.*
NO NEED TO BE SO TIMID, DETECTIVES. EVEN *SPECTRAL SIMIANS* KNOW TO *BEWARE...*
OH NO.

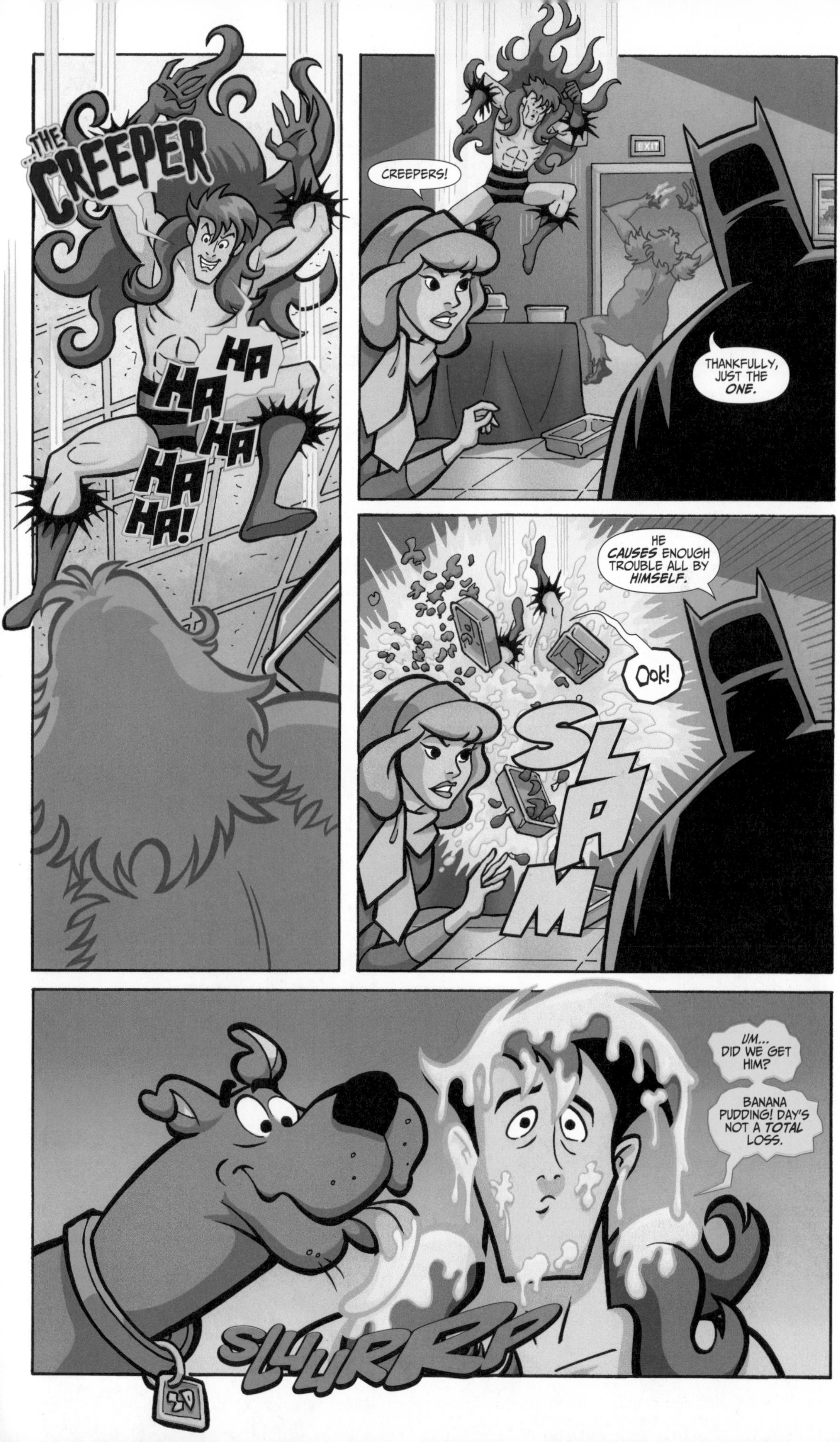
...THE CREEPER
HA HA HA HA HA HA!
CREEPERS!
THANKFULLY, JUST THE ONE.
HE CAUSES ENOUGH TROUBLE ALL BY HIMSELF.
Ook!
SLAM
UM... DID WE GET HIM?
BANANA PUDDING! DAY'S NOT A TOTAL LOSS.
SLUURRP

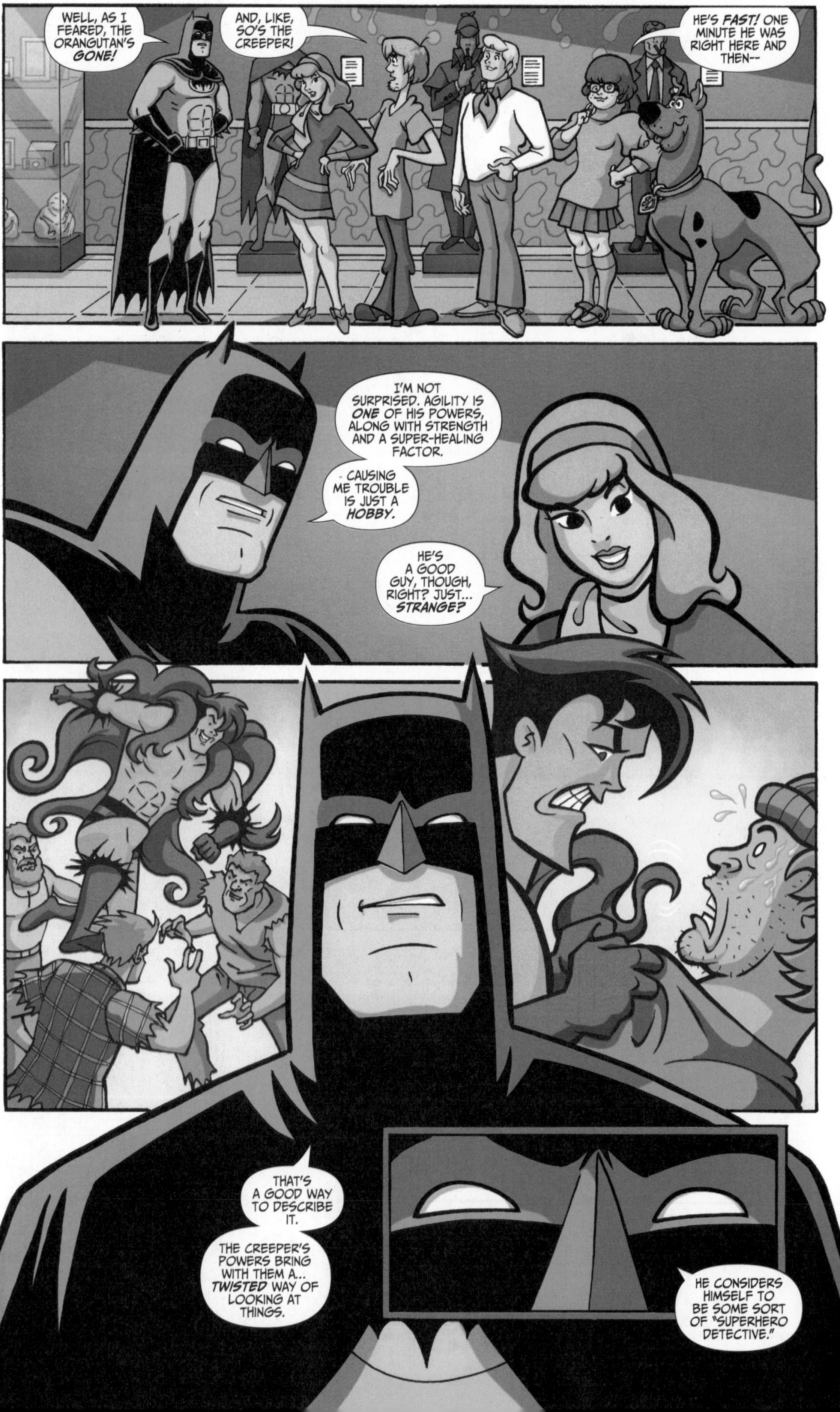
WELL, AS I FEARED, THE ORANGUTAN'S GONE!
AND, LIKE, SO'S THE CREEPER!
HE'S FAST! ONE MINUTE HE WAS RIGHT HERE AND THEN--
I'M NOT SURPRISED. AGILITY IS ONE OF HIS POWERS, ALONG WITH STRENGTH AND A SUPER-HEALING FACTOR.
CAUSING ME TROUBLE IS JUST A HOBBY.
HE'S A GOOD GUY, THOUGH, RIGHT? JUST... STRANGE?
THAT'S A GOOD WAY TO DESCRIBE IT.
THE CREEPER'S POWERS BRING WITH THEM A... TWISTED WAY OF LOOKING AT THINGS.
HE CONSIDERS HIMSELF TO BE SOME SORT OF "SUPERHERO DETECTIVE."

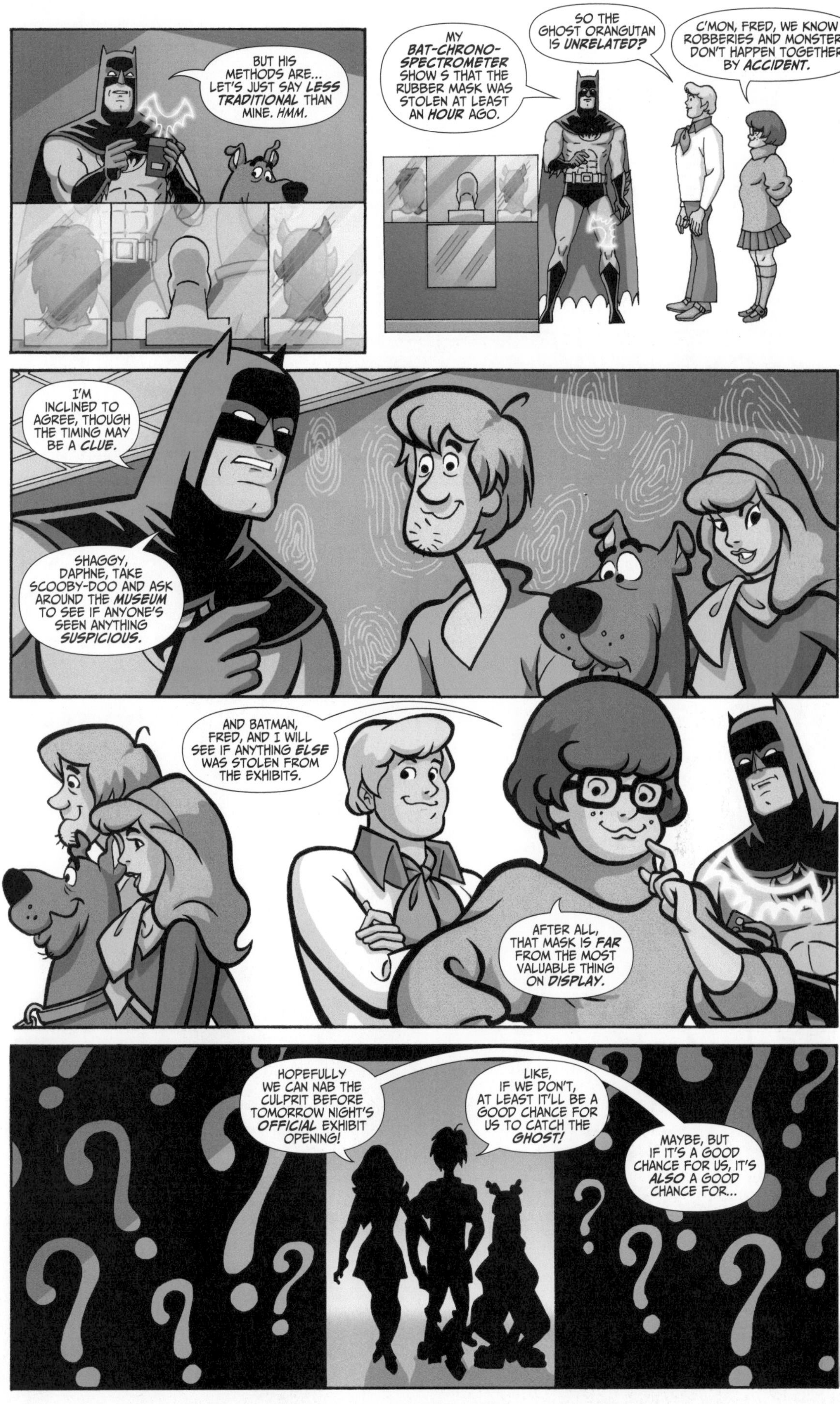
BUT HIS METHODS ARE... LET'S JUST SAY LESS TRADITIONAL THAN MINE. HMM.
MY BAT-CHRONO-SPECTROMETER SHOW S THAT THE RUBBER MASK WAS STOLEN AT LEAST AN HOUR AGO.
SO THE GHOST ORANGUTAN IS UNRELATED?
C'MON, FRED, WE KNOW ROBBERIES AND MONSTERS DON'T HAPPEN TOGETHER BY ACCIDENT.
I'M INCLINED TO AGREE, THOUGH THE TIMING MAY BE A CLUE.
SHAGGY, DAPHNE, TAKE SCOOBY-DOO AND ASK AROUND THE MUSEUM TO SEE IF ANYONE'S SEEN ANYTHING SUSPICIOUS.
AND BATMAN, FRED, AND I WILL SEE IF ANYTHING ELSE WAS STOLEN FROM THE EXHIBITS.
AFTER ALL, THAT MASK IS FAR FROM THE MOST VALUABLE THING ON DISPLAY.
HOPEFULLY WE CAN NAB THE CULPRIT BEFORE TOMORROW NIGHT'S OFFICIAL EXHIBIT OPENING!
LIKE, IF WE DON'T, AT LEAST IT'LL BE A GOOD CHANCE FOR US TO CATCH THE GHOST!
MAYBE, BUT IF IT'S A GOOD CHANCE FOR US, IT'S ALSO A GOOD CHANCE FOR...

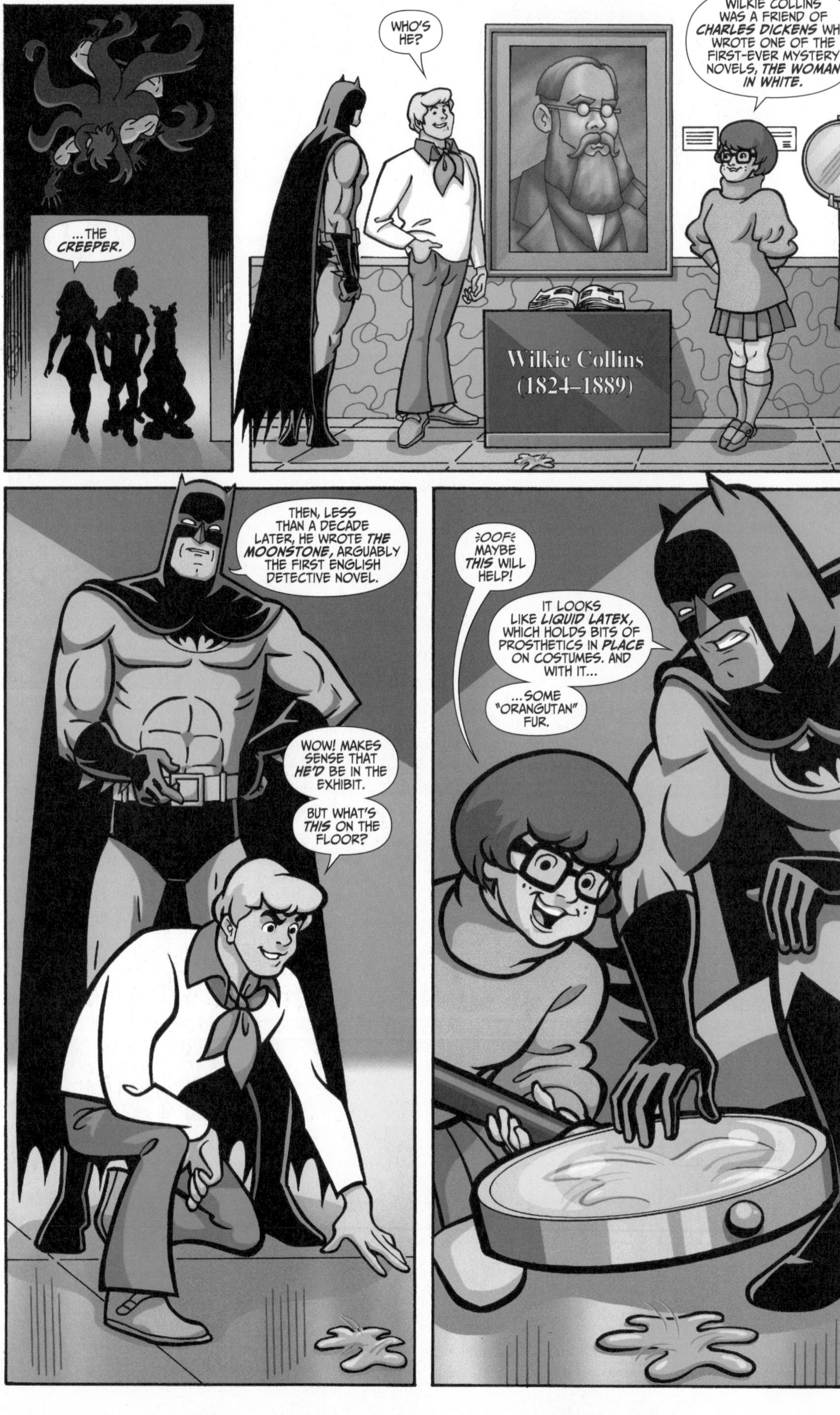
...THE CREEPER.
WHO'S HE?
WILKIE COLLINS WAS A FRIEND OF CHARLES DICKENS WHO WROTE ONE OF THE FIRST-EVER MYSTERY NOVELS, THE WOMAN IN WHITE.
Wilkie Collins (1824–1889)
THEN, LESS THAN A DECADE LATER, HE WROTE THE MOONSTONE, ARGUABLY THE FIRST ENGLISH DETECTIVE NOVEL.
WOW! MAKES SENSE THAT HE'D BE IN THE EXHIBIT.
BUT WHAT'S THIS ON THE FLOOR?
OOF MAYBE THIS WILL HELP!
IT LOOKS LIKE LIQUID LATEX, WHICH HOLDS BITS OF PROSTHETICS IN PLACE ON COSTUMES. AND WITH IT...
...SOME "ORANGUTAN" FUR.

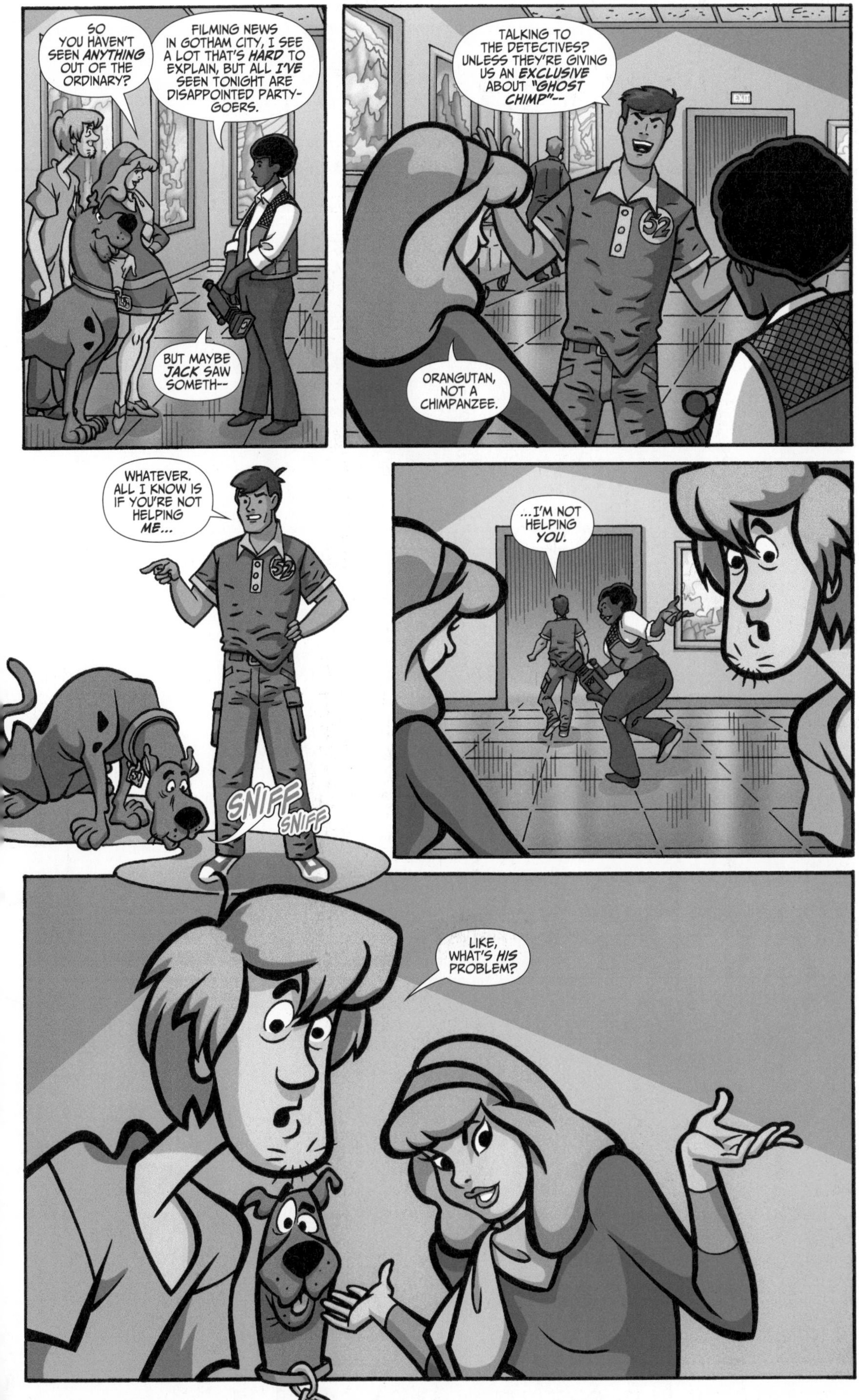

SO YOU HAVEN'T SEEN *ANYTHING* OUT OF THE ORDINARY?
FILMING NEWS IN GOTHAM CITY, I SEE A LOT THAT'S *HARD* TO EXPLAIN, BUT ALL *I'VE* SEEN TONIGHT ARE DISAPPOINTED PARTY-GOERS.
BUT MAYBE *JACK* SAW SOMETH--
TALKING TO THE DETECTIVES? UNLESS THEY'RE GIVING US AN *EXCLUSIVE* ABOUT *"GHOST CHIMP"*--
EXIT
ORANGUTAN, NOT A CHIMPANZEE.
WHATEVER. ALL I KNOW IS IF YOU'RE NOT HELPING *ME*...
SNIFF SNIFF
...I'M NOT HELPING *YOU*.
LIKE, WHAT'S *HIS* PROBLEM?

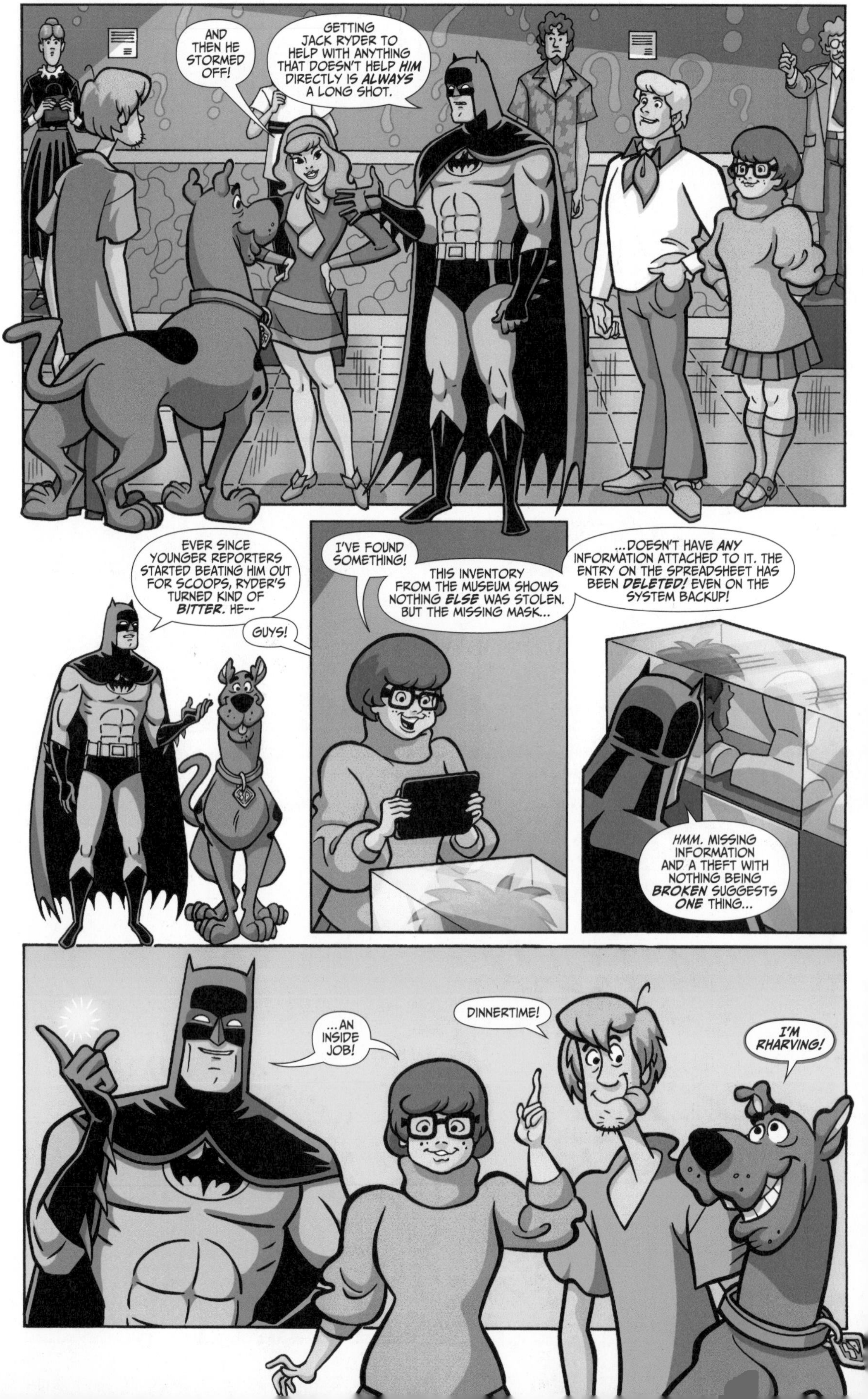
AND THEN HE STORMED OFF!
GETTING JACK RYDER TO HELP WITH ANYTHING THAT DOESN'T HELP HIM DIRECTLY IS ALWAYS A LONG SHOT.
EVER SINCE YOUNGER REPORTERS STARTED BEATING HIM OUT FOR SCOOPS, RYDER'S TURNED KIND OF BITTER. HE--
GUYS!
I'VE FOUND SOMETHING!
THIS INVENTORY FROM THE MUSEUM SHOWS NOTHING ELSE WAS STOLEN. BUT THE MISSING MASK...
...DOESN'T HAVE ANY INFORMATION ATTACHED TO IT. THE ENTRY ON THE SPREADSHEET HAS BEEN DELETED! EVEN ON THE SYSTEM BACKUP!
HMM. MISSING INFORMATION AND A THEFT WITH NOTHING BEING BROKEN SUGGESTS ONE THING...
...AN INSIDE JOB!
DINNERTIME!
I'M RHARVING!

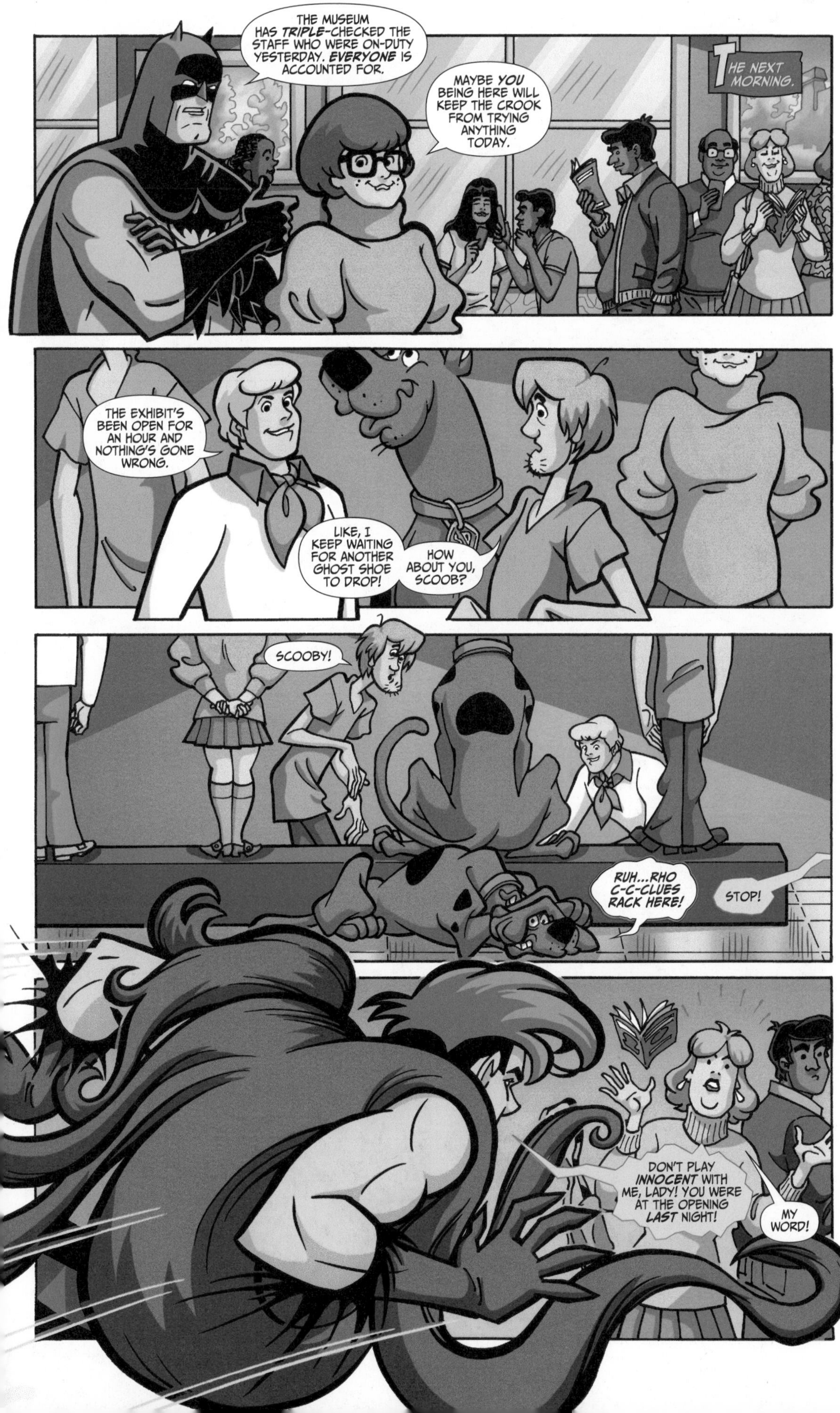
THE NEXT MORNING.
THE MUSEUM HAS TRIPLE-CHECKED THE STAFF WHO WERE ON-DUTY YESTERDAY. EVERYONE IS ACCOUNTED FOR.
MAYBE YOU BEING HERE WILL KEEP THE CROOK FROM TRYING ANYTHING TODAY.
THE EXHIBIT'S BEEN OPEN FOR AN HOUR AND NOTHING'S GONE WRONG.
LIKE, I KEEP WAITING FOR ANOTHER GHOST SHOE TO DROP!
HOW ABOUT YOU, SCOOB?
SCOOBY!
RUH...RHO C-C-CLUES RACK HERE!
STOP!
DON'T PLAY INNOCENT WITH ME, LADY! YOU WERE AT THE OPENING LAST NIGHT!
MY WORD!

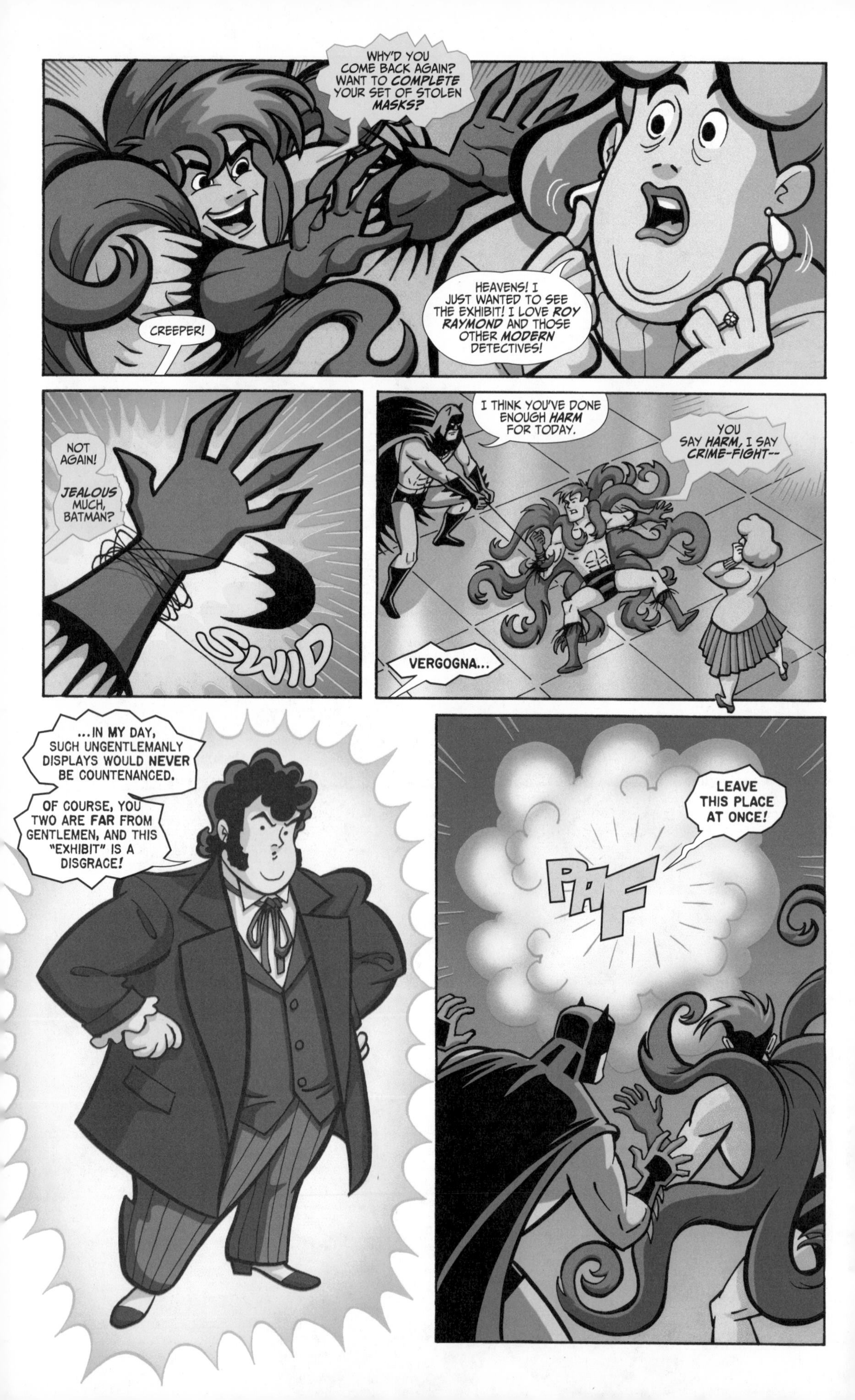
WHY'D YOU COME BACK AGAIN? WANT TO COMPLETE YOUR SET OF STOLEN MASKS?
HEAVENS! I JUST WANTED TO SEE THE EXHIBIT! I LOVE ROY RAYMOND AND THOSE OTHER MODERN DETECTIVES!
CREEPER!
NOT AGAIN!
JEALOUS MUCH, BATMAN?
SWIP
I THINK YOU'VE DONE ENOUGH HARM FOR TODAY.
YOU SAY HARM, I SAY CRIME-FIGHT--
VERGOGNA...
...IN MY DAY, SUCH UNGENTLEMANLY DISPLAYS WOULD NEVER BE COUNTENANCED.
OF COURSE, YOU TWO ARE FAR FROM GENTLEMEN, AND THIS "EXHIBIT" IS A DISGRACE!
PAF
LEAVE THIS PLACE AT ONCE!

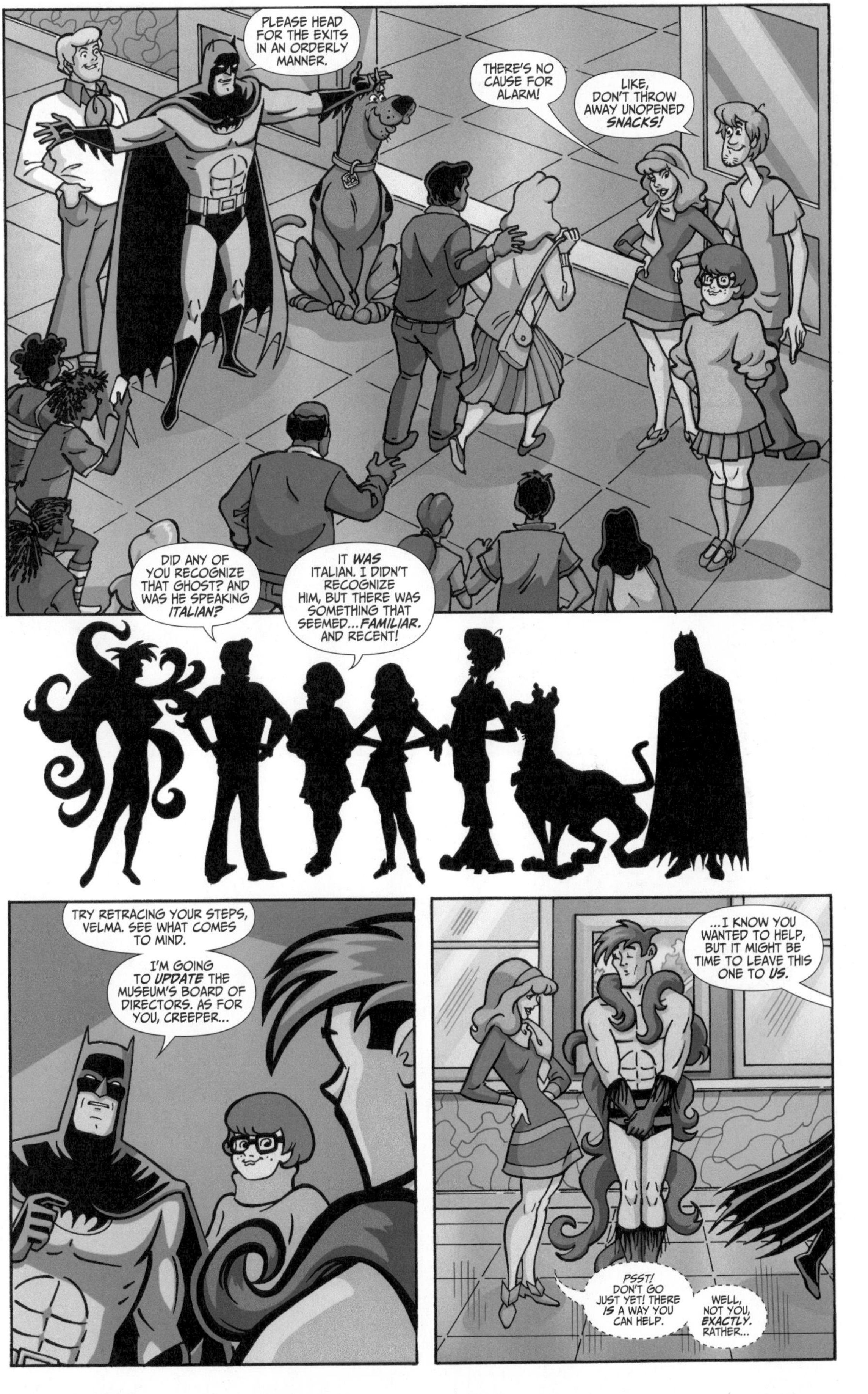
PLEASE HEAD FOR THE EXITS IN AN ORDERLY MANNER.
THERE'S NO CAUSE FOR ALARM!
LIKE, DON'T THROW AWAY UNOPENED SNACKS!
DID ANY OF YOU RECOGNIZE THAT GHOST? AND WAS HE SPEAKING ITALIAN?
IT WAS ITALIAN. I DIDN'T RECOGNIZE HIM, BUT THERE WAS SOMETHING THAT SEEMED...FAMILIAR. AND RECENT!
TRY RETRACING YOUR STEPS, VELMA. SEE WHAT COMES TO MIND.
I'M GOING TO UPDATE THE MUSEUM'S BOARD OF DIRECTORS. AS FOR YOU, CREEPER...
...I KNOW YOU WANTED TO HELP, BUT IT MIGHT BE TIME TO LEAVE THIS ONE TO US.
PSST! DON'T GO JUST YET! THERE IS A WAY YOU CAN HELP.
WELL, NOT YOU, EXACTLY. RATHER...

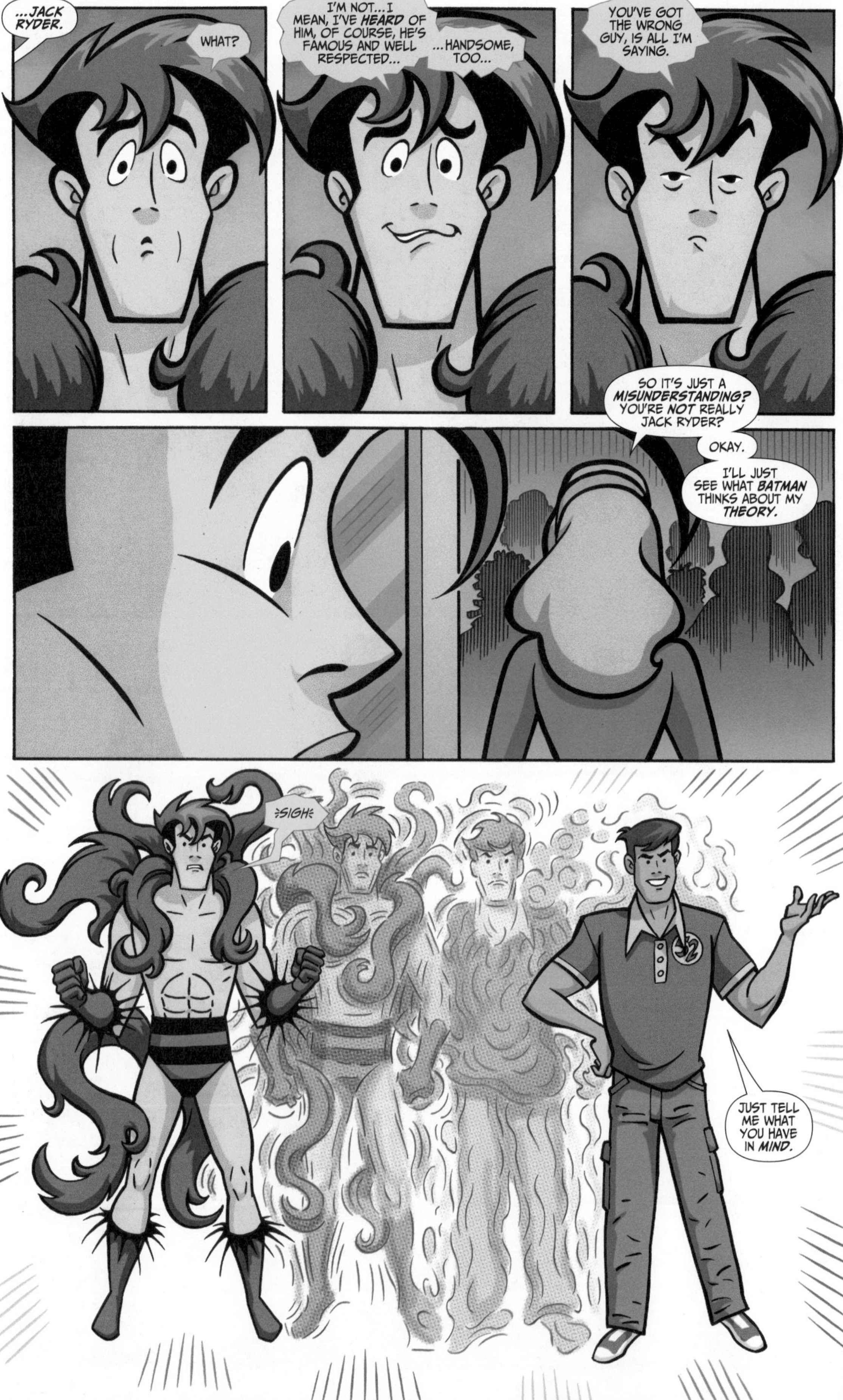
...JACK RYDER.
WHAT?
I'M NOT...I MEAN, I'VE HEARD OF HIM, OF COURSE, HE'S FAMOUS AND WELL RESPECTED...
...HANDSOME, TOO...
YOU'VE GOT THE WRONG GUY, IS ALL I'M SAYING.
SO IT'S JUST A MISUNDERSTANDING? YOU'RE NOT REALLY JACK RYDER?
OKAY.
I'LL JUST SEE WHAT BATMAN THINKS ABOUT MY THEORY.
SIGH
JUST TELL ME WHAT YOU HAVE IN MIND.

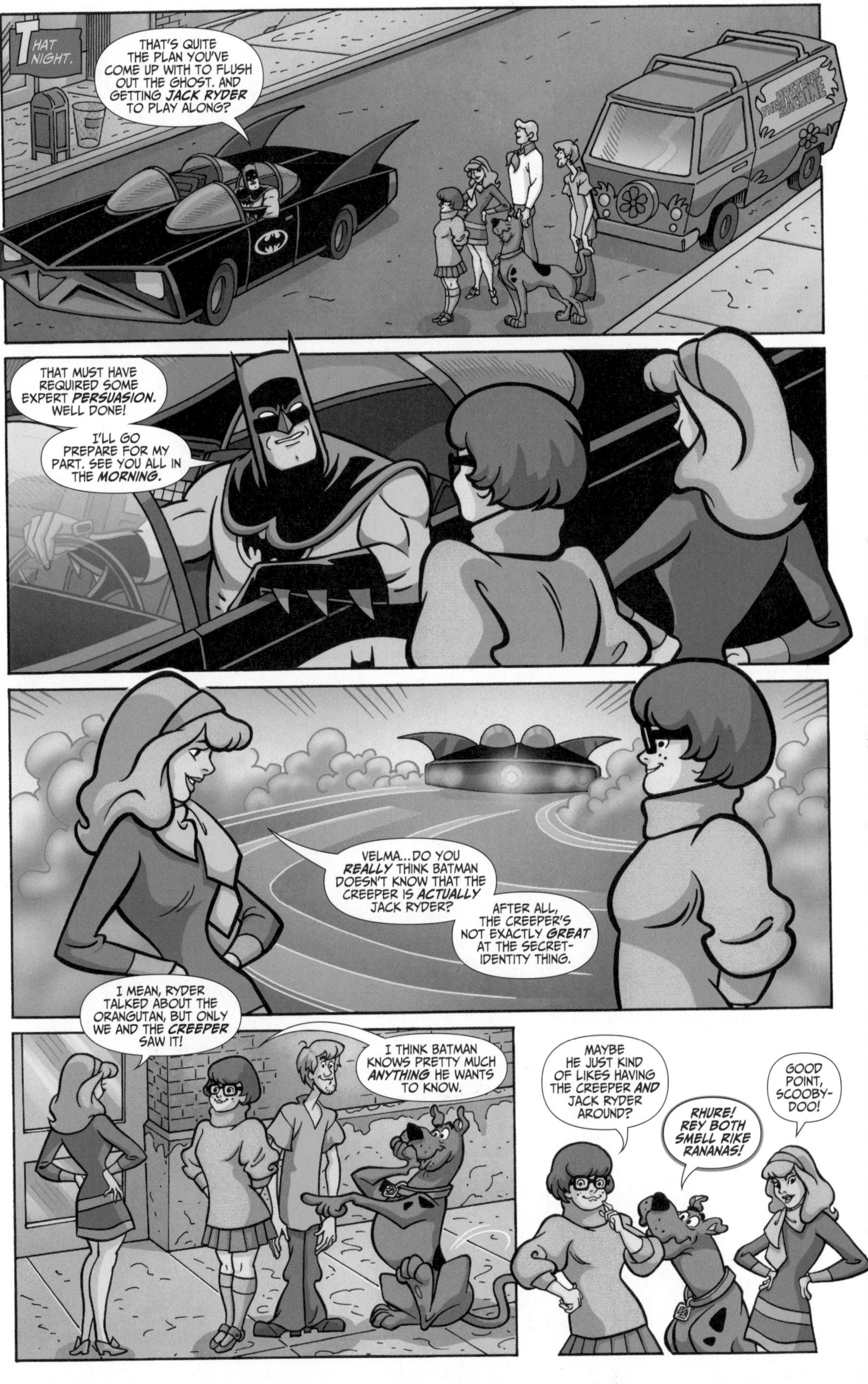
THAT NIGHT.
THAT'S QUITE THE PLAN YOU'VE COME UP WITH TO FLUSH OUT THE GHOST. AND GETTING JACK RYDER TO PLAY ALONG?
THE MYSTERY MACHINE
THAT MUST HAVE REQUIRED SOME EXPERT PERSUASION. WELL DONE!
I'LL GO PREPARE FOR MY PART. SEE YOU ALL IN THE MORNING.
VELMA...DO YOU REALLY THINK BATMAN DOESN'T KNOW THAT THE CREEPER IS ACTUALLY JACK RYDER?
AFTER ALL, THE CREEPER'S NOT EXACTLY GREAT AT THE SECRET-IDENTITY THING.
I MEAN, RYDER TALKED ABOUT THE ORANGUTAN, BUT ONLY WE AND THE CREEPER SAW IT!
I THINK BATMAN KNOWS PRETTY MUCH ANYTHING HE WANTS TO KNOW.
MAYBE HE JUST KIND OF LIKES HAVING THE CREEPER AND JACK RYDER AROUND?
RHURE! REY BOTH SMELL RIKE RANANAS!
GOOD POINT, SCOOBY-DOO!

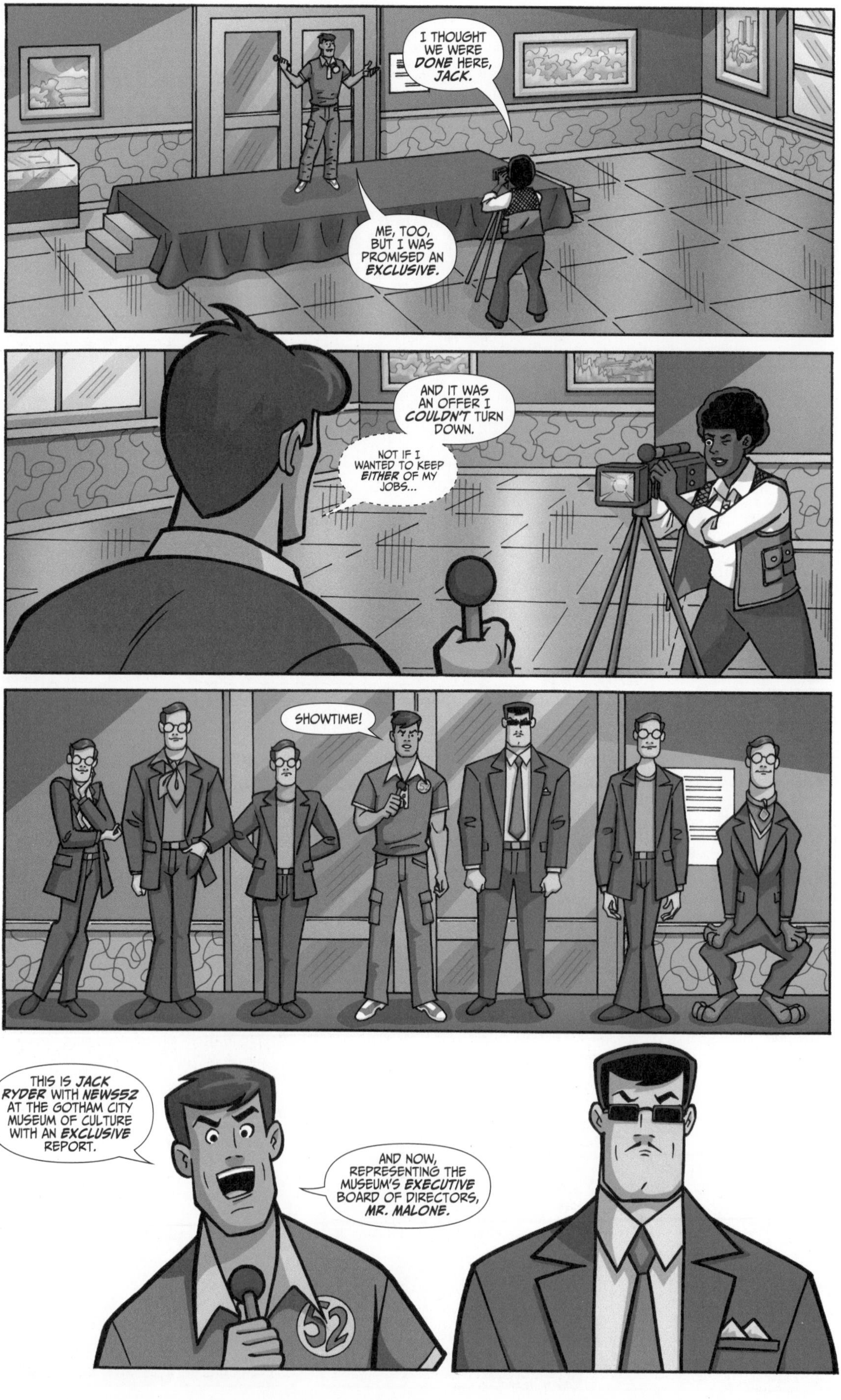
I THOUGHT WE WERE DONE HERE, JACK.
ME, TOO, BUT I WAS PROMISED AN EXCLUSIVE.
AND IT WAS AN OFFER I COULDN'T TURN DOWN.
NOT IF I WANTED TO KEEP EITHER OF MY JOBS...
SHOWTIME!
THIS IS JACK RYDER WITH NEWS52 AT THE GOTHAM CITY MUSEUM OF CULTURE WITH AN EXCLUSIVE REPORT.
AND NOW, REPRESENTING THE MUSEUM'S EXECUTIVE BOARD OF DIRECTORS, MR. MALONE.

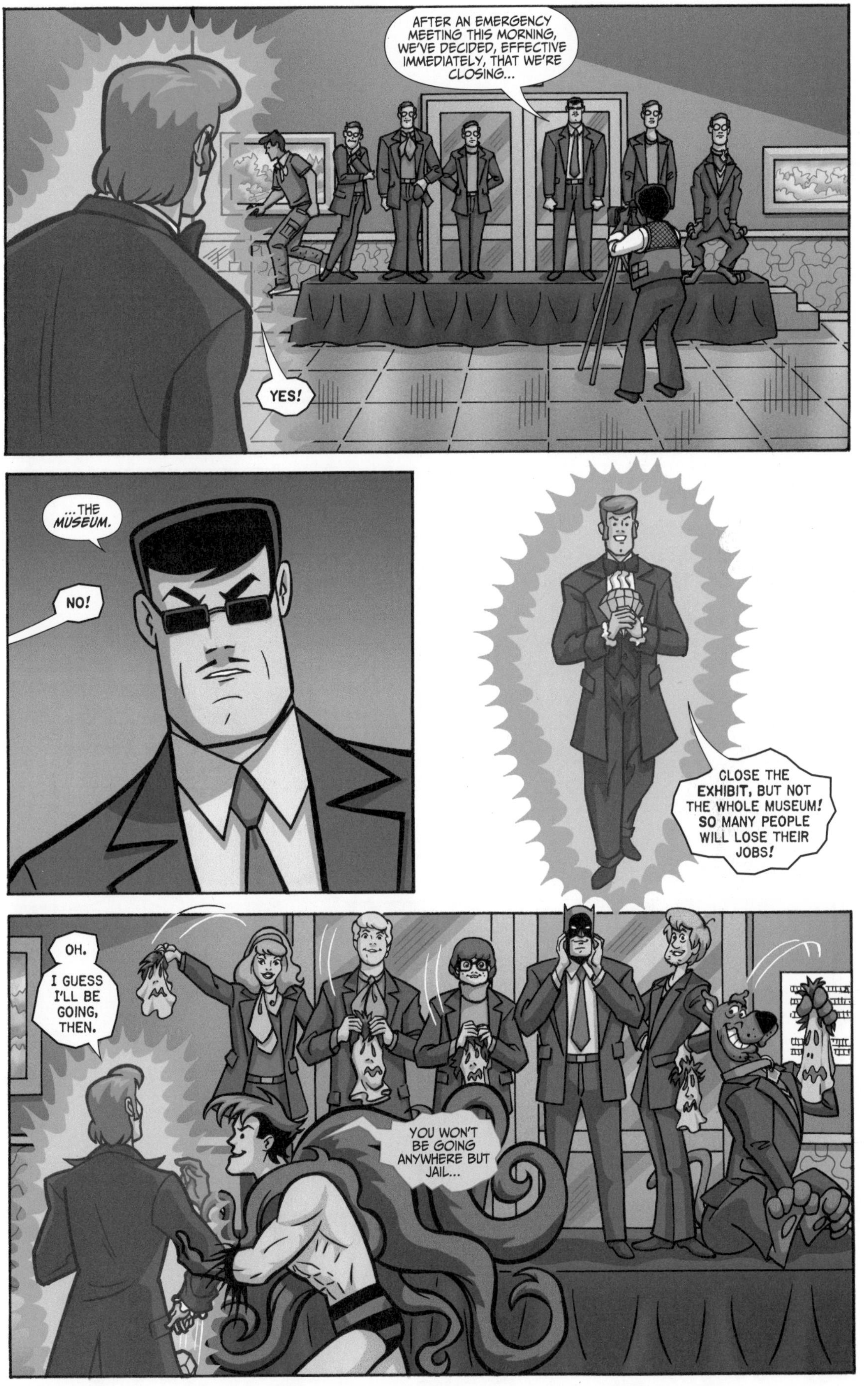
AFTER AN EMERGENCY MEETING THIS MORNING, WE'VE DECIDED, EFFECTIVE IMMEDIATELY, THAT WE'RE CLOSING...
YES!
...THE MUSEUM.
NO!
CLOSE THE EXHIBIT, BUT NOT THE WHOLE MUSEUM! SO MANY PEOPLE WILL LOSE THEIR JOBS!
OH. I GUESS I'LL BE GOING, THEN.
YOU WON'T BE GOING ANYWHERE BUT JAIL...

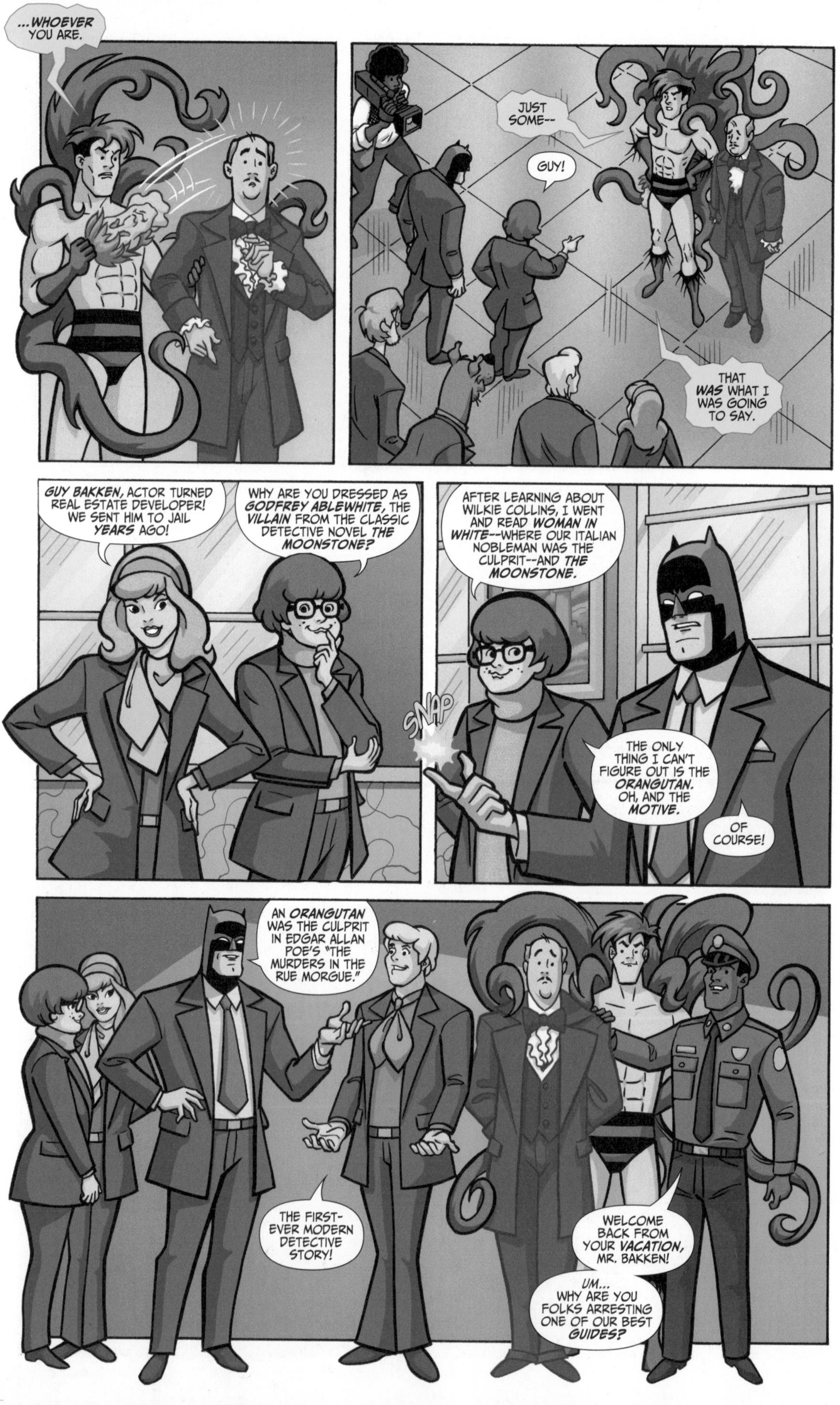
...WHOEVER YOU ARE.
JUST SOME--
GUY!
THAT WAS WHAT I WAS GOING TO SAY.
GUY BAKKEN, ACTOR TURNED REAL ESTATE DEVELOPER! WE SENT HIM TO JAIL YEARS AGO!
WHY ARE YOU DRESSED AS GODFREY ABLEWHITE, THE VILLAIN FROM THE CLASSIC DETECTIVE NOVEL THE MOONSTONE?
AFTER LEARNING ABOUT WILKIE COLLINS, I WENT AND READ WOMAN IN WHITE--WHERE OUR ITALIAN NOBLEMAN WAS THE CULPRIT--AND THE MOONSTONE.
SNAP
THE ONLY THING I CAN'T FIGURE OUT IS THE ORANGUTAN. OH, AND THE MOTIVE.
OF COURSE!
AN ORANGUTAN WAS THE CULPRIT IN EDGAR ALLAN POE'S "THE MURDERS IN THE RUE MORGUE."
THE FIRST-EVER MODERN DETECTIVE STORY!
WELCOME BACK FROM YOUR VACATION, MR. BAKKEN!
UM... WHY ARE YOU FOLKS ARRESTING ONE OF OUR BEST GUIDES?

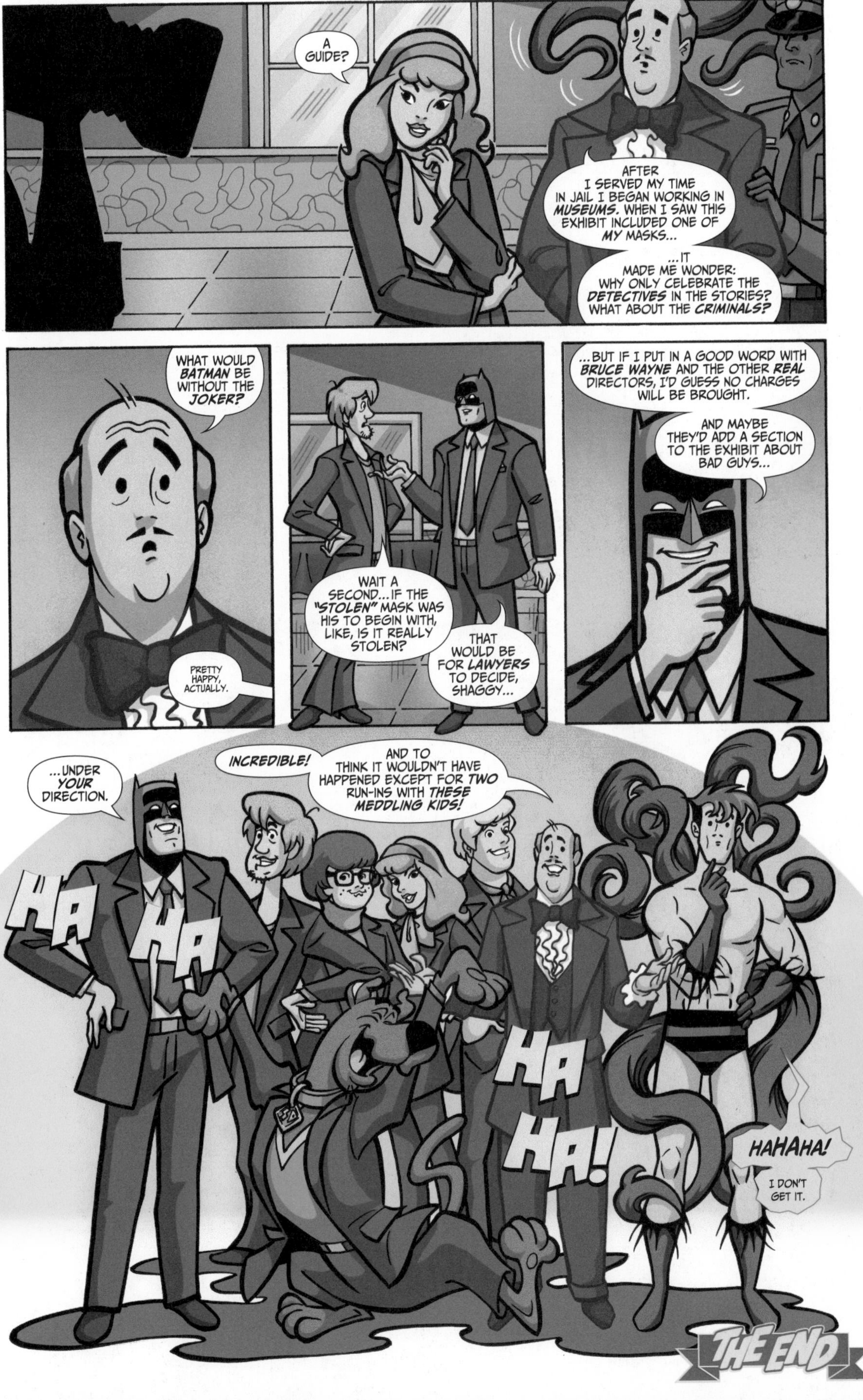
A GUIDE?
AFTER I SERVED MY TIME IN JAIL I BEGAN WORKING IN MUSEUMS. WHEN I SAW THIS EXHIBIT INCLUDED ONE OF MY MASKS...
...IT MADE ME WONDER: WHY ONLY CELEBRATE THE DETECTIVES IN THE STORIES? WHAT ABOUT THE CRIMINALS?
WHAT WOULD BATMAN BE WITHOUT THE JOKER?
PRETTY HAPPY, ACTUALLY.
WAIT A SECOND...IF THE "STOLEN" MASK WAS HIS TO BEGIN WITH, LIKE, IS IT REALLY STOLEN?
THAT WOULD BE FOR LAWYERS TO DECIDE, SHAGGY...
...BUT IF I PUT IN A GOOD WORD WITH BRUCE WAYNE AND THE OTHER REAL DIRECTORS, I'D GUESS NO CHARGES WILL BE BROUGHT.
AND MAYBE THEY'D ADD A SECTION TO THE EXHIBIT ABOUT BAD GUYS...
...UNDER YOUR DIRECTION.
INCREDIBLE!
AND TO THINK IT WOULDN'T HAVE HAPPENED EXCEPT FOR TWO RUN-INS WITH THESE MEDDLING KIDS!
HA HA
HA HA!
HAHAHA!
I DON'T GET IT.
THE END

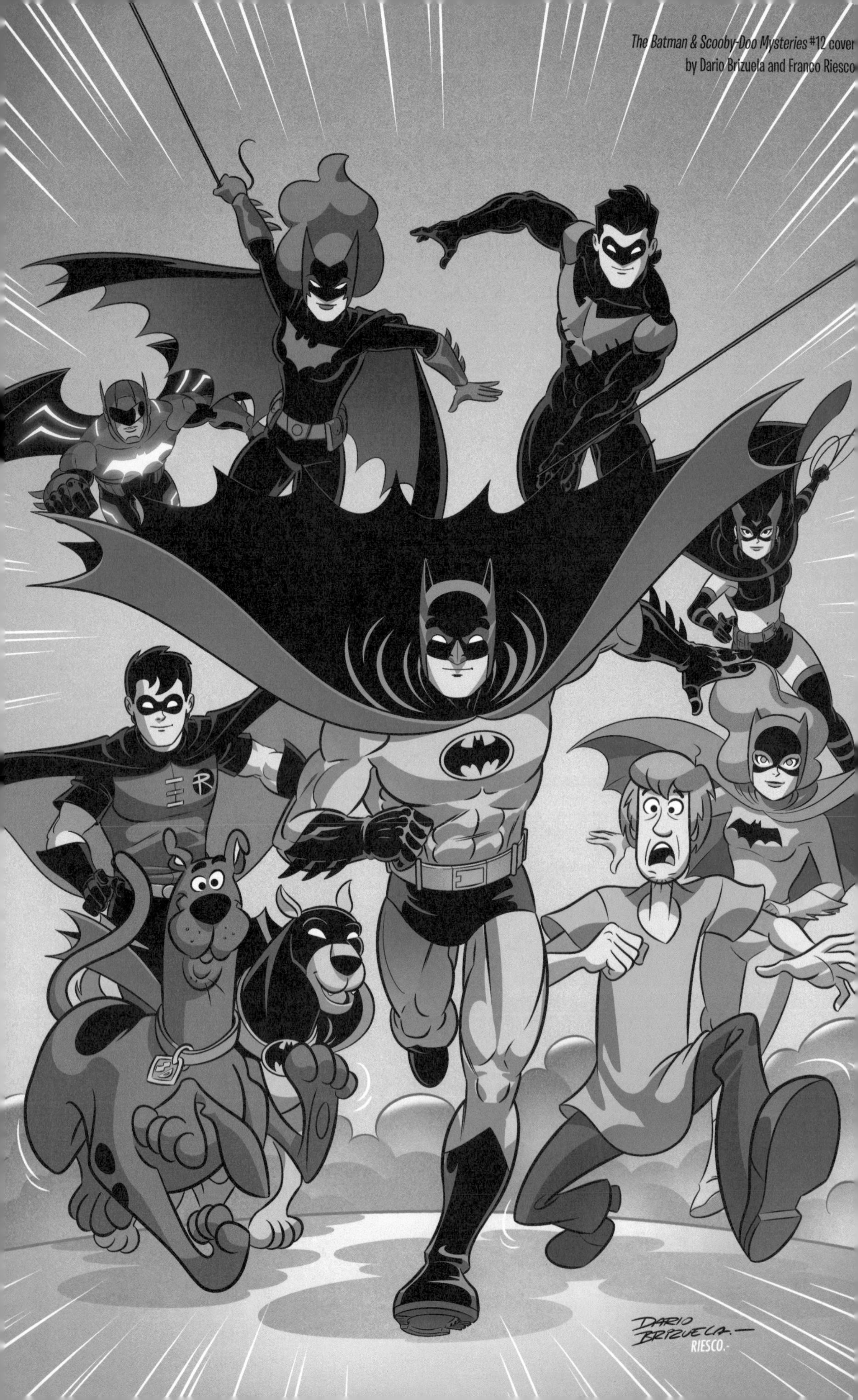
DARIO BRIZUELA—
RIESCO.-

The Batman & Scooby-Doo Mysteries #12 cover
by Dario Brizuela and Franco Riesco

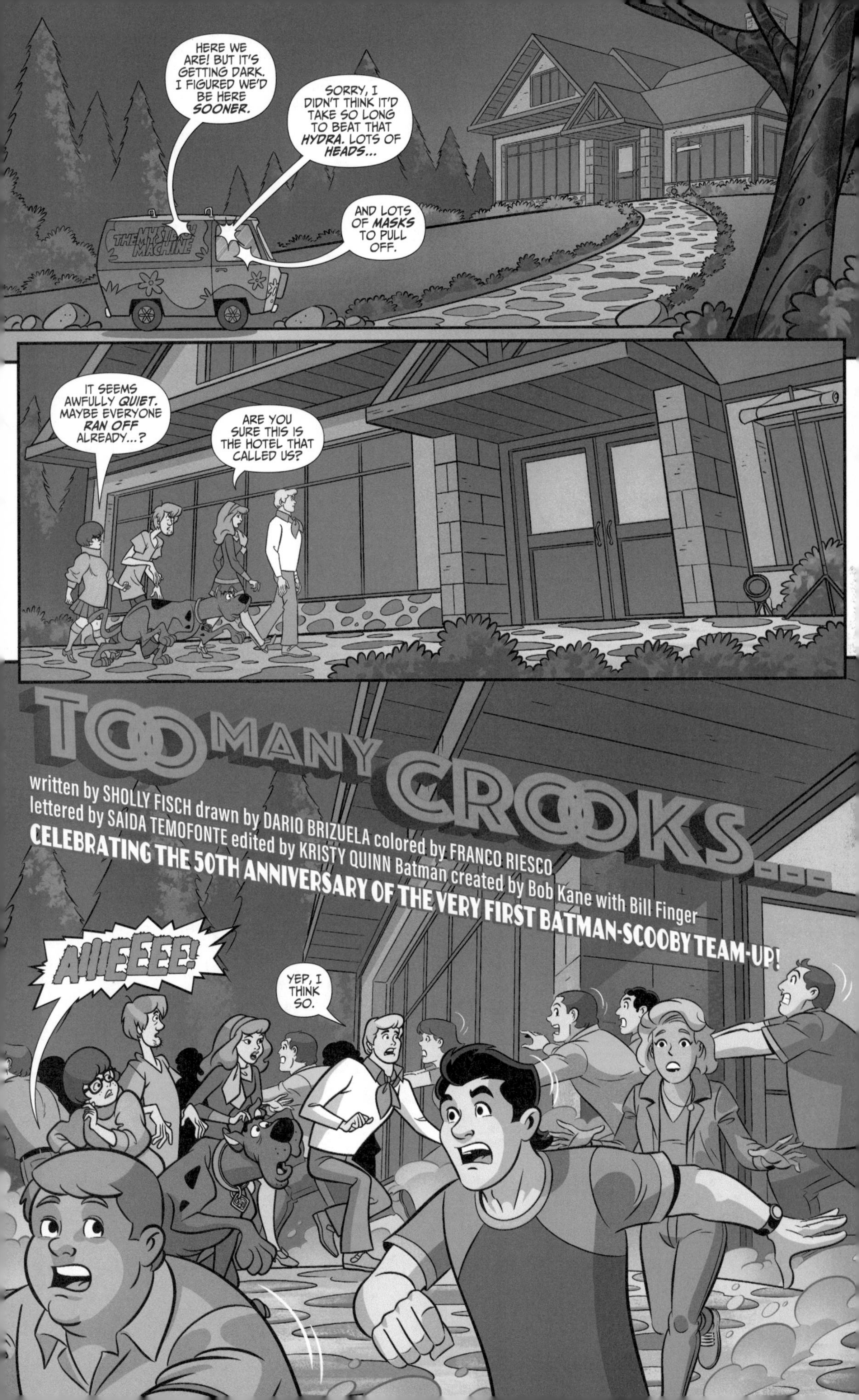
HERE WE ARE! BUT IT'S GETTING DARK. I FIGURED WE'D BE HERE SOONER.
SORRY, I DIDN'T THINK IT'D TAKE SO LONG TO BEAT THAT HYDRA. LOTS OF HEADS...
AND LOTS OF MASKS TO PULL OFF.
THE MYSTERY MACHINE
IT SEEMS AWFULLY QUIET. MAYBE EVERYONE RAN OFF ALREADY...?
ARE YOU SURE THIS IS THE HOTEL THAT CALLED US?
TOO MANY CROOKS...
written by SHOLLY FISCH drawn by DARIO BRIZUELA colored by FRANCO RIESCO
lettered by SAIDA TEMOFONTE edited by KRISTY QUINN Batman created by Bob Kane with Bill Finger
CELEBRATING THE 50TH ANNIVERSARY OF THE VERY FIRST BATMAN-SCOOBY TEAM-UP!
AIIIEEEE!
YEP, I THINK SO.

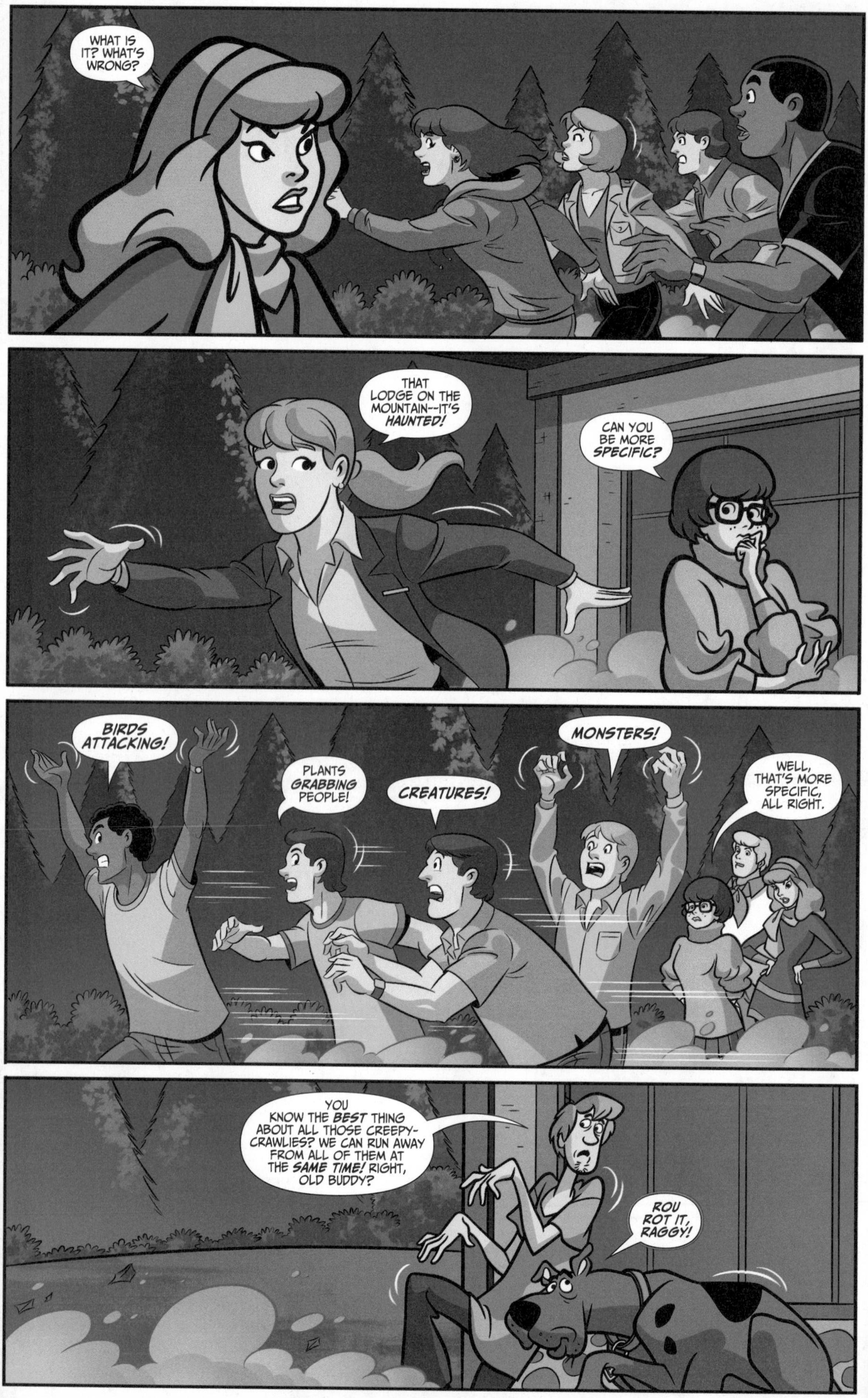
WHAT IS IT? WHAT'S WRONG?
THAT LODGE ON THE MOUNTAIN--IT'S HAUNTED!
CAN YOU BE MORE SPECIFIC?
BIRDS ATTACKING!
PLANTS GRABBING PEOPLE!
CREATURES!
MONSTERS!
WELL, THAT'S MORE SPECIFIC, ALL RIGHT.
YOU KNOW THE BEST THING ABOUT ALL THOSE CREEPY-CRAWLIES? WE CAN RUN AWAY FROM ALL OF THEM AT THE SAME TIME! RIGHT, OLD BUDDY?
ROU ROT IT, RAGGY!

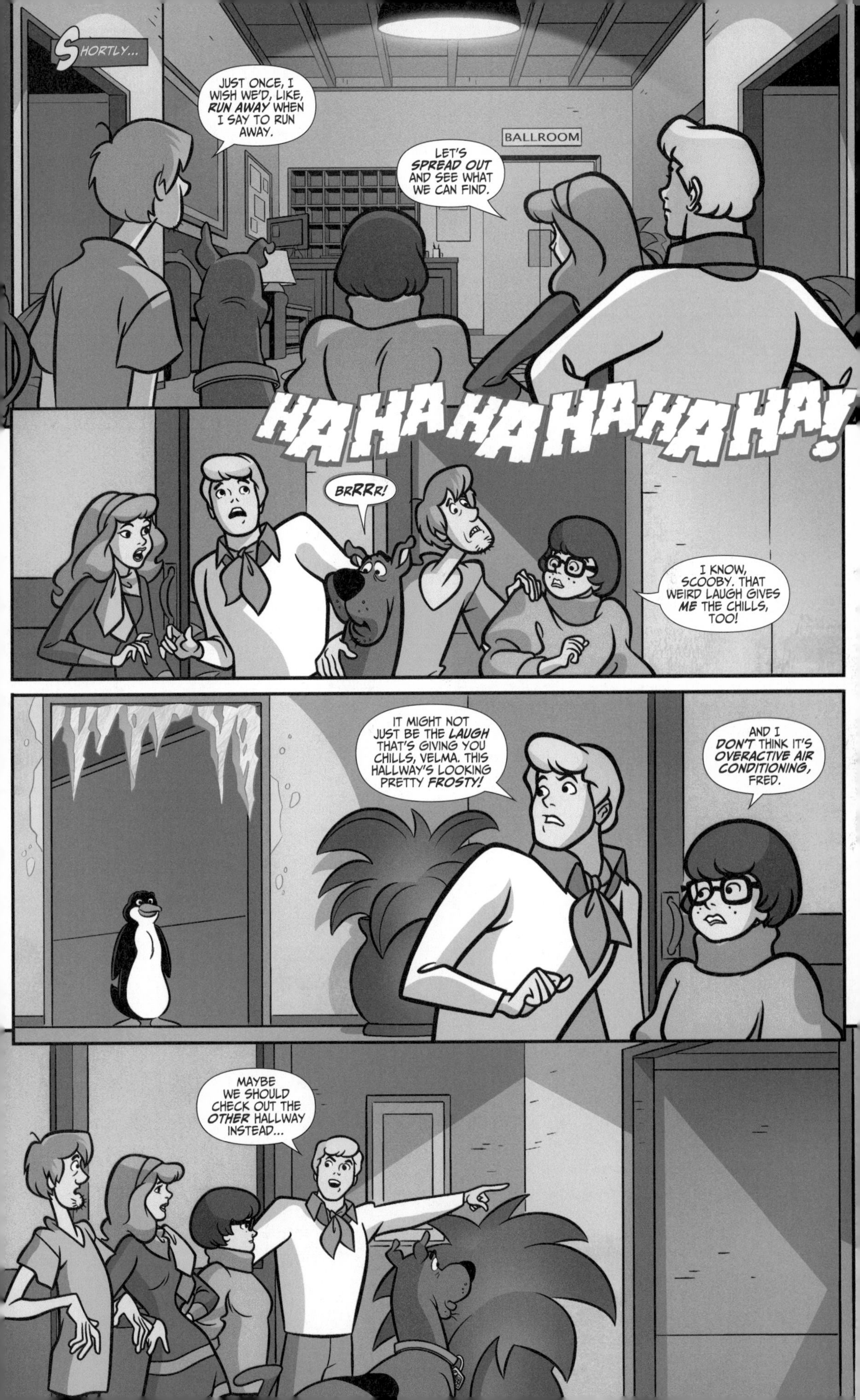
SHORTLY...
JUST ONCE, I WISH WE'D, LIKE, RUN AWAY WHEN I SAY TO RUN AWAY.
BALLROOM
LET'S SPREAD OUT AND SEE WHAT WE CAN FIND.
HAHAHAHAHAHAHAHA!
BRRRR!
I KNOW, SCOOBY. THAT WEIRD LAUGH GIVES ME THE CHILLS, TOO!
IT MIGHT NOT JUST BE THE LAUGH THAT'S GIVING YOU CHILLS, VELMA. THIS HALLWAY'S LOOKING PRETTY FROSTY!
AND I DON'T THINK IT'S OVERACTIVE AIR CONDITIONING, FRED.
MAYBE WE SHOULD CHECK OUT THE OTHER HALLWAY INSTEAD...

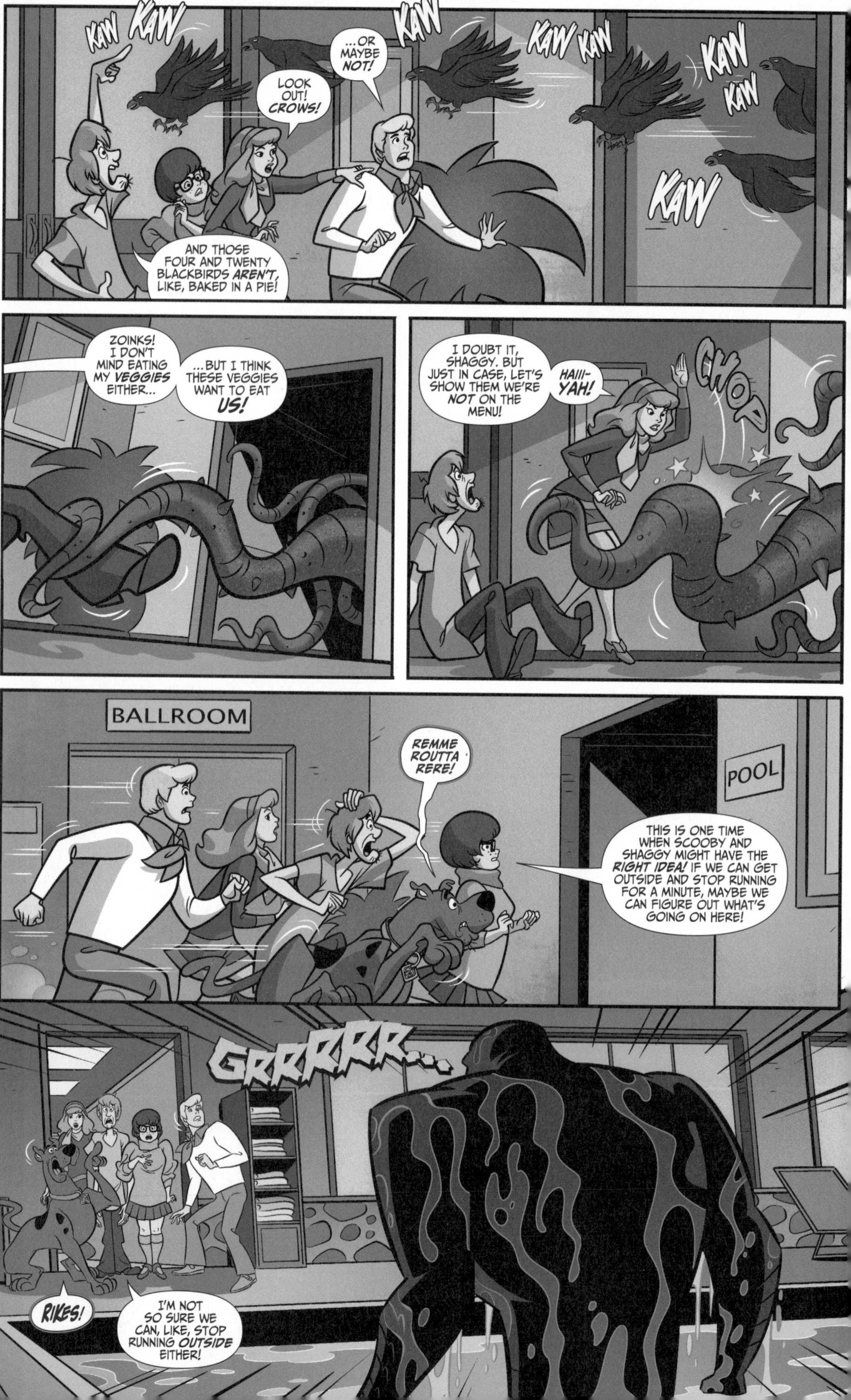
KAW KAW
KAW
KAW KAW
KAW KAW
KAW
LOOK OUT! CROWS!
...OR MAYBE NOT!
AND THOSE FOUR AND TWENTY BLACKBIRDS AREN'T, LIKE, BAKED IN A PIE!
ZOINKS! I DON'T MIND EATING MY VEGGIES EITHER...
...BUT I THINK THESE VEGGIES WANT TO EAT US!
I DOUBT IT, SHAGGY. BUT JUST IN CASE, LET'S SHOW THEM WE'RE NOT ON THE MENU!
HAIII-YAH!
CHOP
BALLROOM
REMME ROUTTA RERE!
POOL
THIS IS ONE TIME WHEN SCOOBY AND SHAGGY MIGHT HAVE THE RIGHT IDEA! IF WE CAN GET OUTSIDE AND STOP RUNNING FOR A MINUTE, MAYBE WE CAN FIGURE OUT WHAT'S GOING ON HERE!
GRRRRR...
RIKES!
I'M NOT SO SURE WE CAN, LIKE, STOP RUNNING OUTSIDE EITHER!

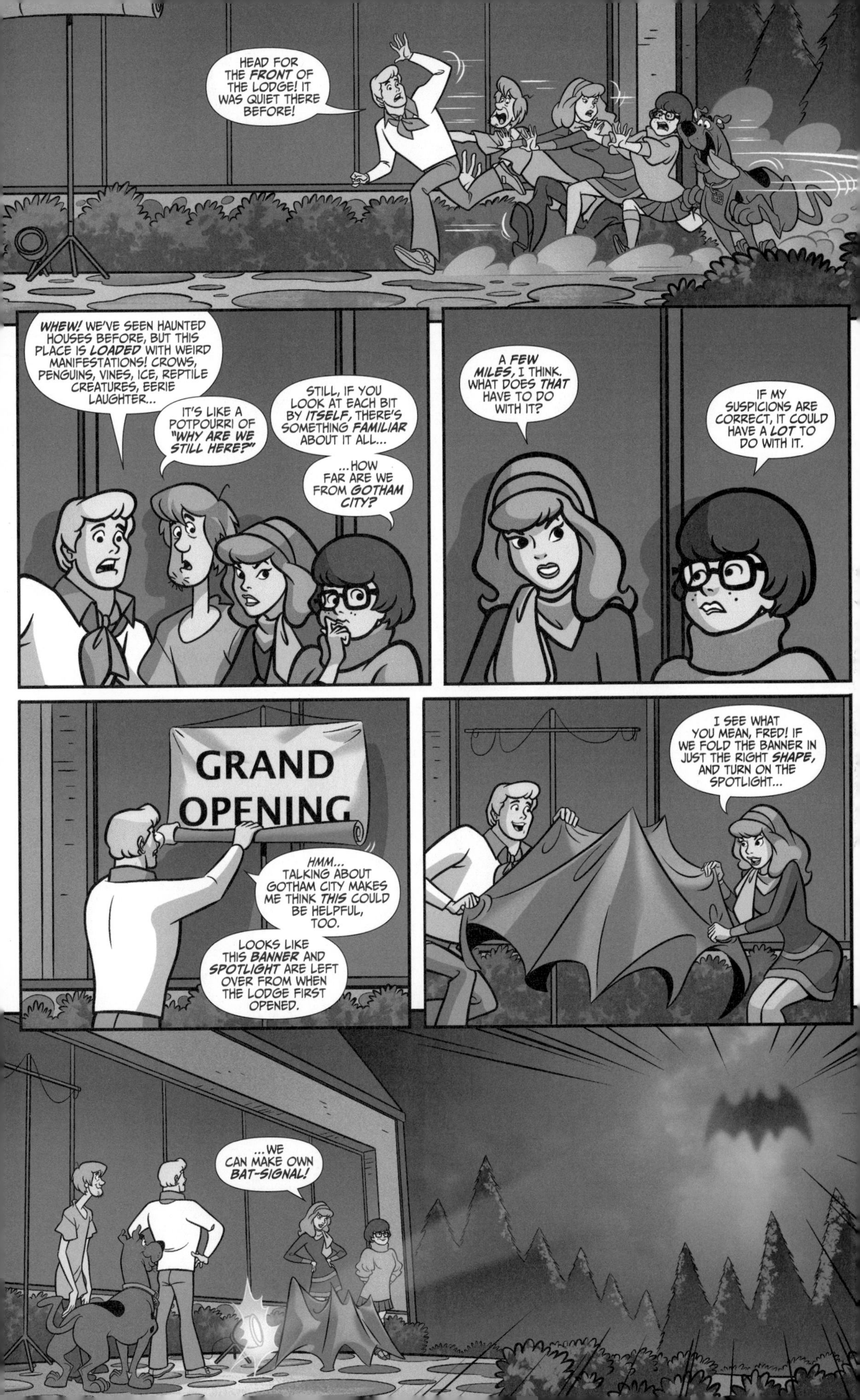
HEAD FOR THE FRONT OF THE LODGE! IT WAS QUIET THERE BEFORE!
WHEW! WE'VE SEEN HAUNTED HOUSES BEFORE, BUT THIS PLACE IS LOADED WITH WEIRD MANIFESTATIONS! CROWS, PENGUINS, VINES, ICE, REPTILE CREATURES, EERIE LAUGHTER...
IT'S LIKE A POTPOURRI OF "WHY ARE WE STILL HERE?"
STILL, IF YOU LOOK AT EACH BIT BY ITSELF, THERE'S SOMETHING FAMILIAR ABOUT IT ALL...
...HOW FAR ARE WE FROM GOTHAM CITY?
A FEW MILES, I THINK. WHAT DOES THAT HAVE TO DO WITH IT?
IF MY SUSPICIONS ARE CORRECT, IT COULD HAVE A LOT TO DO WITH IT.
GRAND OPENING
HMM... TALKING ABOUT GOTHAM CITY MAKES ME THINK THIS COULD BE HELPFUL, TOO.
LOOKS LIKE THIS BANNER AND SPOTLIGHT ARE LEFT OVER FROM WHEN THE LODGE FIRST OPENED.
I SEE WHAT YOU MEAN, FRED! IF WE FOLD THE BANNER IN JUST THE RIGHT SHAPE, AND TURN ON THE SPOTLIGHT...
...WE CAN MAKE OWN BAT-SIGNAL!

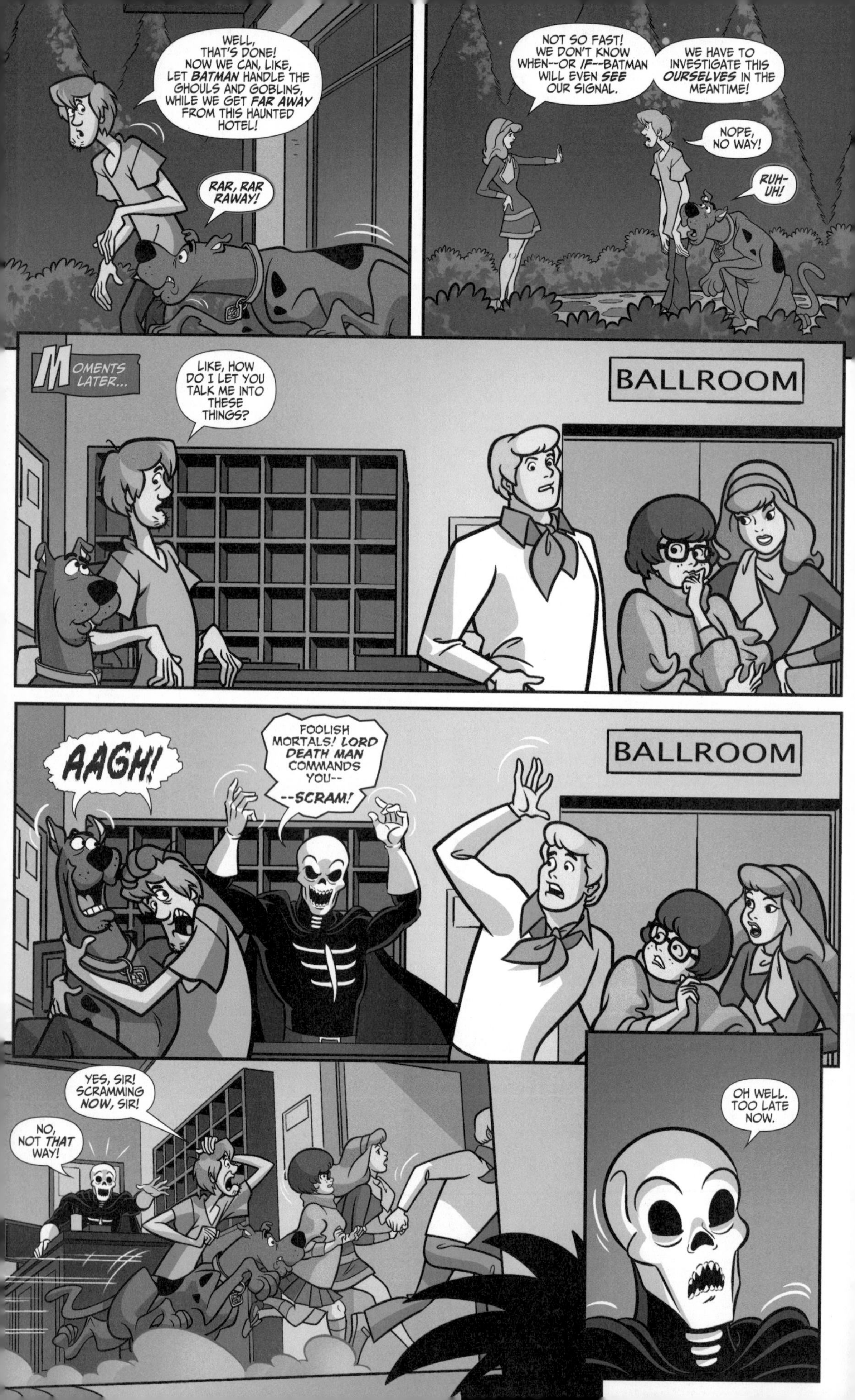
WELL, THAT'S DONE! NOW WE CAN, LIKE, LET BATMAN HANDLE THE GHOULS AND GOBLINS, WHILE WE GET FAR AWAY FROM THIS HAUNTED HOTEL!
RAR, RAR RAWAY!
NOT SO FAST! WE DON'T KNOW WHEN--OR IF--BATMAN WILL EVEN SEE OUR SIGNAL.
WE HAVE TO INVESTIGATE THIS OURSELVES IN THE MEANTIME!
NOPE, NO WAY!
RUH-UH!
MOMENTS LATER...
LIKE, HOW DO I LET YOU TALK ME INTO THESE THINGS?
BALLROOM
AAGH!
FOOLISH MORTALS! LORD DEATH MAN COMMANDS YOU--
--SCRAM!
BALLROOM
YES, SIR! SCRAMMING NOW, SIR!
NO, NOT THAT WAY!
OH WELL. TOO LATE NOW.

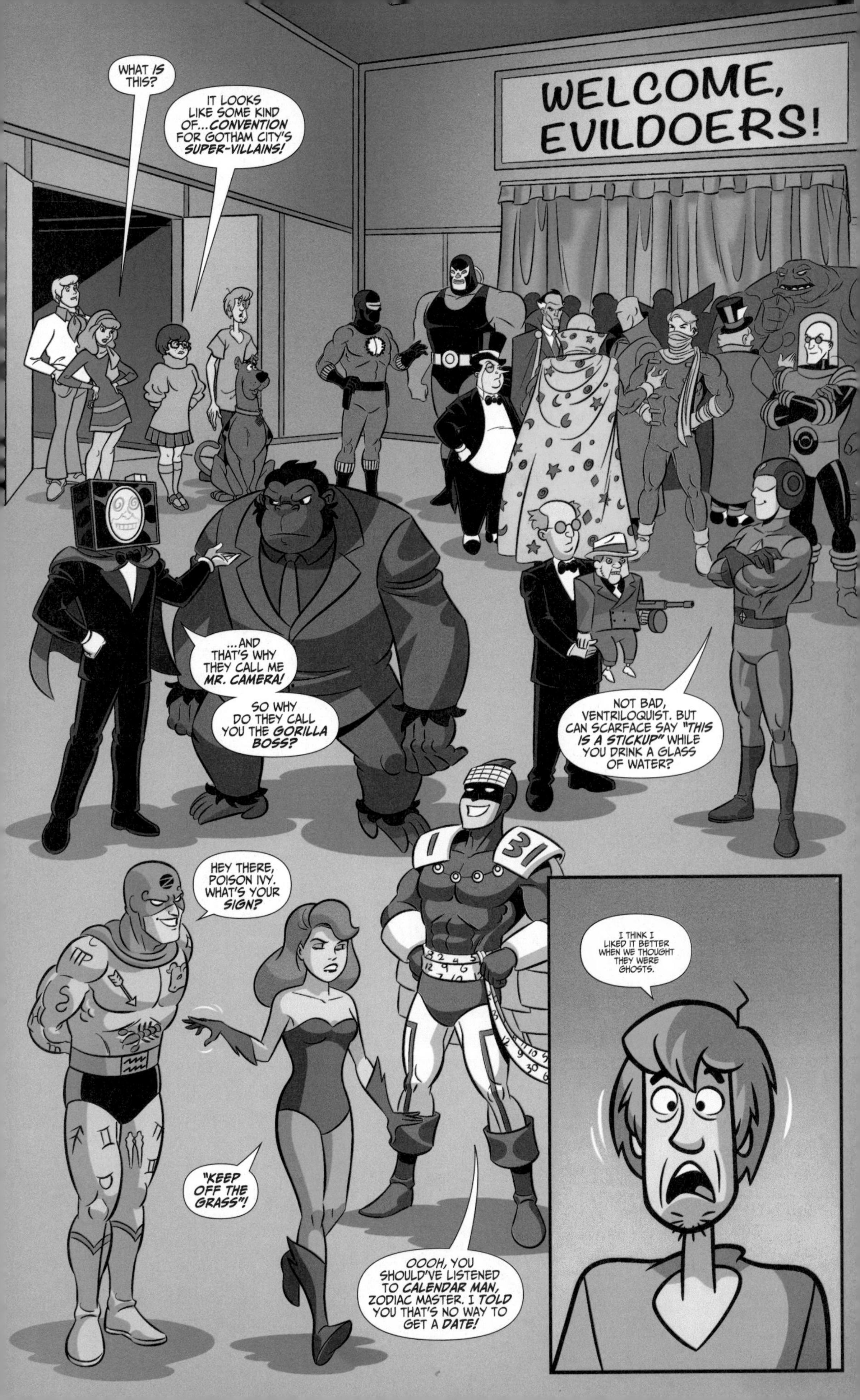
WHAT *IS* THIS?
IT LOOKS LIKE SOME KIND OF...*CONVENTION* FOR GOTHAM CITY'S *SUPER-VILLAINS!*
WELCOME, EVILDOERS!
...AND THAT'S WHY THEY CALL ME *MR. CAMERA!*
SO WHY DO THEY CALL YOU THE *GORILLA BOSS?*
NOT BAD, VENTRILOQUIST. BUT CAN SCARFACE SAY *"THIS IS A STICKUP"* WHILE YOU DRINK A GLASS OF WATER?
HEY THERE, POISON IVY. WHAT'S YOUR *SIGN?*
"KEEP OFF THE GRASS"!
OOOH, YOU SHOULD'VE LISTENED TO *CALENDAR MAN*, ZODIAC MASTER. I *TOLD* YOU THAT'S NO WAY TO GET A *DATE!*
I THINK I LIKED IT BETTER WHEN WE THOUGHT THEY WERE GHOSTS.

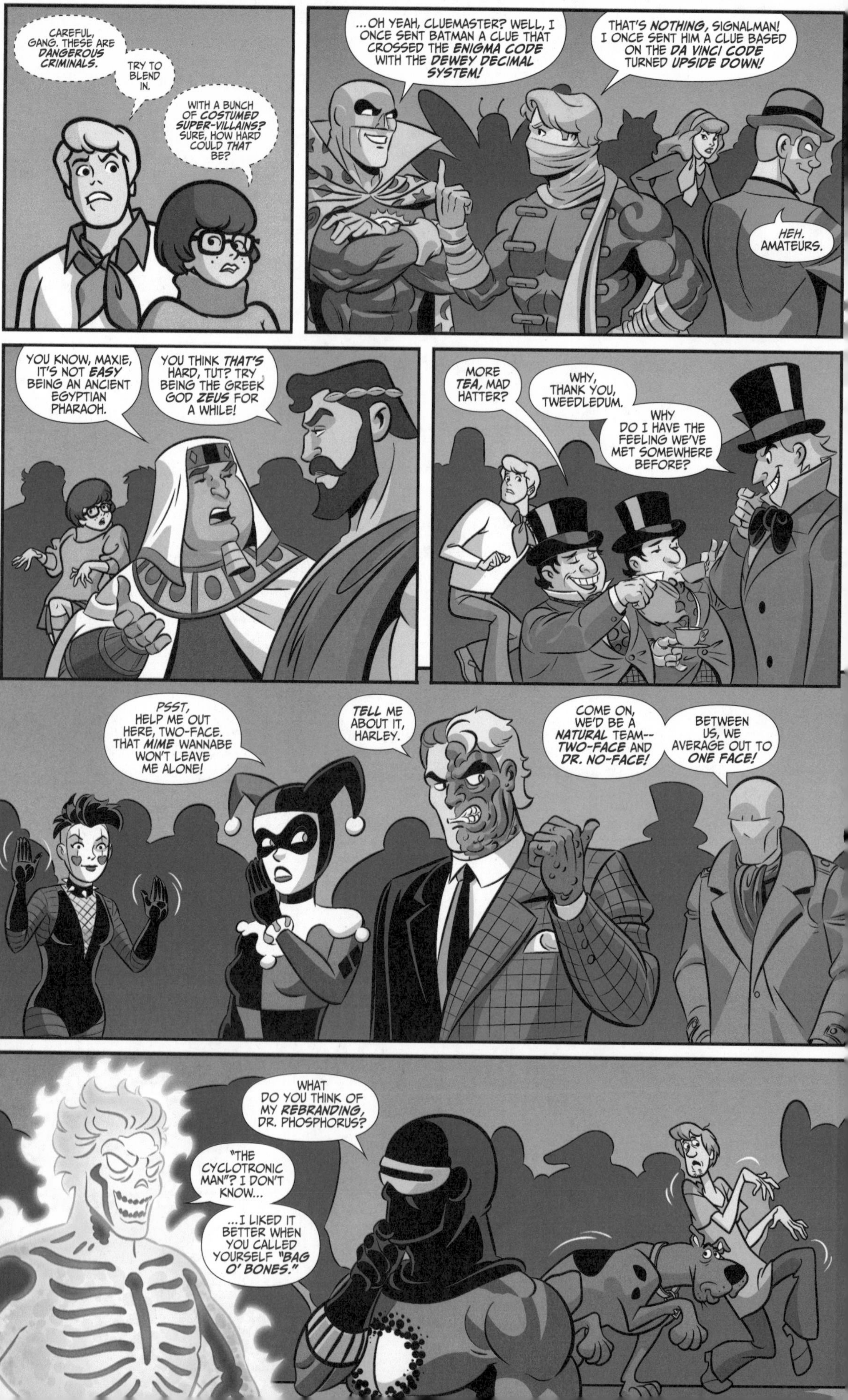
CAREFUL, GANG. THESE ARE DANGEROUS CRIMINALS.
TRY TO BLEND IN.
WITH A BUNCH OF COSTUMED SUPER-VILLAINS? SURE, HOW HARD COULD THAT BE?
...OH YEAH, CLUEMASTER? WELL, I ONCE SENT BATMAN A CLUE THAT CROSSED THE ENIGMA CODE WITH THE DEWEY DECIMAL SYSTEM!
THAT'S NOTHING, SIGNALMAN! I ONCE SENT HIM A CLUE BASED ON THE DA VINCI CODE TURNED UPSIDE DOWN!
HEH. AMATEURS.
YOU KNOW, MAXIE, IT'S NOT EASY BEING AN ANCIENT EGYPTIAN PHARAOH.
YOU THINK THAT'S HARD, TUT? TRY BEING THE GREEK GOD ZEUS FOR A WHILE!
MORE TEA, MAD HATTER?
WHY, THANK YOU, TWEEDLEDUM.
WHY DO I HAVE THE FEELING WE'VE MET SOMEWHERE BEFORE?
PSST, HELP ME OUT HERE, TWO-FACE. THAT MIME WANNABE WON'T LEAVE ME ALONE!
TELL ME ABOUT IT, HARLEY.
COME ON, WE'D BE A NATURAL TEAM-- TWO-FACE AND DR. NO-FACE!
BETWEEN US, WE AVERAGE OUT TO ONE FACE!
WHAT DO YOU THINK OF MY REBRANDING, DR. PHOSPHORUS?
"THE CYCLOTRONIC MAN"? I DON'T KNOW...
...I LIKED IT BETTER WHEN YOU CALLED YOURSELF "BAG O' BONES."

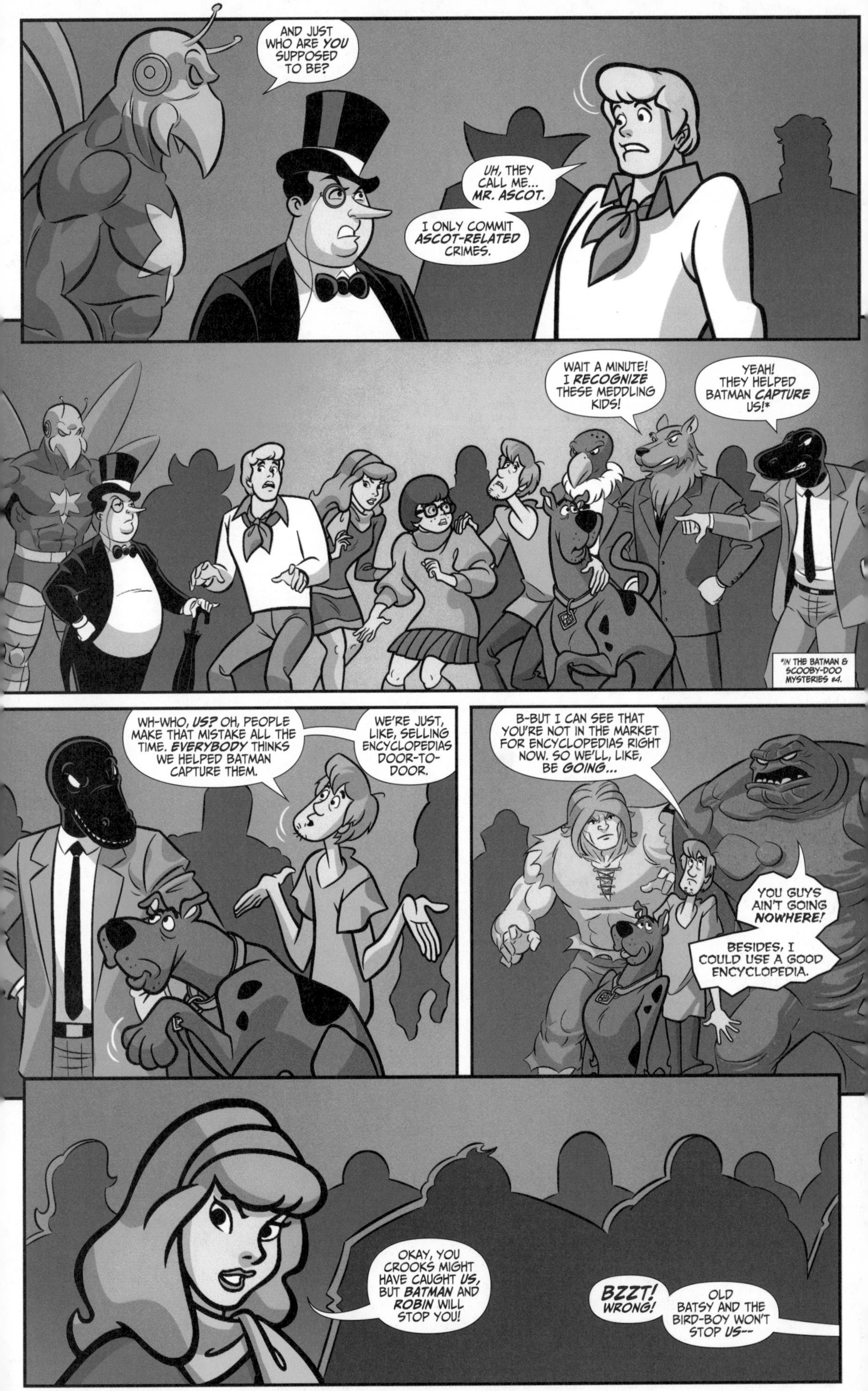
AND JUST WHO ARE YOU SUPPOSED TO BE?
UH, THEY CALL ME... MR. ASCOT.
I ONLY COMMIT ASCOT-RELATED CRIMES.
WAIT A MINUTE! I RECOGNIZE THESE MEDDLING KIDS!
YEAH! THEY HELPED BATMAN CAPTURE US!*
*IN THE BATMAN & SCOOBY-DOO MYSTERIES #4.
WH-WHO, US? OH, PEOPLE MAKE THAT MISTAKE ALL THE TIME. EVERYBODY THINKS WE HELPED BATMAN CAPTURE THEM.
WE'RE JUST, LIKE, SELLING ENCYCLOPEDIAS DOOR-TO-DOOR.
B-BUT I CAN SEE THAT YOU'RE NOT IN THE MARKET FOR ENCYCLOPEDIAS RIGHT NOW. SO WE'LL, LIKE, BE GOING...
YOU GUYS AIN'T GOING NOWHERE!
BESIDES, I COULD USE A GOOD ENCYCLOPEDIA.
OKAY, YOU CROOKS MIGHT HAVE CAUGHT US, BUT BATMAN AND ROBIN WILL STOP YOU!
BZZT! WRONG!
OLD BATSY AND THE BIRD-BOY WON'T STOP US--

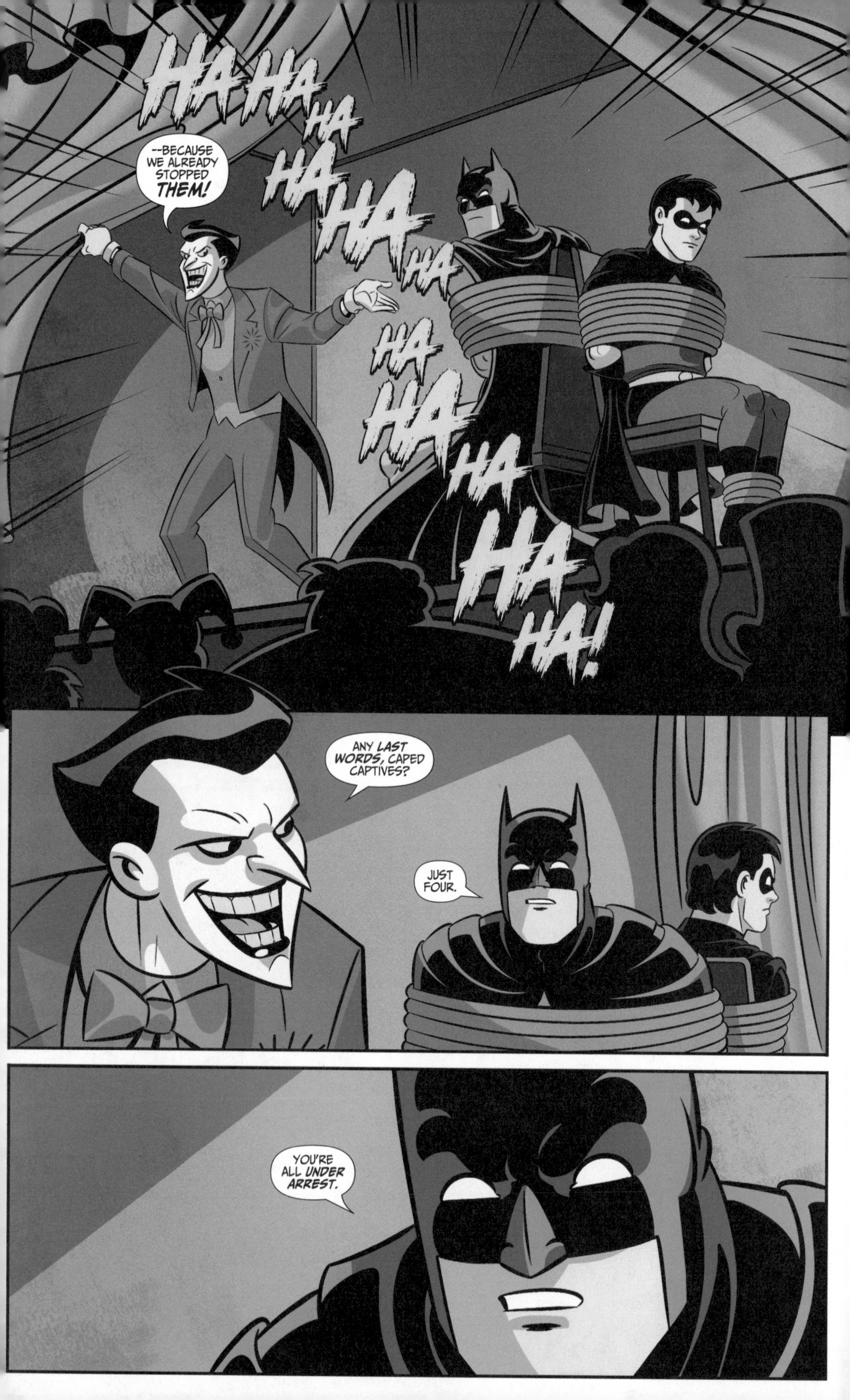
--BECAUSE WE ALREADY STOPPED THEM!
HA HA HA HA HA HA HA HA HA HA HA HA HA!
ANY LAST WORDS, CAPED CAPTIVES?
JUST FOUR.
YOU'RE ALL UNDER ARREST.

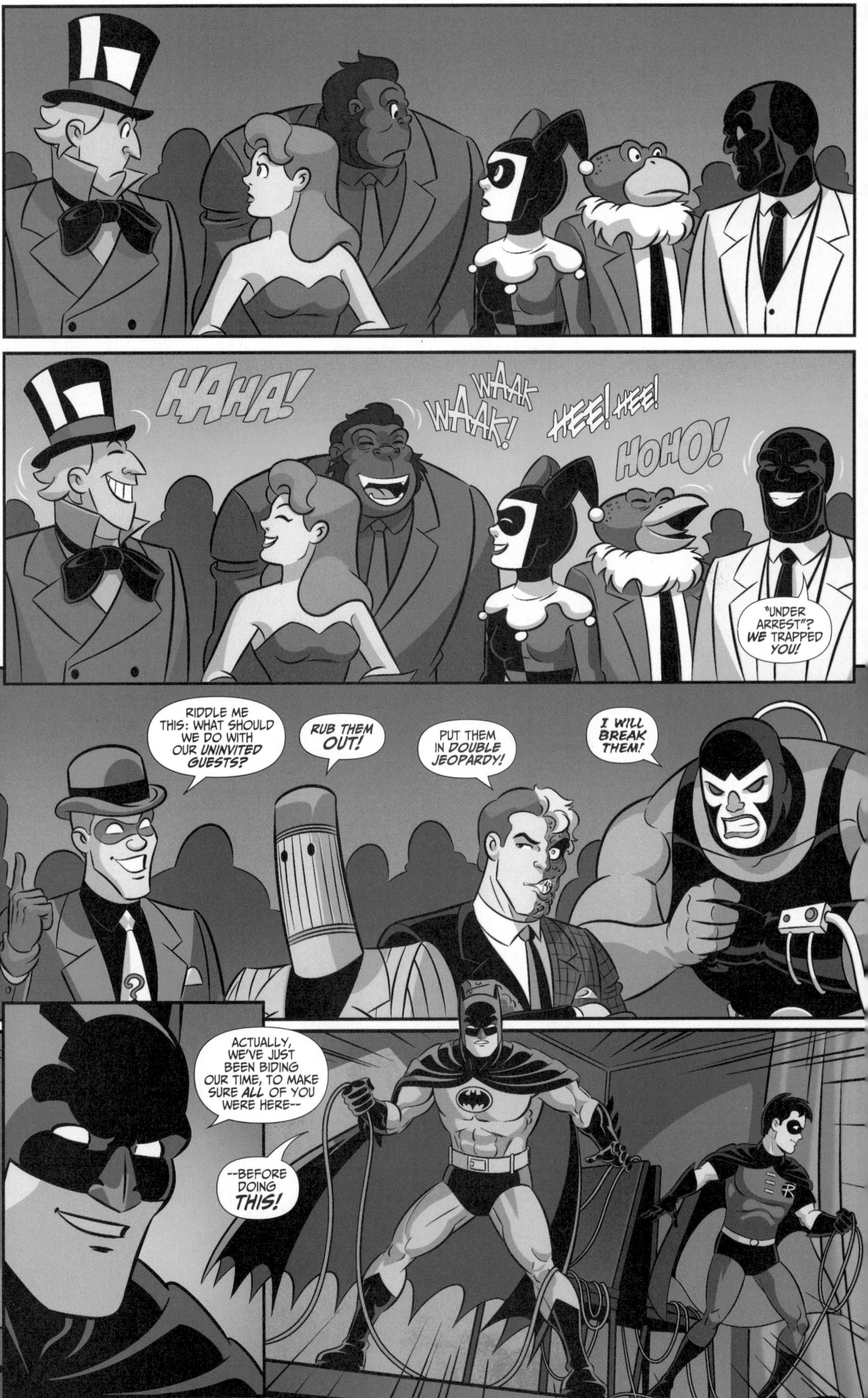
HAHA!
WAAK WAAK!
HEE! HEE!
HOHO!
"UNDER ARREST"? WE TRAPPED YOU!
RIDDLE ME THIS: WHAT SHOULD WE DO WITH OUR UNINVITED GUESTS?
RUB THEM OUT!
PUT THEM IN DOUBLE JEOPARDY!
I WILL BREAK THEM!
ACTUALLY, WE'VE JUST BEEN BIDING OUR TIME, TO MAKE SURE ALL OF YOU WERE HERE--
--BEFORE DOING THIS!

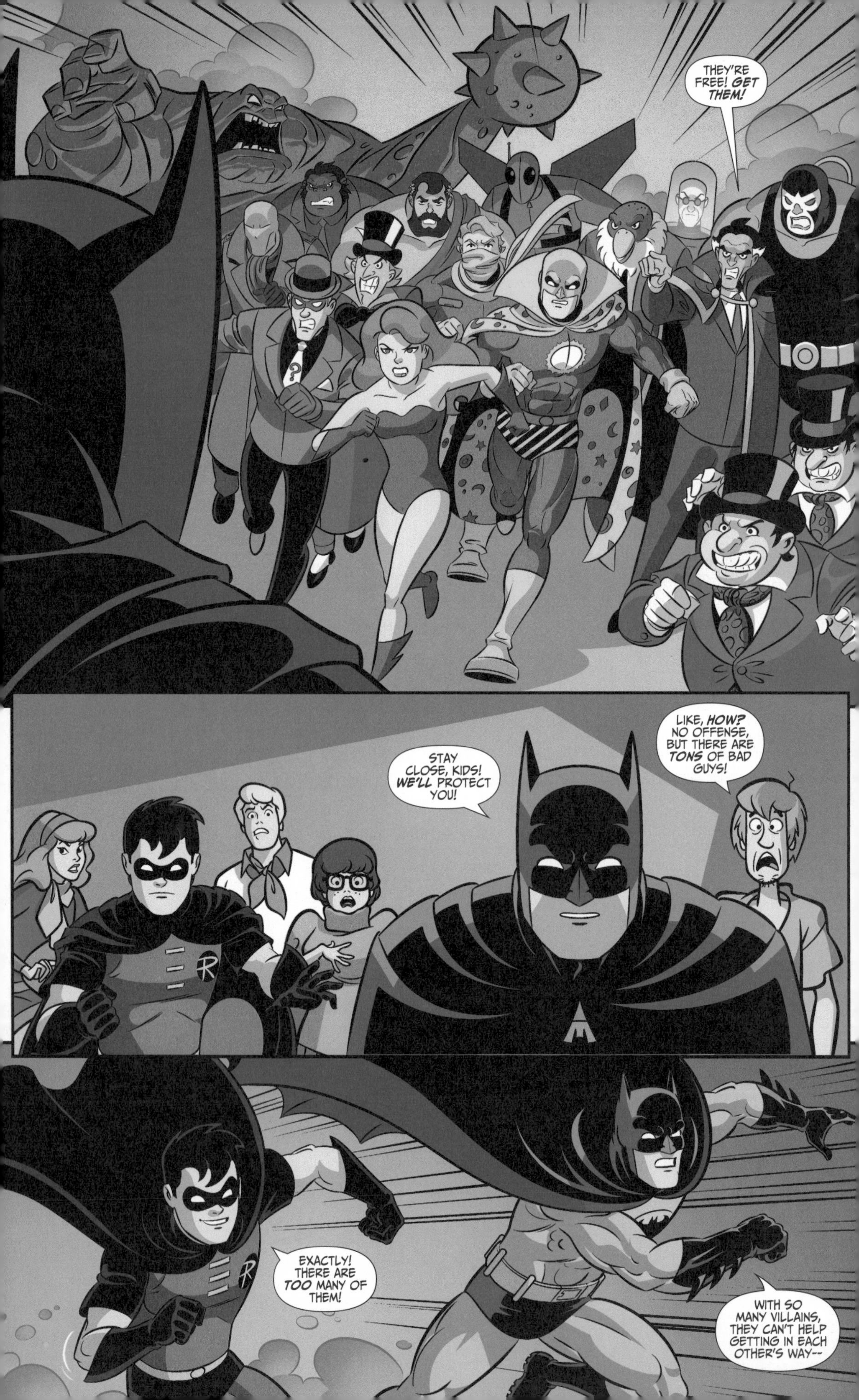
THEY'RE FREE! GET THEM!
STAY CLOSE, KIDS! WE'LL PROTECT YOU!
LIKE, HOW? NO OFFENSE, BUT THERE ARE TONS OF BAD GUYS!
EXACTLY! THERE ARE TOO MANY OF THEM!
WITH SO MANY VILLAINS, THEY CAN'T HELP GETTING IN EACH OTHER'S WAY--

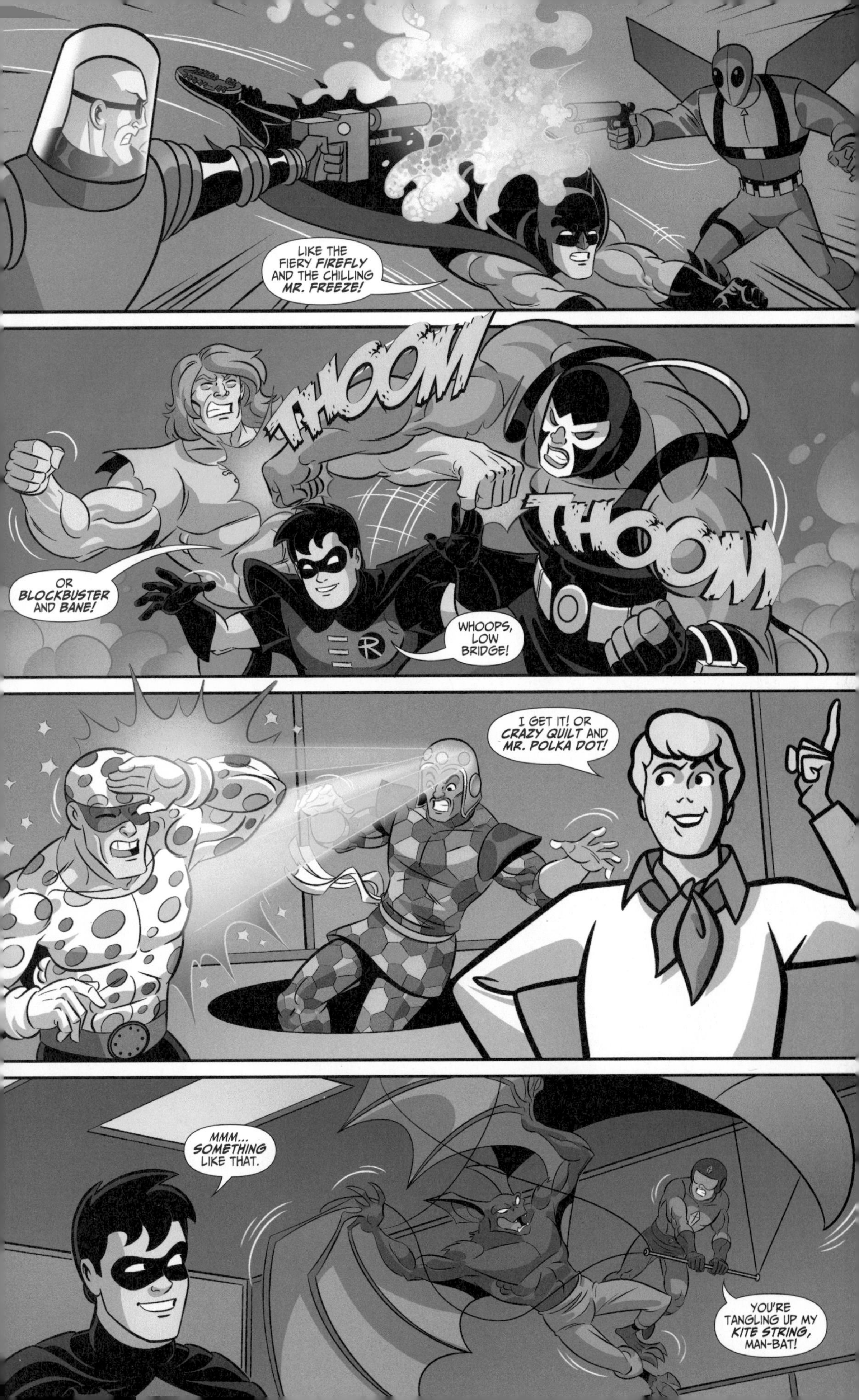

LIKE THE FIERY FIREFLY AND THE CHILLING MR. FREEZE!
THOOM
OR BLOCKBUSTER AND BANE!
THOOM
WHOOPS, LOW BRIDGE!
I GET IT! OR CRAZY QUILT AND MR. POLKA DOT!
MMM... SOMETHING LIKE THAT.
YOU'RE TANGLING UP MY KITE STRING, MAN-BAT!

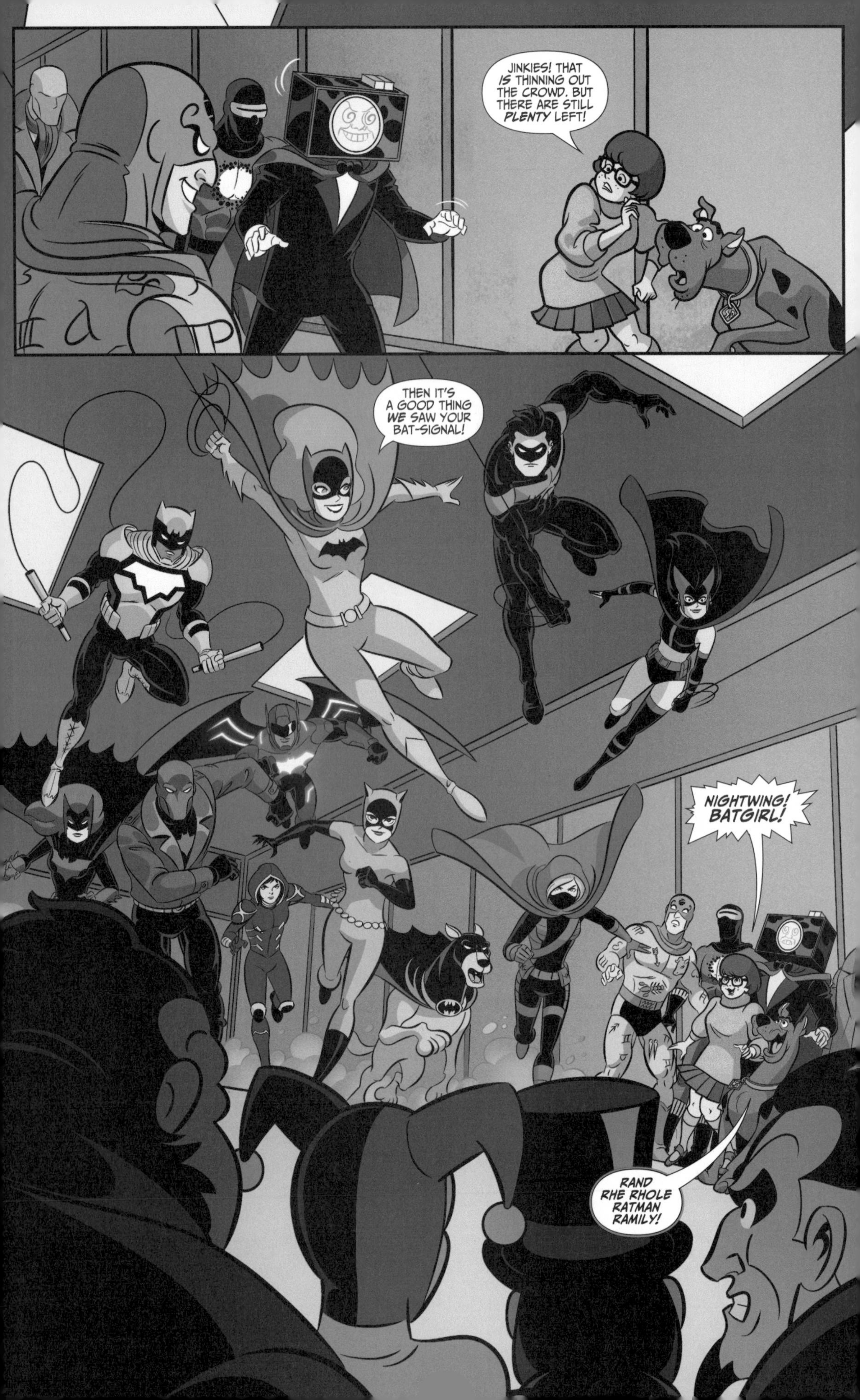
JINKIES! THAT IS THINNING OUT THE CROWD. BUT THERE ARE STILL PLENTY LEFT!
THEN IT'S A GOOD THING WE SAW YOUR BAT-SIGNAL!
NIGHTWING! BATGIRL!
RAND RHE RHOLE RATMAN RAMILY!

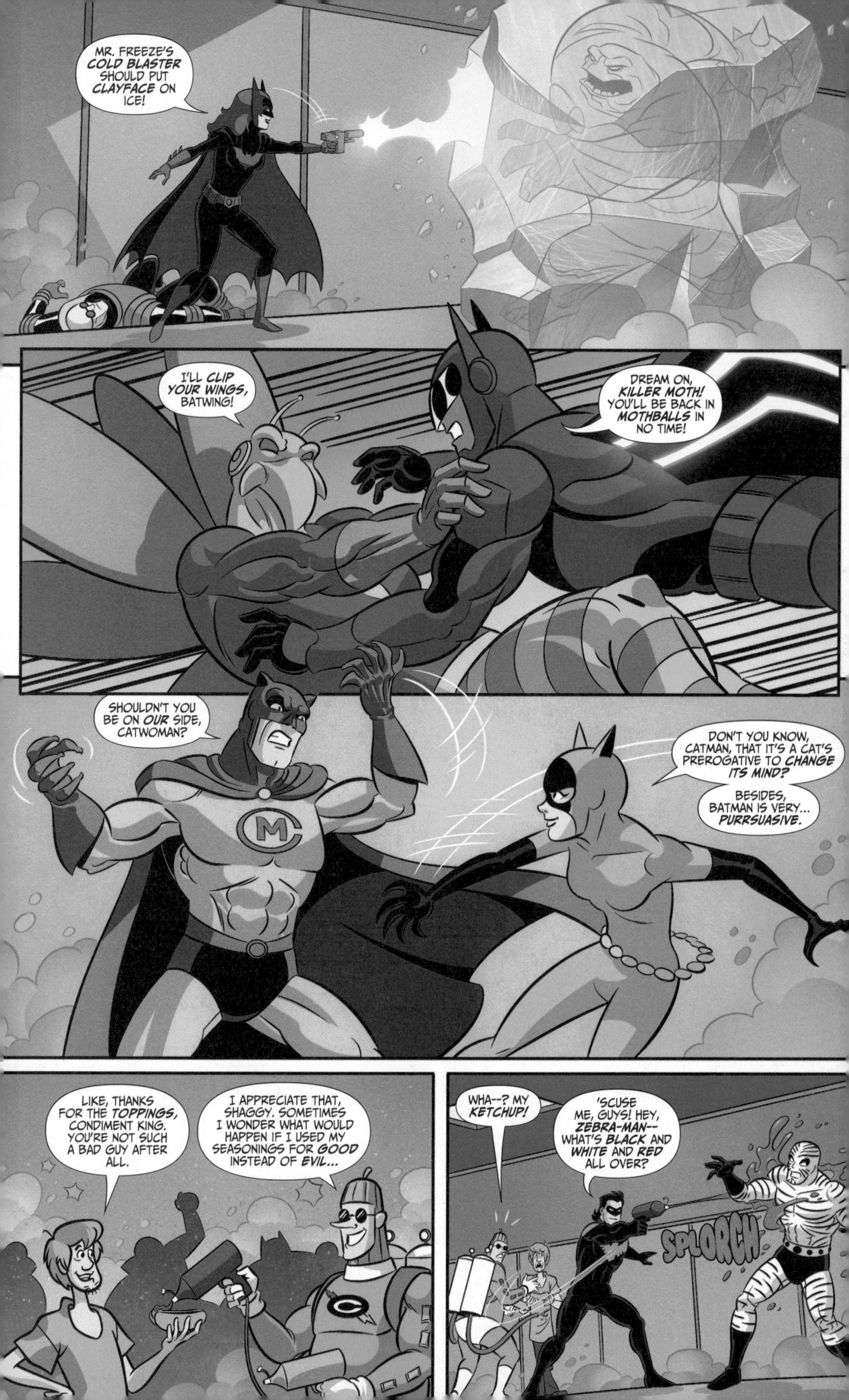
MR. FREEZE'S COLD BLASTER SHOULD PUT CLAYFACE ON ICE!
I'LL CLIP YOUR WINGS, BATWING!
DREAM ON, KILLER MOTH! YOU'LL BE BACK IN MOTHBALLS IN NO TIME!
SHOULDN'T YOU BE ON OUR SIDE, CATWOMAN?
DON'T YOU KNOW, CATMAN, THAT IT'S A CAT'S PREROGATIVE TO CHANGE ITS MIND?
BESIDES, BATMAN IS VERY... PURRSUASIVE.
LIKE, THANKS FOR THE TOPPINGS, CONDIMENT KING. YOU'RE NOT SUCH A BAD GUY AFTER ALL.
I APPRECIATE THAT, SHAGGY. SOMETIMES I WONDER WHAT WOULD HAPPEN IF I USED MY SEASONINGS FOR GOOD INSTEAD OF EVIL...
WHA--? MY KETCHUP!
'SCUSE ME, GUYS! HEY, ZEBRA-MAN-- WHAT'S BLACK AND WHITE AND RED ALL OVER?
SPLORCH

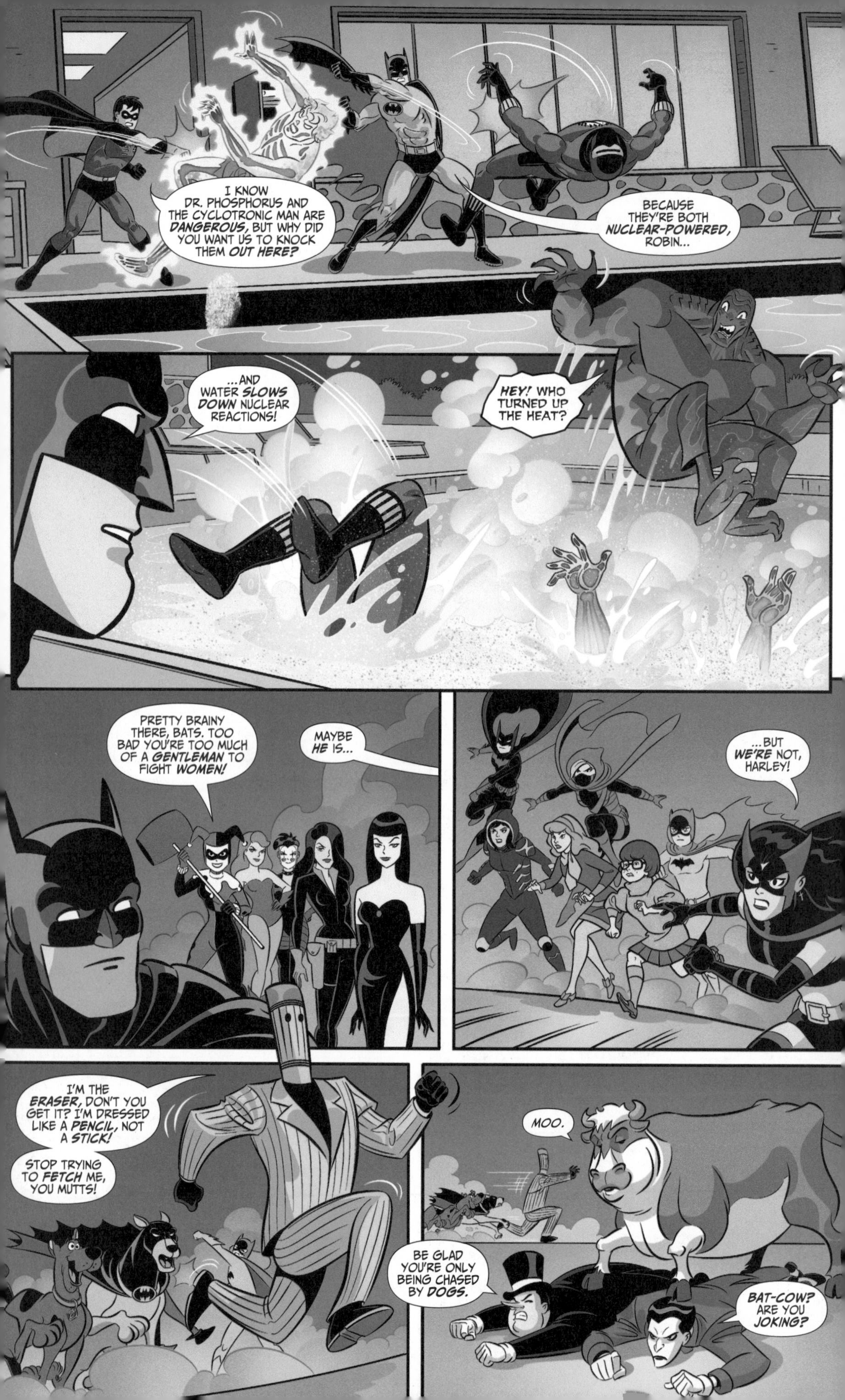
I KNOW DR. PHOSPHORUS AND THE CYCLOTRONIC MAN ARE DANGEROUS, BUT WHY DID YOU WANT US TO KNOCK THEM OUT HERE?
BECAUSE THEY'RE BOTH NUCLEAR-POWERED, ROBIN...
...AND WATER SLOWS DOWN NUCLEAR REACTIONS!
HEY! WHO TURNED UP THE HEAT?
PRETTY BRAINY THERE, BATS. TOO BAD YOU'RE TOO MUCH OF A GENTLEMAN TO FIGHT WOMEN!
MAYBE HE IS...
...BUT WE'RE NOT, HARLEY!
I'M THE ERASER, DON'T YOU GET IT? I'M DRESSED LIKE A PENCIL, NOT A STICK!
STOP TRYING TO FETCH ME, YOU MUTTS!
MOO.
BE GLAD YOU'RE ONLY BEING CHASED BY DOGS.
BAT-COW? ARE YOU JOKING?

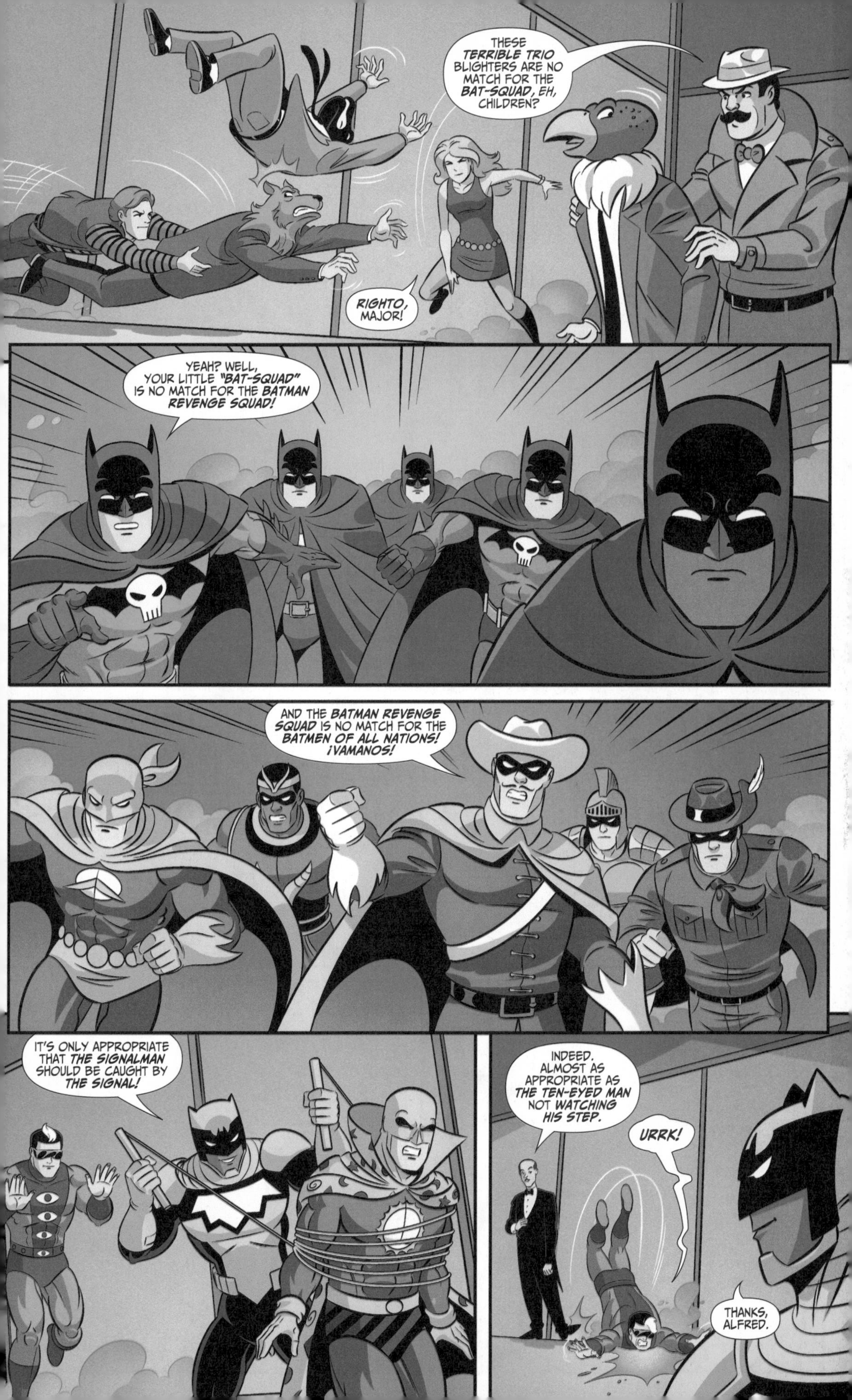

THESE TERRIBLE TRIO BLIGHTERS ARE NO MATCH FOR THE BAT-SQUAD, EH, CHILDREN?
RIGHTO, MAJOR!
YEAH? WELL, YOUR LITTLE "BAT-SQUAD" IS NO MATCH FOR THE BATMAN REVENGE SQUAD!
AND THE BATMAN REVENGE SQUAD IS NO MATCH FOR THE BATMEN OF ALL NATIONS! ¡VAMANOS!
IT'S ONLY APPROPRIATE THAT THE SIGNALMAN SHOULD BE CAUGHT BY THE SIGNAL!
INDEED. ALMOST AS APPROPRIATE AS THE TEN-EYED MAN NOT WATCHING HIS STEP.
URRK!
THANKS, ALFRED.

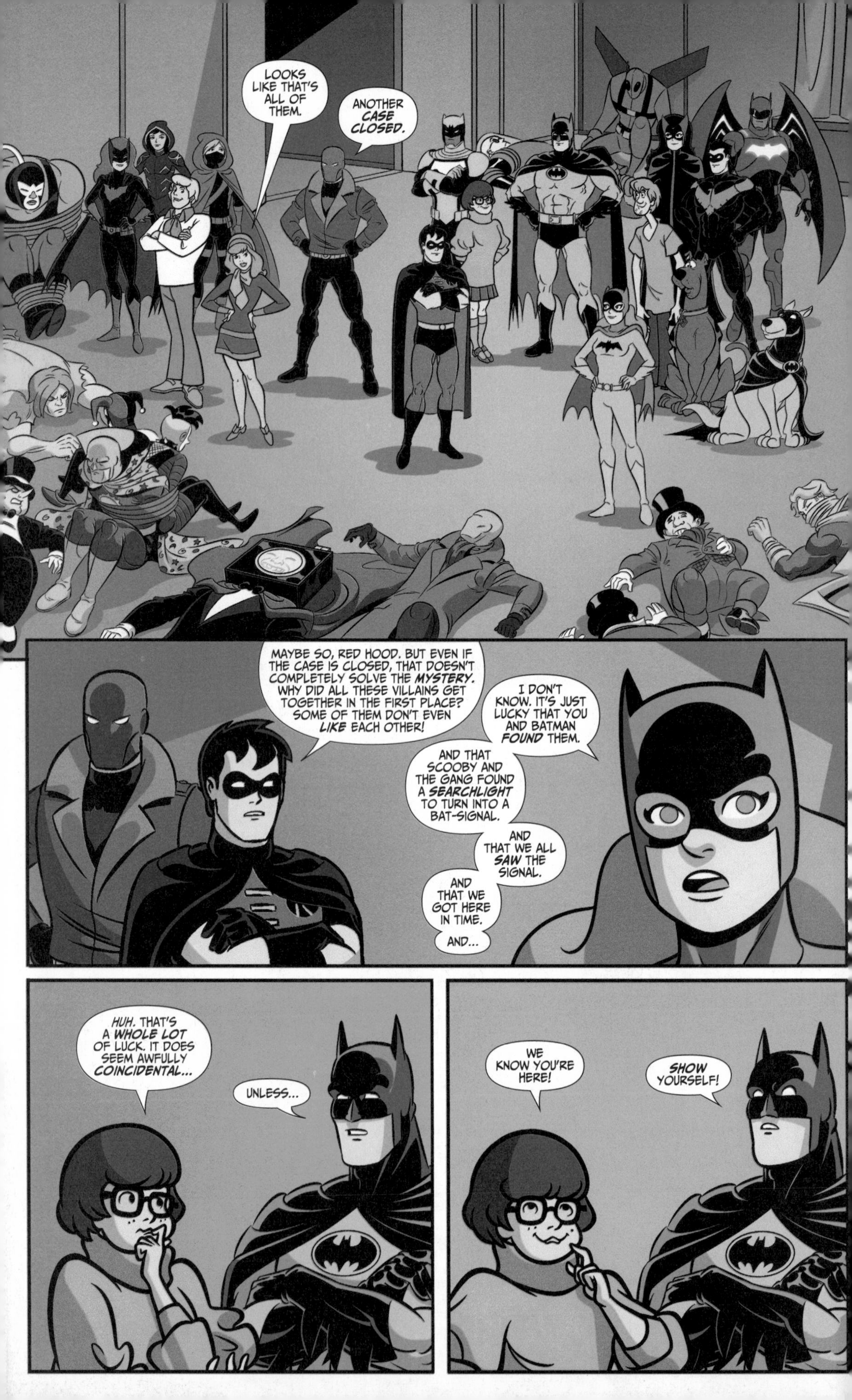
LOOKS LIKE THAT'S ALL OF THEM.
ANOTHER CASE CLOSED.
MAYBE SO, RED HOOD. BUT EVEN IF THE CASE IS CLOSED, THAT DOESN'T COMPLETELY SOLVE THE MYSTERY. WHY DID ALL THESE VILLAINS GET TOGETHER IN THE FIRST PLACE? SOME OF THEM DON'T EVEN LIKE EACH OTHER!
I DON'T KNOW. IT'S JUST LUCKY THAT YOU AND BATMAN FOUND THEM.
AND THAT SCOOBY AND THE GANG FOUND A SEARCHLIGHT TO TURN INTO A BAT-SIGNAL.
AND THAT WE ALL SAW THE SIGNAL.
AND THAT WE GOT HERE IN TIME.
AND...
HUH. THAT'S A WHOLE LOT OF LUCK. IT DOES SEEM AWFULLY COINCIDENTAL...
UNLESS...
WE KNOW YOU'RE HERE!
SHOW YOURSELF!

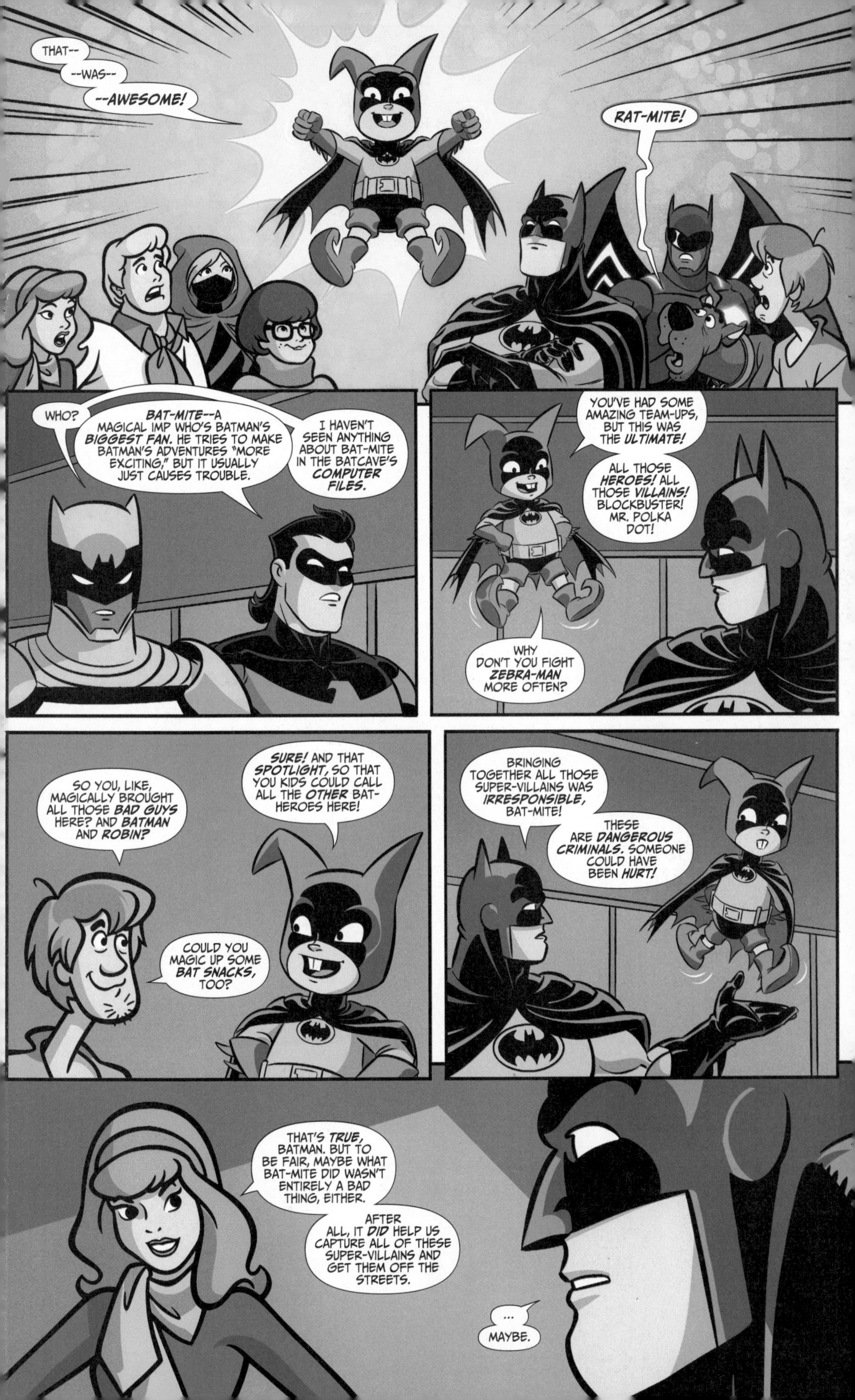

THAT--
--WAS--
--AWESOME!
RAT-MITE!
WHO?
BAT-MITE--A MAGICAL IMP WHO'S BATMAN'S BIGGEST FAN. HE TRIES TO MAKE BATMAN'S ADVENTURES "MORE EXCITING," BUT IT USUALLY JUST CAUSES TROUBLE.
I HAVEN'T SEEN ANYTHING ABOUT BAT-MITE IN THE BATCAVE'S COMPUTER FILES.
YOU'VE HAD SOME AMAZING TEAM-UPS, BUT THIS WAS THE ULTIMATE!
ALL THOSE HEROES! ALL THOSE VILLAINS! BLOCKBUSTER! MR. POLKA DOT!
WHY DON'T YOU FIGHT ZEBRA-MAN MORE OFTEN?
SO YOU, LIKE, MAGICALLY BROUGHT ALL THOSE BAD GUYS HERE? AND BATMAN AND ROBIN?
SURE! AND THAT SPOTLIGHT, SO THAT YOU KIDS COULD CALL ALL THE OTHER BAT-HEROES HERE!
COULD YOU MAGIC UP SOME BAT SNACKS, TOO?
BRINGING TOGETHER ALL THOSE SUPER-VILLAINS WAS IRRESPONSIBLE, BAT-MITE!
THESE ARE DANGEROUS CRIMINALS. SOMEONE COULD HAVE BEEN HURT!
THAT'S TRUE, BATMAN. BUT TO BE FAIR, MAYBE WHAT BAT-MITE DID WASN'T ENTIRELY A BAD THING, EITHER.
AFTER ALL, IT DID HELP US CAPTURE ALL OF THESE SUPER-VILLAINS AND GET THEM OFF THE STREETS.
...
MAYBE.

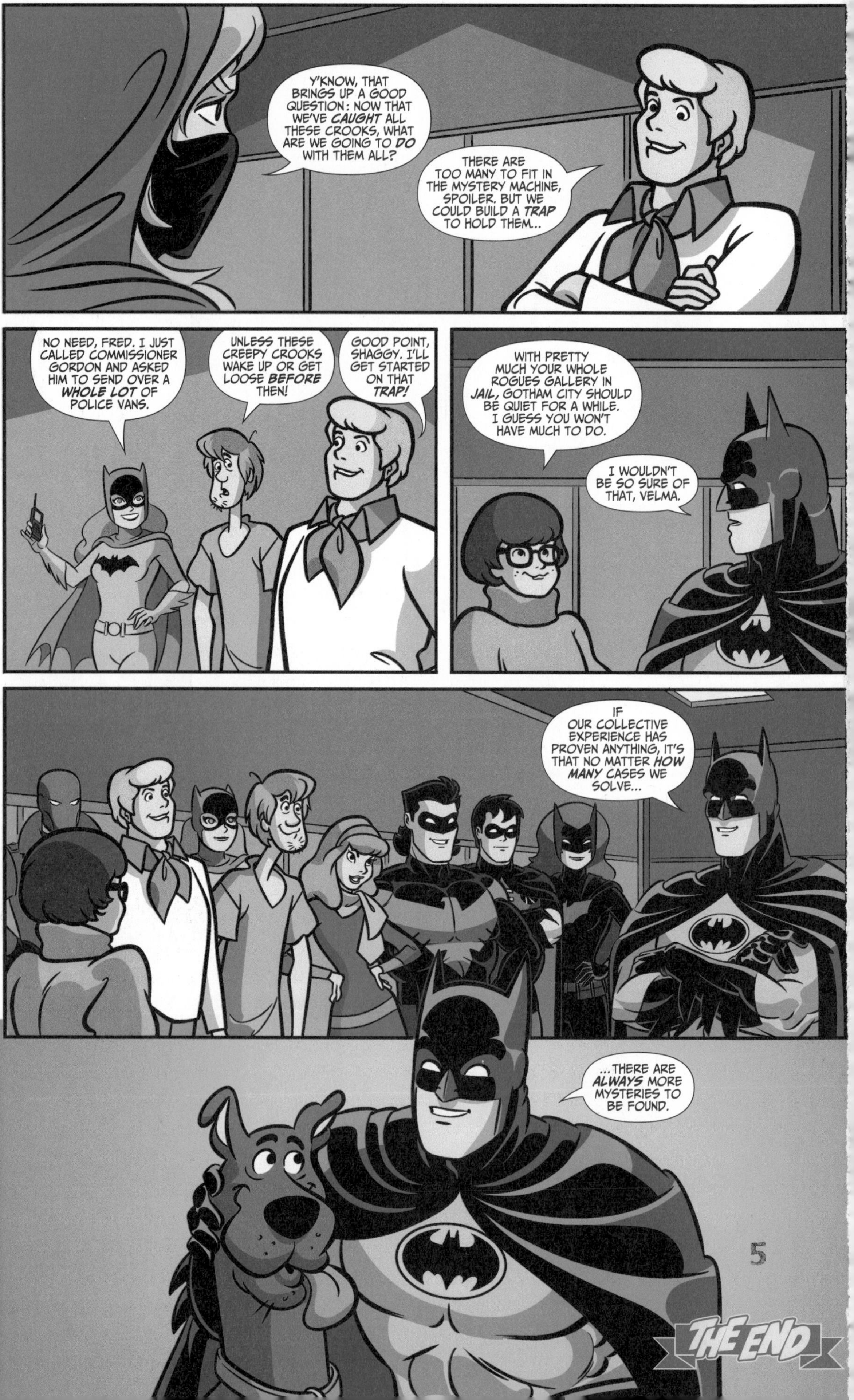
Y'KNOW, THAT BRINGS UP A GOOD QUESTION: NOW THAT WE'VE CAUGHT ALL THESE CROOKS, WHAT ARE WE GOING TO DO WITH THEM ALL?
THERE ARE TOO MANY TO FIT IN THE MYSTERY MACHINE, SPOILER. BUT WE COULD BUILD A TRAP TO HOLD THEM...
NO NEED, FRED. I JUST CALLED COMMISSIONER GORDON AND ASKED HIM TO SEND OVER A WHOLE LOT OF POLICE VANS.
UNLESS THESE CREEPY CROOKS WAKE UP OR GET LOOSE BEFORE THEN!
GOOD POINT, SHAGGY. I'LL GET STARTED ON THAT TRAP!
WITH PRETTY MUCH YOUR WHOLE ROGUES GALLERY IN JAIL, GOTHAM CITY SHOULD BE QUIET FOR A WHILE. I GUESS YOU WON'T HAVE MUCH TO DO.
I WOULDN'T BE SO SURE OF THAT, VELMA.
IF OUR COLLECTIVE EXPERIENCE HAS PROVEN ANYTHING, IT'S THAT NO MATTER HOW MANY CASES WE SOLVE...
...THERE ARE ALWAYS MORE MYSTERIES TO BE FOUND.
THE END